Ukiah scanned throu _____ ___ ___
dering. Who were these people? Why were they
watching silently in the dark? Who was Hex? How
did he know Dr. Janet Haze? Ukiah found no answers in the short cryptic conversation. It was only
as he started for the third time, from the very beginning, that he realized something amazing.

The conversation hadn't been in English.

With his odd photographic memory, he could recognize and name many languages: Spanish, German,
French, Japanese, Chinese. It wasn't any of these. It
had been so familiar to him that he had translated it
unconsciously. Odder yet, he could find no instance
when he had heard it spoken. The knowledge was
there, deeply buried, lost but not forgotten.

The only time in his life he could not recall with
complete clarity was his early childhood. Who were
his real parents? Where had they gone? How had he
ended up running with the wolves? The answers had
always been lost behind a veil of unremembering darkness.

He sat up in the hospital bed to stare out his window, across the dark landscape of Oakland to Schenley Park.

They knew the town where he had been found. They
spoke a language he knew from that dark forgetfulness.
They claimed he was one of them.

He had to go now, while the trail was fresh, and
find these people. . . .

ALIEN
TASTE

Wen Spencer

A ROC BOOK

ROC
Published by New American Library, a division of
Penguin Putnam Inc., 375 Hudson Street,
New York, New York 10014, U.S.A.
Penguin Books Ltd, 27 Wrights Lane,
London W8 5TZ, England
Penguin Books Australia Ltd, Ringwood,
Victoria, Australia
Penguin Books Canada Ltd, 10 Alcorn Avenue,
Toronto, Ontario, Canada M4V 3B2
Penguin Books (N.Z.) Ltd, 182–190 Wairau Road,
Auckland 10, New Zealand

Penguin Books Ltd, Registered Offices:
Harmondsworth, Middlesex, England

First published by Roc, an imprint of New American Library,
a division of Penguin Putnam Inc.

First Printing, July 2001
10 9 8 7 6 5 4 3 2 1

Cover design by Ray Lundgren
Cover art by Fred Gambino

To Don Kosak,
the original Max Bennett.
Cover me—I'm going in.

CHAPTER ONE

Monday, June 15, 2004
Pittsburgh, Pennsylvania

It was going to storm soon. Ukiah Oregon could smell the rain on the wind. He felt the tension on his skin as he leaned out the Cherokee's passenger window. He saw it on the far horizon over the skyscrapers of Pittsburgh.

He leaned back in the window, brushing his long black hair out of his dark eyes. His partner, Max Bennett, was filling the cab as usual with noisy confusion. Max alternately shouted at his wireless phone, the stalled traffic, and the net pages giving him traffic updates. Over it all, the KQV news station droned on with the news of the day.

"Kraynak. Detective. Yes, I'll wait. Veterans' Bridge is not clear, you stupid thing!" This was at the Cherokee's navigation computer, whose traffic updates were lagging far behind real life. "Now tell me why we've been sitting here for ten minutes. I'm trying to merge, honey, move your ass!"

The last was directed at a white Saab in the left-hand lane, which, unlike theirs, was creeping forward.

"It's going to rain soon," Ukiah interjected into the

confusion. "If Kraynak wants us for tracking, we're running out of time."

Max Bennett snorted at the comment, his attention divided between muscling the Cherokee into a hole in traffic and the sudden return of the Pittsburgh Police operator. "What did you say? Are you sure you're saying those names correctly? It's K-R-A-Y-N-A-K, Kraynak. Yes, I'm certain that's with a K." He tapped the Cherokee's screen to consult an Internet page. "Would his badge number help? I could give you his Social Security too. I can even get his wife's maiden name. Yes, I'll hold. I told Kraynak it was going to take us an hour to get into Oakland, but he sounded so wired that I don't think he listened."

After a moment, Ukiah realized that Max was talking to him. "And he didn't say why he wanted us?"

Back when Ukiah started to work with Max, they were usually chased away from police crime scenes, like mink chased from the wolves' kill. Even as their reputation for solving the difficult missing-person cases grew, they were never contacted directly by the police. Occasionally they would learn that the officers on the case recommended them to the desperate families. This was the first time the police had called them, even if the police involved was one of Max's Gulf War buddies.

Max shook his head. "He didn't go into details. He just said that he had a job for us and not to worry about getting paid, that he'd cleared it with his captain." His eyebrows jumped as the operator came back on the phone. "I know he's not in his office, that's why I'm talking to you. I need to be patched to his radio. Damn, why can't the man join the modern age and get a wireless phone?"

Ukiah leaned back out the window, pushing Max's confusion into the background to be examined later.

His attention had been captured by a cat in the white Saab ahead of them. The Saab had New York plates, a Duquesne University window decal, and was packed full of boxes and plants. A Manx cat, looking like a small bobcat, sat on the back seat ledge, a bored veteran traveler.

In Pittsburgh, he often saw dogs in trucks, hanging out the window, nose to the wind. Mom Lara would love cats at the farm, but Mom Jo's wolf-dogs had always made that impossible. Except for a short-lived kitten and a few alley strays, Ukiah's experiences with cats were ones inside other people's houses, peering contentedly from a sun-basked window. At least this cat was riding in an accepted cat fashion: paws curled under and eyes partly slitted with a mix of idle speculation and contempt. Yet it was so—odd—to see it in a car.

In typical cat fashion, the Manx yawned and started to groom, ignoring him completely. A moment later the Saab found an opening in the breakdown lane and illegally sped away. Max tried to follow, but was beaten by a bread truck that immediately stopped, unable to squeeze past the UPS truck in front of them.

"Max, why do people keep cats as pets?"

"God if I know."

"Why do people keep any pets? Well, I understand dogs and I guess cats kill mice, but why snakes and hamsters? Why keep turtles?"

"This is not a conversation you have with someone who was up half the night on a cheating husband stakeout. Oh, not the puppy dog eyes."

"I don't have puppy dog eyes. Wolf eyes maybe, but not puppy dog."

"Okay, okay." Max sipped at his 7-Eleven coffee, made tan by equal parts sugar and cream. "It could be that humans are pack animals. As we got civilized, the need for a pack disappeared but not the desire. If you live out in the woods with no one else around, you get lonely, sometimes even loony. Even living in the city, without family or friends, you feel alienated."

"Get a pet, instant pack. But why only humans? You'd think if it was a good thing, other animals would do it."

"There's that sign language gorilla. It has a kitten. Gorillas in the wild don't keep cats. You get civilized, you get pets. Oh Jesus, what's this?" Max frowned at the Cherokee's GPI navigator display as it beeped and added a traffic hazard directly in front of them. "What the hell is that orange blimp supposed to be? Ukiah, can you see what's in front of us?"

Ukiah hung far out his window to see around the brown UPS truck in front of them. Fifty feet ahead, a tanker truck leaned at a drunken angle, a trail of flares set out behind it. "There's a truck broken down in this lane."

Max cursed and jammed on his left-turn signal. "I told him your bike was at the shop and that I had to run out and pick you up at your moms'. I said it would take an hour and a half, and he sounded like he was going to have hysterics. So I told him an hour and that he'd have to fix any speeding ticket I got. I should have known better. I should have said it would take two hours. No, I should have told him to forget it. I've got a bad feeling about this case. Kraynak's in Homicide now. What the hell does Homicide want with us?"

"Do you suppose that's a mark of an intelligent race—that any aliens we find will have pets too?"

Max snorted. "Aliens? I told you not to watch

those TV shows. They're all made up. They'll rot your brain."

Ukiah closed his eyes and considered what had brought aliens to mind. He relived the last few minutes, tuning out this time the cat and the car, along with Max's ranting. There, suddenly loud without the other noises to mask it, was the radio. The top news story had been the Mars mission preparing to land. "They were talking about Martians on the radio. They said," he repeated the words now echoing in his memory, "in 1996, the first evidence of life on Mars was found on Earth. This week we might find life on Mars."

"Thank god!" Max exclaimed as the bread truck finally squeezed by the UPS truck into the breakdown lane. He pushed the Cherokee through the opening, almost touching bumpers with the bread truck. "They're talking about tiny micros, Ukiah. Like that pond scum stuff."

"So, would intelligent pond scum have pets?"

Max cuffed him without taking his eyes off the traffic. "Don't be silly. Heads up, we're here."

They had swung around the Hill District, cruised along the Monongahela River, then taken the Oakland exit to one of Pittsburgh's many pocket neighborhoods growing on the hillside, competing with the determined scrub woods. Max drove to a narrow street of brick row houses backed against Schenley Park. The street was blocked off from the main road by a police cruiser, its doors open as if suddenly abandoned, its lights strobing in the early dusk. As Max eased the Cherokee around the cruiser, the storm winds shifted and brought the stench of death their way. Ukiah went still in the close quarters, overwhelmed by the sudden chaos before him.

The narrow street was lined with abandoned police

cars, their radios a crackling, harsh chorus. The row houses had identical worn faces. Everyone's attention pointed to one lone door, through which a stream of people poured. The coroner's wagon came up behind them and stopped, blocking the street.

"You okay?" Max asked, pulling up in front of a neighbor's driveway. It was the only parking space on the street.

Ukiah pulled himself back enough to nod. "There's more than two people dead in there. The walls must be painted with gore."

"I hate the case already. Don't worry, I'll do the talking. Just keep your shit together and your head down." Max muttered. "There's Kraynak."

Despite having quit cold turkey three months before, including the cigars on their poker nights, the big policeman was breathing smoke like a dragon as he jogged up to them. He motioned them brusquely out of the car.

"It's bad?" Max asked.

"Shit like this doesn't happen in Pittsburgh. New York, every other day. L.A., twice daily. But not here, not like this. Someone carved up three girls, Carnegie Mellon students, and took the fourth woman for a walk, we think. If they did, we need to find her pronto. Shit is about to hit the fan."

"Damn it, Kraynak, a multiple homicide! Why call us?"

"Because you're the best at what you do. We've got a dozen men in Schenley Park, even flew a helicopter with heat-tracking equipment over the son of a bitch and came up with zilch."

Max gave Ukiah a "you still game?" look and Ukiah nodded back. "Okay. Some ground rules." Max jerked his head toward Ukiah. "He needs room to work—clear the house. He touches anything he wants, nothing hands off. If he leaves the house, he gets backup, at least two good runners."

"You don't ask much, do you?"

"If she was here and they walked her out, he'll be able to tell you."

Kraynak regarded them with angry eyes as he took another deep drag on his Marlboro. "Shit." He flung the butt onto the pavement and ground it dead with his foot. "I'll go see if we can clear the place. Coroner won't like it. They think they're God on murder cases."

As Kraynak stalked away, Max turned to study Ukiah. "You can do this."

"I know, but I'm starting to get your bad feelings. This is going to be a scary one."

Max winced and looked away. "You heard him, they took a woman. She might be alive. If she is, you're going to be her only hope. We've got lots of backup on this case. When you find her, we'll just step aside and let the police finish the case."

Ukiah trembled, feeling like every part of him wanted to fly in separate directions. Excitement, fear, and nervous energy rushed through him like a storm wind.

Max patted him and went to the back of the Cherokee to pop the tailgate. "Come on, let's get geared up."

Ukiah clipped on his headset and ran a VOX check. The periscope camera showed a clear picture on Max's laptop. Max unlocked the gun box and pulled out the pistol tray.

"No rifles. Take your Colt. I want you to have stopping power."

"I hate guns."

"You're going to take your .45 and your Kevlar."

Ukiah frowned but strapped on his kidney holster.

The bulletproof jacket, for once, felt comforting, a strong hug to keep him in one piece. The storm wind whipped dead leaves out of the park, tainted with the presence of death from the row house. His bare arms tingled with reports of punctured spleens and spilled bowels. He rubbed at them to give them something else to consider.

Max was clipping on Ukiah's tracer when Kraynak returned with his captain. She was a solidly built blonde with sharp quick eyes. She was frowning as she stopped before the two private detectives. Her eyes inventoried their gear.

"So this is the boy raised by wolves." She snorted. "Kraynak, I don't know how I let you talk me into this. Are you really that good at finding missing persons?"

This was directly to Ukiah, so he answered instead of letting Max do the talking. "On walkouts, I'm a hundred percent. If they got in a car, I'm only running at forty percent."

"One hundred." The captain whistled. "Then let's hope that they stayed on the ground. Kraynak tells me you need room to operate."

Ukiah nodded. Max added in, "He works better if there's no distractions. This is very detailed work. Lots of people moving around will muddy the trail."

The captain sighed. "I'll give you twenty minutes to work the house. Forensics has been through, but the coroner wants to start on the bodies."

Ukiah frowned at the time limit. With multiple bodies, he would need that long just to work out who was there and which woman was missing. Surely there was a way to cut his search down. "Why do you think they walked out the woman?"

"The neighbors say that all four women were home, three blondes and a brunette. We've got three blonde bodies." The captain held up an evidence bag holding a driver's license. "The missing brunette is Doctor Janet Haze. Her purse and keys are inside. There were kids playing in the street all day. No one saw anything come or go by the front door, so the killer probably came in the back. Oh piss, the media is here."

The media took the form of a truck with the local TV station logo painted on its side and a dish transmission tower on top. It pulled up and stopped, almost touching bumpers with the police cruiser blocking the street. The captain flagged over a uniformed policeman and sent him to stall the news crew. "We need to find her, Wolf Boy, and we need to find her fast. Once this hits the air, I'll have every parent of thirty-odd thousand college students in a panic."

If the killer came in the back, he probably left by the back door too. Yet Ukiah still needed a baseline on the missing woman, which meant he'd have to go into the house. "Okay, let's go."

The first woman was sprawled by the front door, a bloody trail showing that the police had shoved her sideways as they forced the front door. Her scalp hung in tatters, and she was missing fingers where she had tried to protect her head with her hands.

Ukiah swallowed a wave of nausea and fingered one of the wounds, finding traces of dense steel. "Have you found the weapon?"

"Nope." Kraynak answered him from the porch. "Never seen wounds like these before either. Thin like a knife, but with amazing force. You usually get this amputation with axes and such."

Ukiah scanned the room, then nodded his chin toward a piece of black lacquered wood on the wall. "Sword rack for a *katana*."

"A what?" Kraynak asked.

"Japanese sword." Max answered, stepping over the body to tap on the rack. "The sword is missing. It looks as if someone was a rabid Otaku. That's a fan of Japanese animation."

"Damn," Kraynak swore. "I thought that was some kind of weird coat rack. Well, we didn't find any sword, so the killer took it with him."

Max bent to point out a length of hollow wood. "Left the sheath."

"We'll dust that for prints." Kraynak pulled on a disposable glove. He picked it up and dropped it into a long clear plastic bag.

The second dead woman was in the cluttered living room. Ukiah examined it and moved on. The third was in the kitchen and the back door hung open, its doorknob bloody. He returned to the front hall, earning a puzzled look from Kraynak in the doorway.

"I'm not sure who I'm looking for yet," he explained, and detoured upstairs to examine the bedrooms. The three on the second floor were unmarked by the chaos of the first floor. He moved through them, checking the clothes and the bedsheets to establish which dead woman belonged to which empty bedroom.

"There's an attic bedroom." Max tapped a door in the hall.

"That's hers, then."

Max opened the door, revealing narrow, steep stairs leading upward. The smell of a young woman bloomed out, tainted with the odor of sickness. Pillows that had been set on the bottom step plopped out onto the hall floor. Stepping over the pillows, Ukiah led the way up into the cramped bedroom. The dormer window was thrown open, and the oncoming storm winds played with a black blanket

serving as a curtain. A desktop computer sat on a
desk, its plug dangling over its dark monitor. Small
dinosaurs made of K'NEX guarded an open book. A
ragged stuffed rabbit sat at the head of the unmade
bed, ears drooping, wearing an overlarge green tur-
tleneck sweater. A normal bedroom of a normal
woman, but there was something that sent shivers
down his spine. Something was wrong. Something
was out of place, but he couldn't place what.

"Our twenty minutes are almost up," Max said
quietly from the attic door.

He checked the bed, closing his eyes, ignoring all
background noise to focus on the sheets. They were
good quality, one hundred percent cotton with a
thread count of three hundred. The woman was in
her mid-twenties, tall, dark hair, eyes a deep blue. She
had been sick—the sheets were still slightly damp
with sour sweat, and there were signs her white
blood cell count had been high. He frowned as he
found odd fractures in her DNA, hard twists he had
never felt before.

He pulled himself up out of the focus. If he didn't
find her soon, she would be dead. He trotted down
the steps, murmuring "Got her" to Max as he
brushed by his partner.

The wooden back porch looked unpromisingly
clean of evidence. He dropped to his knees and ran
his hands over the flaking gray wood. Bare wood.
Dirt. Asphalt. Crushed grass. He hit a blood trace
and grew still. Two blood types, mixed together. He
identified the first: the woman at the front door. The
second came from the woman in the living room. He
hazarded a guess that the blood had mixed on the
sword blade and dripped onto the wood. There was
a faint smear of blood beside the first trace. He fo-

cused on the worn wood, found the faint outline with his fingertips. A small woman's shoe, right foot.

He crept forward, running fingers before him. On the rough cement steps he found the barest print from the small shoe, again right foot. He moved down to the parking pad, sniffing the still warm stone to help catch the faint trail on the broken asphalt.

Suddenly one of Max's hands was in front of Ukiah's eyes, and the other on his shoulder. Dimly, he realized Max had been talking to him. On the porch had appeared young, fit, uniformed policemen— their backup.

"Got it?" Max asked.

Ukiah recalled what Max had said, what he had been too focused to hear. "These yahoos want you to play base command since their men aren't equipped with GPI tracers. You won't be coming into the park, but I've got the promised backup. You've put one of our spare tracers on them, so you'll be able to keep us together. I'll try not to outrun them. If we get out of the park, I'm to wait till you can move the Cherokee closer."

"Good." Max patted him on the shoulder. "What did you find?"

"She walked out." He considered the placement of the feet. "No. Ran. Her feet are far apart, barely touching the ground. She's running, running quickly."

"Running for her life." Max swore. "Wait for my mark, then go on, and be careful."

Ukiah watched him go, feeling uneasy and weird. They often split up, especially if the trail was old but well marked. Ukiah could then track at a run, and Max, who was almost twenty years older, used the GPI tracer and the Cherokee's navigational computer to drive to points intersecting his route. At the trail's end, the 4x4 and its cargo were usually vital to getting their client out alive.

I've worked without Max behind me, he told himself, *I can do it again.*

But he didn't like it. Not now, not with a killer on the loose.

"Okay, Ukiah, I'm at the Cherokee, you can go."

Across the parking pad and the alley of mostly mud and occasional ancient cobblestones there was a wall of trees and weeds, the edge of Schenley Park. The woman's trail led to a break in the weeds, which screened a well-beaten path. Dusk was full on them and night was hiding in the woods.

Ukiah went down the path quickly, bent nearly in half, hands occasionally patting when eyes and nose failed him. The woman's footprints vanished on the hard-packed dirt, but blood was sprayed unevenly along the trail as the killing sword was swung in pace with running feet. But who held the sword? He had yet to find the killer's track.

Behind him, coming like a herd of moose, his police backup scrambled to follow. Dimly he was aware of Max's voice over his headset, marking his progress via the tracer and coordinating with the police dispatcher. His focus, however, stayed on the blood.

The blood trail left the footpath, turned, and followed an animal run through scrub trees. Ukiah ran half-crouched under the bowed branches. The run burrowed deeper into the thick, uncut growth, a strange haven of wilderness at the heart of the city.

A sharp whistle sounded in his ear piece, and he paused. "What is it, Max?"

"You lost your posse back there. You don't have backup. Don't get too focused or you might walk into something deadly."

"Okay, Max."

Ukiah considered stopping completely, but he could hear his backup, loud and clumsy, moving quickly closer. He had visions of trying to track while they crowded around him. So he pressed on, skittering down a steep hillside. In the gully below, he found the woman's footprints again, pressed deep into the mud. She had scrambled up the other side and paused beside a large tree. There, where the sword would have hung at her side, was a pool of blood. Another set of footprints, a heavy man with large feet, came from the right, following the stream. The woman had stepped behind the tree, letting the man past.

"Max." He whispered, suddenly aware of the rustling storm wind blocking his hearing. Ukiah crept forward, hating what he was sure he would find.

"I hear you, Ukiah."

She followed the man once he had passed, walking over his footprints. "Max, I think the woman is the killer. She's got the sword."

"Are you sure?"

Fifty feet through the heavy woods, she had followed the man, then killed him. Ukiah crouched beside a dead uniformed policeman, hacked and sliced with brutal efficiency. "She killed a cop. I just found his body. There's no one else out here but me and her."

"Get out, Ukiah."

There was a tingling awareness in the center of his back and he turned quickly.

The woman crouched amid the underbrush, her eyes so bright the whites seemed to shine. "You're one of them. Aren't you? I could feel you coming, like a light moving through the darkness, a thousand million voices screaming at once. You're one of them."

"Shit," Max's voice hissed in his ear. "Ukiah, I see her."

The woman gave a wild laugh, full of insanity. "God, how do you stand it? They won't shut up. I won't shut up. *Look! Look! See! See!*"

"Ukiah, get out of there." Max's voice had gone flat and cold.

"You didn't tell me it was going to be this way. That I couldn't even sleep because I *had* to listen to them breathe. Even when you can't hear them, you have that damn blood river flowing in your head!"

"Ukiah, just get out."

"How do you stop listening?" She wailed the words, like a trapped animal calling for help. She caught a handful of her tangled hair, thick with weeds and dead leaves, and tugged hard with her bloody left hand. The right still held the glittering sword. "How do you stop listening?"

Ukiah almost stepped toward her, would have if he could have thought of any way to help her, comfort her. But then her eyes snapped back to him, glittering hard as a mink's at the sight of blood.

"You knew this would happen! You planned it! You didn't want the other stuff. All you really wanted was them dead, wasn't it?"

Ukiah held up his hands. "I don't know you. I've done nothing to you."

She gave a high, ragged laugh. "Don't lie to me. I can tell now. I can tell. Goddamn bugs. How can they be so loud and you can't see them? There must be millions of them, but where are they during the day?"

"Ukiah, draw your gun. You're going to need it out if she jumps you."

There was a flash of lightning, and she jumped at him with the speed of a striking snake. He leaped backward, throwing up his arm to ward off the blow. Unbidden came the memory of the fingerless girl. The sword came as a shining arc in the flickering light, and he felt the cut along his arm—sharp, thin pain. He tumbled, reaching desperately for his pistol. As he gained his feet, the sword kissed him again, slicing upward along his unprotected throat. Hot blood pulsed from the wound with the pounding of his heart. He slapped his left hand over his slick throat and blindly pulled the trigger again and again. The gun leaped in his hand, the discharge bright in the rain-cloaked night woods. He saw her twitch and jerk as the bullets struck her. His knees buckled and he fell, still desperately pressing his hand against the cut in his neck.

There was another crack of thunder, swallowing the echoes of his gunfire, and it began to rain.

CHAPTER TWO

Darkness flashed over Ukiah and he was, for an uncounted stretch of time, without touch, sound, sight, or even thought. Strangely, after this absolute stillness of being, when the world blared forth upon his senses at its usual volume, he knew it had lasted several minutes.

He was still sprawled facedown in the night-cloaked woods, his left hand clamped to his neck. Cold rain pounded down on him, mixing the smell of gunpowder with the blood on the torn black earth. A siren wailed in the distance, growing nearer. Heavy bodies crashed through the underbrush to his left accompanied by a dozen hissing, crackling police radios. Helicopter blades thrummed in the air, its spotlight moving through his vision like an angel of death loosed in the woods. Max's voice was ranting over the headset, in midsentence, obviously talking to someone else. ". . . left, God damn you, Kraynak, don't you know your left from your asshole? He's my partner, just let me . . ."

Ukiah was cold but too weak even to shiver. With

rescue so close, he lay unmoving, knowing somehow that any attempt to even try would be futile.

"Damn it, Bennett, you just wait for the ambulance." The headset conversation echoed off to his right, accompanied by the sounds of a large body crashing through the underbrush. "There's no sign of a path and you're going to have to direct them too. I'll find the kid."

"Then go to your fucking left, you're almost to him."

"There is a damn rock in the way, and I'm just going around it."

The helicopter's spotlight raced suddenly toward Ukiah and pinpointed him on the ground, its light so brilliant he felt his spine prickle. A shout went up from the nearby underbrush, and the searchers swarmed toward him, blood clinging to their feet.

"We found him." Kraynak's voice echoed all around him. The big detective paused over Ukiah, muttering softly, "Oh shit."

"Is he alive? How is he? Kraynak, is he all right?"

Ukiah managed to croak, "I'm—" Fine? No, not fine. "I'm here."

"Ukiah!" Max shouted in his ear. "Oh, thank God."

Kraynak dropped to his knees beside Ukiah. "Is this your blood? Are you hurt?"

"My neck," Ukiah hissed, and tried to unclasp his hand to show his wound.

Kraynak stopped the motion, clamping his hand over Ukiah's. "Keep up the pressure. Bennett would kill me if I let you bleed to death. Bennett, where's that ambulance?"

"I've found a service road. I should be able to get it within a hundred feet of you. How is he?"

"Just make it fast."

They kept Ukiah pinned on the ground with their hands and light until the ambulance stopped a stone's throw away on a dirt service road masked by the trees. With the helicopter still thumping overhead, its spotlight blasting the area with harsh brilliance, a gurney was muscled through the trees and mud to him. Then, with surprising care, the policemen lifted him onto the gurney.

As they started their bumpy way back to the ambulance, Ukiah caught sight of the woman, sprawled in an awkward heap not far from where he had lain. His semiautomatic had punched an angry line through her. Her lips were drawn back in a snarl. Her eyes were open to the rain. Yet he sensed something there, some germ of life.

"Max." He could only whisper, hoping that the mike would catch it, that Max would hear where no one in the bedlam would. "She's still alive."

The EMS glanced down at him and frowned at the headset. "Sorry, but I need to take that off."

He tried to protest but he was too weak. A black void seemed to hover at the edge of his vision. He gave up and let the emergency crew take him.

"Well, you look like someone dipped you in a blood bank, but you've only got a scratch."

It was the first time someone had spoken to him, not shouted alien-tongued instructions over his prone body. Over him stood a young resident with retro wire-rimmed glasses, apparently bored with Ukiah now that his life-threatening injury had been disclosed to be a routine laceration.

"It was close," the resident said, keying notes into Ukiah's patient chart. "A half inch longer and deeper, and you would have bled to death in a matter of minutes, but this was only a scratch."

"I'm so cold," Ukiah whispered.

"That's shock." The resident took out a penlight and flicked it in Ukiah's eyes and noted the reaction. "I'm not surprised, considering what you've been through. We've got you on a glucose drip, which should do the trick, and we're going to keep you for observation. First, though, what is your birthday?"

Ukiah blinked in confusion. "I don't know."

The resident frowned and paused to beam the penlight into Ukiah's eyes again. "Do you know what year it is?"

"It's 2004." Ukiah considered the question, unsure what the resident truly wanted to know. "I was abandoned as a child. I don't know my birthday. We celebrate my found day."

"Oh, I see. Sorry. Okay, how about just the year you were born?"

Ukiah shook his head.

"You can't calculate using the year you were abandoned, and how old you were when it happened?" The resident took in Ukiah's steady shake of his head. "Not even roughly?"

"Not even." Ukiah whispered. He wished he wasn't on his back, weak as a newborn cub. He was sure that fact was making the conversation seem more hellish than it was.

The resident frowned and started to talk slower and louder. "I have to fill this in. I can't believe you don't know your age. You say you were abandoned. Abandoned where, when, how?"

"I was," Ukiah sighed and explained with reluctance, "abandoned in the Oregon wilderness when I was"—he shrugged helplessly—"young." He closed his eyes, thought for a minute, and came to an answer the resident might accept. "Three years ago the court recognized me as legally eighteen so I could vote, drive, carry a gun, and apply for a private investigator's license. Well, not all at once, but—you know—that's a rough guess at my age."

The resident gave him an odd, disbelieving look. "Okay. We'll put in that you're twenty-one and that would make a birth date of 1983." Said information was added to his charts. "Place of birth?"

If I said I didn't know, he'll probably just talk slower and louder.

"I was found outside of Ukiah, Oregon, so I was named after the town."

"It will do," the resident muttered. "So you lived alone in the Oregon wilderness for an unknown number of years. Tell me, how the hell did you survive? Were you brought up by Bigfoot?"

"I was raised by a pack of gray timber wolves."

"You're joking." He looked at Ukiah in amazement, his glasses sliding down to the tip of his nose and threatening to fall off. "You're not." He pushed his glasses back up with his right pointer finger and shook his head. "You can't be a feral child. I've read about them, and you are not feral. Feral children are so developmentally delayed by their isolation that they don't develop speech. They rarely learn any socialization skills at all. They tend to have horrible scarring and usually die within years of discovery. There's not a single case of a feral child reaching adulthood."

Ukiah searched for a reasonable answer, then decided not to bother. His own parents had been dumbfounded (and vastly relieved) by his transition from nonverbal wolf boy to professional tracker in six short years. He shrugged instead, wishing the resident would just go away. "Why would I lie?"

The resident regarded him for a long moment and eyed the chartboard again. "Social Security number?"

The resident finished just as Max appeared at the part in the curtain. Max identified himself to the doctor and they conferred beyond the curtain in low whispers. Moments later, Max returned, stowing away a worried look to enter the cubicle with a relieved smile. "Hey! There you are! Boy, you look like shit. Your mothers are going to kill me when they see you."

"Yeah, you're a dead man." Ukiah laughed weakly, then sobered. "The woman. Is she okay?"

Max's face went grim. "She's dead on the scene, Ukiah."

"I thought she was still alive when they were taking me out."

Max shook his head, patting Ukiah earnestly on the shoulder. "They body-bagged her minutes after that, Ukiah. It's okay, kid. You had no choice. She called the game. Sudden death. It had to be you or her."

"What happens now? Will the police arrest me for killing her?"

"She ginsu-knifed four people to death, kid, and started work on you. No one is going to blame you for anything." Max snagged a chair and settled into it. "There will be an inquest after the coroner does an autopsy. The inquest will probably focus on why she went psycho—pinpoint if she was just a nutcase or if she was high on something."

"Are you sure?"

"Kid, I heard the crazy things she was saying over your link. She was completely psycho."

Ukiah tried to recall the conversation and found that there were huge gaps in his normally photographic memory. He remembered clearly the ride down in the Cherokee, the cat in the white Saab, but then the holes started. The investigation jerked and stuttered through his mind. Max telling him to take the .45. The first victim in the hall. The woman's bedroom. Snippets from a film, spliced with darkness. His last memory before waking in the rain was the woman crouching in the shadows, madness glittering in her eyes.

He knew there was more: she had wounded him; he had shot her. He had seen her wounds. He knew he had made them. He could still feel the recoil in his shoulder. The memory of it happening, however, was gone.

"Do you still have a disc of it?"

Max considered and nodded. "I was recording like usual. The disc is still in the deck."

"I need to see it.

"Tomorrow."

"You could bring your laptop computer and . . ."

"No. No. No. Look, kid, two news trucks followed the ambulance to the hospital, and another pulled up minutes after we got here. I need to call your moms and warn them off. You have to sleep. Doctor's order."

After the glucose drip finished, they moved him upstairs, tucked his personal effects into the closet, and started to explain the various room functions. He waved them sleepily away. He had visited Mom Lara when she was in Presby and knew its personal quirks. Alone at last, he closed his eyes and started his night rituals. He scanned and learned the noises of the hospital around him. Once they regressed to background static, he released the flood. The day's events washed over him, every small noise, taste, smell, and sight, repressed until this quiet time. There was a lot of useless stuff stored there. The distant buzz of a tractor as he ate breakfast. The front page of the newspaper that Mom Lara was reading across the table. The news stories and commercials of Max's news radio. The faint smell of the cat in the white Saab. The taste of earth and blood when he woke in the woods. He skimmed the junk and discarded it.

What he wanted most, the memory of the woman, was gone. There were only clean-cut breaks where they had been, as if the woman had sliced them out when she cut him open. He growled softly in frustration. He riffled through the remaining memories of her house. Why had her room seemed so strange? He scanned the titles of her books, CD-ROMs, and music CDs. Her taste in music was much like his, but the books were mostly on advanced robot programming.

Sighing, he flipped through the rest of the house, at least those memories that remained after his surgical memory loss. Only a handful survived. The full flood started again when he woke in the woods. A paramedic arrived to shoulder Kraynak aside, his deep masculine voice hovering only inches over Ukiah. Others moved in orbit around him: various members of the police force, the newly arrived Max, and seemingly the farthest ones out, the news reporters, kept at bay by the faint flutter of police tape. A half-dozen conversations pressed in at once, a jangled chorus that he had simply ignored at the time. He listened to it again, only vaguely interested in the discord.

"Breathing is shallow and rapid. [Jo?] *Get Forensics out here before it rains again.* [It's me, Max] {Going live in five.} [Ukiah's been hurt.] {Four.} Blood pressure is low. {Three.} *Make sure we don't have any accomplices hiding in the bushes.* {Two.} (So?) Appears to have a laceration near the left carotid artery. [No, I don't know how badly.] {One.} (They've killed each

other, for the time being.) Patient is currently conscious and applying pressure. [They're taking him to
the hospital now.] {I'm Paula Kiri with Channel Four
News.} (What the hell is Hex up to? Why did he
have two of his people kill each other?) [No, I don't
know which hospital yet. I'll call you when I find
out.] {I'm live in Oakland with an update of the multiple slayings.} (I'm not sure if he owns them both—
I think the boy might be one of us.)"

Ukiah frowned at the last statement. He was one
of whose? The police? Who was talking? He untan-
gled the conversation from the rest, using direction
and volume to find both parts of the conversation.

"So?" This an adult female, slightly breathless, as
if she had just raced to the scene. Ukiah backtracked
and caught her entrance. She had run almost silently
up to the scene and stopped twenty or thirty feet off,
in the darkness. The storm-whipped wind brought
him the smell of her breath and musky scent, tainted
slightly by car exhaust, cigarette smoke, and gin.

"They've killed each other, for the time being." A
man stood beside the woman. He had been standing
there from the moment Ukiah woke, silent, watching.
A shiver went down Ukiah's spine. Had the watcher
been in the woods the whole time, somehow missed?

"What the hell is Hex up to? Why did he have two
of his people kill each other?" The woman shifted in
surprise and there was the faint creak of leather. He
caught the smell of large cured hide, like Max's
bomber jacket.

"I'm not sure if he owns them both—I think the
boy might be one of us."

There was a long silence that the other background
noise threatened to wash into. He held it back, focusing tightly on the strange watchers in the wood.

"You're right," the woman stated at last, breaking the silence. "He's one of ours."

"I didn't get a chance to get real close, but I don't recognize him."

"I can sense him from here." Another pause. During this one, Ukiah felt something, like a weak electrical current. It set the hair on the back of his neck on end. He flipped back and found that moments earlier, the same sensation had crawled over him. "I don't know, he has the right smell, but something's weird about him, Rennie."

"Everything is weird about this," the man named Rennie answered. "You should hear what his name is."

His name? It was somehow frightening to think they might know his name. As the object of a police manhunt, it wouldn't be totally surprising though.

"His name? I heard them call him Ukiah."

"Oregon." Rennie supplied his last. "Ukiah Oregon."

"Ukiah, Oregon?" Unlike most people, the woman obviously had heard of the town where Ukiah had been found. "Coyote will want to hear about this."

They moved off, not at a walk in the rain-slick night woods, but at an easy run that was as silent as it was quick.

Ukiah scanned through the conversation again, wondering. Who were these people? Why were they watching silently in the dark? Who was Hex? How did he own Dr. Janet Haze? Ukiah found no answers in the short cryptic conversation. It was only as he started for the third time, from the very beginning, that he realized something amazing.

The conversation hadn't been in English.

With his odd-photographic memory, he could recognize and name many languages: Spanish, German,

French, Japanese, Chinese. It wasn't any of these. It had been so familiar to him that he had translated it unconsciously. Odder yet, he could find no instance when he had heard it spoken. The knowledge was there, deeply buried, lost but not forgotten.

The only time in his life he could not recall with complete clarity was his early childhood. Who were his real parents? Where had they gone? How had he ended up running with the wolves? The answers had always been lost behind a veil of unremembering darkness.

He sat up in the hospital bed to stare out his window, across the dark landscape of Oakland to Schenley Park.

They knew the town where he had been found. They spoke a language he knew from that dark forgetfulness. They claimed he was one of them.

He had to go now, while the trail was fresh, and find these people.

CHAPTER THREE

Compared to his life among humans, his childhood with the wolf pack seemed like a time of dreams. He remembered no beginning, no mark of the years passing. Seasons flowed seamlessly into one another. He could pick out a memory, as one would pluck out a stone from the river, examine it, and throw it back to be lost among the other pebbles. Here was the forest fire that had nearly killed him. There was the white wolf that had hated him, and how he had killed it. Fleeing a wounded grizzly. Tricking a wolverine. Timeless perfect memories. Vaguely he could sort them out—which came first, what came later.

He could not even guess how old he had been when he had first joined the wolves. An infant? A toddler? A teenager? He couldn't count the winters and add to an answer. The seasons seemed endless, as if he had run with the wolves before time began.

Time, for him, began when Mama Jo caught him in the humane wolf trap. It seemed as if his whole being had changed that winter night in the steel cage. Each day afterward became clearly marked and marched forward in step with the human calendar.

Thirty-five days they stayed in Oregon as Mom Jo finished up her graduate studies. February 24 through March 6, they drove to Pittsburgh, a trip made agonizingly long due to his nonexistent communication skills, ignorance of the modern world, and lack of basic hygiene habits. He knew the dates of when he learned to dress himself, eat with a fork, and utter his first words.

So his life was divided in half. January 20, 1996, and forward, he could recall everything in a stream of ordered minutes, ticked off by clocks, marked by calendars. Before then, though, remained a mystery. Where had he come from? Who was he? He longed to know, but there was never any true way of learning. Even if he returned to Oregon, there would be no insightful conversations with the wolves. Unlike Kipling's Mowgli, he never truly communicated with the pack. They merely tolerated him and let him feed on the kill.

If he wanted to know, if these people in Schenley Park truly recognized him, then he had to go to them.

He eased the long IV needle out of his left wrist. He hadn't been fully conscious when they put it in and was now amazed at the length. He gave it a grimace and dropped it into the bio-hazard box.

The doctors had cut off his old blood-soaked clothes, dumping everything that had been in his pockets into a plastic bin. Luckily Max had brought his spare set of clothing from the Cherokee. He dressed quietly in the dark hospital room, filling his pockets again. Wireless phone. Coins. Swiss army knife. Wallet. Two lint-covered midget Tootsie rolls. Spare clip for the .45. The pistol itself, though, Max must have taken or hospital security had locked up. He shrugged at the temporary loss—he hated carrying the thing anyhow. Slipping out of the hospital proved to be easy; the halls were nearly empty at night.

At a lope, he headed across Oakland to the park. Fifth Avenue was silent. Forbes Avenue was crowded with students standing in doorways and on the sidewalks; the street beyond was empty, dark, and quiet. He crossed over the bridge between the University of Pittsburgh and the Carnegie Mellon University campus, up the steep hill to the Schenley Park Nature Center. The crime scene had been to the southeast, in an area that might not truly be part of the park proper, but some area too rocky to build on. Pittsburgh held thousands of such thickets—it wasn't unusual to see wild turkeys or white-tail deer within a half-mile of downtown.

He slowed, aware suddenly that he wasn't armed and no one knew where he was.

He crossed the ambulance tracks first, deep ruts ripped into the fresh mud. The service road that Max had found was no more than a wide, level path, not wide enough judging by the number of uprooted saplings. He followed the tracks and came to the trampled killing ground, littered with the wrappers of the drugs the EMS had given him, the Marlboro stubs from Kraynak, spent casings from his .45, countless footprints, and blood. So much blood.

He could tell where the woman had lain, bleeding out her heart's blood. It was as if she was still there. He could sense her as strongly as when she had stood before him, mad, desperate, and accusing.

Just beyond her was the pool of blood from the slain policeman, but it was just spilt blood. No ghost-like impression remained.

His own blood was eerily like the girl's in that he could have found it with his eyes closed. He crouched beside the stain, wondering what it meant.

Why was his blood like hers? Something small stirred on the ground, and with the rustle of tiny feet, it scurried up to his hand.

With a surprised yelp, Ukiah jerked his hand away. The creature paused where his hand had rested, casting about for a scent. He peered hard to make the animal out of the dark woods floor. It was a field mouse, its fur darker than he had seen before. *You're jumping at mice now.*

Still, it was weird. Why didn't it run away? As he crouched there, regarding the mouse, it ran up to his foot. It placed its tiny paws on his shoe and looked up and up at him. Small black eyes gazed into his own dark eyes.

"You are one strange mouse." He considered his choices: walk away or pick it up. Was picking it up safe? It could be sick; rabid animals, he had heard, were fearless. Rabies certainly would explain Dr. Janet Haze. The mouse's coat was smooth and shiny, the sign of a healthy animal. No scent of sickness clung to it. Perhaps it was a pet, hand-cuddled and lost.

In the end, he extended his hand and the mouse scurried into his palm. Holding it seemed the right thing to do. It certainly seemed comfortable with being held. He marveled for a moment at its size, his fingertip dwarfing its head, its forefeet thinner than a broom straw.

The mouse had to have belonged to Janet Haze. She must have been carrying it in a pocket or even loose in her hand. When she was killed, it had gotten lost.

"Why would anyone keep a mouse as a pet?" he asked it. The mouse was closely examining his hands for food. He tucked it into his breast pocket to see if it would ride there—it seemed content—and unwrapped one of his midget Tootsie rolls for it. The smell of chocolate made his mouth water, so he ate the other. Rather than littering, he folded the wrappers tight and slipped them into his pants pocket. He glanced about at the other bits of trash his near death had brought to the clearing, feeling vaguely guilty. The only things he had truly carried there himself were the .45's spent casings, glittering in growing false dawn. He picked them out of the dead leaves and bloody mud. Just beyond the last one he found an odd cylinder of metal, about the length and thickness of a quality ballpoint pen, shoved almost to obscurity into the mud. Janet Haze had handled it in the last moments of her life, her blood staining its matte black finish. He puzzled over it and then slipped it into his pocket.

Birds were beginning to wake. Hunching in their roosts, they started to call and shout at one another, establishing boundaries in case they were forgotten during the night. Ukiah winced. Max would be up soon, checking on him in the hospital. If he didn't want to catch total hell, he'd better find what he had come for and get back.

He oriented himself with where he had lain, then recalled the direction of the overheard conversation. He quickly found where the watchers had stood. It was a rocky point overlooking the clearing. He had to move through the thickest brush in the area to get there, and he was surprised at the ease with which they had come and gone through it. The man's prints were partially obscured by the general trampling, but he had clearly circled Ukiah and Dr. Janet Haze once before the searchers found them, then moved to where he could watch without being spotted. The woman had run down the hill to join the man on the point.

Ukiah paused to look up at the steep hill and thick brush. *She had run straight to him, in the dark, in the rain, without tripping, without calling out for directions.* The hair on the back of his neck rose slightly. He ran his hand over it to lay it back down. *They might know the park well and prearranged to meet here. They might have had night goggles on. There are lots of ways to explain it.*

He pretended he believed that.

They both had worn boots, identical except for size. They had turned and run up the hill together, retracing the woman's path down. He tracked them to the edge of the park. There, in the mud, were deep motorcycle tracks, clear of rain and thus made after he had wakened. He followed the trail of mud down the street until it was a ghost trail, catching it again only as they splashed through puddles, renewing the mud. They had gone toward Homestead, but eventually the tracks gave out.

Ukiah hunched on the pavement, fingering the last drying remains of the motorcycle prints. Part of him thought about going on blindly, hoping to pick up the trail again. The other part of him had caught the rumble of a Hummer, recognized its motor as Max's truck. Mom Jo laughingly called it Max's GI Joe car, but Ukiah noticed that Max pulled it out of storage only when he was trying not to be afraid and upset. Ukiah wasn't sure how a change in cars helped calm Max, but it did—he became bolder and louder, talking often of how the Marines kicked Iraqi butt. Maybe it made Max feel like he was still part of that larger, fiercer force that he had once stood with.

Whatever the reason, if Max had the Hummer out and was looking for him, then Ukiah better stay put and be found. The Max in the Hummer was armed and jumpy, and he had a tongue that could scald milk.

The Hummer leaped suddenly into view. It rushed up and slammed to a stop just short of where Ukiah was crouching in the road. Its squat shape and round headlights reminded Ukiah of a mean-tempered wolverine. The driver's window slid down, exuding a wealth of information in odor. Max leaned out and regarded him with a strangely unreadable gaze. Somehow this was worse than the cross outburst Ukiah had been expecting.

"Get in," Max finally said.

Ukiah went round to the passenger side and climbed in.

The .45 in Max's shoulder holster was freshly cleaned. The cigar smoldering in the ashtray was cherry-flavored. There was fresh oil on Max's shoes from when he stopped to refuel the Hummer. These stenches did nothing to mask the reek of his fear. Ukiah hunched miserably quiet on his side of the truck, afraid to break the silence and yet hating it.

Max wrenched the Hummer through a tight U-turn and headed across town.

"How did you find me?" Ukiah finally asked.

"Tracer. I was feeling paranoid so I tagged your jeans." Max tapped his laptop sitting open beside him, its screen scrolling GPI maps matching the streets they were roaring down, still dutifully marking Ukiah's position.

Max was silent for a moment, then in more of a statement than a question asked, "There was someone else in the woods, wasn't there? You went back to check them out."

Ukiah nodded. "How did you know?"

"A call from the police got me out of bed about an hour ago. Someone killed the coroner on duty and snatched the woman's body from the morgue. Apparently the FBI has gotten involved in this for some reason. They called the hospital to check on your status—and found out you were missing at the three A.M. bed check. Missing woman. Missing private detective who killed her. Police called me to see if I could shed some light on this coincidence. I activated your tracer and you're running around Schenley Park in the frigging dark." Max pulled off his baseball cap and swatted Ukiah with it. "*What the hell were you thinking!*"

At least this was the Max that Ukiah was expecting. This was the Max he knew. "I needed to study the trail before it got ruined by another rain."

"You need to get your head examined! Why the hell didn't you call me?"

"Because you wouldn't have let me out of the hospital."

"Damn right!" Max snapped. "This isn't our normal case of find the kid snatched by his loser father or a stupid messed-up runaway. Something big and ugly is going on here, Ukiah. I ran a check on the girl—Dr. Janet Haze had a top-secret clearance. They don't give those to whacked-out drug users. Even if they did, we're talking cum laude from MIT. You don't make grades like that while messing with drugs. I watched the recording, and she's tripping deadly on something and acting pretty surprised about the matter."

The light ahead changed to red, and Max slammed the Hummer to a stop. He turned to glare at Ukiah. "Someone slipped her something really nasty. Someone snatched her body, all her body parts and even her blood samples. The night-duty coroner happened to be in the way, and from what I gather, someone messed him up good before killing him. And what are you doing? You're chasing after that damn someone without a gun or backup or even one fucking person who knows that you're not safe in the hospital!"

"Sorry, Max."

"Sorry won't cut it because it won't cut it with your moms when you get yourself killed. Sorry, Jo. Sorry, Lara. I dragged your child out into the big bad world and got him killed. That will go over just great."

Ukiah hated it when Max treated him like a kid. He hated it more than anyone else treating him like a kid—maybe because Max had been the first to treat him like an adult. Somehow Ukiah never saw one of these "that was amazingly stupid" speeches coming. Things would be going fine and then suddenly he'd be jerked back to the wrong side of the kid/adult line.

"I promise I won't do it again," he said, meaning it. "If I feel the need to chase after someone, I'll carry my gun and I'll make sure I have backup."

"That's what I want to hear," Max grumbled, geared down to first, and started out as the light changed. "The police said, when I found you, I was to bring you down to the coroner's office."

"Why?"

"Actually, they said there or the police station, and the station seemed too close to being arrested, so I opted for the coroner's."

A McDonald's was coming up on the corner. At the sight of the sign, Ukiah's stomach rumbled, reminding him that he hadn't eaten since lunch yesterday. "Can we pull through the drive through and grab something to eat first?"

Max didn't answer, but veered hard into the McDonald's parking lot. Three minutes later, they

pulled out, with Max eyeing the pile of food on Ukiah's side of the Hummer. "Hope you don't regret
that when we get to the coroner's."

There was mass confusion at the morgue. Max announced their arrival to the first uniform they saw,
but the man shrugged and directed them inward.
"From the sounds of it, the FBI wants you."

Even if the path to the killing hadn't been clear,
Ukiah could have found it by following the smell.
The last door opened to an autopsy room in complete
disarray and splattered with blood. The body of a
middle-aged black man was huddled in the far corner, his lab coat soaked red by his blood. The damage
reminded Ukiah of a wolf pack kill: the gut ripped
open, the intestines pulled out, the blood-gorged
heart and liver eaten first. Parts of his face were eaten
down to expose white bone.

Max cursed softly, an obscene chant that often
called on his God, who apparently didn't mind having his name taken in vain.

"You two the private detectives I wanted to see?"

It was a voice like Mom Jo used on the wolves, a
strong steel voice that demanded an answer. They
turned to face the young woman bearing down on
them. Compactly built, she came only up to Ukiah's
chest. She projected strength without the little yap-
dog frenzy that Ukiah found in a lot of small people.
She wore a torn heavy metal T-shirt and worn jeans
that fit her snugly. Most of her hair was short and
glossy black. One of her forelocks, however, was
twice as long as the rest and dyed a vibrant purple,
and hung down over her gray eyes. She turned to
one of the forensic people to indicate that they could
go, and flashed Ukiah a look at her .357 pistol in a
kidney holster. She turned back to the private detec-

tives again, flipping the violet hair out her eyes. She was in her mid-twenties, but had the air of someone in complete authority.

Max eyed her blue jeans, T-shirt, and dyed hair. "I didn't hear that the agency had gone casual on the dress code."

"I was working undercover," she stated in a feminine version of "just the facts" impassiveness. She took out her FBI ID and flashed it at them. "Special Agent Indigo Zheng, Pittsburgh field office."

"Maxwell Bennett, Bennett Detective Agency." Max had his hands in his jeans pockets and didn't bother to take them out to shake—a sure sign he was in a bad mood. "This is my partner."

Max paused for a beat to let Ukiah introduce himself. Max insisted on Ukiah giving his own name; "establishing a strong presence," he called it. They practiced it until it was smooth, but Ukiah would rather let Max do the talking.

"Ukiah Oregon." Ukiah shook hands like he was taught and left Max to deal with the agent. In the name of learning, Max had once gotten Ukiah into an autopsy, so he was faintly familiar with the layout of the room and the procedures that the coroner would have followed.

The first step would have been to draw blood samples. Ukiah found the vials labeled JANET HAZE scattered across the appropriate table. They had been dusted for fingerprints and left, so he felt free to pick one up.

Tiny sharp teeth had gnawed through the rubber top. Four hairs lay almost invisible inside. He tapped them onto his hand. They were—mink fur? No, something close to a mink, some animal related to it. The teeth marks matched that of a mink cousin. The strong musk odor coming from inside the vial also confirmed that it wasn't a mink, but something close. He eyed the small glass cylinder with its gnawed-open top. Mink and weasels were common in Oregon's Umatilla National Park where he ran with the wolves, but at a morgue in downtown Pittsburgh?

The second step would have been to remove the vital organs. He found the neatly labeled, semirigid bags, but they too had been gnawed open. This time it was apparent, at least to him, that the damage had been done from the inside out. In the organ bags were more minklike hairs. He noticed this time the lack of blood. There was no residue, no blood cells, no organ cells—only the stray hair. He studied the labels. *Janet Haze, heart, weight 3.4 pounds, extreme damage from advanced viral infection noted.*

She had been sick? He checked his memory and found only black holes. He sighed and examined the vials for blood traces. They had the same lack of residue, yet the labels stated that blood had been placed inside. He doubted that it was a case of labeling the vials and bags prior to use. The dead coroner would have been under pressure to do it by the book. He theorized that the mink cousin had licked the bags clean, but there wasn't any sign of saliva.

So someone had dumped the bags of their contents, washed them well, and then sealed animals inside. Yeah, like that made sense!

Mystified, he studied the room. The first true sign of blood was two feet in front of the vital organ table. It belonged to the coroner—he assumed, then caught himself. It didn't belong to Dr. Janet Haze. The subject had been male, black, and mature, so maybe it did belong to the coroner. There were faint traces of drugs in the blood, ones he recognized from experience to be heart medication.

More blood of the same type splattered the floor in increasing amounts, leading to the coroner's body.

The coroner had died slumped against a wall, knocking a ventilation grate askew with his last struggles. His feet almost touched the table where Dr. Janet Haze would have lain, cut open and gutted. In metal trays were the dissection tools: large knives, bone saws, and one small circular saw to cut open the skull. In a steel bowl were two twisted lumps of .45-caliber bullets.

He found countless little footprints in the pool of congealing blood, trampling over each other until they had become a blur. Here and there, though, he could pick out individual prints. He used his pinkie to measure the prints. Five. Six. Maybe seven individual animals. Over and around the body they had gone, tearing and eating. But where had they gone? They had to have gone somewhere. He felt the hair on the back of his neck lift slightly; the whole situation was creepy. He ran a hand across the apparently clean section of the floor, hoping to hit a blood trail too faint to see.

Agent Zheng walked over and placed a foot in front of his searching hand. "Is this some version of good cop, bad cop? Talkative PI, silent PI?"

He leaned back on his haunches to look up at her. The foot had been a firm "stop it," but there was no anger in her face or body. "I don't talk much."

They regarded each other. She had a strong face, sharp lines, and hard angles, tightly composed to neutrality. Only her large eyes were slightly readable, and they seemed narrowed in vague suspicion. What had she and Max been talking about? Ukiah reviewed their conversation and found that someone had also broken into police evidence and stolen everything held there. Their recording from his head

camera was the only shred of evidence left on the
case, and she was concerned whether it was safe
from theft too.

"I was told," she said, "that you left your hospital
bed sometime after two A.M. Since I was already here
at the morgue at 2:15, it's doubtful you had anything
to do with this murder."

"I can't believe you're considering my partner as
a suspect!" Max snarled behind Ukiah. "We were
called in by the police without a clue as to what was
going on. Mr. Oregon was almost killed by your top-
secret scientist, and was confirmed in the hospital
when this murder happened. How dare you try to
stick the blame on him?"

"The facts remain," Agent Zheng replied quietly,
"he killed Dr. Janet Haze and he left the hospital in
the middle of the night."

"He's got seventeen stitches in his left arm and
five in his neck! The shooting was self-defense. And
what if he did leave? There's no law that says you
have to stay in the hospital once checked in."

Agent Zheng ignored him. "Mr. Oregon, will you
please explain to me yourself why you left the
hospital?"

He considered what to tell her. At least part of the
truth seemed safe enough. "There was a man and a
woman in Schenley Park. The man was at the crime
scene before my backup arrived—they stepped onto
his footprints, not vice versa. He didn't actually come
close enough to touch either one of us, but he did
walk around our bodies. Then he moved off and was
joined by the woman. They wore leather jackets and
boots common to bikers. They ran to the edge of the
park where they had two motorcycles, Japanese high-
performance machines, the man's a nine hundred
and the woman's a six hundred."

One of her eyebrows lifted. With someone else, the gesture would have been unremarkable. In her, it was a shout of surprise. "How do you know this?"

He hated lying, but he'd learned there were limits to what people believed. "When I came to, he was there, but I was too faint from blood loss to tell anyone. When I felt better, I went back to track him."

"Your head camera will confirm or deny this." Was it a warning or a question?

"I don't know if he'll show up on the recording," Ukiah said. "It was dark and raining, but I could sense him moving around. You can hear a black dog walking in the woods at night, but you can rarely film him."

"I see." She showed no hint of believing or disbelieving him. "And were you able to track him?"

"Not far. Their wheels were muddy, thus leaving tracks, but the mud eventually gave out and I lost them."

"Any other questions?" Max interrupted, motioning to Ukiah to get up. "Come out to our truck, and I'll make you a copy of the disc now. Then, if you don't mind, Mr. Oregon has had a rough twenty-four hours, and I should take him home."

She considered them, first Max and then Ukiah, with her somber gaze. "No more questions for now."

Coroner personnel were waiting at the door as they exited. Agent Zheng indicated that she was done and they could remove the body. Max led the way back through the morgue.

Ukiah found himself in step with Agent Zheng despite his longer legs. He wondered if she believed him, if she was suspicious of him still. What did she feel? Why did he care? Why, for that matter, was she even involved in the case? "Agent Zheng, I don't understand why the FBI is involved. This is a straight murder case to be handled by the local police, isn't it?"

"Not completely." Agent Zheng gave him another measured, unreadable look. "Doctor Haze worked for a company with several ongoing top secret projects. A month ago, her immediate superior was killed and Doctor Haze took over his position. We think his death was accidental, but there were some suspicious details and the case is still open. We had our net filters scanning all law databases for anyone connected to the company, and it alerted us when the police filed their initial reports."

"What I don't understand, why was a doctor living with three college students?" Max asked.

"Janet Haze only recently received her doctorate," Agent Zheng said. "She had been roommates with the other three for the last four years."

They emerged from the dim building into the parking lot. The cement was still damp from the night rain. It glistened in the bright morning sun. The police cars were gone and the Hummer squatted alone, waiting unmolested for their return.

"A Hummer?" Agent Zheng studied the truck. "How does a small-time detective agency afford one?"

"Good fortune in a previous life," Max grumbled, remotely unlocking the truck. Opening the driver's door, he leaned in and slotted a blank optical disk into the computer.

"Previous life?" Agent Zheng opened the passenger door before Ukiah reached it, leaning in to eye the Hummer's interior. She waited for an answer, but Max rarely talked about his life before becoming a private detective. "You have it loaded for bear."

"I like it that way." Max ejected the copied disc and held it out to her. "I made a copy of the disc yesterday and gave it to the police, but I guess that's gone. What's here in my truck is a copy too—the original is in a secure place. Myself, Mr. Oregon, and the agency's lawyer know how to access the original." Which meant it was in the floor safe at the office. "Now, can you let Mr. Oregon in so I can take him home?"

She stepped back, turning to let Ukiah into the Hummer. She gazed up at him, and he thought he saw a sudden wistfulness in her gray eyes. She held out her hand. "Mr. Oregon."

He took her hand and they shook firmly. "Agent Zheng."

He got in and shut the door, fastening his seat belt out of habit. Max started up the Hummer and they pulled out of the parking lot, leaving Agent Zheng standing alone.

It was a long drive from the morgue back to Ukiah's moms' place. Usually Ukiah liked the trip; it let him unclutter his mind of useless junk before rejoining his family. The day before, however, still contained choppy flashes of memory. He could tease nothing new from the time after he woke wounded in the park. There remained only the morgue with its grisly puzzle, and he wasn't sure he wanted to think about it.

Max stayed quiet until they hit I-279 north, running up out of the city. Then he glanced over at Ukiah. "You okay?"

"That was really, really scary, Max."

"What, special Agent Zheng?" Max snorted. "Don't let her get to you."

Ukiah shook his head, running his hand repeatedly down the back of his neck in an effort to get the hair to lie down again. "The stuff in the morgue. I've never seen anything like it."

"It looked pretty gory. So what did you find?"

Ukiah shrugged, having no idea where to start. "Janet Haze was really sick when she died. All her organs had extensive damage to them due to viral infection. Or at least that's what the coroner noted on the organ bags."

"Oh Jesus, I wonder if she was working on a germ-warfare project. Maybe we should get you checked out. If she was exposed to something nasty, you could have been too."

Ukiah pondered his own body. "I don't feel sick. Hungry again. And I could use a nap, but I'm not sick." A memory came to the surface—her room filled with K'NEX toys and books on robots. "Anyhow, she worked in robotics, not biology."

"What else?"

He sat for a long time considering what to tell Max.

Max shot him a puzzled look after the first minute or two of silence. "That weird?"

"Far as I can tell, Max, all her internal organs"—he shrugged with helplessness—"changed. They became weasels or mink or something. They attacked the coroner and killed him."

"Yeah, that's weird." Max nodded, then screwed up his face trying not to scowl or laugh. Ukiah wasn't sure which. "Changed into weasels? Are you sure? Even if they did, how could those little animals kill a man?"

"Scout's honor." Ukiah retold how the residue blood and organ cells were missing and that all the bags contained was animal fur. "And the coroner had a heart condition. I figure it probably would be scary enough to kill someone."

They fell silent for a few moments. They hit where I-279 merged with I-79 and worked their way into the traffic.

"What really freaks me out is the fur," Ukiah finally admitted. "But I think it's the real proof of the organ changing somehow. There were two sets of DNA active in it. One set was the weasels' DNA. The other set was Dr. Janet Haze's."

Max shot him a look that he had given Ukiah often over the years. Ukiah wasn't sure what emotions hid behind the look. Max had used it only once on someone else, a con artist that could steal your wristwatch while you were checking the time.

"So," Max muttered after a while. "They cut out Doctor Haze's organs and set them aside. Poof, they turn into a pack of rabid weasels and attack the coroner. Like any sane human being, he's scared silly and drops dead and they eat him." Max considered the run of logic. "Okay, it hangs together in a twisted *Outer Limits* kind of way. I suppose you could even say that after all that effort to change into a weasel, one would be very hungry and snack on whatever was at hand. Then what happens? Where do they go, and what happened to the rest of her body?"

"I don't know, Max. Agent Zheng stopped me before I could get into seriously tracking them. But I got to thinking. If her vital organs can change into weasels, why can't all of her body? The coroner had knocked the grill off the air vent. They're little, they all could have gone into there."

They glanced at each other. After more than three years of working together, they had developed a full language of expressions. The look they exchanged was an agreement not to talk about it for a while. Ukiah looked away to stare out the window at the passing landscape.

They were almost to their exit before Max found a semisafe subject. "So, tell me about these people in Schenley Park that you went haring off after? You didn't tell Agent Zheng everything."

"How could you tell?"

"Oh, after you learn wolf body language, you're as clear as water."

Ukiah wasn't sure if Max was joking or not. "Well, after I killed Doctor Haze, I passed out—"

"After she sliced you open, you passed out," Max corrected him with a light cuff. "Shock does that to people. Which reminds me." He pulled over onto the shoulder. "Let's have a look at that cut."

Ukiah sighed and winced as he peeled up one edge of the bandage.

Max set the Hummer's hand brake, leaned over, and peered closely at Ukiah's neck. "Take the bandage all the way off," he commanded and pulled the Hummer back into traffic.

"Really?" The Hummer was sadly lacking in vanity mirrors.

"The cut looks better than that huge bandage. If you're feeling okay enough to run all over Schenley Park in the middle of the night, then we might as well do damage control with your moms. It's a good thing you heal so quickly."

Ukiah considered the truth of this and started to coax up the sticky bandage. "Well, I passed out. When I came to, there were police and the helicopter and everything."

"Yeah?" Max was obviously puzzled as to where Ukiah was leading.

"And there were these two people, standing off where I couldn't see them, talking about me." He recounted the discussion completely. "I went back to Schenley Park to look at the tracks. It was creepy how they could move through the thick brush, in the dark rain, at a full run, without anyone noticing them."

"This case gets better and better." Max leaned over and cued up the disc on the Hummer's deck. "I didn't pay any attention to your headcam after you went down. I was glued to the GPI screen. When I watched the recording this morning, I turned it off after Haze dropped. Your watcher might be on the disk."

The screen hissed with static and came up with the chaotic jumble of police cars outside the apartment building. "Testing Ukiah's VOX." His own voice always startled Ukiah. The timbre was wrong and slightly higher than he expected. "Testing, 1, 2, 3. How's that?"

Max sounded like Max at least. "Good, it's coming through clear. There's my channel good and strong. We're go."

It was the first time Ukiah had ever really watched one of their recordings. Usually his memory was so much fuller and clearer. This time, however, there were holes in his memory. He and the camera went into the building. Despite state-of-the-art steadycam, the view was jittery and vaguely fish-eyed. The lack of smell and touch, the limited view, and the reduced sound left Ukiah feeling more and more frustrated. Finally he started to skip through the tracks, letting time leap forward in huge bounds. He would watch the disk later, maybe. He hated the gaps in his memory, but he didn't want to relive the case right now.

He found the end, his gun flashing again and again, set the recording to play normally. The camera showed only part of Janet's unmoving foot. There was silence in the foreground except for the hiss of rain. Max's voice continued in the background.

"Ukiah! Ukiah! Kraynak, Ukiah's down and not responding. The fucking girl got him with the sword. I think he's hurt bad. I'm coming in."

This started a heated argument between Max and Kraynak, which Ukiah tuned out. He considered the angle of Janet Haze's body and what he remembered of the footprints in the mud. If he were right, then the male watcher would enter in the upper right-hand corner of the screen.

"When I went back to the crime scene, his tracks put him right here." He tapped the screen, and at that moment lightning lit up the woods. "There! Did you see him?"

"Ukiah, I'm driving. I didn't see anything."

Ukiah clicked the recording backward frame by frame. For one frame only, a man stood in the brilliant light, facing the camera but starting to turn. "There's the guy."

From the angle, it was hard to tell how tall the man was. He was lean—rangy was what Mom Jo would call it—with shaggy, grizzled hair and dark eyes. The flash of brilliance had drained his face of color, making it all stark angles and shadows. Ukiah guessed at an age range of mid- to late-twenties.

Max glanced over and shook his head. "Doesn't ring any bell except he wasn't any of the police running around last night. None of the media either. Here." He pulled off onto the shoulder again. "Why don't you drive?"

They switched places, and Max tried not to wince when Ukiah ground the gears starting out. Max worked at pulling a usable headshot from the recording, muttering, "I've got to let you drive more often. It's the only way you're going to get any better."

"I could go to the defensive driving school. The ad looked like fun."

Max laughed. "It's in California. Two days ago your moms might have let you go, but today, I doubt it."

"So when do I get to stay an adult all the time and not have to go back to being a kid?"

Max shrugged. "It's weird with parents, Ukiah. There's shit I don't tell my dad because I don't want to deal with his fatherly outrage."

"Yeah, but he can't stop you from doing what you want."

"No. He can't. There! One clean mug shot. Let's see what we can pull up on our friend the peeping tom."

Ukiah got off I-79 at the Evans City exit, whipsawed down 528 to the small town itself. Town, both blocks of it, was quiet as they drove through. They were approaching the long twisting drive back to the farm when Max swore. "Oh hell, this just gets better and better. Pull over and listen to this. Our friend in the park is Rennie Shaw, and he comes with Mr. Uck stickers. 'Armed and considered dangerous.' 'Do not approach.' 'Report all contact to the FBI.' He's suspected of arson, auto theft, burglary, carjacking, drug dealing, drug smuggling, oh I see—we just go down the alphabet. Homicide. Manslaughter. Murder. Look at all those outstanding warrants for arrests. Wanted for questioning in the death of FBI agents. Wanted for questioning in the disappearance of FBI agents. Wanted for questioning . . ."

"What about arrests and convictions?"

Max scrolled downward. "Looks like they've never managed to catch and hold him." Max suddenly killed the window and started to type. "Let's hope that I'm consistently paranoid."

"What do you mean?"

"This man, this very bad man, is curious about you, and he knows your name. I'm doing a search on your name to see what he can learn about you."

Ukiah glanced up the driveway to his mothers' house. "He's not coming here?"

His driver's license photo came up on the Pennsylvania Motor Vehicle database. Name: Ukiah Oregon. Address: 145 Maryland Avenue, Pittsburgh. He blinked at it and pulled out his wallet to check the hard copy. "The office address?" He flipped through his wallet. His private detective license. His weapons permit. His motorcycle registration. "They're all to the office."

"Technically, my house. Gifts of my paranoia. We were heading into Annie Krueler's kidnapping trial when we started to establish your identity. I wanted to make sure you were safe from any stray idiots, so we put my house down as your residence. If anyone official questioned it, we were going to say you lived with me."

Three years ago he had been too ignorant to even notice the oddity of his paper trail. Now he knew where the holes could develop. "What about next of kin? Who to contact in case of emergency? Life insurance beneficiary?"

"We figured all the angles. I'm listed for next of kin, emergency contact, and beneficiary."

"Mom Jo agreed to this?"

"She hated it. You would have thought I was trying to steal you with legal mumbo-jumbo, but Lara pointed out that it was for your safety and Cally's."

"So the farm is safe?" Ukiah shifted the Hummer down into first.

Max nodded, but the worried look remained.

CHAPTER FOUR

Tuesday, June 16, 2004
Evans City, Pennsylvania

His five-year-old sister, Cally, was in the front yard when they pulled up, playing with a mix of Tonka trucks and Barbie dolls in the sandbox. She sprang to her feet and ran to the Hummer shouting, "Ukiah's home! Max is here!"

She slammed into Ukiah's legs and hugged them hard, giggling as if all the joy of the world was flowing in her. "You're home! You're home! Mommy said you were sick and might not be home for a while."

Ukiah tousled her curly black hair, soft as puppy fur. "I got better and Max brought me home."

"I'm so glad. I prayed special for you last night. Do you think God heard me and made you better?"

"I'm sure of it, pumpkin." Ukiah shook his head, amazed at how much Cally seemed to love him for how little time he had spent with her over the last three years. He left in the morning before she was awake and often worked days in a row, doing stakeouts or traveling cross-country for out-of-state jobs. Yet every time she saw him, she showered him with a child's pure, strong love.

It amazed him more because when she was born,

he had been miserably jealous of her. Envious of the time his moms took caring for her. Covetous of the love they showered on her. Resentful that they never seemed angry with her. His moms and the farm had been his whole world, and Cally had suddenly appeared to take it all away. He'd sit in his tree house and sulk whenever she was awake.

His change of heart had come when he started to work with Max. It gave him a new, all-consuming world to explore. Slowly he left his childhood behind, and at some time arrived at being an adult. The farm was still a comforting retreat, but it wasn't his life. With no need to compete, he'd been able to stand Cally's presence, then welcome it.

Mom Lara came out of the house and hugged Ukiah warmly. She smelt of yeast, sweat, and honey. Her gold hair was swept up into a bun, and flour streaked her face. White hand prints—her own and Cally's little ones—decorated her blue jeans and crisp linen shirt. "Oh Ukiah." She gave him a radiant smile. "I'm so glad you're home in one piece."

"Thanks, Mom."

She turned, one arm holding Ukiah securely, to look up at Max still in the Hummer. "Where do you think you're going?"

Max tried his normal dodge. "I just ran Ukiah out. I was heading back to the office."

"You look worse than Ukiah, Max. We're grilling steaks for dinner tonight and having a picnic. Why don't you stay, take a nap, and eat with us later?"

She merely stood there, smiling up at him. As always, Max sighed, tucked the Hummer's keys over the visor, and climbed down to join them on the lawn. "You made your potato salad?"

"Of course I did." She kissed Max on the cheek in greeting, wove her free hand into his arm and guided them toward the house. "I was making bread to celebrate the Mars landing, so the house is beastly hot, but it's nice out on the porch."

An hour later the house was silent.

Mom Lara took Cally off to pick strawberries at a neighboring farm. Max was dozing on the porch hammock. Ukiah slipped into the house and cut off a still-warm heel of bread, smeared it heavily with blackberry jam, and ate it with a glass of cold milk. Done in from the night before, he went yawning up to his room.

Mom Jo's family once had been well-to-do, and the old house was a huge three-story Victorian with breezy rooms filled with sunlight. The entire attic was his, although he owned little more than a bed and a dresser. He had been too old for toys when Mom Jo found him; too illiterate for books; too solitary for most sports equipment. For a long time it had been one large empty echoing room. Mysteries and criminology books—spillover from his work— were starting to fill up the vast space. On the one tall wall, he had hung framed newspaper clippings, awards, commendations, and letters of thanks from the people he had found—lives he had saved. He fingered them, trying to drive away the strange hollowness the latest case formed in him.

All these cases, he told himself, *and I've only done good. One bad case shouldn't taint it all.*

Memory was an odd thing. It felt like he had always been Max's partner, but there was a definite day that he went from a part-time tracker to a full partner. Max had taken his moms by surprise by announcing that his promotion was a done deal. Memory being what it was, he also recalled that had been the last time his moms sent him to his room. He had lain in bed listening to his moms and Max shout at one another, arguing about his future.

"You went behind our backs!" Mom Jo had shouted for the third time.

"If you want to see it that way, then there's nothing I can say to change your view, but I didn't."

"What gives you the right to—?"

"Can we get off my rights and all this other shit and talk about what is important? He's eighteen, or close to it as far as we can tell. What is he going to do for the rest of his life? What can an ex–wolf boy who has no education, no driver's license, no birth certificate, no Social Security number—no legal identity at all—do? Nothing! What would happen to him if you both were killed in a freak accident? People would fall over themselves to adopt your daughter. Ukiah? There would be nothing. No one takes an eighteen-year-old in, the welfare system won't recognize him, and if you don't do something to get him set up in work, he won't be able to take care of himself. You're all he has right now. If there were a fire in the house tonight or a car accident tomorrow, he'd be screwed. I learned the hard way that shit happens unexpectedly."

They were shocked to silence. That was as close as Max ever got to talking about his dead wife. After several minutes of the silence, Max started again, much quieter.

"He needs a means of taking care of himself. I can take him on as a partner. He'd make good money with full benefits, including a retirement plan."

Ukiah remembered a moment of silence, which probably meant Mom Jo and Mom Lara were doing their marriage telepathy thing and communicating only in glances. "Are you sure he could qualify for a PI license?"

Ukiah had let out a deep sigh of relief, surprising himself with how much he wanted his moms to say "yes," "maybe," or even "we'll think about it and let you know."

"You've told me he reads and writes at a high enough level to pass a GED. I can help him study for the Pennsylvania Private Investigator licensing test. If he can pass a GED, with his memory, the licensing test shouldn't be any problem. He'll have no trouble with the physical. Bonding might be trickier with his weird background. But to get it all started, you have to go to the courts and get him recognized by the United States legal system. You have to get him recognized as a legal adult. You have to get him a Social Security number."

He hadn't thought Mom Jo would go for all of it. She hated and feared "the system." He had heard her whisper more than once to Mom Lara, "If they ever knew Ukiah wasn't legally adopted, they would take him away from us." When he had been younger, he had had nightmares about "they." He had been amazed that she said yes.

Memory being what it was—three years later and almost asleep on his bed—Ukiah realized that probably the only reason his moms had said yes was because Mom Lara had been told she might have only weeks to live.

Cally woke him for dinner. She crawled onto his bed and hugged him awake with more sharp knees and hard elbows than a human child should have. She gave him a blackberry jam kiss, a sticky smile, and then demanded a horseback ride down all three flights of stairs to the yard.

He recalled his last thoughts before going to sleep and the horseback ride went down into Mom Lara's rose garden to visit the grave of one Miss Pretty Lightfoot. Sometime over the years the rock marking the grave had been moved. If Cally even remembered the burial, she gave no sign. To have the memory of a child—he wondered what it was like.

The ride went to the big wraparound porch where his moms and Max were laughing. His feet boomed on the painted wood floor, so he made a complete circle of the porch, making the most of the effect. Finally he collapsed onto the top porch step to drop Cally off.

"Again!" Cally cried, half-choking him with one of her misplaced bear hugs.

Mom Lara saved him by gently prying her off. "Cally, honey, it's almost dinnertime. Go wash your face and hands."

Mom Jo gave him a hug and let him go with a "Now let me look at this." She tilted his head aside to look at his neck.

"It's nothing, Mom."

"Nothing? An inch over or wider—" She shook her head and scowled first at Ukiah and then at Max. "Sometimes—"

"Mom, I'm fine." He grinned at her, silently vowing that she would never see the disc in Max's Hummer. "I cut myself worse than this the first time I shaved."

They heard a shout of laughter from inside the house, and Mom Lara called, "You have to admit Jo, he did."

With that, it was over—the least amount of fuss they had ever put up over him being hurt while working.

They had steak, medium for Mom Lara and mooing for Ukiah, Max, and Mom Jo. Cally announced proudly she had picked all the salad ingredients, and the mangled vegetables showed it. Max talked Mom Lara through grilling summer squash instead of her normal pan-fry. Mom Jo brought out a bottle of wine and a glass of grape juice for Cally. Dusk fell and the yard became bejeweled with fireflies. Cally begged a jar off of Mom Lara and went off chasing the gleaming insects.

Ukiah sat on the porch, watching her play, drinking the wine with the other adults. *When did I become one of them?* It had happened sometime when he wasn't looking. Was it this year? Last year?

When he had arrived, he wasn't sure, but he could recall the signposts along the road. The first had been certainly Max taking him on as a partner. The second probably had been buying his motorcycle. If he was going to work full-time with Max, he had to be able to commute into Pittsburgh daily. Max and his moms took turns teaching him how to drive, with some vague notion he'd drive Mom Lara's '95 Neon to work. He found the whole process of driving a car awkward, and it left Mom Lara without a car all day. He pitched the idea of the motorcycle to Max first, pointing out that he had ridden dirt bikes on the farm for years. He could put a down payment on a brand-new, reliable machine with his first paycheck and only use Mom Lara's car on days of bad winter weather. It took a while to get Mom Lara over the amputation rate in motorcycle accidents, but his moms agreed. Max drove him to the bank and then to the dealership, but he let Ukiah pick and buy his machine, stepping in only at the end to haggle down the price and help fill out the registration paperwork.

Another signpost had been his moms telling him but not Cally that Mom Lara had a brain tumor and might not survive the surgery. Ukiah was never sure if this was a blessing or a curse. Cally had remained happily ignorant the day of the surgery while Ukiah was sure he'd die of worry.

Another had been when he discovered that the medical bills were driving his moms into bankruptcy, so he used his paychecks to pay off the debtors. At first they protested, but he pointed out that if he was working, he should pay rent and his share of the food. Then he extended his health benefits, covering Mom Lara as part of his family, something Mom Jo couldn't do, despite their marriage.

Mom Jo took Cally off to bed and then went to exercise her pack of ten wolf dogs. Mom Lara was in the kitchen, watching the Mars mission on the NASA channel as she washed up dishes. Max sat rocking back and forth on the glider. Ukiah lifted the wine bottle to pour himself another glass and discovered it was empty.

He glanced over at Max, realizing that he had been quiet for some time. Max was a quiet, introspective drunk. "You okay?"

Max waved a hand at the empty bottle. "I never know when to stop anymore."

"Staying the night then?"

"Looks like it."

Ukiah stood, holding out his hand to Max. "Want a hand up?"

"I guess so."

In the guest room, as he helped Max with his shoes, Ukiah realized how much Max had become part of their life. His alarm clock was on the nightstand. A change of his clothes was in the dresser. His spare toothbrush hung in the guest bathroom.

"There are times," Max said quietly, "that I wish

one of your moms would marry me. I wish that this was my place, that these were my kids, that this was my life. When I was young, this was the life I wanted, it was the life I thought I was going to live, it was the life I worked hard to have."

Ukiah wasn't sure what to say. He gripped Max's shoulder, a little ashamed at the inadequacy of the gesture. "I'm sorry."

"Kid, if you ever find a girl that loves you, that you love, grab hold and never let anything happen to her."

"I will."

"Good night, kid," Max muttered, sprawling out onto the bed.

"Good night," Ukiah whispered, and closed the guest room door on Max's quiet misery.

Downstairs, he heard the click of dishes and soft drone of the news. He drifted down to the kitchen. "Anything I can help you with, Mom Lara?"

"No, thank you, dear." She patted his cheek with a soapy hand without taking her eyes from the kitchen television. The NASA channel showed an odd still picture of closed-quarters machinery. In a small side window, Mom Lara was watching the local news channel. More thunderstorms rushing down on Pittsburgh. "I'm just puttering around during the communication delays. The ship's landed on Mars and they'll be dismounting the rover soon." Her eyes were sparkling with excitement. She was always so vibrant when she talked about stars and planets. He wondered how she ever gave up her work to raise Cally. "Is Max staying the night?"

"Yeah."

She sighed slightly, rinsing the soap from her hands and drying them on a tea towel. "He was never meant to live as a bachelor. He's one of those men that needs a wife and kids to be happy."

"I know."

"Does he ever talk about starting to date again? It's been almost six years since his wife was killed."

Ukiah shrugged. "He didn't look at women before, but lately he's been checking them out. He asks me occasionally what I think about certain women, you know, a waitress at Ritter's diner, one of the 7-Eleven cashiers."

"What do you tell him?"

"The truth."

"Ukiah, your truth is so brutal at times. I hope you've tried to be nice about it."

"Well, I try."

"Good boy." She turned back to the TV. The weather ended without the Mars shot changing. A remote story started up with a pretty blonde reporter playing with a rover prototype apparently developed locally.

He frowned at something wrong, out of place. Then he remembered. He had put a mouse in his pocket earlier. He tented his breast pocket and looked in. The mouse was gone. When had he lost it? In Schenley Park? At the morgue? In the Hummer? When he took his nap? He grimaced at the thought of losing it in his bedroom—Mom Lara would freak. Surely if he had had it until he had gotten home, it would have moved around, tried to get out, or otherwise drawn his attention to it. He must have lost it earlier, probably when he was tracking and too focused to notice its escape.

The obligatory local take on the world news over, the studio reporters came on the air, their faces grave. "Early this morning deputy coroner Earl Frakes was killed while conducting an autopsy on a woman suspected of murdering her three roommates and a policeman."

Ukiah turned away from the television, wishing he could tune it out. "Mom Jo still running the dogs?"

The television continued on behind his back. "Janet Haze had been killed in a police shootout yesterday. Police say that they believe Haze acted under the influence of a hallucinogenic drug. We go live to Hap Johnson on the scene."

"Um-huh." Mom Lara murmured, eyes on the main screen as the uncoupling countdown started.

Ukiah glanced out the kitchen window to see if he could spot his other mom. The moon was a few days from full; it coated the wheat fields beyond the yard in soft silver. In the center of the field stood his oak. The tallest tree on the farm, it had been his sanctuary since the first day he arrived here. Its leaves tipped with moon glow, but his tree house was lost in the dark shadows of the night.

"Thanks, Ashley," the remote, Hap Johnson, was saying. "I'm here at the county morgue, where early this morning deputy coroner Earl Frakes was the victim of a grisly murder—"

Ukiah felt the desperate need to escape the television. "Good night, Mom. I'm going to go out to my tree house. Don't wait up for me."

"Okay, honey."

He strolled out to the tree, climbed the battered ladder up to the large platform built in the massive limbs. He hadn't been out to it in months. Strange how he used to all but live up here. When Mom Jo first brought him home, he'd hid from punishment up in the branches of the oak. The tree house had been built as a compromise, a place for Mom Jo when she came out to comfort him. He hid up here for days after they brought Cally home from the hospital. His first conversation with Max had taken place here.

He stretched out on the worn boards, still slightly warm from the sun. He was never sure why the tree made him feel so safe. It was something inside him buried too deep to touch. Maybe it was open sky, removed from all the chaos and noise of civilized life.

There was something digging in his side. He reached into his pocket and found the ballpoint pen thing from Schenley Park. He scowled at it. What was this? Was it of any importance at all? Too many mysteries had been dropped on him today. This one he didn't care about. He slipped it into his stash hole for safekeeping, then rolled over onto his back to stare up through the branches at the night sky.

The stars filled the sky; Mars glittered like a bright star. The night insects were deafening, and Ukiah could only think of Haze, her eyes wild, shouting about them. Why had Rennie Shaw said Ukiah was one of them? How could he have anything in common with a man like that? Yet few people in Pittsburgh—in Pennsylvania—recognized Ukiah's name as the name of a place. "Ukiah," they would say, "is that a family name?"

The kitchen screen door squeaked open, banged shut. Minutes later Mom Jo came up the ladder. She paused on the top rung to peer over the edge at him.

"You mind company?"

Ukiah patted the board beside him, and she climbed up the rest of the way.

"Mars is bright tonight." He pointed out the planet.

She nodded, her chin eclipsing the constellation Cassiopeia from his sight as she did. "Lara can't take her eyes off the news cast." She suddenly pointed off to the far eastern horizon. "Shooting star, make a wish."

I want to know who I am. The sudden, clear desire went through him as painfully as the sword cut. He shuddered from the thrust, and Mom Jo reached out to smooth his hair.

"You okay?"

"Mom, tell me again about how you found me."

She sat silent in the darkness, only her scent marking her as his mom. What had his real mother been like? "I was a grad student." She started at the same point she always did. "A wolf pack had been sighted in Oregon's Umatilla National Park, the first time in almost sixty years. I jumped at the chance to do my thesis work on them. When I arrived, I discovered their situation was desperate. It had been a hard winter. The park's elk herds were overcrowded and starving. Due to the deep snow, snowmobile trails proved to be the easiest paths for the elk to follow. The trails lead down into cattle and sheep country. Where the elk went, the wolves followed."

The familiar tale was normally comforting in its cadences. This time he waited impatiently for new information, something to shed light on who he was.

"The Oregon wildlife department was using humane cages to try to capture straying wolves and relocate them. My job was to monitor the cages, checking each day to see if any wolves had been captured. One day I went and found a boy inside the cage, growling with wild eyes and chewing on the bait like he hadn't eaten in weeks—"

"No," he interrupted her. "Not the way you usually do. Tell me as an adult."

"What do you mean?"

He shrugged. "I know you don't trust the government, but why didn't you tell someone that you

found me? Didn't you wonder if someone was looking for me?"

She thought about that, stroking his hair. "Well, I
guess, I didn't tell anyone because I was young and
arrogant. I never questioned that I could civilize you,
that me adopting you was the best thing for you,
and that I could give you everything you would ever
need. Part of it was, back then, it wasn't possible for
Lara and me to have our own children, and it was
unlikely that the state would let two women adopt.
Deny something to someone, and that becomes their
focus. We wanted a child so much—"

She laughed and hugged him tight. "My Mowgli,"
she whispered, rocking him. "At first I figured that
if someone was careless enough to lose you, then I
deserved to keep you as your finder. But then we
had Cally. Raising an infant changes you. You see
things so differently. I started to have nightmares
that we went camping and we would wake up in
the middle of the night and Cally would be gone."

She had never told him this before. He held silent
beside her, afraid to talk, to break the confession.

"I knew that I would never, ever stop looking for
Cally if I lost her, not to the day I died. I realized
then your mother and father might still be looking
for you, never giving up hope. So I hired a private
detective."

A memory clicked into the framework of her story.
The Cherokee pulling up to the house for the first
time. Max, then a mysterious, tall, lean stranger, getting out and scanning the front yard with new eyes.
That long summer evening, sitting in the tree house
with Max, answering one odd question after another.
*Have you ever lived in another house? Do you remember
eating cookies when you were little? When you were little,
did you watch television?* "You hired Max."

She laughed softly. "Yeah, Bennett Detective Agency. I picked Max because of his yellow page ad. It said 'Specializing in Missing Persons.' Odd how little decisions become so important later on."

He recalled those first meetings with Max. Max had tried every angle to dredge up information. Ukiah only remembered then what he remembered now—the endless seasons of running with the wolves. Any previous time he had ever spent with humans, however long or short, was gone.

"Did he go to Oregon?" Even as Ukiah asked, he knew Max would have gone. Max loved to dig until he found the hidden truth. He would have searched missing-persons databases, using age progression/regression photos with pattern matching algorithms. When electronic means failed, Max would have visited every police station in Oregon, reviewed old regional newspapers, and talked to every local who would chat. He might have even hacked spy satellites and searched the park itself from orbit—looking for what, only God knew. "Did he find anything?"

"No." She breathed, as if she knew how much he wanted her to say yes. "No one ever reported a child matching your description missing in the United States or Canada."

Why wouldn't his parents make a report? It occurred to him that perhaps they were dead. A scenario unfolded in his mind. A car accident on a deserted road. The parents killed instantly. A young child—a toddler? an older child with a head wound?—wanders off. When the car was found with the dead parents, would anyone realize that a child was missing?

It was too horrible to bear. *Things like that don't happen.* But he knew they did. It had happened to Max, who came home from a business trip to find his new house mysteriously empty, his beloved beautiful wife gone forever, her body not found until months later.

He hugged Mom Jo tight, trying to drive away the nightmarish thoughts.

Mom Jo patted his back. "It doesn't matter, though. It only means that you're mine forever. I'll never have to give you up to someone else. At least, till you get married."

As usual, Max was slightly late for breakfast as he spent half an hour in the guest room making phone calls on his wireless phone. He came down the steps as he finished up the last call.

"We'll be by later to pick it up. Bye."

"My bike's done?" Ukiah guessed.

"Yeah."

"Pancakes, Max?" Mom Lara asked, flipping the last ones off the griddle.

"Yes, thank you." Max settled down into one of the kitchen chairs as Mom Lara set a stack of pancakes before him. "You're going to have to teach Ukiah how to cook like this, Lara. Currently his idea of cooking is popping frozen waffles into a toaster."

"He'll learn." She collected Cally's empty plate. "Cally, go wash your hands and get your shoes on. When Jo and I first moved out of the dorms, I needed a cookbook to boil eggs. Come on, Cally, we're running late."

"I'll get the dishes, Mom," Ukiah volunteered as he finished his pancakes.

"Thanks, love." She kissed his cheek as she snatched up car keys and a stack of books. "I should have never stayed up to watch the landing. Remember to lock the door."

She and Cally swept out of the house a minute

later. As Ukiah washed the breakfast dishes, Max and he discussed their various open cases. He had been taking a semivacation while the breakdown of his motorcycle stranded him at the farm, doing odd jobs about the house as he made dozens of time-consuming long-distance calls to cross-check background information. He had noted all his findings on his PDA and uploaded them to Max.

Max had been working with their two part-time detectives, Chino and Janey, on a surveillance case. He had E-mailed Ukiah several updates. It was, however, the first time they could compare insights and gut feelings. Max finished up his stack of pancakes and brought his plate up to the sink.

Ukiah washed it quickly, set it with the other plates in the dish rack, and dried his hands on a tea towel. "So what's up for this morning? We pick up my bike first, or what?"

Max led the way outside, pausing on the wide porch. "I realized last night that it's been almost a month since our last target practice. I think we should drive to the back forty and get in a solid hour."

Ukiah grimaced, locking the front door behind him. "I hate guns."

"The .45 saved your life yesterday." Max cuffed him as they walked to the Hummer. "You let your skills go rusty, and next time you won't be so lucky."

Ukiah reluctantly nodded. The kick of the .45, the muzzle flash lighting the woman's eyes, the report mixing with her scream flashed through his mind. *When did I start to remember that?*

While Max drove to the back of the farm to the target range, Ukiah reviewed the day before. All his memories were complete now. Some were cloudy, as if seen through fogged glass, but intact. Why couldn't he remember them when he was in the hospital and could now?

It was a short bouncy trip to the target range, a long flat field on the very edge of the farm. At the one end of the field, the land dipped to the creek bottom and the neighbor's property line. At the other, the hundred-year flood plain line rose sharply. It was into that deep soft bank that they shot.

Max wheeled the Hummer around so the tailgate faced the bank and killed the engine. In the cool morning sun, nothing stirred in the field except occasional grasshoppers. "Quiet."

"Me or the field?"

Max considered, swinging open his door. "Both."

"Max, did you ever kill anyone?"

Max gave him a surprised look. "I killed that Crazy Joe Gary."

"Oh yeah."

No wonder Max looked surprised. Joe Gary was the whole reason they started to target shoot. It had been a bloody turning point in Ukiah's life—only three years ago, and yet seemingly in some other lifetime. Before that case, Max had worked mostly solo, only showing up to fetch Ukiah for rare tracking cases. There had been no talk of "partner" and never even a question of Ukiah carrying a gun. Then Max had taken him out to find a hiker lost on the Appalachian Trail. It was a difficult tracking job on rock, gravel, and hard-beaten dirt paths with hundreds of other searchers confusing the trail.

They were twenty miles from nowhere when Ukiah discovered a clear set of tracks and the truth of the woman's disappearance. She had been force-marched by a man to his secluded cabin. They found out later that the man was Crazy Joe Gary. That he was built like a bear. That he had more guns than

Max. And much later, that he had two dozen dismembered skeletons buried about his cabin, and one cut-up Boy Scout in his refrigerator.

But they didn't know all of that.

When they found the cabin, they called the local police on Max's wireless phone. A woman on the other end politely explained that all her officers were out on foot searching for the missing hiker, and it could take hours to get someone to them. It was then that the screaming started, horrible terrorized screams. Max decided to storm the cabin, counting on surprise and a drawn gun to win the day. Being Max, he also set up a backup plan. He gave Ukiah his spare .45 and told him to stay outside unless things went bad.

Maybe if they had known more about Crazy Joe Gary, they would have waited for the police backup. Maybe not. As it was, Max crashed into the cabin barely in time to stop Gary from bashing the woman's head open as the first step in a much practiced slaughtering ritual. Gary had stood, sledgehammer in hand, slack-jawed at Max's entrance. His shock lasted for only five heartbeats, then he exploded into action.

A minute later, Ukiah stood over the half-conscious Max, eye to eye with Joe Gary's rifle. He patiently explained that he could pull his trigger just as fast as Joe Gary, that the .45's slug would kill Gary just as quick as the rifle's bullet would kill Ukiah, and that they would simply both be dead.

Unfortunately, crazed killers don't have the strongest grasp on logic, and Ukiah had never fired a gun before. From the bloody desperate gunfight that followed, two things were born: Ukiah's hate of guns and Max's insistence that the boy learn how to handle them. Yesterday, though, had been the first time since Crazy Joe Gary that he actually fired his gun during a case.

Actually, Ukiah reflected, a third thing had come out of that gunfight. Without lead up or fanfare, Max asked him if he wanted to be a full-time private detective. Of course he said yes. After his moms also said yes, but before his identity was fully established and all his various licenses granted, Max took him on every case, patiently explaining everything that went into being a private detective, and began introducing Ukiah to all as "his partner."

Not that Ukiah remembered everything that happened on that day. There were holes in his memories leading up to the gunfight. Neat bullet holes in his recall. The paramedics had said memory loss was common for accident victims. Those missing memories stayed lost. Why had the memories of Janet Haze come back?

Max coded open the Hummer's gun safe. "You know, Crazy Joe Gary, he was a lot like that girl. A killer on the loose and your life on the line. I know it feels bad knowing that you killed someone. I've been there, it's horrible."

"Gary was different." Ukiah hadn't been bothered by Gary's death—but was it because he hadn't fired the killing bullet? No, that wasn't it. Maybe because instead of just his life against the killer's, it had been Max's life and the woman's versus the killer's. Had it become noble then, a selfless act to be honored?

He realized that Max was sitting on the Hummer's tailgate, watching him like he was worried about him. It wasn't something Max did often, and it made Ukiah uncomfortable.

"Joe Gary was different than this girl," Ukiah repeated, and struggled to put into words the gut feelings he had. "He was a monster long before we showed up. If you hadn't killed him—" Suddenly the words seemed like a lie. To be fair, Ukiah should own the bullets he had put into Joe Gary. "If *we* hadn't killed him, he would still be killing people. But this woman, she seemed so—lost. I don't think she had ever hurt anyone before in her life. There were teddy bears in her room, Max. She seemed furious that she had killed those people, and she seemed to think someone had done something to her to make her kill them. What if someone *had* done something to her—gave her some drug? What if I hadn't killed her, and the drug wore off and she went back to being just a woman and not a monster?"

"What if, what if, what if." Max shook his head. "The 'what ifs' will drive you insane if you let them. Much as you hate the idea, Ukiah, you only had one choice: if you wanted to live, you had to kill her. You had a split second to make the decision at gut level, and you wanted to live. There is nothing horrible about wanting to live, Ukiah. There is no creature on this earth, on that deep gut level, that doesn't want to live."

"I could have wounded her."

Max scowled at him. "What did I tell you about using a gun?"

"If you are going to shoot, shoot to kill. Otherwise you'll miss your target completely and you might as well not have pulled the trigger."

"I know you can remember that—and the entire Pittsburgh yellow pages, if you wanted. But it can't be memorized words, it has to be embodied actions. You did the right thing with that girl. You fired your weapon and hit twice in the torso. But you need to do it next time, and the time after that, or you'll be dead. You're not a good enough shot to wound someone in a battle like that, kid. Maybe in a few years, but not now."

"I don't want there to be a next time!"

"Kid, we're hired to help people. We find lost people. We find kidnapped people. We save people from tight jams. But sometimes, like with Crazy Joe Gary, we have to fight the bad guys before we can save our client."

Max's phone rang and he flipped it open. "Max Bennett." Max's face grew dark as he listened to the person on the phone. "Agent Zheng, we've already told you all we know on this case. If you don't mind, we don't want anything further to do with it." He stood and started to pace. "If you missed the news flash, my partner was almost killed by Doctor Haze. What? No. That won't be necessary. We'll meet you at our office in an hour."

Max growled and looked like he wanted to pitch the PCS out into the field. "Damn bitch. Well, get in the truck, the FBI wants us in town to 'discuss the case' now."

"What wasn't necessary?"

"Agent Zheng said if we didn't want to come to town, she'll drive out to wherever we were."

"I don't want the FBI out here. Mom Jo would freak."

"That's why we're meeting her in town."

CHAPTER FIVE

Bennett Detective Agency was a silent testimony to how much Max had been worth in his "previous life." It was located a block off boutique-infested Walnut Street in the posh Shadyside neighborhood, in the downstairs of a sprawling five-bedroom Victorian home. The floors were cherry, the walls chestnut burl paneling, and in the entry was a massive grandfather clock that filled the house with solemn, even ticking.

When Ukiah started to work with Max, the downstairs and most of the upstairs had been empty. Once, in a semidrunken state, Max explained that he and his wife had lived for years with broken hand-me-down furniture in tiny apartments. When success finally brought in money, they had bought the small mansion, thrown away the old furniture, and planned to slowly fill the house with beautiful antiques. The grandfather clock had been their only purchase before Max's wife's death.

Since then desks, chairs, a conference room table, wooden filing cabinets, and other office equipment slowly filled the downstairs. Max's office was in the den with floor-to-ceiling built-in bookcases. He had a desk once owned by Frank Lloyd Wright (a reference that failed to impress Ukiah until Max drove him down to Fallingwater) and a two thousand dollar "executive" chair. Ukiah's desk was much less impressive, but he usually used it only to stay out of Max's hair while he did the paperwork that ran the agency.

Agent Zheng was standing on the front porch when they pulled up. Her car, identified by its government plates, was a silver four-door Saturn. Ukiah parked the Hummer on the street instead of pulling around to the garages behind the office, since he and Max planned to pick up his motorcycle after the interview. Besides, he wasn't the best at slotting the wide truck into the standard-size garage. He had driven, in part to get in his needed practice, but mostly to let Max search hither and yon for information on Agent Zheng.

Max winced as Ukiah rode over the curb on his last pull forward. "Well, that's all that seems to be on-line about our Agent Zheng. Not much to go on. One smart cookie that gets results—too bad it's our balls she's trying to break."

"Be positive." Ukiah turned off the Hummer and pocketed his keys. "We haven't done anything wrong."

"Kid, you're just too naive for your own good."

He grinned at Max. "Don't know how, hanging around with you all the time."

Max shook his head, smiling. "Let's get this over with."

Agent Zheng nodded to them as they came up the walk. "Mr. Bennett, Mr. Oregon. Thank you for seeing me."

"You didn't give us much of a choice," Max grumbled, unlocking the front door and leading the way into the house.

Ukiah hung back to let Agent Zheng enter first. She paused to give him a long study, working upward. Without comment, she gazed at his comfortable hiking boots, moss-colored slacks, white linen button-down short-sleeve shirt, and thick black hair, still damp from his hasty shower but neatly combed. It probably seemed like a drastic change since she had seen him last. When he had gotten home yesterday, he'd discovered he looked like he'd been rolled over most of Schenley Park. Dirt coated all his exposed skin. Dead leaves floated in his hair. The spare clothes from the Cherokee had been full of holes, stained with black cave mud, then slightly shrunk in an attempt to get them clean. His night romp through the muddy park had only made his appearance worse.

Reflecting back on Agent Zheng's undercover blue jeans and torn heavy-metal T-shirt, Ukiah supposed that neither of them had been at their peak at the morgue. This morning Agent Zheng wore an expensive-looking black pantsuit and a white silk blouse. All of her hair was raven black. The one long lock swept like a wing, silky and controlled, down from her forehead to her neck. Her makeup was crisp and her perfume—a musk, warmed by her body heat—was light to the point of elusive.

Agent Zheng finished her inspection and brushed past him. His skin tingled with the nearness of her passage. She followed Max, scanning the rooms as they moved through them, expressing neither surprise nor pleasure. She was almost impossible to read, and Ukiah wasn't sure if this was good or bad. It spoke to him, though, of being centered, achieving a tight focus that couldn't be wavered.

Max opted for his office, taking the position of power behind the large desk. Ukiah leaned against the wall to Max's right, facing them both. Agent Zheng accepted the visitor chair, a stylishly sleek chair that decorated her well.

"All right, Agent Zheng, you wanted to discuss the case. We're here. What is there to discuss?"

She plunged straight to the heart of the matter. "We studied your disc frame by frame, and we found one frame to be of most interest."

Ukiah glanced at Max, and a name seemed to be shouted between them—*Rennie Shaw.*

Agent Zheng laid out a blown-up version of the mug shot Max had used. "This is Rennie Shaw. I will be frank with you. This is a very dangerous man. He belongs to a loose organization of motorcycle gangs. These gangs span the country. They are the Demon Curs, the Hell Hounds, the Devil Dogs, the Wild Wolves, and the Dog Warriors."

"Kind of stuck on the canine motif." Max, as usual, did the talking for the partners.

"Yes they are. As a collective, they call themselves the Pack. Rennie Shaw is believed to be the leader of the Dog Warriors, perhaps of the entire Pack. It is a tight-knit group, rigorously exclusive and extremely cunning. Authorities rarely can arrest a member, and they never stay in custody long. The Pack has a reputation as extreme escape artists. They have been known to vanish without a trace from maximum-security holding cells. Authorities have tried to cut deals with captured members—reduced sentences and such for inside information—but no offers have ever been taken."

"Could be they knew they could get out without taking a deal," Max stated dryly.

"Yes. But it is unusual that in a group of this size,

no disgruntled members have ever come forward. Despite the apparent lack of communication between the various gangs, not a single undercover agent has ever been able to penetrate their society. Everything we know about the Pack comes from extensive interviews from eyewitnesses. Another unusual aspect of the Pack is that many of the members are untraceable. No birth certificates. No Social Security numbers. No official records."

Ukiah squirmed. This sounded uncomfortably close to himself three years ago. "So how does the Pack link in with Janet Haze?"

"We don't know." She indicated the photo. "This is the only clue we have that they are involved. If Doctor Haze, however, was given some type of dangerous drug, it could have easily come from the Pack."

"So the Pack gives her drugs," Max ticked off points on his fingers, "watches her freak out, and checks to see if she's dead in the woods, and later steals her body. Murdering escape artists fit the bill to what went down yesterday."

"Yes, it does." Agent Zheng said "After finding this photo, we started to investigate the possible link between Doctor Haze's work and the Pack yesterday morning. Within an hour, one of our agents vanished without a trace." She flipped a second photograph onto the table. A solemn man in his thirties with "I'm the FBI" stamped invisibly on his forehead. "Wil Trace was one of the best agents we had; an agent with ten years of organized crime and gang experience. He was quick on his feet and level-headed."

Had. Was, Ukiah noticed. *She is already using past tense.*

Max leaned far back in his chair, almost as if he was trying to distance himself from the missing FBI agent. "I think I can see where this is going, and I don't like the destination."

"In the past," Agent Zheng went on, "the Pack held law officials they'd captured for several days. Usually, the Pack either subverts them or simply makes them vanish. If they have Wil Trace, and he's still alive, we have to find him before they try either."

"No." Max made defecting motions with his hands. "This is a case for the FBI and police. Not for us."

"He has a wife and three children."

Max tapped his finger on the FBI seal on the file folder that had held the photographs. "He's an FBI agent who knew the risks."

"Max," Ukiah interrupted quietly, "shouldn't we at least hear what she wants?"

Max shot him an angry glare. "Don't fall for that wife-and-three-children bit, kid. She's got the whole FBI organization behind her. They don't let their agents fall through the cracks. Every law agency in the state, in the country, has been brought to bear on this."

"You're right," Agent Zheng admitted. "They have. But we're desperate, time is running out, and we're not even sure if it is the Pack that took Special Agent Trace."

Ukiah frowned—he'd thought Pack involvement was a given. "What do you mean?"

Agent Zheng turned to him. "There's no logical tie between Doctor Haze and the Pack. Nor was Wil Trace even investigating the Pack. He was searching Doctor Haze's home for some clue to her death. His car is still parked outside the house. Neighbors remember him going in, but didn't see him leave. We've turned the house upside down and found nothing. We've searched the neighborhood and Schenley Park. Nothing. Mr. Oregon has proved that he could find a trail where no one else can. He's our last chance to find out what happened in that house."

Ukiah glanced at Max.

"Don't give me that look." Max made a rude noise. "Okay, okay. But we aren't doing this for free."

"You will be paid. What are your rates?"

"If I read this right, this is a tracking job," Max explained. "We charge a flat rate of one thousand dollars a day on normal tracking jobs. Since this case has proved to be unquestionably dangerous, we'll want two thousand dollars a day."

Agent Zheng tilted her head slightly. "That seems high."

Max snorted. "If you wanted us to do a background check on a guy before dating him seriously,"—her records had listed her as single—"it would be one hundred dollars an hour plus expenses. It would take a couple of days. We'd present you with a detailed report of exactly who you were about to sleep with and a bill for easily over one thousand dollars."

Her eyes jumped to Ukiah. She shifted slightly in the chair as if uneasy and then relaxed, gaining her center again. "I see you've been doing your homework."

"We like to know who we're dealing with, Agent Zheng." Max flashed her a roguishly pleased smile. "Tracking is a different ball game with a different rate chart. It's quick, it's dirty, it's dangerous, and we're the best in the business. Much as we like to help people, this is a business. Because of yesterday, our insurance rates went up another notch, and we'll need a lawyer to make sure that, in all this chaos,

Mr. Oregon isn't charged with Janet Haze's death just to neaten things up."

She nodded slowly. "I can authorize your fee."

Max reached into his desk drawer and pulled out their standard tracking contract. He wrote FBI in the client's blank and noted the danger rate of $2000. He signed the bottom and pushed it across to Agent Zheng.

She signed in a controlled neat cursive. "You'll start immediately and I'll be coming with you."

Max shrugged, sliding over to the copier to make her a copy. "I'm curious, though, Agent Zheng. I got the impression yesterday that you didn't trust us."

"I didn't." There was no apology in her gaze. "You were complete unknowns acting in a suspicious manner. Since then I have had a chance to do a background check."

"And?" Max looked up with intense interest.

"Your highest praise was—'If my kid was missing, I'd want them on the case.' "

"And the lowest?" Ukiah asked, getting a scowl from Max.

She looked at him for a silent minute before answering. " 'The kid is creepy to work with, but he's always right.' "

She wanted to ride with them in the Hummer. Max motioned Ukiah into the back so she could sit in the front, away from all the gear Max had in the back. Not for the first time, Ukiah wondered if all the military hardware Max had was totally legal.

Ukiah leaned forward and noticed that her hair was scented with honeysuckle. Her one long bang swept down to the white curve of her neck. She noticed that he was staring at her and turned to meet his gaze. He expected her to say something, but she merely looked back at him silently. Her eyes were somber and still, moonstones of gray.

Max noticed her turn in her seat, then glanced at Ukiah in the rearview mirror. "When Ukiah looks at you, you stay looked at."

"I've noticed."

Max glanced again in the rearview mirror and turned onto Janet Haze's street.

"What was that all about, kid?"

"What was what?" Ukiah checked his .45 and slipped it into his kidney holster. The day was hot and the flak jacket uncomfortable, but he knew Max was too edgy to let him go without.

"The looking." Max snapped shut the chamber of his gun and put it into his shoulder holster.

Ukiah shrugged and slipped on his headcam. "I don't know. I was just looking at her and she looked back."

"You—I understand." Max shook his head. He flicked on his handheld tracking system and checked the signal. "I've got you." He slipped the tracking system into his pocket. "I'll leave the deck on the Hummer. I mean, you *look* at people. That's what I remember most about the first time I met you— the look."

"What do you mean?"

"Kid, you've got a look that—like I said—one stays looked at. That first day, I came up the tree-house ladder and was eye to eye with your look. Pow, straight to the core. I almost climbed back down and dropped the case."

Ukiah shook his head, giving Max a grin. "Max, I have no idea what you're talking about."

"Of course not. People don't do it back to you. Check it out sometime, though—you make a lot of people damn nervous by it, especially the guilty ones."

"She wasn't nervous. She just looked back."

"Which has me damn nervous."

Max slotted a new disk into the Hummer's deck. "Max VOX test. Testing. Testing." He tapped the colored signal strength bar on the monitor. "I'm coming through loud and clear. Give me a test."

"Ukiah VOX test. Test 1–2–3–4."

"That's lousy—you're barely in the yellow." Max reached up and tugged on Ukiah's headset. "Try it again."

"Ukiah VOX test." Ukiah grinned. "Hey diddle diddle, Max jumped over the moon."

Max shook his head, laughing slightly. "You're in the green. Let's go."

Max slammed the Hummer's door and locked it by his remote. Together they went up the steps to join Agent Zheng by the door. She had unsecured the police barrier tape and pushed open the broken door.

As she stepped cautiously inside, Max caught Ukiah by the shoulder. "Just because Agent Zheng is with us, that doesn't make her an automatic good guy, kid. Remember that. Don't rely on her, don't expect her to cover your back."

Ukiah nodded. "Okay, Max." A thought occurred to him and he smiled. "Not one of the good guys? Max, haven't you noticed? Agent Zheng is a girl."

Max cuffed him on the shoulder and went on into the house.

The bodies had been removed. The bloodstains remained. Ukiah crouched in the threshold as he remembered doing the day before. Slowly he scanned the entry. His memory skipped back and forth between his normally laser-etched recall and his slightly fuzzy regained memory. "Lots of people been in here since the day before yesterday, things are shifted around, not by much, but enough."

"Like what?" Agent Zheng asked, pulling out a PDA to take notes.

"That piece of carpet." It was a two- by three-foot carpet sample used to catch dirt at the front entrance. It was stained a rust color by blood. "It had been under the one girl when I first arrived. It's over there beside the stairs now."

He tilted his head sniffing, suddenly aware of a draft and a familiar smell.

"What is it?" Max asked.

He stepped inside and swung the door shut. Behind it was an obvious basement door. He cracked it slightly and the strong odor of animal musk swept up from the basement.

"You weren't in the basement," Agent Zheng commented behind him.

Ukiah glanced back at her. "They kept mink in the basement?"

"Ferrets." Agent Zheng scrolled her PDA file backward and read. "There were three ferrets found in cages in the basement, one male and two females. According to friends, they belong to Janet Haze, and normally she kept them in the attic with her. A day prior to the murders, she asked her roommates if she could move them to the basement, complaining that they made too much noise. The ferrets were removed the evening of the murders by the Allegheny Animal Control Department and taken to the humane shelter on the North Side."

"And they're still there?" Max tried to sound casual while he gave Ukiah "the look."

"I checked on them yesterday afternoon," Agent Zheng admitted.

Ukiah shut the door uneasily. "Too much noise? She seemed really bothered by noise."

Agent Zheng nodded. "It's been found that in psychotic individuals there is an inability to filter out background noise. It's theorized that it's a chemical imbalance that literally drives the person insane by overloading their senses. In your recording, Janet Haze repeatedly asked you how one stopped listening."

Max caught his eyes and shook his head, as if warning Ukiah not to say anything.

Haze had been asking the wrong person, Ukiah thought instead of saying. When they had first started working together, Max asked him often if he was listening. It had puzzled Ukiah since he didn't go around with his fingers jammed into his ears. Slowly he had learned that other people couldn't recall things they hadn't paid attention to, while Max had learned that Ukiah always listened.

Ukiah glanced about the entry hall. Other than the basement, there was the living room and the stairs leading out of the hall. "Where first?"

Agent Zheng indicated upstairs. "Since the bodies were on the first floor, it's the most disturbed. It probably would be best if you start with her room."

Ukiah started up the steps and had almost reached the top when a thought hit him. *Why did Agent Zheng check on the ferrets yesterday afternoon?*

He paused at the top of the steps and watched Agent Zheng follow him up. Should he ask her? What would he say if she asked why he was so interested in the ferrets? If Janet Haze's ferrets were still at the humane society, then they weren't the ferrets at the morgue. Assuming, of course, they hadn't broken out, had a midnight feeding frenzy, and returned to their cages to look innocent. Unlikely, but so far everything about the morgue was unlikely.

The window to Janet's room was shut, and otherwise at first the room seemed unchanged. He stood at the center of the room and did a slow scan. To her credit, Agent Zheng stood patiently at the steps, without a hint of growing impatient. Max pulled out a cigar and chewed on its unlit end.

When Ukiah found the first missing item, Max caught the change in Ukiah's expression. "Found something?"

Ukiah stepped forward to tap a crowded bookshelf. "There was a bottle between these two books, shoved the whole way back to the back wall. It was one of those small drug bottles. It had a label with the word 'Imuran.' "

Agent Zheng and Max both pulled out their PDAs, and uplinked to the web. Max whistled as he found the information first.

"Imuran, generic name azathioprine, manufacturer—hmm—Indication: organ rejection after liver transplantation; severe, active, otherwise unresponsive rheumatoid arthritis. It's an immune-suppression drug." He did a further search as Agent Zheng nodded in agreement. "Janet Haze hadn't undergone organ replacement surgery anytime in her life. I wouldn't think you'd put someone with severe rheumatoid arthritis in the attic bedroom."

Ukiah shook his head. "She didn't have arthritis."

Agent Zheng tilted her head slightly. "Was she taking it, or giving it to someone else? Was any gone at all?"

"The bottle was half full and there were needles beside it. One used, and about three still in sterile wrappers." He cast his mind back to Janet Haze crouched in the shadows of the woods. 'She had needle marks on her arms.''

Agent Zheng made notes on her PDA, an infinitesimal frown touching her face. It was a slight crease between her black eyebrows and the hardening of her eyes. She glanced up to see Ukiah watching her, and the frown smoothed away.

"Anything else?" Max asked.

Ukiah shrugged. "All the books and papers have been shifted. It's as if someone took down each book, one by one, and replaced them. They're in the same order, but they're staggered differently." He held his hand over a piece of paper to indicate it without touching it. "This piece of paper was on top like this, but over here. As far as I can tell, at the moment, they are all here, but it's harder with the paper."

Agent Zheng took out latex gloves and slid them on. "I'll check through the books. If they needed to move every book, then maybe they didn't find what they were looking for."

"Maybe your agent, Wil Trace, moved the books," Max suggested.

Agent Zheng nodded slowly. "It is possible but unlikely. I normally wouldn't on a case involving the Pack. They usually limit their contact to in-person conversations and rare telephone calls. The searcher was probably looking for something written: a letter, prescription, a photograph, or something like that. I don't think Wil Trace would have put in the effort either."

Max produced a pair of latex gloves and pulled them on. "Let's split this bookcase up while Mr. Oregon finishes his search."

So they did, taking one book out at a time to flip through them. A half hour passed in silence.

Max finished his half first, having flipped quicker

through the books. He stretched and roamed the room. "Any luck, kid?"

"I only saw the top layer of papers, so I can't tell if anything from a lower layer is missing. There seems to be only one paper missing; a piece of legal tablet paper with the word 'substitutions' written across the top. I can recreate it, but it's all ASCII to me."

"If you write it down, I'll find someone who will understand it," Agent Zheng said. "There's something odd about these books. Janet read science fiction in her spare time; they account for all the worn paperbacks mixed in with the textbooks. But these other books she took out of the library. By the due date stamped inside, I think she borrowed them only a day or two before her first sick day at work. *New Advances in Aging. Aging: Facts and Myths. Methuselah's Children: New Age Treatments for Aging.*"

"*Immortality: Myth and Legends,*" Max added, slipping a book out from under a pillow. He sat on the edge of the bed to flip through it.

Ukiah stretched muscles sore from leaning over the desk. "Why would a twenty-something be reading up on aging?"

"You have to admit that it's ironic that she'd be dead within a week," Max commented, then made a sound of discovery. "What do you make of this?"

Agent Zheng and Ukiah came to look over his shoulder at the worn photograph he held. It was a black-and-white photo, older than any Ukiah had ever seen, of a dark-haired man. He stood under a great arch that proclaimed "New York City's World's Fair." While he was obviously the subject of the photo, a great number of people had been caught passing under the arch.

Ukiah glanced at the photo and felt the hair on the back of his neck start to rise.

Agent Zheng shook her head. "Anything on the back?"

Max flipped the picture over but it was blank. "No."

"I doubt the searcher was looking for that." Agent Zheng unfolded from the bed and returned to the bookcase. "It looks like it might be a family photograph, maybe Janet's grandfather. Just in case, I'll run it through the FBI labs and see what they can deduce."

While her back was still to them, Ukiah caught Max's hand and flipped the photo back upright and then pointed to a face that sprang out of the crowd. In the mass of faces blurred by movement, one man alone was still, and thus clear. He stood a good thirty feet back, his face no larger than Ukiah's pinkie tip in the photo. He stared toward the photo's subject with crystalline hatred. It was Rennie Shaw.

Max stared at the photograph and then glanced at Ukiah. "Is this who I think it is?" was plain on his face. Ukiah nodded to him. Max indicated Agent Zheng with his chin. Ukiah shrugged, unsure of what the special agent would make of the impossible appearance of the Pack leader.

"I would be interested to know what the lab has to say about it." Max handed the photograph to her. "Could you keep us apprised?"

"You believe it's more important than I think?" There was no indication that Agent Zheng was demeaning their opinion. It seemed like an honest question.

"It's the only out-of-place thing we've actually put our hands on," Max pointed out.

"This evidence by omission is hard to work with,"

she admitted. She took a hand scanner from her purse, connected it to her PDA, and ran the photograph through it. The scanning complete, she put the scanner away and uploaded the scanned photo to some distant computer. "There, that will get them started."

Ukiah started to rise, putting out his hand to catch the bedpost. He stilled as his fingers ran over a patch of blood. He closed his eyes to pick through the information his senses were relaying to him on the smallest levels. Almost by reflex, he compared the new sensations to ones he learned by trial and error. Here was the marker for male. There was the indication of European white. The loosing strands hinted at middle age. Max told Ukiah often that what he did was impossible—and also not to try and explain his abilities to anyone in detail. People, Max said, could handle "Indian trackers," and "psychic detectives," but probably not be able to cope with—whatever he was. What would Agent Zheng say if he explained his talents to her?

Until he talked to Max and made sure it was okay, he said instead, "There's blood here."

Max came to eye the bedpost. "Oh damn, that's not good."

Ukiah moved his hand slowly down the post. "The smear goes the whole way down. Someone has made an effort to wipe it up." He ran his hands over the dark-painted hardwood floors. "There was blood on the floor, too, but not a lot. Some hair too. It seems like a head wound, blunt force to the head." Crouched on the floor, he scanned the room. "If he was attacked in this room, and the attacker left the weapon behind, what was he hit with?"

"Why do you think it got left behind?" Agent Zheng asked.

"There's nothing missing," Max answered for him. "How about the classical heavy acrylic award?"

Ukiah picked up the clear acrylic award but found it innocent of blood. "No."

Agent Zheng stood staring at the floor. "If the body fell here, the attacker would have stood here and"—she reached down to nudge a pair of roller blades tucked under the desk—"these would be close at hand."

Ukiah examined the heavy wheel base. The right blade was clean, but he found blood and hair caught under the rims of the left. "This was it. Someone hit Wil Trace in the head with this."

"And took his body out the back," Max added, "if no one saw him leave the front."

"Or the body is still in the house," Ukiah amended.

Agent Zheng shook her head. "We've checked the house."

From the attic window, Schenley Park stretched out as a canopy of green. Max looked out over the treetops and shook his head. "I'm starting to hate that park."

Ukiah crouched on the same path that Janet Haze had taken two days before. To him the passage of Wil Trace's body was clear. "You said that your people checked the park?"

"There wasn't any indication that he went into the park."

Ukiah glanced up at Max. "Can't you see this?"

Max shook his head. "It's just a bunch of footprints to me. What is it?"

Ukiah forgave the FBI somewhat. It seemed to him as if they should be perfect and infallible. The path was there, why hadn't they seen it? "A man came this way, carrying something extremely heavy. See how deep his footprints are on this piece of level ground, compared to the others? Here, here, and here—blood. It's going to be easy to follow, but it's a day old."

"Might as well see where it goes." Max took out his pistol and checked its clip.

Agent Zheng nodded too, so they started down the dirt footpath.

Unlike Janet Haze's earlier trek, the blood trail followed the path to one of the park's wide graded trails until it came to the edge of Panther Hollow. There Wil Trace's abductor cut through shallow woods to a set of train tracks. The railroad, they discovered, forged through the heart of Oakland, almost unseen, hidden by the folds of land, bridges, and tunnels. Ukiah had heard the train occasionally, the rails singing, but never traced the engine's almost invisible route before. They walked through the narrow gorge between the Carnegie Museum and Carnegie Mellon University and found a tunnel. On the other side of the tunnel, the gorge continued. The Oakland traffic hummed high overhead on bridges crossing the ravine. Ukiah recognized the buildings perched above them and thus the streets crossing the bridges: Center Avenue and Baum Boulevard. It meant they were only a few blocks from the office.

Just before the railroad dipped down to join the busway, the blood trail climbed up the steep embankment to street level. It was a hard scramble, leaving Ukiah impressed with the strength of anyone who could do it with a body slung across one shoulder. They were in a bleak area. The street was deserted despite the fact it was full daylight. The buildings stood empty, windows boarded up, signs torn away.

The blood trail led to a door hanging askew on its hinges. Max caught Ukiah's shoulder before he entered, pausing him. Max had his pistol out, pointed skyward. He indicated Ukiah's gun with his eyes and a frown. Agent Zheng held her pistols skyward too, apparently also unwilling to enter the building unarmed.

Ukiah slipped his Colt out of his kidney holster, made sure the safety was on, then nodded his readiness.

The door opened to a large room, the far wall a bank of windows through which hazy sunlight barely cut through filthy glass. Dust coated the floor like a gray carpet. A host of footprints marched through the dust; dozens of people had entered and left the supposedly abandoned building.

Max moved cautiously into the large room. Agent Zheng followed behind. Ukiah stalked behind, stiff-legged, the hair on the back of his neck rising. Something was wrong. He moved slowly forward, straining to identify the sense of danger, to give it a shape, a name.

Except a few broken chairs, the only furniture in the room was a battered desk set under the bank of windows. Marks on the floor indicated that there had been an elaborate cubicle system in the vast room. Offices lined the side walls, executive claims on privacy.

"The attacker carries Wil Trace to this center support." Ukiah called the trail as he found it, his eyes only half on the marks in the dust. "He puts him down. Wil Trace lies here, awakes, and starts to crawl. The attacker drags him back and ties him to the support."

"Trace is alive?" Surprise colored Zheng's voice.

"He was. There's no more blood." What was the

danger? "The wound has stopped bleeding and the attacker doesn't hurt him again. Other people come in two groups. The first group walks around Agent Trace. There are three men and the attacker. The second group wears biker boots. They wander around the room; it seems at random. There are five men and a woman in the second group."

"The second group sounds like the Pack." Agent Zheng said. "Who are the first group, though?"

Ukiah shrugged helplessly.

"They put something on this desk." Max pointed at the disturbed dust on the desktop.

Ukiah nodded, following the tracks to the desk. "The one that brought him here put something here and retrieved it. A pen or pencil. See, these are his fingers sweeping through the dust to pick it up." Ukiah frowned at the feather-fine track across the desk. The pen or whatever had rolled across the slightly slanted top. He stooped and looked under the desk. A hypodermic syringe glittered under the desk. "This doesn't look good."

"What is it?" Max asked.

"A syringe, and it's been used." He fished it out. On the tip of the needle, he found human blood. "It was used on Wil Trace."

Max drifted off, checking into the nearest empty executive office. He had his PDA out, digging through the Internet. "This wasn't a random spot. They knew this place was empty and considered it a safe meeting place."

"Can you tell what he was given?" Agent Zheng asked tentatively, doubt clear in her voice.

Ukiah pulled out the plunger and touched the tip, then slipped his pinkie into the cylinder. It had been used twice. At one time it had been filled with a complex pharmaceutical that he took to be the missing immune-suppression drug. The second substance was a bloodlike protein that triggered memories of Janet Haze's oddly broken DNA. He frowned. Agent Trace was injected with blood?

He sensed something then and grew still, unable to name it. The feeling of something horribly wrong struck him again. This time he got the impression there had been something he overlooked, a warning left unrecognized. He cast back over the last few hours, trying to spot it. A black car had been parked near the office that morning. It had been in the alley behind Janet Haze's house, parked and empty three houses down.

The second set of tracks leading into the building, those of the Pack's, led in but didn't go back out.

The Pack had followed them to Janet Haze's, then raced ahead to this building, and waited.

It was an ambush.

There was a slight noise from Agent Zheng, a sharp inhale of surprise, but it hit him like a shout. He spun and found Rennie Shaw barely ten feet away, dressed in fatigues, shotgun in hand.

How did he get so close without me sensing him?

The Pack leader had turned too as Agent Zheng gasped, leveling his shotgun at her.

"No!" Ukiah flung himself in front of her.

A boom like a cannon filled the enclosed room and the blast hit him square in the chest, throwing him backward through the air. He hit the ground tumbling from the force. It hurt less than he expected Then he remembered he was wearing the flak jacket. If he could have breathed, he would have laughed.

He started to get up, gasping for breath. He had been kicked by an elk with less force. Rennie was coming on, chambering another shell. There was something about the Pack leader's face, his eyes.

Ukiah suddenly realized that for Rennie, no one else existed. Rennie was here to kill him.

Ukiah scrambled backward on all fours, discovering he'd lost his .45, gasping hard for a breath that wouldn't come. Rennie lengthened his stride, brought down the shotgun, aimed at Ukiah's head.

Max suddenly appeared behind Rennie, pistol shoved against the back of the Pack leader's head. "Drop it! Drop it or I'll blow your brains out."

Rennie froze. Just then, Ukiah sensed others in the building, hiding in the shadows. Even as he looked about for them, groping still for his pistol, they emerged from the ring of executive offices. Six in all, armed with shotguns. Like Rennie, they were intently looking at Ukiah.

"Put your guns down!" Max shouted, nudging the back of Rennie's head. "Do it or I'll kill him."

Ukiah heard the clunks of shells being chambered.

"Drop your gun," Rennie told Max, "or we'll kill you too."

Too, because they had come only for Ukiah.

"Back down, Max." Ukiah forced the words out of his bruised lungs and then gasped for another breath. "They just want me. Back down and let them have me."

"Over my dead body, son."

That was uttered from the heart and not from the mind. *Damn it, Max, don't start thinking like that. I don't want you dead too.*

So he lied to Max. "They're not going to hurt me, Max. You know I've told you weird shit in the past, and I've always been right." He struggled for breath. "Back down, and none of us will be hurt."

He looked up at Rennie, met his eyes squarely and silently pleaded to him. *Don't tell him the truth. Let him believe me. Don't let him force you into killing him.*

Max let out a long sigh and slowly lowered his gun. "I hope you're right, kid."

Pack members moved in, stripped Max of his weapons, and put him on his knees, hands on his head. There was a sudden uneasiness in the Pack members.

A large Native American man stepped beside Rennie. "He's the one, isn't he?"

Rennie shrugged and motioned Ukiah up onto his knees. The Pack leader stepped forward to catch the neck closure of Ukiah's flak jacket and, in one hard pull, tore it open. The edge of the shotgun blast had punched through the fabric above the Kevlar plate. Blood trickled from a pellet embedded in his collarbone. Below it, a fist-sized bruise was already shading to black.

Rennie pressed his fingers into the wound and then licked the blood from his fingertips. "He's the one."

The Native American shook his head. "Coyote must be wrong about this."

"Maybe. Maybe not. We can't afford to be wrong." Rennie looked down at Ukiah. "What say you, boy?"

"Do what you want to me," Ukiah whispered earnestly, "but not here, not in front of him. Leave them here and finish this wherever. I beg you, don't hurt them."

Rennie stared down at him, a long unreadable look. Finally, he reached into the baggy pockets of his fatigues and pulled out an aerosol can. He flipped the can's lid off in a practiced flick of the thumb, then kicked Ukiah solidly in the chest. As Ukiah gasped for breath, Rennie aimed the can into Ukiah's face and pulled the trigger. Green gas blossomed out to kiss Ukiah's lips. The smell was sweet and suddenly distant. He tried not to inhale, but the gas was down deep in his lungs already, making him cough and sputter, sucking down more as he did. Ukiah managed to think, *At least this won't hurt much,* then the world canted sideways and darkness closed in on him. Strangely his hearing remained, like a stereo left on after the lights were turned off. There was a low moan from Max, a deep utterance of despair.

"What do we do with them?"

"Can't make the boy a liar. Cuff them to a post, then follow."

Ukiah marked their movement by sound. They moved remarkably fast for being burdened with his body. The run ended with the beep-beep of a car answering a remote and the thunk of a trunk lid popping open. A moment later he felt carpet against his cheek and hands roughly searching him.

"What the hell is this?"

"A camera," Rennie answered. "It's probably got a remote recording system, probably in the Hummer."

"Should I double back and get the recording out of the truck?"

"No," Rennie commanded. "This was supposed to be a slash, not a grab. We don't have time to clean up the loose ends. Just strip him down, be sure to get everything, then we go."

They pulled off his headcam and its power unit. They took his wallet and his phone, tossing them into the bushes from the sound of it. They found the tracer clipped to his jeans, ripped it free, and smashed it. He was left completely untraceable and defenseless.

"That's it," Rennie said. "Gather the Dogs. We'll meet at the den at midnight."

The trunk lid slammed down, entombing him.

This was supposed to be a slash, not a grab.

So he had been right. They had planned to kill him, but something had gone wrong. Something was not what they expected, but what? He searched for the reason he was still alive, for clues to keep himself alive. He recalled only a handful of unreadable looks and obscure remarks. He didn't even know why they wanted to kill him. *I'm dead,* he finally admitted to himself. *You don't get grabbed like this and survive— but at least I saved Max.*

CHAPTER SIX

Wednesday, June 17, 2004
Unknown location

He was in the trunk for hours. There were mysterious starts and stops. Finally they drove over a rough road and stopped for good. The car doors opened and shut. The drug had worn off slightly; he could open his eyes and make a slight whimpering noise. The trunk lid was unlatched and lifted. He tried to bolt, but none of his muscles responded. He lay instead, looking helplessly up at Rennie Shaw.

The Pack leader was what Max called a Black Irish, with black hair and intense blue eyes. There was something hard and fierce about his face. His broad nose, strong chin, and sparse black eyebrows molded into something that could have been anger or hate or fear. Ukiah couldn't read him, couldn't tell what lay ahead.

It was full night and the warmth of the day was gone. By the fishy stench and soft murmur of water, one of Pittsburgh's three rivers ran close at hand. He filled his lungs with the damp air and knew it was the Monongahela. He listened hard and caught the faint rumble of roller coasters from Kennywood

Amusement Park, the happy screams of those paying to be frightened.

Behind the Pack leader stood an old warehouse. Ukiah knew the type well. It had been built when steel was king, then stood empty since the king had died. It was over five hundred feet long, essentially one endless room. Its windows were huge banks of one foot square pieces of glass, numbering in the hundreds, filthy, mostly broken.

If it was like countless other warehouses, it was surrounded by empty buildings and bordered by the river. If the drug ever wore off to the point he could scream, no one would hear him.

A woman came to stand beside Rennie. She had long black hair, dark worried eyes, and a full mouth pressed tightly shut, as if she didn't like or approve of what was about to happen.

"It's wearing off," she said. He knew her voice. She had been the other watcher in the woods. "Should I dose him again?"

"No Hellena." Rennie gripped Ukiah's wrist and yanked him easily up into a fireman's carry. "I want him awake. I want him scared."

As Ukiah flopped on the large man's back, he caught a glimpse into the car's interior. Keys glittered in the ignition. A wire fence ran around the weedy parking lot, but no gate blocked the exit to a badly paved street. If he could get free, here was his way out. He forced himself to relax, to wait. Next time would be his last chance.

The Native American was waiting just inside the door. Rennie swung around toward the Native American, giving Ukiah an idea of the hugeness of the building. A circle of spotlights flooded the center, like a boxing ring, only slightly larger. The echoes measured the darkness, bouncing back as mere ghosts of their former strength.

"Bear," Rennie murmured quietly to the other man. "Get my shotgun from the car. You and Hellena—keep hold of your shotguns too. Make sure they're fully loaded."

"What are you going to do with him?"

Ukiah couldn't read the inflection. Had that been a question or a challenge?

"Just fetch my gun and keep yours ready."

Rennie carried him to the circle of lights and let him down to the floor a lot gentler than he expected. The floor was concrete, with a century of dust and pigeon droppings layering it. As Rennie rolled him onto his face, Ukiah gave a test wiggle of his arm. It moved slightly, a halfskip motion on the cold concrete. Rennie caught his wrists and snapped cold handcuffs on them.

There were others now—Ukiah could sense them in the darkness—twenty if one counted Rennie, Hellena, and Bear, moving closer. They were wary and unsettled. *There might as well be neon signs: "Bad shit going down."*

Bear appeared with two shotguns. Rennie hauled Ukiah up to his knees, tripoding him with his hands cuffed behind his back. Once he was sure Ukiah wouldn't pitch over, he took one of the shotguns. He backed up, leaving Ukiah at the center of the lights and the watching eyes.

"Coyote!" he bellowed, reminding Ukiah of a monster summoning in a B-rated movie. "Coyote! I've got Prime's son down here!"

Son? They knew who his father was? They wanted to kill him because of his father?

Footsteps sounded from above, where a finished loft area must be hidden by the lights. Hinges creaked. Ukiah felt instead of heard the body jumping. The presence raised the hairs on the back of his neck. With the slightest of sound, the one they called Coyote landed just inside the circle of light.

He was a tall man, corded muscle, hair short and grizzled. He stared at Ukiah with gold eyes, and Ukiah could feel the hatred like a wave of heat. In his hand Coyote held a fire ax; and plain as if he spoke, his thoughts were of hacking Ukiah's body into small pieces and feeding them to a roaring fire.

Every fiber in Ukiah's body tried to bolt. His torso jerked backward and his legs heaved him halfway up before the drug weakness sent him sprawling onto the concrete. He managed to land on his side, at least, instead of his face. Instantly he tried squirming away, but his muscles were all noodles again. Coyote shifted his hold on the ax and stalked forward. Again his thoughts were clear—on his side, Ukiah was in the perfect position for a beheading. Ukiah whimpered in fear, too scared to be ashamed of the weakness. *Dear God, don't let him near me!*

There was a loud boom and the concrete between Ukiah and Coyote smoked. Behind Ukiah, Rennie chambered another shell into the shotgun. "We need to talk, Coyote."

The man lifted his eyes briefly to Rennie. "I told you to kill him where he stood. If you don't have the heart for it, I'll do it gladly."

"You might be wrong about this. Or you might be right. He might be what you fear. If he is, we'll do what you plan. But I think you're wrong. The Pack should decide."

"I'm not wrong. He must be killed. There is no deciding, there is only doing."

"We say there is," Rennie snapped and was immediately echoed by Bear and Hellena. A growling agreement rippled through the others as well.

Rennie is for not killing me? There's a chance?

Coyote circled Ukiah, and Rennie moved at the same time—keeping the helpless boy between them. "What is the question here? Is there any question that he's the one? Is there?'

Apparently not; the Pack remained silent. A spark of hope that had lit with Rennie's apparent mutiny was quickly dying. *They are all madmen.*

"You know as well as I that Prime didn't want to make this child in the first place." Coyote continued, his voice a deep rumble. "You know he planned to destroy it while it still was growing in its mother's womb. You know that he thought it would be killed when he blew up the ship."

So his father was a madman too.

"I know. I know," Rennie agreed. "But do you know what strikes me most about our Prime? He was an asshole. He panicked easily, he acted without thinking, and he never thought things the whole way through. Look at the mess he's made of us. On the one hand, here, we've got honest concern, a possible monster is in our midst and we should kill it before it spawns. On the other hand, the Pack is all that is left of Prime, and that makes us the boy's father. Prime assumed that his child would be a monster— but was he right?"

Coyote waved Rennie's argument away. "The possible dangers outweigh the chance we might be wrong."

"What danger? He's been in this city for three years that we know of. Three years under our noses. What has he done? Nothing!"

"You offer this as proof?"

"No, I don't." They continued to circle Ukiah

slowly as he lay sprawled in the dirt. "This I offer as proof. He knew what we came for. He read us right away, and he knew. You could feel his terror. Did he beg for mercy for himself? Did he plead for his life? No. All he cared about was the safety of his partner. You know what Hex would have done! You've seen his work from here to Oregon. There's no Ontongard in the boy. You're wrong about this child."

"Boy! Child! You know how old he is."

"Look at him! Just look!" Rennie cried, pointing at Ukiah with a stiff angry finger. "He's a boy, a teen-ager maybe, but not an adult. He's still gangly limbed and smooth-skinned. It will be years before he reaches his true height and weight. He's just a boy. *A Pack cub!* I know what Prime expected to crawl out of that girl's womb. I've had nightmares about it since I joined the Pack. But this isn't it."

Ukiah cringed inside at the image Rennie was painting. *What are they talking about?* Just as he thought he understood them, the conversation would cant at some odd angle.

"I can't allow him to live." That was clear enough. "He will not leave this place alive."

"Coyote!" Hellena was equally adamant. "You harm him against our will and we'll tear you apart. We can feel his fear, and we will not let you hurt him."

"You are my Get!"

There, the conversation tilted again.

"And there are days," she growled in return, "I would gladly tear your throat out for that alone."

"So you're willing to risk everything on the smell of a cub's fear?"

"First and foremost, he's Pack," Rennie started. "We'll test him like any other new Pack member. If he passes, he lives. If he fails, he dies. It's the way the Pack has always been."

There was a roar of approval for this plan. Coyote growled, then nodded. "So be it. Hellena, you're best at this. You do it."

Hellena handed her shotgun to Rennie and walked to Ukiah, sprawled helplessly on the floor. He watched her come, trying not to show the fear skittering inside. She caught him by the shoulders and righted him back onto his knees. For a moment he thought she was going to undo his handcuffs, but she left his hands locked behind his back.

Sure that he was stable, Hellena cupped his chin with her right hand, cocking his head back to look up at her.

"Take a deep breath," she commanded, brushing his bangs out of his eyes with her left hand. Her dark eyes locked with his, her dark hair spilling forward as she looked down at him. "Again."

Together they took a breath and released it. He felt a slight tickling on his forehead, as if a spider had landed there. He thought for a moment it might be her left hand, but it was cupping the back of his head.

"Now, this is going to hurt."

It was all the warning he got. The tickling point became a knifepoint of pain that lanced into him. He screamed and bucked, but she held him firmly, her eyes locked on his. He couldn't shut his eyes. He couldn't look away. The knifepoint reached bottom and twisted and . . .

. . . *it was late summer, the stars sharp and clear as they ran down an elk. He ran easily behind the alpha male. He had no tooth or claw to take down the buck, but he could herd it as well as . . .*

. . . *he was faint with hunger but the grizzly still was*

at the foot of the tree. Currently it had overturned a rock bigger than his whole body, and was foraging for ants under it . . .

. . . Mom Jo gasped, her breath turning to clouds in the cold. "Oh my God, it's a boy! Jesus, he's naked." . . .

. . . "Ukiah!" Mom Lara clearly was between anger and laughter. "Where are your clothes? It's snowing out there. Get in the house. We wear clothes outside. No, no no, you only do that in the potty" . . .

His mind was a television with a billion channels. Flip. Flip. Flip. Memory after memory. Those dark eyes locked on his were gone. The room was gone. Reality was his memories, as if he was living that moment over again. He felt the sharp pain of Crazy Joe Gary's bullet again. He burned in rage as a wolverine stole his dinner. His life went forward and back, moving at a furious rate.

He could sense the Pack, distant, watching, somehow reliving these memories with him. Vaguely he realized that the woman was searching for something, could sense in a moment that she hadn't found it and would flick away the unwanted memory, pulling up another.

. . . Cally's face appeared, framed by the window in his bedroom. She was crying and lifted up a still furry body. "Miss Pretty Lightfoot is sick!" . . .

Ukiah's heart jerked at the memory of that day. He expected to flick to the next memory, but they stayed on this one.

He rubbed at bleary eyes to focus on his sister's beloved pet. Obviously it had tried to corner around a stone wall at high speed and failed. Part of its scalp and skull had been lifted away, as if by a rough-toothed rasp. Its tongue protruded through its sharp teeth, and its eyes were dull. "Oh Cally, I'm sorry. Miss Pretty Lightfoot is dead."

"Dead?" She looked at the rabbit, puzzled. "She has batteries? Can you get her new batteries?"

"No, no, pumpkin. Bunnies don't have batteries." What a day to be stuck baby-sitting. Why couldn't his moms be here? Oh yes, they went to the hospital for—but the thought aborted, avoided completely. "Miss Pretty Lightfoot is like Miss Marker, your Sunday School teacher. Do you remember, she died and we buried her at church?"

Cally stared to cry. "I don't want to bury Miss Pretty Lightfoot and never see her again."

He closed his eyes hard on the thought of never seeing Mom Lara again. No. No. Things will be fine. What to do about the damn rabbit? "Pumpkin," he tried again, this time trying something he'd overheard at church. "Cally, if we don't bury Miss Pretty Lightfoot, how is she going to go live with God? You want her to be happy, and what would be happier than to be with God?"

It stopped his sister in midscream. "She won't go to heaven if we don't bury her?"

Ukiah winced and tried to imagine all the ways this conversation could go wrong. "Wouldn't you be upset if one person said you could go but someone else wouldn't let you?"

Cally was a study in serious thought. "We should bury Miss Pretty Lightfoot. Can we do a funeral? Pray and sing and then have cake and punch afterwards?"

He was puzzled about the cake and punch until he remembered that was how the Sunday School teacher's funeral had gone. "Sure, pumpkin."

So they dug a hole in Mom Lara's rose garden using a shovel and garden trowel. They emptied the last of the oatmeal into a plastic sandwich bag and used the round container as the coffin. Cally demanded that some of Mom Lara's prize roses be picked and put in with Miss Pretty Lightfoot. Ukiah complied, sure that this once his mothers would only want Cally to be happy.

They knelt together in the freshly spaded earth. Cally pressed her hands together and intoned like Reverend Brown, "Now we pray." Ukiah mimicked her pose, intending only to sit silent beside her. Instead he found himself praying silently with intensity that amazed him. "God, let Mom Lara be okay. Let them get out the tumor that's making her so sick and let her come home. I don't want her to leave us. I don't want Mom Jo to cry. I don't want Cally hurt. Please, God, don't let her die."

. . . And he was kneeling on the cold concrete of the huge warehouse, tears running down his cheeks. Hellena held him still in the vise grip but her eyes no longer were locked with his. She was looking at Rennie, some silent communication going between them. Rennie glanced about the ring of the silent watchers, collecting the unspoken vote.

"The boy," Rennie turned to Coyote, "lives. He's part of the Pack. We won't let you harm him."

The eyes of the Pack turned toward Coyote, cold determination almost like a wall between them and him.

Coyote's gaze swept over them, disapproving. "So be it. Be warned, I don't think Hex can corrupt a Pack member, but this one, this one he would try very hard indeed to corrupt."

He walked across the warehouse and out the door. Hellena released her vise grip, stepping forward to support Ukiah with her body as he sagged wearily forward. It was gray outside instead of dark, he suddenly realized, and remembered that sometime during the night there had been a thunderstorm. The search through his memories had taken hours.

I'm going to live?

Rennie shook out tight muscles and yawned widely, cracking his jawbone joint and his neck. "Damn cold bastard."

"Do you think he'll do anything behind our back?" Hellena murmured, still intent on the closed door.

Rennie considered it for a minute. "No. I think if he wasn't truly convinced of the boy, he would have taken us all on. He saw that I was right, but he won't admit it." He came to hug Hellena, towering over her. He looked down at Ukiah leaning exhausted against her.

I'm going to live?

Rennie nodded and handed off his shotgun to Bear. "Thanks for the backup."

"You walk the edge, Rennie." Bear muttered, shaking his head. "Watch you don't fall."

"Don't wake the sleepers." Rennie patted him on the shoulder.

"Don't wake the sleepers." Bear headed out the door, following Coyote.

Rennie flashed an amused grin at Ukiah. "How do you feel? Can you talk yet?"

Ukiah wet his mouth and tried. "Um, yeah, I can talk. I feel like shit."

"How about your legs? They work yet?"

"Maybe." Ukiah managed to stand, but it was obvious he wouldn't stay that way.

"Nope, not quite." Rennie caught him, steadied him long enough to undo the cuffs. Then, with another practiced yank, he had Ukiah in a fireman's carry. "Since you managed to stand, I'd say the gas will wear off shortly."

He carried Ukiah easily out to the car. Rain still beaded on the finish, and puddles reflected the light. Rennie opened the passenger door with his free hand and dropped Ukiah into the passenger seat. The Pack leader tucked in his feet, fastened his seat belt and shut the door. A growing sense of relief was washing through him as Rennie got in and started the engine.

They're not going to kill me. He's actually going to take me home.

That relief was enough for several minutes. He leaned against the glass, okay with the silence. When Rennie turned onto the parkway, heading for downtown, instead of crossing through Squirrel Hill to reach Shadyside, Ukiah shifted uneasily. *Maybe he's not taking me home.*

Rennie glanced at him. "I'm assuming the FBI will be watching your office. Their missing agent has them riled as hornets with a broken nest. I'm dropping you on the bus line downtown. You can catch a bus or call your partner."

Unbidden came the memory of Wil Trace's face. A wife and three children. Ukiah sighed and glanced at Rennie. "Did you take the FBI agent?"

Rennie shook his head. "We're the obvious bad guys, aren't we? The Pack isn't what it looks like, though. We're the heroes in a war—a long, hard, bitter war."

"Against who?"

"Someone a lot better at covering their asses than us. FBI doesn't have a file on them, doesn't have a clue. They've taken the FBI agent, but we don't know why. They're up to something, something big. All we do know is that Janet Haze was part of it, but she's vanished."

"Who are they?"

Rennie glanced over at him, then shook his head. "You need to stay out of this war. In many ways, you're the goose that lays the golden eggs. If the other side found out about you, they wouldn't rest until they had you. You might think the Pack is harsh, but remember this. I had compassion enough to leave your partner alive. The Ontongard would have put your hands around a gun and made you blow out his brains just for fun."

"How can I avoid them if you don't tell me who they are?"

"I can't because I don't know. They change their names, they hide in shadows, and the only time we interact is to kill each other. I can't tell you who, but you'll know them."

"How?"

"When your hackles rise, and you get caught between running from or tearing the throat out of a person, you'll know—he's one of them."

Rennie pulled to a stop beside the Steel Plaza T-station. He reached over, undid Ukiah's seat beat, and opened the door. Ukiah half expected a shove next and slid out under his own power. His legs were still wobbly, and he clung to the door.

"That's it? You're not going to explain anything that just happened? Who the hell was Prime, other than my father? Who was my mother? Is she dead? What kind of monster did you expect me to be? How did Hellena do that memory thing, and why did you decide to let me live?"

"I would tell you, boy, but sometimes it's a mercy not to know. What was done to your mother"—Rennie shook his head—"it's not a good thing for someone to know about themselves. Go on, go back to your life, and stay clear of everything that touched Janet Haze's life."

Ukiah stepped back, teetering until he caught hold of a bus stop sign. "You've got to tell me more."

Rennie looked at him, long and hard. "I don't know if I can explain. I've never had to. Usually when you join the Pack, you receive the Pack memory. You're Pack but you're not. I wouldn't even know where to start. Call your partner and go home. Don't wake the sleepers!"

The sedan leaped forward, the passenger door slamming shut. Ukiah watched it go until it vanished and then glanced around. A public phone stood only a dozen feet away. Feeling like a toddler, Ukiah let go of the bus stop sign and staggered to the phone.

Max answered his phone on the first ring. "Bennett."

"Max, it's me."

"Where are you?"

"Downtown, outside the Steel Plaza T-Station, on Sixth Avenue."

"You safe?"

"Yes, I'm safe."

"Hold on, I'm on the parkway heading into town. I'll be there in a minute."

It was nearly to the exact minute when the Hummer slammed to a stop beside the bus stop. Max leaned over and opened the passenger door. Ukiah climbed shakily in.

"Are you okay?" Max regarded him worriedly.

"All things considered—yeah." He slammed the door closed and slumped into the seat.

Max found first gear, swung the Hummer back around, and started down Sixth Avenue again—only much slower. "How did you get away from the Pack?"

"They let me go."

Max glanced at him in surprise. "Just like that?"

"You sound disappointed."

"Hell no, but—" Max glanced at him and something went unsaid, something rooted in the kidnapping, borne of fear and desperation. Max veered away from it, and Ukiah was glad. Things were too raw and painful from those moments. "I just can't believe they went through all that just to talk to you."

Ukiah gave a dry laugh. *This is what true relief feels like.* What he had felt before was the lessening of terror. "Oh, I guess you could call it talking." *If your idea of a discussion includes an ax, shotguns, and a debate on whether the prodigal son should be cut up and served for dinner instead of the calf.*

"What the hell did you talk about?"

"It was a slight family disagreement that they wanted to settle."

"Family disagreement? Wait a minute! It was the name they twigged on first. Do you mean that it was the Pack that lost you in Oregon? Is that what all this insanity is about?"

"Yes. I think. They claimed that my father had been part of the Pack, a man called Prime. I don't know how they could be sure I was his son, but they were dead sure."

"I don't get it. If that's true, why did they come to kill you?"

How did he know? Oh yes, the headcam. "Do what you want to me but not here, not in front of him . . . finish this wherever." "This was supposed to be a slash, not a grab . . ." *Oh the joys of modern technology.*

"I'm sorry, Max. I had to get you to back down. I just had to."

Max shrugged but didn't look at him. "Well, actually, you were right. None of us were hurt. But if they had killed you—"

He lapsed into silence, and they drove along Fort Duquesne Boulevard, trying to work their way around the always present construction. Max suddenly swore, glanced at his watch, and then handed Ukiah his wireless phone. "You still have time to catch your moms at breakfast."

Whenever work kept him out overnight, he tried to call them during breakfast. "Do they know?"

"I trust you too much, Ukiah. You said that the Pack wouldn't hurt you, and I couldn't stop believing you, even after we viewed the disc. I was waiting for news, one way or the other, before telling them."

Ukiah flipped down Max's speed dial list to his moms' number. The phone rang twice and then Mom Lara, her voice slightly guarded, answered. "Good morning, Max, what's up?"

"It's me, Ukiah, Mom."

Her tone changed completely. "Ukiah! Why are you using Max's phone?"

"Lost mine," he said truthful. "I'm just checking in. How are things at home?"

"Things are fine. Yes, yes, it's Ukiah." This was to Cally, who was talking excitedly in the background. "Cally wants to talk to you." Before he could reply, the phone was traded off, and Cally was saying, "Ukiah, could you get me a new doll?"

"A new one? What's wrong with your old ones?"

"Ranger ate them last night. GI Barbie, Dr. Skipper, and the Beddy Bye twins."

Mass carnage. Ukiah found himself laughing soundlessly. "Okay, pumpkin, I'll get you a new doll, but you've got to take better care of it or Ranger will eat it too."

Max rolled his eyes and mouthed, "You spoil her rotten."

"Thank you, Ukiah. I want a—"

"Pumpkin, I can't promise you a certain doll. You'll have to be happy with the one I get, okay?"

There was a long little-girl silence of unhappiness, and then, "Okay, I'll see you tonight. I love you." And Cally hung up.

Ukiah laughed out loud and handed Max back his

phone. "I owe her, Max, otherwise Mom Lara would have got around to asking questions about what kept me out all night."

They had, Ukiah noticed, crossed the Monogahela River and were running alongside the Ohio River.

"Max, where the heck are we going, anyhow?"

"The FBI called me. A body showed up in an arson fire. They wanted me to come down and see if I could identify it as you."

"Well, it's not me. You could call and tell them that."

"Yeah, but they also found where the Pack stripped you down. They have your phone, your wallet, your Colt, and your keys. I thought you might want those back."

Fire trucks and city EMS crews had been added to the familiar jumble of police cars. Between the rain and fire hoses, the gutters ran deep with black water. The fireman scowled at Max and his intrusion, but the EMS crews recognized them from search and rescue cases. News of Ukiah's kidnapping had already spread among them, and their relief at seeing him was obvious. They pulled him aside and instantly noticed the shotgun wound. Before he realized what they intended, they cut away the rags of his shirt, cleaned all his wounds, and covered him with sterile bandages in every imaginable size.

Max was laughing as they strolled on to the crime scene.

"What?"

"Oh, you look like GI Barbie after Dr. Skipper gets done with her."

Ukiah winced and paused to check out his reflection in a fire engine's side mirrors. The bandages stood out on his body, a vivid patchwork of white on deep tan. "Ugh," he muttered at his reflection, then laughed. Mass carnage. "Ranger ate GI Barbie last night."

"He got GI Barbie?" Max put his foot up on the truck's bumper and leaned on his knee. "Too bad. I loved her crew cut and army fatigues. Your Mom Jo is twisted."

"She just doesn't want Cally to accept the stereotypical feminine roles." He tried to see what they had put across his back. When had he hurt that anyhow? His recall told him it was when the shotgun blast had sent him cartwheeling across the floor, he had hit something sharp that managed to slip down his Kevlar collar.

"So why give her dolls at all?"

"She wouldn't if she could, but Cally loves dolls. I think Mom Jo is slightly scandalized by it."

Max laughed, then spotted someone beyond the front of the fire truck. "I didn't think this was inside the city limit, but it must be—there's Kraynak. Hey! Kraynak!"

Max half stepped, half leaped over the water-filled gutters to meet Kraynak in the street. Kraynak looked pale and slightly bruised about the eyes. The smell of vomit clung to him. "Bennett, oh man, I'm sorry about your—" Kraynak went wide eyed in surprise as Ukiah came around the front of the fire truck to join Max. "Where the hell did you find him?"

"He found me." Max produced a cigar, snipped off the end, and lit it.

"It's what I'm good at," Ukiah added.

Kraynak caught Ukiah by the shoulder and gave him a little shake. "It's good to see you in one piece. They told me that it might be you in there, and it made me sick. Damn good to see you."

"Thanks." Ukiah was pleased to know Kraynak

truly meant it. There was no denying the large cop had been physically sick recently.

"I'll have you taken off the missing list then." Kraynak gave him a pat and let him go. "We ID this body, and hopefully that will be two off the list. I wish the FBI would get their ass in shape and stop falling off the edge of the earth. It's blowing our crime rate off the chart."

"What do you mean?" Ukiah asked.

"Didn't you tell him?" Kraynak eyed Max then explained. "Another one vanished late last night, around ten o'clock. A Special Agent Warner."

Ukiah's stomach had tightened as Kraynak talked. The tension released when the Homicide detective named the missing FBI agent. For a moment he had been worried that Agent Zheng was the kidnapped agent. Somehow the news was easier when it involved someone he didn't know. He felt sudden sympathy toward Kraynak dealing with the arson victim.

"Speaking of FBI, have you seen Agent Zheng?" Max put up a plume of cherry smoke. "She's got all of Ukiah's stuff that the Pack took off him."

"Oh, yeah, you're working with the Famous Bitch of Ice, the F-B-I." Kraynak used his fingers to emphasize the initials of Agent Zheng's nickname. "She doesn't get angry. She doesn't get upset. She just gets cold. Today we're talking arctic icebergs—huge, cold, and silent."

"So where's the iceberg?"

"Around back of the house." Kraynak pointed to the narrow alley between the houses. "The fire started in an old coal cellar in the back corner of the basement. One of the neighbors was awakened by the start of the thunderstorm. She was sitting in her bedroom window, watching the lightning, when she saw a black sedan pull up to this abandoned building. Four men got out and carried a struggling fifth person into the house. She called 911. When we got here, the basement was fully involved. The whole back half of the house is gone."

"What made them think it was Ukiah?" Max asked.

"The MO was vicious," Kraynak explained. "They set the victim on fire alive. We could hear screaming when we arrived, but you couldn't get close. I was close to puking before the FBI showed up with their possible ID. I'll be eating breakfast a second time later today."

Ukiah shook his head. "I don't get the connection."

"You got snatched by the Pack." Max played connect invisible dots with his smoking cigar. "This is a Pack-like crime. Two stepping-stones and then a giant leap makes the victim you."

Kraynak nodded, tapped out a Marlboro, and lit up. "We had a case just like this one last year. Tied up the victim, killed him, burned his house down around him. Just like here, they used a gel fuel, spread on the body. Neighbors there identified two Pack members at the scene."

What a family I've just been adopted into! "You haven't arrested them?"

"Got to catch them to arrest them." Kraynak sneered. "Got to find them to catch them. No one knows where the Pack hides out."

"Up the Mon." Ukiah supplied, feeling slightly traitorous. "In a warehouse on the south shore, down river of the steel mill, and close enough to hear Kennywood."

Kraynak noted it on his PDA. "It might help. They tend to move base constantly. I would think that after you—" he stopped and looked up in puzzlement. "How did you get away from them?"

After Max's reaction, Ukiah felt sheepish admitting the truth. "They let me go."

"The Pack?" Kraynak stared at him in disbelief.

He nodded, then indicated the smoldering house. "Also, I doubt that they did this."

"Why not?"

"They were busy with me. At midnight the whole Pack was at the warehouse, and the meeting didn't break up till about an hour ago."

"You sure all of them were there and that they stayed all night? There's like twenty of them known to be in Pittsburgh."

"There were twenty-one in all there." He closed his eyes and searched his memory. All through the test, he could sense the presence of the pack. "No one left."

Kraynak made another note, shaking his head. He considered the patchwork of bandages on Ukiah. "You okay?"

Ukiah nodded.

"The FBI says what went down in Oakland was supposed to be an execution, but the Pack changed their minds. Why did the Pack want you dead, and why didn't they kill you? Why did they kidnap you, hold you for ten hours, and then let you go?"

It was a question that would be repeated until he answered it. Kraynak might be a friend, but he was still a police officer. The FBI would want to know. Max. His moms. He glanced at Max, who was trying hard not to show how much he wanted to hear the answers. Ukiah sighed; at least both Max and the police would hear it at one telling.

"It turns out my father was part of the Pack. Apparently he never wanted me to be born. So when the Pack discovered I was living here in Pittsburgh, their leader decided to fulfill my father's dying wish."

Kraynak whistled, writing into his PDA. "Oh, that's twisted."

"Lucky for me, most of the Pack wasn't happy about this. They saw me as an honorary member. So Rennie Shaw changed the plans in Oakland, grabbed me, and called a meeting of the Pack. They had a heated discussion, complete with axes and shotguns." He veered completely around the memory search—he couldn't explain it, so why mention it? "Around five o'clock they voted to let me go."

Kraynak blew out his breath and looked at Max.

Max looked away, scuffing at the ground. "How close was the vote?"

"Don't know, they didn't tell me the tally."

"Christ, kid," Max said, "let's get your stuff and go on vacation."

Ukiah nodded. "That driving school in California is sounding better and better."

Kraynak added a note or two to Ukiah's statement. "I'll upload your statement and take you off the missing-persons list. You want to press charges?"

Ukiah laughed. "Can't press charges if you can't arrest them."

Kraynak scowled darkly. "True! True! Still miracles happen."

Ukiah sighed. "If you catch them, I'll press charges."

"Good kid." Kraynak smiled. "Take care, keep your head down and your ass covered."

"You too."

"Oh yeah, by the way, I like the buff and bondage look."

*   *   *

On the other side of the house, they found the mouth of a fiery hell. The back of the building gaped open, cave black and smoking inside. Max paused to survey the damage done to the house. Ukiah scanned the crowd of people gathered here and found Agent Zheng standing alone, watching the police forensic team moving through the rubble. She wore a black raincoat that stirred in the heat currents, her face solemn, her raven hair rain-slick but drying in the furnace blast of the smoldering building.

He started toward her, wondering what she was thinking. What went on in her mind? As he reached her side, she noticed him approaching, then recognized him.

Her face transformed for a moment with surprise and something that could have been joy. She was suddenly beautiful, all the hard lines softening to the point that looking at her took his breath away. She put out a hand to him and he took it. "Ukiah!" She breathed his name, gripping his hand warmly. "I'm so glad that you are alive! How did you get free?" She touched the bandage over the shotgun wound on his chest. "Are you seriously hurt?"

"The Pack let me go." He gave her a pared-down version of his release. "I'm not hurt. The EMS crews got carried away with the bandaging."

She looked away when he started to explain, regaining her control again. "So the question remains, who is this that died in the fire? Do you know?"

Ukiah shook his head, puzzled. "How would I know?"

"Did the Pack mention the agents they are holding? Did you see them? Are they alive?"

"No. I asked about them. The Pack says that there's another gang in town, one that operates in very covert methods. Rennie Shaw claimed that the other gang had the FBI agents. If this victim proves to be one of your agents, then Rennie was telling the truth."

"Why do you say that? Are you sympathetic with them now that they spared your life?"

He gave it a study. "No. I just know that they claimed all the Pack was there, and the number present agrees with the number of Pack in Pittsburgh. I know none left from midnight to five o'clock when this happened. They didn't set this fire. If an FBI agent was killed in this fire, then they told the truth."

She considered him with her unreadable gaze. She was like a deep, still pond. His kidnapping and return were stones thrown in, made their ripples, and were gone without a trace. He found it soothing after the raw emotions Max contained. If he needed, he could perfectly recall that one true flash of emotion on her face, the firm warm grip of her hand as she welcomed him.

A uniformed policeman came up out of the rubble and made his way to them. "They're bringing up the body now."

Agent Zheng acknowledged him and turned to Ukiah. "Do you think you could identify a burned body the way you can identify blood?"

It amazed him that she so easily accepted his abilities. Most people refused to believe, even after he nailed one piece of evidence after another. Others found him creepy and shied away as if he was going to harm them. There was no uneasiness in her, no fear, only calm expectation.

He found himself nodding. "Yeah, I think so."

Max drifted up. "Get your stuff yet?"

"Working on it." Actually he had forgotten to ask. Perfect recall didn't mean one couldn't forget.

Agent Zheng handed him his Colt carefully and

then pulled his phone and key ring out of her rain-coat pocket. "Here." She pressed them into his hands and then pulled his wallet from her coat breast pocket. "There was a photo of you taken by a professional photographer in your wallet. I took it for our fact sheet. I don't have it on me right now. Sorry."

"Oh, that picture." He cracked his wallet and found the empty slot among his credit cards and other photos. "We use it for our advertising. Don't worry about it. Max is the photographer. We print up copies whenever we need them. I don't need it back."

The body came then, interrupting anything she would have said in reply. They had it in a body bag already, but the bag looked far too flat to hold an adult body. Agent Zheng stopped them and un-zipped the bag.

The body looked like an Egyptian mummy; flesh sunk down to bone or missing altogether. Limbs had separated from the body, cooked until the joints parted with the gentle movement of lifting the victim into the bag. The skull was missing the jaw, the mouth open in an endless scream, hair and flesh burned away to the blacked bone.

Ukiah reeled backward. *Had Kraynak seen this? No wonder he was sick.*

"Are you sure about this, kid?" Max murmured at his elbow.

Ukiah nodded and put out a hesitant hand to touch the coarse burnt flesh. It was difficult, the fire had changed the structure so that he could barely recognize the familiar form. He knew, though, and his eyes filled with tears.

"Who is it?" Agent Zheng asked quietly.

"Janet Haze."

*   *   *

He and Max drove in silence back to the office. He went upstairs to the bedroom unofficially considered his and got a clean T-shirt. When he came downstairs, he found himself drifting through the rooms as Max made countless calls. Ukiah recognized the pattern after the first few calls. Max had contacted anyone that could have helped find Ukiah or avenge his death. His partner was now spreading the news of his safe return.

He raided the kitchen and found he was hungrier than he thought. In the refrigerator was leftover General Tso's Chicken, which he heated and ate. It seemed to trigger a tidal wave of eating. He thawed a porterhouse steak in the microwave and broiled it. He made a box of instant au gratin potatoes, fried all the eggs lining the fridge door, and cooked a package of frozen corn in the microwave.

Max came in for coffee as Ukiah was finishing off the ice cream bars and eyed the remains of his lunch. "Call it a day, go upstairs, and sleep."

"I was going to do some work after I finished," Ukiah protested.

Max laughed at him, glancing at his wristwatch. "If you want, I could set a stopwatch for when you crash and burn. You can sleep at your desk or you can sleep upstairs in a bed. Doesn't matter to me."

"I wasn't going to sleep." But a huge yawn suddenly forced its way out.

"You got the shit beat out of you yesterday, and you didn't sleep last night. Trust me, I know you. After eating like that, you're always asleep in five minutes. So, you've got four minutes and counting."

"Okay. Okay." Ukiah held up his hands in surrender. "Don't let me sleep all day, though. I want to go home tonight and be with my folks."

"I'll get you up in time to get your bike," Max promised.

Ukiah returned to his bedroom. Max had had it furnished after the fourth time work or weather had forced Ukiah to spend the night sleeping on the floor rather than make the long trip home. Actually Max had turned the project over to an interior decorator and had written the whole thing off on his taxes as a business expense. It had a queen-size sleigh bed, heavy cherry nightstands, and real oriental rugs over the hardwood floors. Over time, more and more of Ukiah's things had gravitated there. To a casual observer, it would seem he actually lived there.

It was comfortable and familiar, but it wasn't home.

He woke by himself at three o'clock. The afternoon sun was full on the bed, blasting it with heat. He woke from a nightmare about being burned alive. It did not help to know that if he had failed the Pack's test, he could easily have been toast today. He stumbled into the bathroom to scrub the previous day's experience from his body: the dirt, the death, the fear, and all the countless bandages. The bruise on his chest and the pellet wound were completely healed (and he assumed the ones on his back were too), thankfully gone without a trace before his moms could see. The Ukiah in the fogged mirror afterward looked completely sound and familiar—one would never know his whole viewpoint of life had been scrambled.

He dressed in clean clothes and came down the sweeping staircase as Max was trotting up.

"Hey!" Max stopped. "I was coming up to wake you. I've got to go check in with Janey and Chino."

"I was going to walk over and get my bike and head home."

Max nodded, starting down the steps again. "I need you here tomorrow early, like seven thirty. Okay?"

"Okay. What do you think I should tell my moms?"

Max winced. "I don't know. Something of the truth, but probably not the whole truth. The whole truth is just too hairy. Jo would want to know about your father, if nothing else."

Ukiah had to admit that was true.

Max snapped his finger and pointed to Ukiah. "Don't forget, get a doll for Cally."

Ukiah almost missed a step. "I forgot! Thanks for reminding me."

Max wearily shook his head. "I'll never figure out how you can quote back the yellow pages and forget little shit like that all the time."

"I have to think of it before I can remember it, Max. I wasn't thinking about dolls."

"Whatever. See you tomorrow. Drive carefully, and take your gun."

Ukiah stopped at the front odor. "My gun?"

"Your gun. Two times in two days is too close. I think you should wear your gun full time for a while."

Ukiah opened his mouth to argue and shut it again. Max looked weary and older than his thirty-eight years. His moan of despair as the Pack gassed Ukiah replayed in his mind, and touching the burnt remains of Janet Haze followed on its heels. Things had turned dangerous in Pittsburgh. Now wasn't the time to be running around unarmed, especially if he was going home to his family. Slowly he nodded. "Okay, I'll get my gun."

          *   *   *

While there were shopping areas on his way north to his moms, they required him to go miles out of his way and deal with suburban sprawl. Walnut Street, however, ran between his office and the motorcycle repair shop; it was a sudden explosion of boutiques in the otherwise serenely upscale neighborhood of Shadyside. The five or six blocks represented some of the trendiest stores in the entire city. The little stores with their expensive, eclectic goods crowded together, making real estate prices high and parking impossible. Ukiah started at one end of the street and worked his way down, growing more and more dismayed.

There were dolls to be found. One store sold voodoo dolls complete with certificates of authenticity at a frightening price (and even more frightening, a curious brush of fingertips revealed that human blood stained the cloth body.) Another shop stocked Peruvian fertility charm dolls. The Japanese dolls in silk kimonos were charming, but unpractical at the level of abuse Cally practiced on her toys. He thought he had lucked out at one store with an entire shelf of Barbie dolls on display, only to discover that they wore hand-stitched original designer clothes. And no, they wouldn't sell the Barbie dolls naked.

On one of the side streets among the Walnut Street–wannabes, he discovered a Native American arts store. The door stood open while the sign firmly announced, "closed." Half the shelves stood empty, and the floor was crowded with unopened boxes marked dream catchers, fetishes, and Navajo blankets. One box near the door had been opened to reveal a collection of dolls in beaded dresses.

A gray-haired woman stocking the shelves caught sight of him standing in the doorway. "I'm sorry.

The air-conditioning is broken, so I opened the door, but we're not ready for business yet."

He pointed down at the dolls. "I've been in every shop in the neighborhood looking for a doll for my little sister. The dog ate her complete collection last night and I promised her a new one."

"Oh dear! Ate them all?" She gave a laugh. "Well, we're set up for credit purchases, but not for cash. If you have a card, I could sell you one."

"American Express?" He took out his wallet to find his card.

"We take all the major ones." She picked up the box of dolls, carried it to the checkout counter, which doubled as a jewelry display case. "I think these are all the same, despite the fact the dresses are all hand-beaded." She laid out five to confirmed their identical nature. "Take your pick."

He picked up the center doll. Hair black as his own decorated the doll, tied into two long braids. Black eyes blinked at him as he inspected the brightly beaded dress. A wealth of information came from the thin leather and tiny glass beads. A Native American woman had made the dress. He fingered her genetic ghost—black-haired, dark eyed, dusky skin—so many of his own traits that he wondered about his parents. "I'll take this one."

"Let me wrap it for you," the storekeeper said, producing a small box. "Then I'll have to find my charge slips. They're here someplace."

The doll hidden away inside the box, Ukiah glanced about for the charge slips. His attention was caught, however, by a collection of small stone statues of various animals in the display case.

"These are beautiful." He breathed, bending down to examine them closely.

"Those are fetishes made by the Zuni Indians."

The storekeeper lectured as she wrapped the doll's box in silver wrapping paper. "Each animal has a different power. The belief is that if you own that animal, and you treat it with respect, the animal will share its power with you. The bear is health and strength. The mole protects underneath; the Zuni bury it beside their crops but it's considered *the thing* to have it placed in the foundation of a new house. Um, the frog is fertility and rain."

Perhaps it was his upbringing, but the wolf statue seemed to be the best. Carved from a blue stone, its eyes captured perfectly the steady patience of a hunting wolf. It reminded him, somehow, of Agent Zheng's even gaze.

"What power does a wolf share with you?" he asked.

The storekeeper set the wrapped present before him. "Wolf, mountain lion, and badgers share the power of hunters, if you're going after something."

A hunter—like Agent Zheng. "May I buy the wolf fetish too?" Impulse moved him to get it as a gift for her, when he wasn't sure if he'd ever see her again. "It doesn't need to be wrapped."

"Certainly." She unlocked the display case and took out the stone statue. Wrapping the fetish in cotton, she slipped it into a small bag. "May I ask, are you Native American?"

"I think I am," Ukiah admitted. "I was"—he decided not to go into his upbringing too deeply—"adopted. I don't know my true parentage."

"Oh." She took his charge card and swiped it through her machine, then checked the back to see if it was signed. "Ukiah Oregon. What a clever name. I've been there. A tiny little town. There's a reservation nearby of Plateau Indians."

"Really?"

"The Cayuse, Umatilla, and the Walla Walla tribes. Nice people. They make beautiful baskets. I have some that I'll be unpacking later. Perhaps you would like to come back and see them."

He signed the charge slip. "I'd like that. Thank you."

Putting the bag with the fetish into his pocket, he left carrying the doll box, thinking about his parentage. Certainly his parents hadn't been a love match. The Pack all but said that his father meant to kill his mother while she was still pregnant with him—for that was the only way to kill an unborn child by blowing up a ship. But his father hadn't killed her. Was it because he had a change of heart (and never got around to telling the Pack) or had his mother survived the murder attempt and escaped unnoticed? If it was the latter, it certainly explained why he was abandoned into the wilderness to fend for himself.

It was a depressing thought, so instead he took out the memory of Agent Zheng greeting him at the fire and relived it in glorious detail.

"Hey, Wolf Boy!" Mike hollered in greeting as Ukiah strolled into the dark confines of the repair shop. The mechanic beamed through a layer of grease. "I expected you yesterday!"

Mike never seemed to be able to talk much lower than a full shout. Max said it probably indicated a hearing problem. Ukiah thought it just indicated the level of Mike's exuberance—his cheerful moods and constant grin certainly seemed to back Ukiah's guess.

"I—I had some trouble yesterday." Ukiah laughed at how trivial his explanation made his experience sound.

"Really? You have a tracking job?"

Ukiah reluctantly nodded. "The FBI hired me to find one of their missing agents."

"That Trace fellow? They lost another one last night. Warner! It's all you hear about on the news! How did it go?"

"I got kidnapped by a biker gang."

"You're shitting me!" Mike shouted. "Get out! Why would a biker gang kidnap you? You know all that shit about biker gangs being tough dudes is just a lot of hype! Hell, my aunt and uncle are part of the Hell's Angels."

"This was the Dog Warriors."

Mike's constant grin dropped from his face and he whispered. "Oh shit, man, are you okay?"

"Yeah. They didn't hurt me."

"I don't know what the fuck you did to piss them off, Wolf Boy, but don't mess around with those dudes. Most bikers are regular joes. Yeah, they'll get drunk sometimes and brawl, but who doesn't? Bikers work nine to five, eat macaroni and cheese with the wife and kids, and spend their evenings sitting on the couch watching TV while drinking a cold one. They're just everyday people—weekend warriors and all that. But, shit, the Dog Warriors! You're talking paramilitary hard asses. They don't have another life except being mean SOBs. Stay far, far away from those dudes!"

"I plan to," Ukiah said, then wondered if he truly meant it. There were so many questions that Rennie didn't answer. Questions already niggling at him. How long could he stand not having the answers all the while knowing that the Pack held the knowledge he wanted? "Besides, they kind of made me an honorary member."

"Get out!" Mike shouted. "You, a Dog Warrior? You're the man!" Mike held up his hand for a high five, and Ukiah slapped his palm. "My friend, the Dog Warrior!" Mike laughed as he went to his desk to pick up a key ring. "I'll send my bill. Here's your keys."

Ukiah caught the keys that Mike threw to him. He kept his bike keys separate from the rest. Home, office, office garage, the three company cars, and still others made his key ring an impressive collection of keys he was afraid to leave jiggling out in the open as he drove down the highway. "Thanks, Mike."

Mike followed him out to the street, where his bike sat gleaming bright red in the afternoon sunlight. Ukiah stuffed Cally's present into the seat storage, then swung his leg over the seat. The smile dropped off Mike's face again. "Look, kid, an honorary member or not, don't get messed up with the Dog Warriors more than you have to."

Ukiah made a vague promise. "I'll try not to."

He crossed Veteran's Bridge to catch I-279 heading north. His mind worked over the day's events as he drove. He shied away from the actual kidnapping, the emotions too raw there. Strange how he could still feel so bad about lying to Max when it saved all of their lives. Perhaps it came from a fear that Max would no longer trust his word completely. Shifting forward in time to the point where Rennie opened the car trunk, he reviewed the Pack and his trail.

The sensations that were Rennie rolled through his mind again. The smell of leather, hot oil, engine exhaust, sweat, and surprisingly, wolf. Like Janet Haze, Rennie had the odd fractured DNA, an odd jumble of genetics seemingly smashed together. Ukiah picked at it trying to make sense of it. Here—the normal pattern for a white, young adult male. There—something that seemed like a wolf. Underscoring it was something hard, jagged, strange—and yet uncomfortably familiar.

He moved forward to Hellena's first touch. He focused on her skin and found the same fractured DNA. Odder yet, as he picked over it, the similarities grew too many to ignore. Hellena seemed like a twin to Rennie. True, she was female, and of more Italian descent than Rennie's Irish, but the jumbled pieces— that hard strange something—matched perfectly. It seemed as if someone had taken the same base and just overlayed Rennie and Hellena onto it.

He wished that he had touched one of the other Pack members, or at least touched something they had handled. He recalled their scent, and found, as a collective, a weird mix of man and wolf. He realized that all during the test, he'd been aware of the Pack movements even as his eyes were locked on Hellena. He felt them stalk through the darkness behind him, their presence a tingle like static electricity on his skin. No, not quite on his skin—on some part of him that existed just above his skin that he never noticed before, an invisible layer of sensitivity.

Shuddering, he backed away from the thought, returning instead to the sense of familiarity to Rennie's and Hellena's twin base DNA pattern. Was it only Janet Haze's genetic pattern that triggered this déjà vu? He recalled it and found a few points of common reference in that of the Pack members'. He ran the length of the Pack genes, trying it against the various recent samples he had experienced. Wil Trace? No. Agent Zheng? No. The kidnapper of Wil Trace? Hmmm, his pattern matched Janet Haze's almost exactly, just as Rennie's and Hellena's had been near twins.

Then the obvious hit him, and he checked.

It was his DNA that he was thinking of.

Not twined like Rennie and Hellena, but definitely a match to the Pack members and not that of Janet Haze and the mysterious kidnapping Other. Only where their pattern broke, jumbled, and tumbled in odd confusion, his genetic pattern was a seamless whole.

"He's just a boy," Rennie had shouted. *"A Pack cub! I know what Prime expected to crawl out of that girl's womb, I've had nightmares about it since I joined the Pack. But this isn't it."*

The Pack, he suddenly realized, wasn't a biker gang. It was a family. His family.

In the end, he didn't have a chance to tell his moms about his kidnapping or his newfound family. Cally was sitting in wait for his arrival and ambushed him at the door. He made the mistake of admitting that he had remembered the doll, but forgot it outside with his bike. From then on, chaos reigned until he took her outside to open her present.

"An Indian princess." Cally breathed in delight as the last piece of silver wrapping paper had been reduced to shreds and the top of the box flung aside. "Thank you, Ukiah, she's beautiful."

The doll also earned him one of Cally's choking, misplaced hugs.

Far off, he could hear the whine of a motorcycle. Linked so closely to the Pack, it suddenly seemed like a menacing noise. The unknown rider turned at the end of the farm's long driveway and started up it, slower now, the engine more of a growl. It sounded like an angry animal, and it sent his heart pounding.

He pried Cally off and tried for one of Mom Jo's commanding voices. "Go in the house, Cally." Amazingly, she went without fuss.

He unholstered his pistol, checked his clip, and walked to where the old stone wall and one of the pines gave him cover. The motorcycle climbed the slight grade and shot into the driveway too fast. The rider saw almost too late that the road ended here and braked hard, half sliding, sending up a spray of gravel.

The rider gave the sprawling yard, the far kennels, and the great old house under the massive oaks a long study, working the throttle slightly to keep the engine running. Ukiah leaned against the pine, studying the rider. The bike wasn't a big one, yet large for the rider, so it was a small woman. Ukiah breathed deep and filtered out the gas fumes and hot oil for her scent. It was Agent Zheng. He shook his head. Why was she here? Mom Jo was going to freak.

She came to the end of her sweep and saw him standing in the shadows. Her mirrored visor reflected his image, and he was surprised how fierce he looked. She killed the engine, put down the kickstand, and pulled off her helmet.

She combed her hair back out of her eyes. "Is this place Max's too?"

"What are you doing here?" He couldn't keep from growling. "How did you find it?"

"Your cell phone. When I called Max yesterday, this is the cell he was in, and this is where you trotted back to this afternoon, so I came out to see what was out here."

"Why?" He put his pistol away.

She marked the fact he had been armed, but replied without a comment on it. "Because in the last two days I've spent most of my time wondering where you were and if you were still alive. I wanted to fill in the holes of what I didn't know about you, just in case this trend continues. Why are you so angry?"

He sighed, letting go of his anger. "This isn't Max's place. It belongs to my family. I don't want anything to do with this case to touch their lives. They don't even know what happened to me yesterday. They think I worked last night, called in at breakfast as usual, and came home for dinner."

"Your records don't say you have a family."

He hopped over the stone wall to cross the driveway to her. "That's to keep nosy FBI agents out of their lives."

A smile touched her eyes for a moment. "Is not." She hung her helmet on the handle bars and dismounted the bike.

"Is too." Ukiah crossed his heart. "Scout's honor."

She crossed her arms, cocking her head as she looked up at him. "Were you ever a Boy Scout?"

"Yeah." The scouting experience had ranged from horribly stilted interaction to great fun. It had taught him a lot more about people than the crafts and skills he was trying to learn. He supposed he also took the moral lessons a little more to heart than was recommended. "I gave it up to work with Max."

"So, why don't you want nosy FBI agents here?"

"You ask a lot of questions."

"That's what I'm good at. So why the no-fed zone?"

He shook his head; she was persistent. "Look, I was never adopted officially. Until I became of legal age, my Mom Jo was afraid that the government might take me from her. It doesn't matter much now that I'm a legal adult. Old habits are hard to break, though."

"I see." She walked to the stone wall and sat down with her back to the house, looking out over the land.

"Beautiful place. You know, your mom probably had nothing to worry about if she had consent letters from your birth mother."

"I was abandoned." He sat beside her. "Mom Jo found me in Oregon. She actually probably broke all sorts of laws bringing me across the country to Pittsburgh."

Agent Zheng shook her head wearily. "Yes, she did break the law. Several federal laws. Okay, Boy Scout, I see why you don't want FBI agents here. How old were you? An infant? One? Two? How did she know you were abandoned and not lost?"

Ukiah laughed. "I was about twelve, it was the middle of winter, I was naked, and I was eating the guts out of a dead rabbit when she first laid eyes on me. It was a pretty good bet that I hadn't gone missing over lunch."

"Rabbit guts?" She raised an eyebrow at him, open disbelief on that unreadable face.

He had to smile and push it, enjoying being able to read her at last. "Oh yeah. See, I was being raised by a pack of timber wolves, and we considered the guts the best part. It had been a hard winter, so a whole rabbit to myself was actually terrific."

She cocked her head, trying to decide if he was telling the truth or not. "Do you tell a lot of people that story?"

"Actually—" he sobered, "I think you're only the second person. Max was the first."

She looked away. "I've been told your nickname is Wolf Boy and the police jokingly call you 'the boy raised by wolves.' It would seem you've told a lot of people that story."

"Oh, I tell them I was raised by wolves, but I've never told them about not having clothes on and eating the rabbit guts. You have to tell people something, sooner or later: why you don't know what it's like to be a normal kid with trick or treat, Christmas, birthday parties, school, proms, losing your baby teeth, getting your shots. Why you don't remember a cool kid's show that everyone your age watched when they were ten. Why you miss tons of culture references from old commercials, political scandals, world events—"

She turned her luminous eyes back to him. He stared into them, trying to find her again.

"If you just say, 'I don't remember,' they keep feeding you clues, like they can trigger the memory in you. When they find out you have a photographic memory, you can't even say, 'I don't remember,' because then they know you're lying, but they don't realize what part you're lying about. So you admit it, not as the first thing you say to them, but some time early on. I was raised by wolves, I ran with a pack of timber wolves, I don't know what it's like to be a normal child."

He fell silent. There was a slight softening about her eyes, as if she believed him. He'd have to be content with that, for now.

"So how did you end up working with Max?"

"Mom Jo hired him to see if he could find out who I was, and he couldn't. The first day he was here, though, doing background questioning, we took a walk and ran across a trail of a man setting traps on the farm. I tracked the man for over a mile at a trot to catch him at his truck. Max ran him off. About a week after my case panned out, Max was hired to find a little boy. John Libzer, sixteen months old, vanished from his yard, gone for two days without a clue."

"You found him?"

Ukiah nodded. "He followed a neighbor's cat

across the street and into a wood lot. There was the bore hole for an oil well there, no more than this wide." He put his hands out to illustrate. "You wouldn't have thought a kid could fit down it, but I could smell him."

"I know this case," she said softly. "I reviewed it when I came to Pittsburgh. I spoke to the agent who worked it. He said he'd been through that lot twice and never saw the hole. I don't remember hearing about you, though."

Ukiah shrugged. "Well, my moms weren't home when Max came out and asked me to help him. He knew the FBI was involved and knew how Mom Jo felt about them, so as soon as I'd found Johnny, he called 911, gave Mr. Libzer his bill, and got me out of there. My moms were pissed, but we watched the whole rescue, and they cried when the firemen got Johnny out alive. After that, I tracked with Max part-time, about once every two weeks. Then three years ago, Max asked me on full time."

"After the Joe Gary shooting."

"What do you know about that?"

"Mr. Bennett's past is about as interesting as yours. Veteran of the Gulf War. Military police. College graduate via the veterans' college fund. Co-founder of a highly successful Internet software company, providing business savvy to his computer genius partner, being bought out at age thirty-two for more money than most people dream of making in a lifetime. Beautiful wife goes missing and police are suspicious of the husband, as always, but the husband was touring California at that time, doing speaking engagements on his success. Besides, everyone who knew them says they were madly in love, newly rich, and looking forward to starting a family. Three months later, the police still had turned up nothing, so Mr. Bennett hired a private detective. A week later the car and missing wife were dredged up from Lake Arthur, where it's easy to slide a fast car off the road and into deep water. Mr. Bennett buried his wife, became a private detective, and devoted his life to finding lost souls. Very poetic."

At first he thought she was being sarcastic about Max, then realized that no, her eyes had deepened and her voice had softened. She had been touched by Max's desperate attempt to make his world right.

"You've done your homework."

"Besides the suspicion of his wife's disappearance, the only other blemish on Mr. Bennett's file is the manslaughter in self-defense of one Joseph Gary. The local police records seem almost purposely confused, like they helped cover up the fact that there was a second shooter, identity unknown, using a .45. If you go back and question paramedics on the scene, they tell you there were three wounded; a female hiker, a man with a serious concussion, and a boy who'd been shot with a rifle."

"Not one of our better days."

"A week later, your paper trail starts, and you're added as an official part owner of Bennett Detective Agency."

Ukiah looked at her, amazed. "I'm what?"

"He gave you half the company. It doesn't seem like much, until you read the asset list: half-million dollar house, three luxury cars, and enough high-tech surveillance equipment and guns to keep a third world country happy. You saved his life that day, didn't you?"

Max had meant "partner" in a more literal meaning than Ukiah thought. He wondered if his moms knew. He wondered too if Max would ever regret the move. The Max of three years ago was more somber, less willing to look ahead then the Max of today.

Ukiah realized that Agent Zheng was still waiting for an answer, that she wasn't going to let him not answer it. "I don't understand why you're asking all these questions. Why does it matter if I saved Max's life three years ago?"

"I'm asking because I need to know how much I can trust you. Did you save Max's life like you saved mine?"

"I suppose so. I jumped into the way without thinking and got hit instead."

"You got hurt, but the other person would have died."

Ukiah nodded. "I guess. I don't know why you need to trust me. We're so off the case that we're talking about taking a vacation in California. We don't do this kind of stuff. We find people who've taken a wrong turn in their day-to-day life. Like Johnny Libzer, who fell down the well."

"Like Max's wife, who went off the road?"

Ukiah nodded and caught the sound of Cally creeping up behind them. He turned and she darted the last few feet to fling herself into his lap, burrowing her face into the crook of his arm. "Hey, hey, what's wrong."

"Mommy wanted me to come ask you who you were talking to, and see if they were staying for dinner."

"Oh. Well, this is—" "Agent Zheng" wouldn't sit well with his moms, he scanned back for her first name. Agent Indigo Zheng. "This is Indigo. Indigo, this is my little sister, Cally."

"Hello, Cally."

Cally burrowed deeper into Ukiah's lap.

"What's wrong, pumpkin? Can't you say hello?"

She shook her head.

"Cally, what's wrong? Why are you scared?"

"Is she the girl that hurt you so you had to stay in the hospital?"

"No, no, pumpkin. That girl died. Indigo is a law officer. You remember what we've told you. Police men and women are our friends—aren't they?" Mostly.

Cally peered out from the safety of Ukiah's arm, her eyes wide and serious. "Uh-huh."

"Okay, pumpkin. Can you go tell Mom that I'm talking to Indigo, and she's—" He glanced at Agent Zheng.

"—staying for dinner." Agent Zheng finished his sentence.

"Okay." And Cally bolted away.

Ukiah watched her still awkward baby running, wondering when kids made that leap to gracefulness. He looked back and found Agent Zheng—Indigo—studying him intently.

Dinner went well, perhaps because neither Ukiah nor Indigo mentioned that she was an FBI agent. She was good at asking a question and listening to the answer, speaking only to nudge the person into talking more. Mom Jo and Mom Lara talked about female-on-female fertilization, gay marriages in the United States, and Mom Jo's wolf dogs. After dinner, Mom Jo took them back to the kennels, named the dogs, and explained how each had been rescued from an owner that didn't want the half-breed or a humane shelter that mistrusted their wolf blood.

"We've got something viral circulating through the pack, though." Mom Jo ducked into the end cage to check on her most recent addition, a female crossed with a husky. "The newcomers are fine until they start fighting for a pack position. I think it might be blood transmitted."

Ukiah and Indigo left Mom Jo tending the sickly female, and walked out into the night-cloaked fields. He amazed Indigo with his knowledge of the stars.

"Mom Lara has a doctorate in astrophysics. She used to work at the Allegheny Observatory, but she gave it up to have Cally. I know how much she loved it—I'm always amazed at her sacrifice. She has a NASA grant to do special science projects at the local school."

"And Mom Jo?"

"A doctorate in biology. She's head of the Pittsburgh Zoo. I know stars and animals. The Big Dipper is really Ursa Major, which means big bear." As he hoped, she knew the Big Dipper. He used it to point out other constellations. Venus and Mercury had already set. Saturn was too faint to see easily. He guided her to the Gemini constellation and picked out the stars Pollux and Castor as pointers to Mars.

She gazed at the planet for a long time and finally murmured, "It's so small, so far away. It's amazing we've actually reached it. I wonder how the rover is doing."

He laughed. "I had almost forgotten that was going on."

"I can't," she murmured.

Why couldn't she, he wondered, but a streak of light distracted him. "Shooting star. Make a wish."

Her lips moved against the night sky. What had she asked for? What did she want? He wished he knew what she was thinking.

A memory triggered in his mind, and he smiled in the dark. "I bought something for you today."

"Something for me?"

He took the bag containing the wolf fetish from

his pocket and handed it to her. "When I bought it, I wondered if I was ever going to see you again to give it to you."

He repeated what the storekeeper had told him.

She unwrapped it and held it up into the moonlight to inspect it. "And you bought it for me?"

The question confused him. Hadn't he just said that? Perhaps she thought he bought it because he liked it and was giving it to her to make it seem like he planned it all along.

"I like the fact that you can stay so focused on the here, the now," Ukiah said. "Most people I meet get so caught up in the what-was and what-might-be that they spend most of their time reacting to something other than the present."

He reached out to touch the statute in her hand, and their fingertips met. "This wolf has the look of one who is centered. It reminded me of you."

She gazed up at him in long silence, then whispered, "It's beautiful. Thank you."

They walked on along the sea of wheat. They were close, almost touching. Then she reached out to twine her hand in his. Her hand was warm and soft and felt right in his.

"So you're twenty-one."

"That's what we think. I seemed to be between thirteen and sixteen when Mom Jo found me. They picked thirteen to make up for the basic life foundation I missed out on and started to count from there. That was eight years ago, January. I could be older, I could be younger."

"You look like you could still be between fourteen and sixteen—well, not all the time. Most of the time you look about eighteen, and then you suddenly get this puppy-dog look and you're fourteen or sixteen."

"Thanks." They came to the great oak with his tree

house. She climbed up and he followed. "How old are you?"

"I'm twenty-six."

"Older woman," Ukiah observed, laying back on the worn wood to stare up at her as she looked at him. What was she thinking?

"Robbing the cradle," she murmured and leaned down to kiss him. He had seen kissing on TV and always wondered why they did so much of it. Now he found himself almost whimpering with the pleasure of it. Her mouth was warm and sweet, and where her tongue touched him felt electric.

He closed his arms awkwardly around her, his right hand finding the curve of her bottom and his left tangling into the soft richness of her hair. Her body molded itself to his, and he felt all of it, the shape of her breasts, the flatness of her stomach, the inside curve of her legs.

She tugged up his shirt, and he sat up to help her pull it off. She skinned out of hers and they pressed close again, feeling the warm skin on skin. He was amazed at the softness of her skin, the ripple of muscle under it.

"Have you ever done this before?" she whispered, her eyes filled with the moonlight.

"No," he admitted reluctantly. "Most girls I meet are suffering from hypothermia and are in borderline shock."

She gave her deep, rich laugh, running her hands over his chest. "Most of the guys I meet are trying too hard to be you."

"Me?"

"You're strong and silent by nature. They're putting on an act, so they can't keep their mouth shut when something cute hits them. You can get this dangerous look they couldn't get without Raybans."

He kissed her shoulders and neck and the top curve of her breast. "Is it important that I'm dangerous?"

She laughed into his hair. "I rarely get a second date from accountants."

"So I need to be able to walk beside you and not be afraid."

"I think you can."

He looked up and got lost in her eyes.

"I know so little about you." Ukiah found her spine fascinating, the slight ridge of bone under skin.

She rolled over, presenting other fascinating points of anatomy. "What do you want to know?"

He laughed, tracing her small breasts, so unlike a Barbie doll's full featureless chest. "Everything. You were born in Pittsburgh,"—so said her records—"lived here for some time. You barely have the accent, but it's there. Do you like it here or did the agency assign you here?"

"I asked for it. My family is here, and while attending college, then the academy, I started missing them. I think it was because there was no one special to keep me happy in Washington."

"Father, mother, brothers, sisters?"

"Yes. All that and more. Most of them live in the South Hills. My folks wanted me to live at home when I moved back to the area, but I couldn't have taken that."

"They're frightened by what you do. You would have to lie to them constantly if you lived with them."

"Yeah." She suddenly smiled at him, a full wondrous smile. "My dad owns a restaurant; most of my family works there. They're not sure what went wrong with me."

"Nothing. You want to save the victims, punish the bad guys, fight evil, and see justice served."

"You know everything about me."

He laughed. "No I don't. It's just that you're a lot like me. What's your favorite color?"

"Blue, indigo blue, what's yours?"

He considered. "Green, leaf green, grass green."

She reached up and guided him down on top of her. "Favorite food?"

"Indian. Japanese. Cantonese. Like you, I love ethnic food."

She laughed. "How do you know I love ethnic?"

"It's been on your breath every time we've met. Thai, Japanese, Korean."

They fell silent, suddenly intent on making love again.

They fell asleep very late, twined together into one person. They woke, stiff and cold, on the wood floor of the open tree house just as dawn streaked the eastern horizon. Ukiah found his pants as Indigo stretched. His phone claimed it to be 5:30 A.M.

"Max wanted me in the office at seven thirty this morning." He pulled on his shirt and cast about for his briefs. "We're behind on our cases."

She moaned. "I've got a debriefing at eight. If I leave now, I can shower at my gym and review the case notes."

"I'll be surprised if I can think of anything but you today," Ukiah admitted.

Her eyes held a quiet look of joy. She leaned over and kissed him.

It was 5:50 A.M. when he glanced at his phone again. He walked her to her bike. She looked disheveled but happy when he finally could step away to let her go. She coasted her motorcycle quietly down the hill and started the engine at the bottom, lessening its deep sudden growl on the silent morning.

His moms were blessedly still asleep. He crept upstairs to his room and showered, unable to stop thinking about her. Indigo. Indigo with the gray eyes. He dressed quickly, glancing at his bedroom clock. She had fifteen minutes on him, but she didn't know the roads like he did, and she had a smaller motorcycle.

He'd picked one of the more powerful bikes because he'd thought, as a private investigator, there might be times he'd have to go like the wind. He'd never thought it would be because he wanted to catch up to his girlfriend. He kept to a reasonable though illegal speed on the winding country roads, but gunned the bike into the hundreds the moment he reached the flat straight I-79. In minutes he was nearing the I-279 merge and saw the taillight of anther bike. He zipped through the thickening morning traffic and then came level with her.

He was so happy to see her that he didn't mind the mirror visor that cloaked her gray eyes. She shook her head and lifted her hand briefly to blow him a kiss. The traffic slowed slightly at the merge, where police often waited for speeders. They wove through the lagging cars, first Indigo leading and then Ukiah. It was a weird, exhilarating feeling to ride beside her, as if they were two hawks flying together. They swooped and twined into the city. Ukiah followed her into downtown, wanting to look at her eyes one last time before heading off to Shadyside. She stopped outside a parking garage in a loading zone and pulled off her helmet.

He stopped beside her, killed his engine, and took off his own helmet. "Hi there."

A slight tender smile touched her face. "Hi there."

She touched his damp hair and shook her head. "You must have broken the sound barrier to catch up with me."

"I wanted to see you again."

She gazed deep into his eyes and whispered, "You're seeing me."

He kissed her fingertips, the palm of her hand, and then took her in his arms to kiss her lips until a van beeped at them, wanting into the loading zone.

She reluctantly pulled away. "Let's get together for dinner. Come down to my office and get me at five."

"I'll see you at five," he promised, pulled on his helmet, started up his motorcycle, and headed out to Shadyside.

CHAPTER SEVEN

Friday, June 19, 2004
Pittsburgh, Pennsylvania

Ukiah pulled the motorcycle around to the back of the offices, unlocked the fourth garage, pulled up the door, and drove in. He left his helmet on his bike, closed, and locked the door again. His phone read 7:25 as he unlocked the back door and walked into the kitchen. Max was there, dressed for the day, finishing up his breakfast of mushroom and cheese omelet.

"Hi, Max." He opened the freezer, got out a pair of frozen mini-waffles, and popped them into the toaster.

"Good morning." Max folded up his newspaper, then tilted his head at Ukiah. "What's that goofy look on your face?"

"Goofy look?" He bent down to look into the toaster's mirrored surface. His reflection wore a broad smile. "You mean the grin?"

"Yes, the grin."

He shrugged as his waffles popped up. "Guess it's because I'm in love."

"Love? With who?"

"Indigo."

"Who the hell is Indigo? The new girl at 7-Eleven? God, Ukiah, she's ugly."

"Agent Zheng. Indigo Zheng. Isn't it a cool name?" He pulled a plate out of an upper cabinet, dropped the hot waffles on it, and found the maple syrup.

"When did this happen?" Max looked bemused by the news. "You've only seen her, let's see—the morgue, the day you were kidnapped, and yesterday morning—three times."

"Four." He covered the waffles in syrup. "She came out to the house last night."

"She did?" The bemusement vanished, replaced with concern. "How did she find it? How long did she stay? What did you two talk about?"

"She tracked me with the wireless phone system. Ancient FBI secret, apparently." He tore off one of the mini-waffles with his fingers and stuffed it whole into his mouth. "She stayed all night. We didn't do a whole lot of talking," he answered honestly, without thinking, then blushed solid, "not as much as I would have liked, not that I didn't like what we were doing."

Max looked at him a moment, then flipped his newspaper over his shoulder. "You slept with her! I thought you meant 'puppy dog from a distance I wonder if she would date me' in love, not 'I had great sex with her last night' in love! Jesus! Well, that explains all the looking—drooling at the candy store window, so to speak."

"Huh?"

"All her looking at you. I can't believe I didn't see this coming. I forget that to women, you're Mister Joe Studly."

"Me, studly?"

Max laughed. "Take it from someone who was

geek of the week at your age and could spot the guys who would get the girls. You are serious eye candy. The hair, the eyes, the face, the body, the cool bike, the big gun. God, you're a single, female, FBI agent's wet dream. She did a serious background check on you—didn't she?—then came out to see where, what, and why you were hiding out in the boondocks."

"Yeah. She knew stuff I didn't know about myself."

"Like what?"

"That I own half this house. And the cars. And the guns and everything. You never told me."

"I didn't want to make a big deal about it. Still don't."

Ukiah ignored the hint. "Are you sure you won't regret it? I mean, what if you find someone, remarry, have kids, but you've given away half of the house you live in, half of the stuff that should go to your kids."

"Ukiah." Max's eyes went stern. "I don't regret doing it. I will never regret it. If I ever find someone, it will only be because you kept me alive long enough to find her." He got up then and carried his dishes to the sink.

"Sorry."

"You're a good kid, Ukiah." Max stood at the sink, washing the skillet he used for his omelet. "It's a tribute to your character that you worry about me, but really, this house and the agency stuff, is piddling to what I've got in stocks and bonds. Plus, my wife believed in big life insurance policies. Between what I got in the buyout of my first company and her double indemnity insurance payment—" he shook his head "—I couldn't spend it all even if I tried."

While they were tap-dancing on mine fields, Ukiah

figured he might as well hit them all. "Mom Lara says you should start dating."

"I know," Max acknowledged, and left it at that.

They fell into a comfortable silence as Ukiah finished his waffles, raided the fridge for some orange juice, and took his turn at rinsing off breakfast dishes. Max leaned against the breakfast bar, looking at him. "You slept with Agent Zheng," he finally muttered, shaking his head in disbelief. "You, um, used protection, didn't you?"

"She had some with her."

"You sure you can handle this, kid? You're definitely not the first guy she's dated, and you're probably not the first guy she slept with. She could have even lived with a guy for a couple of years at her age."

Ukiah shrugged, putting his dishes into the drying rack. "I have to have a first love sometime. You told me your first love broke your heart, and you lived through it. If it comes to that, so will I."

The cases they had put on hold for Janet Haze's case were what Max called "bread-and-butter work." While not what neither he or Max loved to do, the cases kept the agency afloat. The first was a skip, someone disappearing on a debt. The second was a straightforward employee background check. The third was a background check on a new girlfriend of a wealthy man.

The cases were nothing flashy, and except for the skip, not even vaguely dangerous. After the frantic pace of the week, it was good to settle into something slower.

Max handed Ukiah the folder on the background check. "The girl, Marie Tovin, is coming out clean. Dallento wants us to tail her for a while. His last

sexy young thing kept a boyfriend on the side while
Dallento paid her bills. This is not a way to start a
relationship, in my book, but he's paying the bills."

Ukiah took the folder, his stomach sinking as he
realized that Max's comment could apply to him and
Indigo. He didn't mind Indigo checking into his
background, but Max might hold it against her. "Do
you think it was wrong that Indigo did a background
check on me?"

"Kid, you're talking night and day. A woman in
the middle of a multiple-kidnapping and murder
case has to be careful. She's putting her life on the
line. Dallento wants to make sure that if he buys the
cow, he's the only one getting the milk. You can't
compare the two."

Ukiah opened the folder to look at Marie Tovin's
photo. When he had seen the picture last week, he
had vaguely recognized it as sensual. Today he understood the allure of her sleepy eyes, the taunting
promise of her hand resting on a slipping waistband,
and the sexual act suggested by her tongue toying
with the end of a pencil. "How long does Dallento
want us to follow her?"

"A full week. He's got money to burn. I'll call
Chino and Janey to take up the slack. Go over, make
sure she's home, and then keep out of sight until
Chino and Janey can take over. I'm going to do some
phone calling to see if I can get any kind of a lead
on our skip."

There was a security system on Marie Tovin's
apartment building. Ukiah glanced at it as he strolled
past the main door, trying to hide his interest in it
behind an air of casual indifference. He stopped at
the corner for the light, using the pause to consider

his options. How could he get in without attracting attention to himself?

A few blocks down, one of Pittsburgh's semipermanent street peddlers was hawking bouquets of flowers. Ukiah wasn't sure where the flowers came from. He had never seen the peddler actually set up in the morning or break down in the evening. The man, a sunburnt blond somewhere in his twenties, just seemed to appear each day, his collection of tall white buckets and cheap Styrofoam containers brim full of fresh flowers. During rush hours, the peddler stood on the curb, flowers in one hand, holding up the fingers of his other hand to indicate how many dollars the bundle cost.

Seeing the peddler, Ukiah recalled a ploy he once read about in a murder mystery. Ukiah bought two large bouquets and returned to the apartment building. He waited before the door, arms full of flowers, until someone kindly held the door open for him.

Marie Tovin lived in apartment 395. Standing in the hallway, he could hear a shower running and the chatter of morning radio. Someone was home and awake.

He slipped out of the building again and reluctantly pitched the flowers. There would be no way to keep them fresh enough to give to his moms or Indigo.

At a McDonald's across the street from the apartment building, Ukiah bought a small mountain of food and sat down with the morning paper. He held the paper up so he looked like he was reading it, glanced at the front page, and gazed over the top of the paper at the front door of Marie's apartment building. As he watched the residents come and go, he reviewed the front page in his mind—oh, the joys of a photographic memory.

Yesterday's fire was the headline story. The *Pittsburgh Post-Gazette* photographer had caught Indigo standing with Kraynak before the smoldering building. He smiled at the photo. Taken alone, Indigo looked very aloof and very FBI. Unfortunately, beside the huge police officer, there was something also very doll-like about her. Indigo would probably hate the picture, he decided, but he'd have to clip it. The photo caption read "FBI and City of Pittsburgh Homicide department are working together to solve baffling arson." The story continued onto the next page, but they never named Indigo as the investigating agent. There was a single line which stated, "Haze was killed in self-defense by a tracking expert from the Bennett Detective Agency." He was relieved to find he wasn't being publicly touted as her killer.

He flipped slowly through the paper, memorizing a page with a glance and reviewing it mentally. There were several stories on Wil Trace's and Agent Warner's disappearance. His own kidnapping, however, went without notice. Both Mom Lara and Max read the paper every morning, and neither had mentioned a story on him in yesterday's paper. It looked like he'd escaped the media's attention completely, which suited him fine.

The day was proving expensive for Mr. Dallento. Not only was he paying for a private investigator to follow his girlfriend around town at a hundred dollars an hour, said girlfriend loved to shop at the more expensive shops in Pittsburgh. Mid-morning she had started at Kaufmann's and was working her way across town. Keeping up with her wasn't a problem. The difficulty came with killing time while she shopped without seeming obvious. Ukiah was holding down a table at the Fifth Avenue Arcade shops when his phone chirped.

"Oregon."

"Hey hey hey, Wolf Boy, it's Chinooooo."

"Hey, Chino!"

"Where are you? Max says I'm to help out following a chickchickchickchickie."

When Chino had his mouth shut, he could actually blend into the woodwork. It was an amazing thing to see after talking to him.

"Downtown. The Fifth Avenue Building."

"Hey, I'm almost there. I had to stop at Market Square to meet a friend. I'll have to find a parking place, which could take a while."

"Try to find one quick. After six floors of Kaufmann's, my face is getting too familiar."

"I hear you. Keep your head down and I'll be there as soon as possible."

A testament to parking in Pittsburgh, it was almost a full thirty minutes before he handed Marie Tovin off to Chino and the recently arrived Janey.

Moisha Janey was a tall, black woman with no-nonsense eyes. "I heard through the grapevine," Janey's voice was so low, Ukiah had to listen close to hear what she said, "that you've been accepted into the Dog Warriors."

"In a way."

"I heard that those are some scary dudes not to be messed with."

"Yeah, they are."

"I heard that there's a turf war between them and some scarier dudes, dudes so scary they don't have a name."

"They kind of told me about them."

"They say that last year a Dog Warrior was drinking in a place uptown. They say that one of the other gang came in and they fell on each other without a word, without a thought. They say it was bad shit, like they both went instantly rabid. They say it was weird shit, because neither one spoke, just tried their damnest to kill the other. They say they tore the place apart, killed a policeman who came to break up the fight, and when it was done, the winner burned the loser's body right there, burning the place down to cinders."

Ukiah wet his mouth. "Who won?"

"They don't say." She turned her dark eyes on him. "I get the impression that after the two killed the policeman, no one stuck around close enough to see the end of the fight, but the place was torched and the fireman found a John Doe inside." She rapped on his chest with her knuckles. "You be careful."

She strolled off with the carriage of an African queen.

The Federal Building rose on a wedge of land where Liberty and Grant streets merged at a forty-five degree angle. It was a mid-'70s office building, columns of steel and glass and ugly as hell.

He checked the directory for the FBI offices and found that they took up the sixth floor. Most of the elevators were coming down packed. The only challenge getting on one going up was getting in before the doors closed once the prolonged stampede of down passengers ended.

On the sixth floor he asked the receptionist directions for Indigo's office. He had to surrender his weapon and submitted to a quick search before he was allowed to wander off to find her.

Another female agent was standing in Indigo's door, her body a picture of relaxed friendship as she leaned against the door frame. She spotted Ukiah coming, inventoried him completely with a smile, then whispered into the office. "Stud muffin alert! You should see what's heading our way."

"Fisher." Indigo's voice came from the office, slightly scolding.

Agent Fisher stepped back, expecting him to pass, and was taken aback when he stopped even with the door. "Can I help you?"

Indigo looked up and a smile bloomed across her face. Ukiah's knees felt weak, and he found himself grinning back at her.

Agent Fisher saw his grin, glanced at Indigo, and tsked. "Oh, he's *your* stud muffin. Too bad."

Indigo blushed slightly, and Agent Fisher went away laughing.

"Hi." She gained control of the blush and became her normally composed self.

"Hey. I'm not too early, am I?" Ukiah asked, leaning against the door frame, eyeing her office with interest. The surfaces were almost clear of paper. There were Japanese silk prints on the wall and a red maple bonsai tree before the narrow window.

"I'm almost done." She filed the few pieces of paper into one desk drawer, and produced her helmet from another. "Where would you like to eat?"

"Any place, as long as it's with you."

It earned him the slight Mona Lisa smile.

The phone rang and she picked it up. "Agent Zheng." She listened and then glanced up at Ukiah. "Actually, he's right here." She listened a moment longer. "I don't think that makes him an expert, but I can bring him over." She hung up the phone. "The police would like you to come look over a Pack member for them."

He was slightly startled. "They caught one of the Pack? Who?"

"They didn't say."

Nor did Ukiah recognize the Pack member when they arrived and were shown the two-way mirror with a view into an interrogation room. The member was a tall lanky man, grizzled long hair, and dark eyes, like so many of the Pack. He was clad in a worn pair of leather pants, high biker boots, and a leather jacket with a stylized running wolf.

Ukiah shook his head, watching the man pace back and forth in the small dim room. "I don't recognize him."

"We'd be surprised if you did," the police captain that met them explained. "We believe he's a West Coast member, of the Wild Wolves. He won't admit it, won't tell us his name, and has no ID. We were hoping you could verify if he was a Pack member or not."

Ukiah looked in surprise at the captain. "How would I know?"

"You're the only person in this building that's actually dealt with the Pack. We're going off mug shots and old reports. So, what do you think? Is he a Pack member?"

Indigo was silent and unreadable. Ukiah shrugged and walked up to the glass. As if he knew Ukiah was watching, the man came to stand before the mirror, his lip curling back almost in a snarl. Ukiah studied him, looking for any clue yes or no.

"He looks like Pack," he finally admitted. "But he isn't. I don't know why. There's some gut reaction missing. He's not Pack."

"Are you sure?"

"Almost. I've only dealt with the Pack once. But I'm almost positive he's not."

The captain turned to a plainclothes detective standing beside him. "Bring him in."

The detective walked into the interrogation room, caught the fake Pack member, and brought him snarling out. The fake Pack member glared at Ukiah as the detective parked the man in front of him.

"Take a good look," the captain said. "Are you sure he's not Pack?"

The man glanced at the captain, then sneered down at Ukiah. "Who the hell are you?"

Ukiah gazed at the man. Why was he so sure that this man wasn't Pack? He thought back to Rennie, Hellena, and Bear. There had been something about them, something he had never felt in the presence of other people, something that had gone unnoticed till now. He shook his head as he tried to place it. "No. I'm positive now. This man isn't Pack."

The fake gave him a Pack-like glare for a moment longer. Then the look vanished. It was like watching an actor take off his mask. "How the hell can you tell?"

Ukiah shook his head, still unable to pinpoint it. "You just know the difference."

"This is Detective Robert Cecil." The captain perched on the corner of the table. "He's one of our best undercover agents. He's spent weeks researching the Pack. We wanted to run one last test before he tried to infiltrate the Pack."

"They would eat him alive," Ukiah murmured.

"Are you sure?" the captain prodded. "I've heard about you, that you can be downright creepy the way you can spot things. Are you sure that you're spotting something that would slip past the Pack?"

Ukiah considered the question. He certainly could

tell things that other people couldn't. But what about the Pack? He remembered the way he could tell what had been on Coyote's mind, the clarity of the thoughts as if they had been his own. He shuddered and remembered too the test, the way Hellena seemed to flip through his memories, how he felt the Pack watching, experiencing it with him.

He didn't believe in telepathy, but there was no other way to explain the phenomenon. It was the very reason he never even questioned if the Pack had identified him rightly. The very reason, most likely, they had been so dead sure of who he was. There was a knowing down to the core of one's being. You couldn't deny it. Pack knew Pack. He looked at the waiting policemen. If he didn't convince them without sounding crazy, they would send this man to his death.

"They would know." He wet his mouth, searching for something to add, and found it. "When Rennie Shaw first saw me in Schenley Park, he didn't come any nearer to me than fifteen feet. It was night. There were no lights. It was raining. I was laying facedown in the mud. And he had never seen me in his life. But he recognized me as a Pack member's son."

There was still doubt in their eyes and the way they held themselves.

He found another nail and drove it home. "Everything you've heard about me holds true for the Pack."

They looked at each other, doubt still there, but no longer of what he was saying.

Behind Ukiah, the door flew open. A uniformed policeman in his early twenties stood in the doorway, his eyes wide with excitement. "They've brought in a Dog Warrior! They stopped him for speeding and found one of the missing FBI agents in his trunk! It took about five officers to get him in the wagon, and they've got him in booking right now."

Ukiah was carried along with the flood downstairs. The rookie cop ran most of the trip down backward, explaining details of the arrest. The Pack member had been driving a late-model sedan and gone forty through a twenty-five mile per hour speed trap. There had been two marked cars, a motorcycle policeman, and an unmarked car manning the speed trap. One of the officers had noticed a bloody handprint on the trunk, and they wrestled the Pack member out of the car, handcuffed him securely, and then searched the trunk. Wil Trace was in the trunk, recently dead, covered with vomit. Needle marks covered his forearms. Cans of gel fuel were tucked in around his body, and the speed trap had been mere blocks from a row of abandoned houses.

"The coroner's office already picked up the body, and they're requesting police protection."

The captain grabbed another uniform as they hurried through the halls. "You two go to the coroner's office and make sure nothing happens this time."

They came into booking. Two officers had a tall lean man between them, pressing his fingertips to the mug card.

All the hair on the back of Ukiah's neck went on end, and he slammed to a stop. *Oh, my God!* It was as if fear was poured from a bucket over him, drenching him suddenly and completely. This was the enemy. This was the one to be feared. This was the one to kill if he could. This one would kill without hesitation.

Even as Ukiah started to backpedal, the man gave a pure howl of anger and exploded into a whirlwind of movement.

The man caught Detective Cecil, slammed him to

the wall—then frowned. "You're not Pack!" The man snarled and flung the undercover cop aside, scanning the room. His eyes locked on Ukiah, and knowledge registered there.

Ukiah skittered backward, half falling, half climbing over desks as he encountered them. In his head was Rennie's warning. *If the other side found out about you, they wouldn't rest until they had you.* Like an arrow of death, the man came on, straight at Ukiah, smashing everything in the way to reach him.

Policemen leaped to tackle the killer. Even as the cops reached him, they were snatched up and sent flying, rag dolls before the man's rage. The killer vaulted a desk in a standing jump, landing before Ukiah.

Ukiah yipped in surprise, leaping backward. His memory told him there was an exposed I-beam above him. He caught hold of it. Momentum swung him up and back, and he kicked his pursuer full in the chest. The man tumbled backward onto the floor, and a crowd of policemen piled on top of him. Ukiah dropped down to the floor beyond the cops, jostling to pin down the man's arms and handcuff him.

For a moment the man seemed stopped. Then he came heaving up out of the pile of bodies, shedding policemen. There were screams of pain, the crack of bones, and blood scented the air.

"He's got a gun!" someone shouted.

The man held a service pistol in his hands. He turned toward Ukiah, bringing the pistol up. A dozen officers were yelling, "Put down the gun! Drop it!"

Ukiah stepped back and found himself up against a wall. Behind the man was a ring of police officers and Indigo, all with their weapons trained on the killer. If they missed, though, they would hit Ukiah.

The man leveled the pistol.

A single gun roared behind the man. A hole the size of Ukiah's fist sprouted from the man's forehead. The bullet struck the wall a foot from Ukiah's head. Angry blood and bits of brain sprayed him across the face. The man's knees folded, and he fell hard onto the floor. There was smoke coming from Indigo's gun. Her face was featureless with concentration. Everyone stood, frozen into position, and silence held the room.

The captain broke the silence. "What the hell was that all about?" The room burst into activity again, a sudden roar after the calm. Officers surged forward to pluck the gun from the lifeless hand, check for a pulse, cringe at the spray of gore covering Ukiah.

Ukiah slid down to sit on the floor, leaving a neat outline of himself in blood above him.

The man sprawled dead on the floor. A neat hole punched in the back of his head and the massive wound in the front. His eyes were open, a sightless angry stare at Ukiah. There was, however, the sense of life within him. Just like there had been in Janet Haze.

Indigo came around the desk, her gun still ready. She considered the carnage and uncocked her gun. "Are you okay?"

"I'm fine. Thanks."

She picked up a box of tissues and crouched down to wipe the blood from his face.

"What the hell was that all about?" the captain asked, this time clearly of Ukiah.

"The hell if I know," Ukiah said truthfully. "He knew I was Pack and he wanted me dead—but I don't know why."

Indigo glanced at the dead man and back to Ukiah. "Was he one of the ones that kidnapped you?"

"He's not Pack." Ukiah closed his eyes and focused on her hands on him. "He's part of the other gang Rennie warned me about. The Ontongard. Rennie failed to mention that this other gang could spot me in a crowded room."

"He knew you were in the room before he spotted you," Indigo murmured. "He went at Detective Cecil because of the clothes, but then he realized his mistake. How did he know?"

He opened his eyes and lost himself in her concerned and confused gaze. "The same way the Pack knew I was one of them. The same way I knew Detective Cecil wasn't Pack. There's something I can't describe or explain, but you know."

And then he suddenly understood. *Pack knows Pack. They can spot their own kind—and humans aren't their kind. Everyone in this room was human—except me.*

I'm not human.

It was like taking a fist to the gut. The hard truth forced the air out of him. Facts cascaded down on him, supporting this awful knowledge. His perfect memory. His tracking ability. His heightened sense of smell, hearing, taste. His ability to read people's DNA. Even the fact that he had been raised by wolves and yet became a fully functioning member of society within a few short years.

"No," he whispered in denial, shaking his head. He had assumed for so long that he was different because he was raised among wolves. But he couldn't deny the truth. People called his abilities "creepy" but what they meant was "inhuman." There was no way a human could do everything that he did.

"What is it?" Indigo brought his focus back to her—to her beautiful worried human face.

If I'm not human, what am I?

"Ukiah?"

"I need to get out of here." He scrambled to his feet, fighting the sudden urge to run. *There's no out-running yourself.* He needed time to think. No, he needed information. He needed to know what he was. "I need to find Rennie. I need to talk to him."

"You're going to try and find the Pack?" She had to run to keep up with him as he sought the door. Behind them the police captain was calling to Indigo, reminding her that as the shooter she had forms to fill out and sign.

"I need to know what's going on." He gave her a half-truth, hating himself for lying even that much to her. "In a room full of cops, with a dead FBI agent in his car trunk, all that man cared about was killing me—and I don't know why."

"How do you know that the Pack won't hurt you? You said they almost killed you last time. What if they change their mind?"

"They won't. I'm one of them. I'm under their protection. They consider me a Pack cub." *I'm one of their children.* He remembered Hellena's wistful protectiveness after the test and almost staggered as another truth hit him. *No, I'm their only child.*

They reached their bikes. He pulled off his shirt to scrub away the last of the gore before pulling on his helmet.

"Ukiah, I don't understand." Indigo was picking up her helmet.

"There's a war going on between the Pack and the Ontongard." He threw his bloody shirt into a nearby trashcan and pulled on his jacket. "I don't know what they're fighting about, but I'm stuck in the middle. Already both sides have tried to take me out. Janet Haze and Wil Trace got caught up in it, and they're both dead. I can't stumble around without a clue. The Pack almost killed you and Max. There's a dozen policemen in there wounded because of it. I've got too much to lose. I have to know what's going on."

"I'm coming with you."

"No." He shook his head. "You know I'm safe from the Pack, but you aren't."

"I don't know you're safe until I see it for myself."

He leaned forward and placed his hand on her cheek. "Trust me, Indigo. I will be careful."

She kissed his palm and moved into his arms, holding him fiercely. "I guess this is what I get for not trying harder with the accountants."

They kissed one last time and then she reluctantly stepped away.

"Be careful." She controlled her face, but her eyes were sad.

"I will."

He started moving and he couldn't stop. He rode directionless for a while, panic blinding him to everything but the need to run. He finally pulled off to the side of the road and sat hugging himself.

"Stop this!" he shouted at himself. "Stop. Just find the Pack, talk to them."

Yeah, sure, just find the Pack. The FBI and the police have been trying for years.

"You're a private investigator," he told himself. "You know how to find people. You're the best tracker in the state. You can find them."

Last known address was the place to start. He started up his motorcycle, walked in a tight turn, waited for a break in the traffic and pulled out. His directionless run had left him far east of Pittsburgh. He worked his way back to the Swissvale area. In fits and starts, he found his way to the warehouse.

He parked in the weedy parking lot. A yellow

piece of police tape fluttered on the door frame. The police had come and gone, and someone behind them. Curious neighbors? The Ontongard? Ukiah checked his pistol nervously, then stalked quietly to the dark warehouse. The door hung partially open. He put his back to the wall beside the door and pushed it open while still under hard cover as Max had trained him.

No one fired shots through the doorway. Nothing moved inside the vast darkness. He strained to hear and caught only the far-off tinny music of the merry-go-round at Kennywood. The smell of Pack hung thick as the kicked-up dust, laced with cigarette smoke. He noticed a fresh butt by the door, crouched, and picked it up. Kraynak's saliva tainted the end. He dropped the cigarette butt and eyed the door. Sweat slicked his pistol grip.

He took a deep breath, tightened his hold on his pistol, and stepped into the warehouse. Moonlight dappled the floor. He stalked through the dark, filtering out the hammering of his heart, his own footfalls, the rustle of his own clothing, and listened to the pure silence.

He hadn't noticed the night before, but rooms lined the far back of the warehouse. They had been offices at one time. The Pack apparently used them as living quarters. The windows looking over the river sparkled with a recent cleaning. The floors had been swept, scrubbed, and lived on. He uncovered traces of Pack hair, engine oil, and food. The Pack, it seemed, shared his passion for curried chicken. In the cracks of the wood flooring, he found an earring— a tiny gold dream catcher hoop. Traces of Hellena remained on the sharp stud part, a reminder of the Pack's odd genetic profile. He examined it once again and found what he had missed simply by not under-

standing the clues—hidden under that surface layer
of Hellena lay a core of alien genetics. Rennie had
the identical alien soul, a different "human" veneer.
It was the changing from human to alien that caused
the odd fractures, the discontinuity. Janet Haze and
those that killed Wil Trace, the Ontongard, had the
same kind of jumbling, but they didn't match the
Pack's.

*"I know what Prime expected to crawl out of that girl's
womb." Rennie's words echoed in Ukiah's head again.
"I've had nightmares about it since I joined the Pack."*

What kind of monster did they expect? Was it why
he was the Pack's only child? Surely if the idea of
producing children gave you nightmares, it would
limit how many were born—but only one born to
nearly a hundred men and women?

He cast about for more clues but found the place
devoid of information. The Pack seemed to expect
someone of his abilities to search the rooms. Many
of the surfaces had been scrubbed with a sterilizing
solution. Here and there, Ukiah caught disturbing
traces of Ontongard. The enemy, it seemed, had
searched for the Pack.

Out the back door of the warehouse, he found
where the Pack had ridden off on their bikes the day
before. The mud encased in the wheels took him
three blocks down the rough pavement until the
gang splintered, breaking into groups of twos and
threes and heading out in different directions.

He trotted back to his bike, wondering why the
Pack hadn't torched the warehouse to cover any pos-
sibilities of being followed. Perhaps, he decided, they
planned to make use of it again when their enemies
forgot about it. Would the Ontongard forget, he wondered, or did they share his perfect memory?

*   *   *

The door to Mike's garage was down with a closed sign hanging in one of the narrow slit windows. He knocked hard on the door anyhow, hoping he wouldn't have to waste time finding Mike first.

"I'm closed!" Mike bellowed from within.

"Mike! Mike, I need to talk to you!"

The large door rattled up noisily. Mike squinted at Ukiah through his mask of grease. "Wolf Boy?"

"Mike, I know you told me to stay far, far away from them, but I've got to find the Dog Warriors. It's important."

"Forget it, Wolf Boy. They don't want to be found, so you're not going to find them. They got to stay one step ahead of the law. They don't establish habits. They don't have a normal hangout. They don't stay in one place for long. Bar owners in this part of the tri-states think of them as locusts. The Pack comes to a bar, hangs out for that night only, and then they're gone."

"I need to find them."

"Hell, Wolf Boy, they could be West Virginia, Ohio, or up in New York. They move around."

He considered while Mike stood in the doorway, one hand up on the garage's rolling steel door. "So, you're saying that the only habit they have is that they go from one bar to the next, no order or pattern, and stay there until late."

"Yup."

"So, at this time of night, if I call the bar that they are at, then I'll catch them there."

"If you know the bar. There's hundreds in the area."

Ukiah sighed. "Thanks, Mike."

Mike looked mystified. "You're welcome. You going home now?"

"No, back to the office. I've got phone calls to make."

On the way back to the offices, Ukiah decided to concentrate on the Allegheny County bars. If the Pack and the Ontongard were locked in battle, and the Ontongard were working in and around the city, then the Pack probably wouldn't venture far.

Ukiah recalled Max's telephone calling list for small seedy bars in the local area code and started at A.

"Abby's!" The first number answered cheerfully.

"Are the Dog Warriors there tonight? Any of them?"

The voice gave a shout of laughter. "No, thank God! We haven't seen them in months."

He tried the next phone number in his memory.

He found them at Café Loco. The voice that answered the phone was less than cheery.

"Yeah, they're here."

"Can I talk to one? Rennie Shaw, if he's there, but any of them will do."

He sat drumming his fingers as the voice shouted at Rennie to come answer the phone.

"Who's this?" Rennie growled through the phone a minute later.

"Rennie, this is Ukiah Oregon. You know—you kidnapped me the other day."

"Of course I know you, cub," Rennie snapped. "How did you know we were here?"

"I've been calling bars alphabetically to find you."

"Ah, yes, process of elimination." The tone of his voice lightened. "What do you want, cub?"

"I need to talk to you."

"You're doing that, cub."

"Face to face, Rennie."

There was a moment of silence, except for the muted background noise. "What's wrong?"

"The police caught one of the Ontongard. I was there when they brought him in for booking. He tried to kill me—just like you said the Ontongard would."

"Are you hurt?"

"No."

"Where is the Ontongard now?"

"Dead. The FBI agent with me shot him in the head."

"Damn. He's at the morgue, no doubt." The background noise became muffled as Rennie covered the mouthpiece. Ukiah could hear the Pack leader bark across the room. "Johnny, Ethan. There's a dead Ontongard at the county morgue."

Oh, damn, Ukiah thought, what did I do now?

"Rennie! Rennie!"

The background noise returned to normal. "What is it, cub?"

"They're not going to hurt anyone, are they?"

"No, they're just going to make sure the Ontongard stays put."

Ukiah wished he could believe Rennie. Still, if there was a repeat of Janet Haze, the Pack members would be there to take the brunt of the Ontongard retrieval of their dead.

"Rennie, I need to talk to you."

"Okay, cub, I'll meet with you. Do you know McConnell's Mill?"

"Yes." Ukiah had worked there one too many times. The first three times he found the missing person alive. His fourth case, and the most recent, he had dragged the tiny body of a four-year-old out of the dangerous undertow of the creek that ran through the park.

"Meet us across the gorge from the mill, down in among the rocks—in about two hours."

He pictured the place. "Okay."

"And, cub, please, no cops."

"No cops," he promised.

Max had explained once that the gorge at McConnell's Mill had been formed by a huge wall of ice moving through the area millions of years ago. The whole concept boggled Ukiah's mind. A wall of ice big enough to tumble house-sized boulders out in front of it?

But there it was, in the middle of gentle rolling hills, this gash cut through stone, lined with huge boulders. Paths meandered along both sides of the deceptively small stream. Picturesque cliffs and boulders provided dangerous scrambles and tempting fissure caves. Water-smoothed slick rocks gathered on the shore. In his last case, the little boy had been hopping from stone to stone. Ukiah had sat on the last stone the boy had safely landed on and watched the water flood over the spot where the creek had hidden the body.

Trying not to recall that day, Ukiah drove down to the bottom of the gorge, rumbled across the covered bridge, and up the steep road to the far side. There he found the Pack's bikes parked. He pulled his motorcycle in among theirs and killed the engine.

He pulled off his helmet to hear the ticking of his cooling engine and the *creaka-creaka* of tree frogs. "Rennie?"

"Down here, cub!" Rennie's voice floated up from beyond the cliff.

Ukiah walked to the edge of the cliff and looked down. For a moment, all he saw was darkness. Then his eyes adapted to the night, and he could see Rennie motioning to him. Ukiah glanced about, found a slight path, and cautiously picked his way down to the foot of the cliffs.

Rennie and Hellena were sitting together on a mossy stone, half in a niche made by the two huge boulders that formed this section of the cliff. Rennie grinned at Ukiah as the boy scrambled down to them. The smile faded, though, replaced by a frown.

Ukiah stopped, suddenly wary. "Rennie?"

Rennie came at him faster than he could react, a blur of motion. The Pack leader caught him by the jacket and slammed him hard against the cliff. "You reek of Ontongard and a woman!"

"It's been an interesting day," Ukiah managed, his heart leaping to his throat. Anger radiated from the Pack leader, though Ukiah could not fathom why. "You might think this is funny, but I finally figured it out. We're not human, are we?"

Rennie's eyebrows went up. "You didn't know?"

"I was raised by wolves. I had no idea that I wasn't like normal human children because I was some kind of—hell, I don't even know what I am. Freak of nature? Science experiment gone bad? Alien monster?"

Rennie nodded slowly. "Prime and Hex came to Earth on a ship, a scout ship for an invasion force. We're not of this world. We are only vaguely human."

"And I am the only cub."

"One can only pray." Rennie grumbled dangerously, "Who was the woman?"

Ukiah squinted at Rennie, missing the change of subject. "What woman?"

Rennie roared and pulled him forward to slam him against the cliff again. "The woman you slept with! Who was she? Tell me!"

Fear for Indigo flashed through Ukiah. "No!"

"I saved your life yesterday," Rennie growled in Ukiah's face, "but I can take it just as easily today. Tell me her name."

Ukiah shook his head in denial. "You might have saved my life, but I don't trust you. I won't tell you who she is. If I have to protect her with my life, I will."

"Rennie!" Hellena pulled the Pack leader back. "Ukiah, is she pretty?"

Ukiah eyed the dark-haired Pack woman, wondering if her question was a verbal trap, but finding no harm in answering. "She's beautiful."

"She is special?"

He considered the question, found it safe, and nodded. "She looks at me and truly sees me."

Hellena reached out to touch his face and he flinched, remembering the test, remembering how she had learned all there was to know about him. She tsked him gently and laid the hand on his face. *Do you love her?*

Hellena hadn't moved her mouth, but the words were clear. He closed his eyes against this blatant show of their alien blood. *Would she love me if she knew this?*

"Let him go, Rennie. Our little cub is in love."

Rennie kept him pinned to the wall, a growl rumbling down in his chest. "We missed this woman. There might have been others, all of which he loved."

Hellena glanced back up at Ukiah. *Have there been others?*

No.

"Rennie. He's too human not to seek someone out. Let him go."

Rennie dropped him and stalked away. "I hate this—this not knowing. Is he or isn't he? Is this the true cub or a careful lie? Are we doing the right thing or are we throwing it all to shit because of some wolf instinct we can't ignore?"

"Am I or am I not *what*?" Ukiah snapped. "What is it you think I'm going to do? Why are you trying to kill me half the time, then treat me like your child? How can I lie to you when I don't have a clue to what is going on? Until a few hours ago, I thought I was a fairly normal, twenty-year-old human. Could you for once stop and explain something—anything—to me?"

Rennie eyed him. "Well, for one, you're not twenty years old. You were conceived the first week Prime was on Earth. That was several hundred years ago. We're not sure of the exact date. Coyote was Prime's only Get, and his grasp of time is very weak."

Ukiah reeled. He couldn't be that old, could he? He thought back to his time with the wolves, how he had never been able to count the seasons and tally to some reasonable number. He had thought it many times—it felt like he had run with the wolves since the beginning of time. Miserably, he nodded his head. Yes. This was the truth. "So, Coyote is my brother? No, you said only Get. Where do I fit in?"

Rennie shook his head. "You're Prime's child. A Get is totally different from a child. A Get is something you make. It's an ugly evil thing."

"You make a Get? How?"

"You inject your genes into a human, usually using a syringe filled with your blood." Rennie looked ashamed as he explained. "Your genes act like a virus, spreading throughout the person's body. All of their cells are replaced, one by one, with nearly duplicate cells containing your genes. It hits them hard, like the black plague. Their immune system fights the whole way. Out of a thousand times, maybe one person lives. Most burn themselves out before hitting the threshold—the point where your genetic material can keep the body alive while it stamps out the last of the host's DNA."

Ukiah's mind flashed to the used hypodermic syringes tipped with Wil Trace's blood. "This is what the Ontongard are doing to the FBI agents. They did it to Janet Haze."

Rennie nodded. "We think they're using the immune-suppression drugs to increase the odds of the host surviving."

Ukiah gave him a sharp hard look. "Host? That makes you sound like parasites."

"The worst ever imagined. Prime's people overpopulated their home world and spilled out into the universe, going from world to world, replacing all life with themselves. It was what they intended to do to Earth, until Prime intervened."

A million questions flashed through Ukiah's mind. He fought to ignore them, to stay focused on the issue at hand. "I don't understand. Why are the Ontongard interested in making the FBI agents into Gets? Why did my father make Coyote?"

"Making Gets is all Hex cares about," Rennie snarled. "It's why he came to Earth. It's why we fight him. If he could, he would cover the world with Gets."

"Prime was about to be killed by Hex," Hellena added in a more patient tone. "He was wounded and desperate. He infected everything he spotted in hopes that one creature would survive, would remember, could fight on after he was dead."

Ukiah shook his head. "I still don't understand. If your genes replaced all of the host DNA, then the person basically becomes a copy of you."

Rennie nodded solemnly. *A copy slaved to you. You've wiped away most of its memories, its hopes and dreams, and given it all of yours. How can it be free if all it knows is your desires?*

Ukiah got the impression that Rennie spoke to him mind to mind to reinforce the concept that one Pack member could affect the other's thought. Mental slavery seemed frighteningly possible when thoughts other than your own echoed in your head.

"And my father did this to Coyote?" Ukiah flashed back to his trial with Coyote shouting, "You're my Get!" He turned to stare at Hellena, appalled. "Coyote did this to you?"

"We were all once human," Hellena said quietly. "Now we're thinly disguised copies of Prime." She smiled wistfully at him. "Which makes us all your parent."

Ukiah glanced from Hellena to Rennie. "But why are you different looking?"

"If you replace its diamond with cut glass, the ring will appear almost the same. The fairly simple human cells are replaced with a complex cell structure that can mimic being human. Over time, our appearance drifts toward Prime. Coyote is the oldest of us, and at one time he was a wolf."

"A wolf?" He almost didn't believe, then remembered Coyote's weird golden eyes, his wolf eyes.

"The Pack is still a mess from that little twist," Rennie muttered as he sat down on a stone ledge. "You retain a shell of yourself, ghost memories, like extended déjà vu. If you're left alone to rediscover yourself, you can become independent of your creator. Most of the Pack have recaptured themselves." Rennie put an arm about Hellena's slim waist and pulled her close, glancing up at her. He received a sad smile.

"We prize our humanity over our lives," Hellena

whispered. "Hex holds his Get tight. They're just shadow puppets moving for their maker."

"So where does this leave me? If I'm not a Get but a child, why aren't there any other children? Why did Prime want to kill me? Why do you keep trying?"

"There are a hundred or so Pack members made by Coyote. We abhor what we are and don't create many Get. Hex, while he focuses on creating Get, has only a thousand or so—we think." Rennie grinned. "He empties his veins often for little or no return. When we can track down a Get, we kill it." Rennie caught Ukiah's shocked look. "The human it once was is no longer alive, and each Get represents a possibility for a thousand more. Luckily, it seems that Hex is worried about creating another Prime, a rebellious Get with information enough to destroy everything. He limits himself to what he can keep close at hand, and normally doesn't allow his Get to create others."

"He tried it once, let all his Gets create Gets of their own last century," Hellena added. "Millions of humans died. They thought it was an extremely virulent strain of the flu. So many dead for a handful of Get."

"The biter is that it took so much time to track down the new Gets that they had grown too independent for his taste. He burned them all."

"What does this have to do with being the only child?"

Rennie came to stare into Ukiah's eyes. "Only one in a thousand lives because the alien genetics triggers the body's defenses immediately. The war begins at the injection site and death comes before the alien genes can keep the body alive. There's a way around it. You create a blending of parasite and host. This new genetic material will be accepted by the host until it's too late—when the immune system starts to reject it, the threshold has been reached."

Ukiah was chilled suddenly to his core. "You make a child—an alien father, a human mother."

Rennie nodded. "It required a delicate, sophisticated machine that humans haven't even come close to matching. The machine did the egg extraction, fertilization, genetic manipulation, and implantation. It held the host mother inactive for the period of gestation, suppressing her immune system so her body wouldn't miscarry the half-alien fetus, yet kept her alive for the duration of the gestation. It was a huge machine. On the scout ship, there was only one."

Ukiah started to pace, wrapping his arms about himself, but the cold horror stayed in him. "I was born to take over the human race?"

"You are a weapon of destruction wrapped up as our one and only child. Is there any wonder that we love you yet fear you?"

"Why? Why did Prime even make me?"

"We don't know." Rennie sat watching him pace. "For us, memory is genetic. We're encoded with our creator's memories. Only Prime was badly hurt when he made Coyote and we lose recent memories when we are wounded. It's like someone made paper dolls out of *War and Peace*, and now we're trying to figure out the plot line from what's left."

"Rennie!" Bear came scrambling down the rocks to hold something out to the Pack leader. "The cub's got fleas."

Rennie took a dark speck of plastic from Bear's hand, sniffed, and grimaced. "He sure does. Scatter the Pack."

"Fleas?" Ukiah came to look into Rennie's hand.

The plastic encased a wafer thin computer chip, small battery, and smelled of hot plastic. "What is it?"

"Something with too much to do for as little as it is." Rennie dropped the plastic speck into Ukiah's hand. "It's got to reach all the way up to orbit and tell a spy satellite where a certain Pack cub is going."

Ukiah stared at it in amazement. "She bugged my bike!"

Rennie cocked up one eyebrow. "This *she* wouldn't be the unnamed love of your life?"

"What can I say? I admire resourceful women."

"If she bugged you, someone's following you." Rennie cracked the wafer and tossed it away. "We have to be gone before they get here or it gets real messy."

"Wait. Why do the Ontongard attack us on sight? Who was my mother? How was she killed? What do you remember from Prime?"

Rennie gave Ukiah a slightly bemused look.

"There's too much he needs to know, Rennie." Hellena picked up a battered coffee can and handed it to Rennie. "And not enough time to teach it. Give him a memory."

Ukiah took a step backward despite himself. "Oh, no, not that mind-meld shit."

"That only works when we have time to kill." Rennie indicated with his eyes that Hellena was to leave. "This is the quick and dirty way to hand off memories." He took off the lid, flipped the can upside down to tap out coffee grounds, glanced at the shining interior, and set it on a rock. "This might not work. Your immune system might just destroy it." He flipped out a stiletto knife, the blade bright in the moon light. He made a fist and, in one quick cut, opened the vein in his left wrist. Ukiah winced at the sudden self-violence. "And it might kill you, but I doubt it, not with you being Prime's son."

His blood poured from the wound, at first beating down in a tinny rhythm like rain into the coffee can. The bottom of the can was quickly covered, and the sound became more like water from a faucet.

"Are you going to be all right after losing that much blood?"

"This is nothing," Rennie scoffed, "I'm a first Get from Coyote, who's a first from Prime. I'm closest in the Pack to you, except for Coyote, and he's gone back to the woods. To give it the best chance to work—and at the moment you're in desperate need of it working—I need to be the donor."

"Chance for what to work? What are you doing?"

"I'm giving you a cure for what ails you—ignorance. This is knowledge. If it works, you'll know everything that I know at this moment."

The blood stopped flowing from Rennie's wound. He shook the last drop from his wrist and quickly snapped on the lid. "Now, go someplace you can afford to be sick, because you might be, and not that Shadyside mansion of your partner's. We found you there and so can they. If it doesn't work, come find me without any fleas."

"If I can find you again."

"I have faith." Rennie handed him the coffee can, frowned, took it back, punched holes in the lid, and handed it to Ukiah again. "Don't spill it and don't let it get away."

One last roar of motorcycle engines and Ukiah stood alone in the woods, holding the can of Pack blood.

It took some doing to wedge the coffee can into his seat storage, and he drove home carefully. Carrying it would have been easier, he thought ruefully, if Rennie hadn't put holes in the lid. What was he supposed to do with the blood? Drink it? He shuddered at the thought.

The house was dark when he reached the farm. In the full moonlight he popped the seat storage and lifted the can out. There was no sign of spillage. As he examined the rim, the can tilted oddly, as if the contents suddenly gathered to one side, and it almost flipped out of his hands. He tightened his grip. As he did, the can shifted again, and this time he heard the skittering of small claws.

The smell of blood was gone, he suddenly realized, and another smell seeped out through the holes. He sniffed cautiously. Field mouse.

He stood for a long time in the driveway, holding the coffee can. He had seen Rennie pour his own blood into the can. It was the same can. There had been blood in it.

The mouse skittered loudly in the stillness.

So this is what it meant not be human. It was pretty bad when your own kind could creep you out.

After wandering about the house trying to decide where would be the best place to experiment with the blood mouse, Ukiah decided on his bathroom. The last mouse had vanished without a trace. Until he figured out what he was supposed to do with this one, he would have to be careful with it. The bathroom was small, had only the toilet to hide behind, had no small holes through which the mouse could bolt if it got loose, and the door closed tight to the floor.

Ukiah lifted one edge of the red plastic lid and peered into the coffee can. In the slant of light, the mouse looked back at him warily. It looked like the mouse he had found in Schenley Park, black-furred and black-eyed. The feeling was completely different. Before, it had been as if he had found something fragile that was lost. This mouse was going to hurt him if it could.

He closed the lid and considered the problem. How did one *use* a mouse? He thought blood had been tricky. He set the can into the center of the bathtub and went to flop onto his bed.

Obviously, the Pack and the Ontongard had a strange cell structure when compared to humans. Humans did the normal bleeding/bled routine and that was the end of it. The blood of the Pack, though, seemed to be able to survive being removed from the body. There was Janet Haze and her organ ferrets. There was Rennie's blood mouse. His thoughts went back to the mouse he found in Schenley Park, the way it had come fearlessly to him, as if it were his.

Realization hit him and he slapped a hand over his eyes. *It was mine.*

He had found it where his blood had soaked into the ground. Not as neat a container as a coffee can, but the results had been the same. How many mice had he left scattered behind unnoticed before? Not many, surely, or there would be more holes in his memories. Certainly his lost memories of Crazy Joe Gary still skittered about the cabin in West Virginia. Thinking back, he could remember the surprising lack of blood on the floor when he came to, the small frightened bodies scurrying from hiding place to hiding place. But there had been his maddening hunger that led to the grisly find in the refrigerator, his battle to resist the roasted leg of Boy Scout, and the welcomed arrival of the paramedics. He had paid no attention to his scared, lost memories, never gone back to recover them.

But what about the thousands of cuts, scrapes, and punctures he'd gotten over the years? He had no other memory loss. Why? Maybe the amount of blood mattered—usually he only bled a small amount. Ukiah took out his Swiss army knife and made a shallow slice across his thumb. A pale slit of pain showed on the pad of flesh. Blood seeped up, coloring the line to crimson. He stared, making no move to blot away the blood, rub it away, lick it away, bandage it out of sight, or his favorite—just plain ignoring it until it wasn't a problem. This time he would watch.

The blood flowed, stopped—then slowly seeped back into his flesh where it laid. It took minutes to complete, but in the end there was no sign of the cut except a thin scab he knew would be gone by morning.

From his bathroom came the sound of small claws on metal, amplified by the porcelain bowl of the bathtub. If the mouse Rennie gave him was a holder of memories, then it would explain the reappearance of Ukiah's lost memories after he found the Schenley Park mouse.

Obviously Ukiah used his memory mouse, but how? Last he remembered, it had been in his pocket, and then it was gone. He had already scanned through the morning and then the afternoon of that day. When he tried before, he hadn't bothered checking his sleep memories. They were fuzzy things, mostly of sound, smell, and touch. Occasionally he used sleep memories with books on cassette tapes, but otherwise found them useless. He focused on the long nap in the quiet house. Sure enough, there had been a stirring in his pocket followed by tiny feet running across his bare chest to rest in the hollow of his neck. A warm wetness developed there and then vanished completely.

So, one made flesh-on-flesh contact with the memory and it became part of you. Ukiah remembered the hostile look of the Pack memory. *Yeah, sure.*

It would be easiest to kill it and then hold it. He remembered the carefully created air holes in the coffee can's lid. No. It probably wouldn't work if it was dead.

He went back to the bathroom, closed the door tight, and peeled the lid off the coffee can. The black mouse glared up at him. Reaching into the can with both hands, he trapped the mouse between his palms and lifted it up.

It bit him. The pain was so sharp and unexpected that he almost flung the mouse away. He controlled the reaction and pressed his hands together tighter. The tiny body struggled frantically, tearing and biting with its small razor teeth. He could feel his own blood, hot and sticky, pouring out between his palms. He tried to stop the biting by pressing his palms together even tighter, but this made the mouse scream in a thin, terrified wail.

I hate this! I hate this! I can't do this!

He opened his hands to release the mouse, and it was gone. There were tiny mouse droppings, deep tiny bites, and his own blood covering his palms. No mouse. It worked! Maybe. He had the mouse in him. When could he access the Pack memories it contained? It hadn't been until the next day he had noticed the return of his own memories.

He debated about washing his hands. What if the memory was just a coating at the moment, a bacterial and germ layer that needed to work in? It was a sure sign, he thought suddenly, of how civilized he had become—worried about blood on his hands. He rinsed them lightly as a compromise and threw himself into bed. He realized that he should call Indigo and—

—*Is this Prime's monster?* Rennie crouched among the trees, training his field glasses on the two private investigators standing beside the tan Hummer. *He's just a kid. He doesn't look any more than sixteen. Why does he look so young?*

Another question was, how did he get to Pittsburgh? All the paperwork on the boy started suddenly three years ago, all originating from Pittsburgh. It was as if he had materialized here. Had the Ontongard been involved?

Rennie shook his head. If the Ontongard had brought the boy to Pittsburgh, they would have him locked away, not left him running free with this private detective. Rennie watched as the man patted the boy on the back, gave the kid a smile, and got a grin back. The next-of-kin listing took on new meaning. The two were close. *Oh damn, this seemed so simple.*

Rennie focused on the boy, trying to quell the rising doubt. *He's Pack. I can feel him from here.* There was even a certain facial resemblance. He had Hellena's eyes; same shape, same color. He had the straight black hair common among the Pack. Bear's nose. Rennie's own mouth. It was as if he was the blend of all the Pack members, but Rennie knew it was actually the opposite, it was his traits spread through the Pack. *No, not his, Prime's.*

Rennie watched them walk up the front steps of the new Ontongard's house. He'd been inside and found it a poor ambush site. They would have to wait until the detectives made their way into the park, following the trail of the kidnapped FBI agent. He signaled the others into the park, then checked his shotgun.

This is going to be a bitch. I'm going to sit around the den for days wondering if I took out a child instead of a monster, that I'm becoming like the Ontongard, that somewhere I lost all the humanity that I had left. He gritted his teeth against the inner doubt. *Come on, Rennie, don't start this. Coyote changed you, but you're still human at heart. You know what Prime's child could do to this world.*

Rennie glanced back to the house one last time and immediately wished he hadn't. The two had paused on the stoop, letting the FBI agent enter first. The man had his hand on the boy's shoulder, telling him something of importance. The boy nodded occasionally—silent, attentive, respectful. The speech reached its end. The boy gave his bright easy smile again. The man cuffed him and into the house they went.

Yeah, yeah. Facts don't change though. He looks like a good kid, and I'm going to kill him without even making sure he's the monster we think he is—

Ukiah found his own eyes and looked through them instead of Rennie's. His head was pounding, and he was half slumped over the edge of his bed. The room lurched and started to slowly spin. Something heaved and fought against his stomach muscles, trying hard to expel his stomach contents up the wrong way. He tried to stand, fell instead to the floor. Gagging in the effort to control his bile, he crawled on all fours to the bathroom. Somehow he made the toilet before he started to vomit. There wasn't much in his stomach to bring up. After the initial rush, he hunched over the bowl, dry heaving as if his gut was trying to leap out of his mouth. Finally the heaving stopped and he laid his head on the heavenly cool rim of the bowl.

Oh God, what have I done to myself? I should do something, get someone—

"—made it, Mary, I almost made it." Rennie whispered, his voice in tatters after hours of shouting. He had called for a surgeon at first, then for help in getting the dead horse from his legs, then just for water. "My time is up. I could have come home. Oh, Mary, why'd I leave you and Danny? A boy needs his father."

There was movement in the moonlight. He fell silent, peering into the slants of shadow and silver light.

"Is someone there?" He forced the shout out, each word feeling like a steel rasp against his throat. He coughed in pain but cried out again. "Please, please help me."

A man drifted in and out of the shadows, his footsteps silent, his eyes gleaming like a dog's at night. He went barefooted, with Confederate pants, a white undershirt, and a long Union officer's coat. He came to crouch across the dead horse to gaze at Rennie. "You want my help?"

Rennie flinched back in fear then controlled it. *Think of Mary, Mary and Danny.* He had to wet his mouth twice before managing, "Yes. Please."

The strange man tilted his head back and forth, considering the massive damage to Rennie's body. "What I have to offer might kill you, might not. I vowed I'll never be like them, twist and shape flesh to my needs, but I'm lonely."

The man threw back his head and howled, a deep-chest wolf howl that lifted all of Rennie's hair on end. He had had an uncle that could do what the family thought was a good wolf howl. It frightened all the children. It was a pale, thin thing compared to this—this sound of misery.

"I should be running with litter mates, aunts and uncles, cubs all around and underfoot. I should be running with my mate, watching her grow fat with our cubs. We would howl together and sleep in the sunshine, our bellies full, and our noses tucked under our tails. I shouldn't be here, running alone, hiding from evil among the dead of the petty brothers. I damn Prime for what he did to me, as you will damn me if you take my help."

"Please," Rennie whispered. "I beg you."

The man moved forward on all fours, flowing over the dead horse until his face almost touched Rennie's. "Don't beg. Not for this. This is something to be feared. Say yes, and I'll curse you with my help. Say no, and I'll end your misery with your own weapon."

"Yes, I want your help."

The man crouched there, his gleaming dog-eyes bright, and finally he nodded. The man undid a canteen and held it to Rennie's lips, letting him drink all he could. Food followed, obviously stolen from the dead. When Rennie had eaten and drunk, the man pulled out a slender glass tube with a long needle at the end. He stripped off the coat, tied a tourniquet around his upper arm, and then slid the needle into his arm. The glass tube filled with blood. The man put the tube in his mouth, clenching it between his teeth as he untied the tourniquet from his own arm and tightened it around Rennie's.

"Make a fist," the stranger commanded. After Rennie complied, the man sat still, looking down at the wounded soldier with unreadable eyes.

"I don't want to die."

"Someday you might."

"I'm only twenty-three. I want to live to see my son grow up. I want to live to see my grandchildren and their children. I want to live to see the next century. I don't want to die for a long long time."

"If you survive tonight," The needle slid home, "you won't."

The one known as Prime knew he was going to die. The sled's engine screamed under full throttle, but still Hex gained. Somehow he had been discovered. During his childhood, his training, and the long space flight to this planet, he pretended to be part of the collective mind. He kept hidden that he could stand apart, could see the evil of his father's race, could hate it with a passion, and could conceive and carry out acts of sabotage.

Yet Hex now knew the truth. Prime couldn't remember how. All his recent memories had holes burned through them with the laser rifle. He had gotten away, but the sled's display showed that Hex would catch him soon. Any tactics he had were tattered, almost beyond even recalling them. What had he planned to do? Had he succeeded?

He remembered suddenly that he had helped to create a breeder, almost turned back, and then recalled that he left a bomb on the scout ship to kill the native female and the unborn child. Had it gone off? Had Hex stopped the bomb's countdown?

The only thing certain was he was going to die. He was unarmed and Hex had the laser rifle. He scanned the sled, hoping for any chance to prolong his battle. In a bin beside the seat was a delivery pistol and two score darts, needing only genetic material to make them complete. He nearly tossed them aside as useless. The laser rifle had twice the range. The damage from the darts was easily healed.

Then he stopped, stared at it, sick at the very idea even as he recognized it as his only hope.

He could inject random native life forms with his genetic materials. True they would most likely die than be converted, thus the whole need for a breeder. But if he could make just one Get, Hex could never track it down, not lost among the thousand other creatures in the area.

He had promised himself he'd never spawn himself onto another creature, destroy a viable life to proliferate his own. But if he died, who would stop Hex?

Hating himself, he filled the darts with his blood. He scanned for the natives that Hex had found to impregnate with the breeder, but his luck failed him. All he could find was a pack of four-legged predators, gathered around a kill. Hex was only minutes behind. They would have to do.

Coyote ran, ran howling. Death was in the air. It tore the air. It screamed like hawks. It stung like bees. It was death. Run. Run. Lay panting. Lick the wound. Death was all around. Sick here. Dying there. Death in his stomach, heaving up. The pack was dead. Mourn, mourn the pack!

Rennie reached out and touched Hellena and passed her the message of: *We can't all move in, or he'll sense us coming. Let me get close, nail him once good, and then you can move in to hold off the others.*

She nodded and replied: *The sooner we finish, the happier I'll be. This slashing our own makes me feel like Ontongard.*

Me too, he admitted and broke the contact.

He stalked forward silently. He almost made it, but he'd gotten too focused, and the FBI agent's sudden gasp caught him off guard. Instinctively he turned, aiming the shotgun, and pulling the trigger. Even as the shotgun went off, he swore at himself. She wasn't to be hurt if possible.

But the kid took the bullet. He had been moving even as Rennie aimed, and the blast caught him square in the chest. It tumbled him away and Rennie followed, working the next cartridge into the chamber. There! He had started the killing. Now to make it as quick and as painless as possible. The boy was on his hands and knees, possibly with broken ribs, gasping for breath. Rennie sensed the boy reading him, and saw the knowledge of the execution register in the kid's eyes.

Rennie aimed the shotgun again, hating himself. Since the kid had on a flak jacket, it was going to have to be a head shot, right into those eyes that looked like Hellena's, that smile that had flashed so easily just two minutes before. *To save Earth*, he told himself, *to save all the worlds beyond*.

The partner was suddenly behind him, with a pistol pressed against Rennie's head. "Drop it! Drop it or I'll blow your brains out."

But the kid knew they had come to kill him. It was plain to the Pack that he knew and that it terrified him, even as he begged his partner to back down. The boy raised dark eyes to Rennie, and mentally pleaded. *Don't tell him the truth. Let him believe me. Don't let him force you into killing him.*

Did the boy know that he was truly speaking to them? Was this a ploy? To what end, except to save the man's life? He asked nothing for himself, seemed to expect nothing for himself. Rennie stood staring down at the kid, unsure if the boy was as noble as he seemed, or if he was only very skillful at manipulation.

The pistol to Rennie's head dropped, and a moment later they had the partner stripped and neutralized. The kid was still on the ground, his breathing coming easier now, but the subsonic messages of terror still vibrated up and down the Pack's spine. Rennie could hear the Pack's confusion. *This is the monster? This cub? This has to be one of our lost Get, not the monster.*

Bear, of course, pushed the issue to a head. "He's the one, isn't he?"

How am I to know? he snapped at Bear then shrugged. The smell of blood was coming from the kid. Rennie got him up, the flak jacket open, and wet his fingertips in the kid's blood.

Testing blood from an Ontongard was like sticking a thistle into your mouth. Pack blood tasted like piss and vinegar, bearable, but it bristled and complained at being sampled. Rennie expected something worse than a thistle. A monster should taste nasty. The sharpness of the Pack was in the kid's blood, but it was mellowed, blended, softened. Unlike the jagged broken jumble of DNA that was the Pack's signature, the kid's DNA was a seamless work of art. Human and alien interlocked perfectly. There was no doubt; he was made by an ovipositor.

"He's the one."

Rennie licked the blood from his lips, remembering suddenly the raven-haired girl that was the kid's mother. It explained the boy's good looks and dark eyes regarding Rennie with the same fear as the boy's mother. *Have we focused so much on the father that we missed the influence of the mother?*

Rennie tasted again the perfect blend of human and alien, and checked the boy's maturity. While not a man, the kid was past puberty, a teenager, able to breed, probably able for countless years. If he was the breeding monster they thought of him as, where were the children? All the files and records claimed he was just barely legal age, an upstanding citizen with no rape charges, no paternity suits, no garnered wages to support an unwed mother, no wife, no charges on his credit card to even indicate a girl-friend. How could he be the monster unstoppable breeder if he didn't even have sex?

Coyote had found Rennie dying on the battlefield. Coyote had made him an undying slave, who could be controlled like a puppet on its master's whim. Coyote had sent him out to kill a monster, and he had gone willing. But if Rennie wanted to keep hold of his sliver of humanity, he couldn't do this.

Prime stood in the doorway, eyeing the machine that was contained in the room, that took up the room, was the room. He wished he could just smash it.

Just one! Just one of the hated father race born on this machine could take over this world. All of its seed would be viable. It would spread itself into the native livestock, reproducing hundreds and thousands of times a year. Within its life span it would replace everything that lived. Slower by far than the invasion force Prime had already stopped, but inevitable.

But he couldn't—

—blackness, lost memories—

Prime was running. He had the key programmed and he merely had to hit the row's master lock as he went. Over his link he could hear the countdown for the launch of the scout ship: 88, 89. He slotted the key, waited for the confirm, jerked out the key and ran to the next master lock: 90, 91. He had to get them all: 92. He tripped, almost fell and caught himself on the #1 sleeping unit. The Ontongard inside lay waiting for its wakeup call on the new world. Prime glanced down the row, stretching into dimness. Eight more. He—

—blackness, lost memories—

—he finished the security hack. Turning, he took the impregnation tip out of stasis. Hex's genetic sample floated inside. He slotted the tip into the disposal and flushed it clean. Hurriedly, he flipped it over, jabbed the extractor into his arm vein, wincing at the sharp pain. Once the tip was full, he quickly replaced it into stasis and backtracked through the security hack. He'd have a minute to clear the room, and then security would be reestablished, his visit neatly deleted.

It was a horrible waste of time. He probably would be finished before Hex found a suitable life form, captured an intact female, and brought her back to the scout ship. Even if he wasn't, there would be many chances to kill Hex's fetus before it was born. But he had to plan for the worst case. If things went wrong, a child might be born and let loose on the world. So he used his own mutated genetic material. If everything went wrong, then maybe the child would be a rebel like his father.

But Prime doubted it. The Ovipositor would probably weed out his mutation, reverting his child to what he would have been—one of them. Back on the bridge, he—

—blackness, lost memories—

"—look at what they were defending themselves with." Hex hooted with laughter, holding out short wooden shafts with tips of stone. "I couldn't get the setting right on the stunner and killed most of them, and the rest were male. I got only one female, but that's all we need for now."

The female seemed small, light-boned, motionless, like a bird killed on the wing. Her hair was long and black, glossy under the ship's lights. Her eyes were half open, exposing an exotic eye of white outer ring and a center nearly as black as Prime's. In proportion and shape, she was not much different than his mother's race. Perhaps this was why he found her weirdly beautiful.

So this will be the mother of my child, he thought then caught himself. He must not let his guard slip around Hex. One stray thought, caught and noticed by Hex, would spell the doom to—

—blackness, lost memories—

Hex swung the Ovipositor over the struggling female. "Stun her again or I won't be able to do the insert."

Prime raised the stunner, thought about upping the power to "accidentally" kill the woman, then realized he still needed Hex busy with this. *I'm so sorry, little female.*

There was a crack and flare of the stunner and the woman went limp. Hex nodded, guiding the needle end of the Ovipositor over her bare stomach—

Ukiah bolted upward with a shout. He was in his bed, not in his bathroom. It was daylight out. He found himself clutching his stomach, unable to erase the image of the long needle out of his mind. It was memory, a memory, he chanted, of a time long ago. He looked about the room, trying to fill his vision center with something else. The braided rug on the floor. The coffee can on his nightstand. Max standing at the foot of the bed, looking angry and worried in equal parts.

The last one pushed everything out of his mind, leaving him trembling, weak, cold, and confused.

"Max?" He plucked at his sheets, trying to pull them about his shoulders and failing. "What are you doing here?"

"I've come to find out what the hell you've done to yourself. Pittsburgh isn't a big town, kid. Kraynak called me last night to talk about your shootout yesterday. I tried to call you and your phone was off. I called Agent Zheng and she told me that you'd taken off after the Pack. She was all 'don't worry, we've got him bugged,' but when I checked back later, it's 'sorry, we lost him.'"

"The Pack found the bug. Rennie broke it."

"You're shit lucky they didn't hold it against you."

Ukiah hunched over, holding his head, which banged painfully with the flow of his blood. "Yeah, yeah, they cut me slack because they think I'm a kid and don't know better."

"You are a kid, but you should know better. You promised me."

Ukiah flinched under the stinging words. "I took my gun and I told Indigo where I was going, but I couldn't take backup, Max, not to visit the Pack."

"I figured you were either in deep shit, or here at home with no idea of the chaos you were causing. So I called out here to eliminate the second."

Ukiah returned to his sleeping memories and discovered he had heard the phone, moaned in reply to Mom Jo's soft query, and they had cleaned him up, tucked him into bed, and forced liquids down him. "God, I was out of it."

"So I gathered. They said it looked like food poisoning to them, but they didn't know you'd run off to visit the Pack, or that Doctor Haze was running a full viral infection before she went loony. Now, what the hell did you do to yourself?"

"Rennie gave me the Pack memory. My immune

system was fighting it, but I think they've come to a compromise."

Max moved suddenly from the foot of the bed to his side. He caught Ukiah's chin and studied his face carefully. Worry overcame anger in Max's eyes. "The Pack gave you an unknown drug and you took it?"

Ukiah moaned, rolling his head free. "Max, please. I had to take it. I had to know what the hell was going on. The Pack tried to kill me, you know how close they got. Worse was how close they came to taking out you and Indigo. Rennie warned me, when he was dropping me off downtown, that there was another gang, one that makes the Pack look like puppy dogs. That shootout yesterday was with one of them, Max. I walked into the room, and he chewed through a dozen cops trying to get to me. I had to know what I had gotten into the middle of. I had to know before the trouble followed me out to the farm."

Max understood the beginning of his logic but not the end. "Ukiah, no drug is going to explain gang warfare to you. All they do is get in and screw with your mind."

"I didn't say it was a drug, Max. It was the Pack memory. Actually, it was a mouse. And it did explain everything."

"Memory? Mouse? What's a mouse?"

"A mouse. A little hairy thing, like Mickey Mouse, only more real."

Max reached out to press a hand up against Ukiah's forehead. "I think you're still out of it."

Ukiah pushed his hand away. "I'm not out of it, I only sound like I'm out of it. It's impossible to explain." Ukiah threw back his covers and climbed shakily out of bed. He was starving and dehydrated.

He cast about and found his bathrobe. "You wouldn't believe me anyhow."

Max flung up his hands in exasperation. "So you're not going to tell me? Are you going to leave me wondering again as to what the hell the Pack has done to you this time? Why don't you trust me anymore?"

Ukiah closed his eyes, not sure how they got to this point. There had been a break between them. It had been growing over the last few days, and the whole ground was about to give in. How had he missed it? How did he stop it?

"Max, I don't trust anyone more than I trust you. I don't even trust myself as much as I trust you. Before Janet Haze, I knew I was your partner, Cally's brother, and my moms' son. I loved my job. I loved my life. Then it all went to shit."

He dropped back to sit on the edge of his bed, shaking his head. "It's like I fell through the looking glass. There's a girl turning into ferrets. The Pack does this really weird mind-meld shit to me, where they actually experienced my memories like I was some type of ViewMaster. I'm suddenly telepathic with the Pack! I can read their minds, and they can read mine. Last night I watched Rennie cut his wrist and bleed into this coffee can." He picked up the can and held it out to Max. "When I got home, his blood had turned into a mouse. I held the mouse in my hands, and it merged with my body." He considered the can himself. "Yeah, I really think the mouse bit sums up my life for the last three days. How can I ask you to believe me when I don't even believe myself?

"And all that is nothing to what I learned last night. Oh God, Max. Everything I've ever thought or believed about myself isn't true. I'm not human, Max.

I've never been human. My father was some rebel from an invading alien force. They used this machine to make my mother pregnant. I was supposed to be the first step in taking over the Earth. That's why the Pack tried to kill me. My father made the Pack to stop the invasion, to protect the world, and they saw me as a threat. I'm the only breeder ever born." Ukiah hunched over in sudden misery. "Oh god, Indigo! What am I going to tell her? What if I got her pregnant? We used protection, but what if that doesn't work with me? What if I've infected her? God, how do I tell her I'm some kind of monster?"

"Ukiah, stop it." Max dragged him upright and made Ukiah look at him. "If this was what you were born as, then nothing has changed. You are what you always have been, a good, honest, loving person. I've seen you wade through knee-high muck for sixteen hours to find a little girl. I've watched you burn the soles off your shoes to carry Boy Scouts out of a forest fire. I've pulled you half-drowned out of filling storm sewers because you won't stop looking. You're kind, compassionate, loving, and human. I've always been proud of you and there's no one on this planet I trust more. Nothing has changed."

Ukiah scrubbed at his face, feeling brittle. "What do I tell Indigo? I can't hide this from her. It would be like not telling her that I have AIDS."

"I'm not sure. Come downstairs. Let's get some breakfast. Tell me everything you know, and we'll see what we can figure out."

The fridge was disappointingly bare—one stick of butter, a few tablespoons of sour cream, a dozen eggs, a pint of mushrooms, a gallon of milk, a can of frozen orange juice, a wedge of cheese, a squeeze bottle of chocolate syrup, and a four-pack of AA batteries. Must be Saturday, when Mom Lara cleans out the fridge and goes food shopping. He started with the dry goods instead, washing five potatoes and putting four into the microwave. He ate the fifth raw. He didn't cook the eggs either. He cracked the full dozen into a glass, planning to drink them raw.

Max intercepted the glass. "I hate when you eat this way." He got out a nonstick skillet, poured the eggs into it, added milk, and whipped them well. "Okay, explain."

There were so many angles Ukiah could take. He could start at the very beginning when the Ontongard overpopulated their native planet and reached for the stars. Or he could start with their most recent success, the planet Prime had been born on, a planet with thousands of native species and trillions of life forms, all replaced by the Ontongard. An entire ecosystem reduced to one vast hive mind. He could explain how Prime sabotaged the invasion ship, or how his father failed to act prior to the scout ship departing the main ship, allowing the Ontongard to reach Earth.

He decided instead to start with Schenley Park and Janet Haze, as he should have days ago. He told Max for the first time about finding the mouse and "losing" it and what he realized later as to what had truly happened with it. He recounted the trial completely—memory search weirdness and all.

As Ukiah talked, Max pushed the scrambled eggs about the nonstick skillet until they formed a fluffy yellow mountain. The smell was maddening to Ukiah, and when Max spooned three-quarters of the scrambled eggs onto a plate for him, he ate frantically.

"So you're telepathic with the Pack?"

Ukiah nodded, his mouth full of hot fluffy eggs.

"Why? Do you know?" Max asked.

"Well, I think it has to do with the fact that we're collections of cells, a communal being. The Dog Warriors are one creature with twenty bodies, a continuation of my father. Despite my mother's DNA, I'm genetically very like my father. The Ovipositor tended to favor the alien genes over the native lifeforms when it could. So, in the way that my toe communicates with my nose, I can communicate with the Pack."

"I don't get this toe communicates with your nose." Max set the remaining eggs on the back burner, layered them with cheese, and started to grill a small onion and a cup of mushrooms. Once they were done, he folded them into the cheese and eggs.

"Well, it's hard to explain." Ukiah got up for orange juice. "If you have a skin cell, normally that's what it stays. But with me, if there's a sudden need for heart tissue, the skin cell converts into heart tissue. There's a communication between the cells, working to keep the whole colony alive."

"That's handy." Max got the potatoes out of the microwave and set them in front of Ukiah with butter, sour cream, bacon bits, chives, salt, and pepper. Certain Ukiah was preoccupied with the potatoes, he sat down with his semi-omelet. "So, the Pack agrees with me. You're a good person, not a monster. Go on."

Ukiah launched into the part about the Ontongard at the police station and his realization that he wasn't human. He skipped quickly over his search and hit on the discussion he had with Rennie. "He gave me a memory mouse. It's a weird thing Pack blood does. Basically all our cells are mimicking the human body." He pointed to his forearm. "This patch of cells are mimicking skin and pores and hair. If someone cut a chunk out of my arm, the cells can't survive as skin and pores. They need oxygen, and a way to absorb nutrients. So they communicate with each other, pick a form, and convert into it. The animal they form depends on the size. A small chunk becomes a mouse."

"A large chunk, say a heart, liver, or brain, becomes a ferret."

Ukiah nodded. "Yeah. It has to be something we've handled, something we know down to a genetic level. Janet Haze kept ferrets, so her cells had that genetic blueprint to follow. But the cells aren't too happy being split off. A mouse is easier to kill off than a human. A memory wants to rejoin with the main body."

"Which is why your Schenley Park mouse was so friendly and snuck back in the first chance it got. Why do you keep calling them memories?"

Ukiah sighed, scrubbing at his face. Max's questions were unfolding answers in his brain, huge and complex and instantly realized. It felt so weird to know something without learning it. Worse was trying to explain, because he couldn't just show the path he took to find the answer. "Our memories are genetic, which I guess is a good thing because our cells move around. What was a brain cell today might be a heart cell tomorrow, if I was shot in the chest. Actually, human brain cells are fairly fickle things to start with. Rennie gave me enough genetic material that my immune system could whomp the heck out of it and still have something to absorb. Basically the mouse was viral DNA, and not very happy about being handed over to me. There was a small biological war in my system, but we came to a truce, and I got the Pack's memories attached to my normal DNA sequence."

"Yeah. Right. If your memories are genetic, why did you forget your fight with Haze?"

"It takes hours for memories to be coded down to the genetic level. The information is collected in the bloodstream, and the blood cells handle actual coding and dissemination, so eventually all the cells have the same memories. If you start to bleed, well, it's a crap shoot as to what you lose memory wise, and what you get back, if you can recollect the lost blood via a mouse. That's what happened to me in Schenley Park. I lost memories and got a lot back, but there's details missing. Everything slightly fuzzy. The cells holding that information probably died off, unable to survive being outside my body."

"So you have all of Rennie Shaw's memories?"

"And Coyote's, who had infected Rennie, and my father's memories, who had infected Coyote, and his father's." Eons of memories threaten to cascade out. The older memories were dark things, with no hint of emotions, no thoughts beyond eating and reproducing. Coyote's life as a true wolf was more comprehensible than the early generations of the Ontongard. It was like suddenly being able to communicate with pond scum, able to hear them think out budding, growing, stretching out to cover all available surface.

"You okay?"

"I think so. Basically, the Ontongard came to Earth to replace all life. My father, Prime, was a mutation in that he was an individual. He sabotaged the main invasion ship. He and another of his kind, called Hex, came to Earth on a scout ship, something he tried to stop but couldn't. They landed in Oregon, hundreds of years ago. There was nothing there but Native Americans with bows and arrows to stop them. With the technology on the scout ship, Hex could have still wiped out everything on the planet. So Prime blew up the ship. Only Hex figured out what was happening, and killed Prime. In sheer desperation, my father infected Coyote, to carry on the battle."

"I have to admit one thing." Max got a glass of milk and poured Ukiah one too, adding chocolate syrup to it. "All this is too impossible to believe."

"Except at the day-to-day level," Ukiah said, gazing at the milk.

"What the hell does that mean?"

"You got me milk without me asking, chocolate even."

Max made a frustrated noise. "You would have asked for milk right after I closed the door. You always do when you eat this way. The more calories you take in, the sooner you stop eating, so you got the chocolate."

"And when do I eat like this?"

Max looked at the milk then at Ukiah, emotions warring on his face. "Oh hell, Ukiah, this doesn't mean shit."

"When do I eat like this?"

"When you get the shit beat out of you," Max snapped. "You eat like a pig, sleep like a dog, and in a few hours I'm wondering why I was so worried about you because you look fine."

"But it's not really human, is it?"

Max shook his head. "No, but it still doesn't mean shit. We've done this so many times we don't have to talk about it. Just because we now know why doesn't change anything."

"What am I going to tell Indigo?"

"Depends." Max got up to wash his dish and the pans. "If she's your first love that breaks your heart in a few weeks or months, probably not everything.

She is the FBI, and you could be considered a carrier of a dangerous virus. Ex-lovers are sometimes your worst enemies. But if she's the girl that you make forever with, then you tell her everything."

Ukiah laughed weakly. "So I tell her a little every day for the rest of our lives?"

"Well, that's one way of doing it." Max came to rest a hand on Ukiah's shoulder. "I don't know Indigo the way you do, kid. I won't be living your life. I wish I could tell you to do X, but that might be something I could live with and you couldn't. Take the day off. Go and see her. Think before you say anything. That's all I can tell you to do."

Ukiah sighed. If he had only known a few days earlier, then he could have avoided the problem by not becoming Indigo's lover. The thought, though, made him feel desolate and cold. No, he couldn't stand the concept.

Surely to love was a sign of being human.

Max had a lead on their skip, heading down into Wheeling, West Virginia. He had come out to pick up Ukiah to ride shotgun on the trip. Ukiah tried to offer to still come with Max, but Max firmly turned him down.

"Look, you've had your throat cut, you've been kidnapped—well, shot in the chest and then kidnapped—and had the shit kicked out of you and almost shot, and then been violently ill all in three days. By rights I should just stick you on an airplane for the California defensive driving school, but I don't think running away will be good for you. I'll just get Chino to come with me. Go see Indigo."

"She's probably going to be mad that I didn't call her already. Hell, it's almost noon."

"I called her this morning. I told her that your

moms had called me and you were here, laid low with food poisoning. She was worried, but not mad."

"Thanks, Max."

"I'll be back probably late tonight. It's a two-hour trip down, two hours back, and the normal couple of hours of screwing around. If it gets too late, I might stay the night."

"See you tomorrow, then. Watch your tail."

"Watch your head." Max tousled his hair and got up into the Cherokee. "And keep your Colt on."

"Right." He followed the Cherokee out to the end of the driveway and watched it go down the lane. Clouds as big as spaceships were cruising across the summer sky, and one slid across the sun, throwing Ukiah into shadows as the Cherokee turned onto the main road and headed off for West Virginia.

CHAPTER EIGHT

It took all his courage to call her.

She answered with "Special Agent Zheng" in her steel-hard voice.

"Hi. It's Ukiah." He wasn't sure what to add.

Her voice went warm and concerned. "You okay?"

"Yeah. I'm sorry I didn't call earlier. I hope I didn't worry you too much."

"Max called and told me what was going on. I'm sorry that I bugged your bike without warning you. When it went dead, I was afraid that I might have caused you serious harm."

Ukiah laughed weakly. "We both have our little demons, don't we? I'd like to see you. I'm out at my moms at the moment, but I can be down there within twenty minutes."

"I'd like to see you too, in one piece. How about twelve-thirty, outside my office?"

He checked his watch. It would give him forty minutes to make her office. "I'll be there."

She came out of the Federal building carrying her helmet and riding jacket. He found himself smiling in spite of everything as she walked up to him. Her eyes gleamed with happiness, and she tasted of plums when they kissed.

"I'm so glad you're okay." She handed him her helmet as she pulled on her jacket. "Did you find the Pack? Did they tell you what you needed to know?"

His heart fell with the reminder of what he needed to tell her. She caught it on his face and her brow creased slightly.

"What is it?"

"I found them, they told me. We need to talk. There was so much I didn't know about myself, stuff I found out, that you need to know."

She nodded slowly. "Let's go someplace private, then, and talk."

She pulled on her helmet and straddled the seat behind him, wrapping her arms tightly around his waist.

Private? His first thought was of his tree house. It was a long drive, though, and he wasn't sure how much time they had. She might only expect to take a long lunch. He settled then on the offices. Max was gone and the place would be empty.

She tugged off her helmet as she followed him into the mansion. This time she paused to touch the rich chestnut burl paneling. "This place is so beautiful."

Ukiah nodded, disarming the security system, except for the outside doors. "I didn't know it at first. I'd only been in a few houses when I was a kid, and you've seen my moms'. I thought everyone had great big Victorian mansions. After a year or so of being in and out of people's homes, it suddenly struck me. Wow! This is big and it's elegant and it's beyond what most people could ever hope to own."

She laughed. "Can I have a tour?"

He had planned to tell her the moment the door was shut, but the chance for delay was too tempting. "Sure. This is the foyer. Max and his wife bought the grandfather clock in England on their second honeymoon, a couple of days after his company was bought out. When they got back to the states, they bought this house for someplace to put it."

He took her into the reception area, which still could pass as a living room, and showed her his office. He took her upstairs to peek into Max's master bedroom suite, large enough almost to be an apartment. The guest room. The second-floor laundry. The exercise room, which she shook her head at and commented, "Too many rooms to be filled in any way possible," and he nodded.

He opened the door to his bedroom. "This is my room when I stay in town."

She went in and he followed. She poked her nose into every corner, laughing at one point at the closet full of black T-shirts.

"I wear them constantly," Ukiah said, defending them. "Look, they have 'Private Investigator' written on the back, big and bold, so you can see it from a hundred feet. You don't know how many times it has kept me from being shot. People can recognize me from the back as one of the good guys."

"I was laughing because they look like the FBI jackets I wear on busts."

"Well, Max took the idea from those jackets."

"I'm glad he takes such good care of you." She came and leaned her head against his chest. "I love listening to your heart beat. It's so strong and steady."

He held her tight, breathing in her scent. Her warm hands ran under his shirt to touch his bare skin, and she kissed his neck, his chin, and then slipped her tongue into his mouth. He groaned softly, the gentle torture of loving her and being afraid of losing her. He returned her kisses with passion, lost in the heat, until she guided him to his bed. He hung back, shaking his head. "Oh, Indigo, there are things we should talk about. There are things I need to tell you. Things that after you hear, you might not want me."

"I think I know, and I don't care."

"You can't know. This is impossible, crazy stuff that I can barely believe."

"They did the autopsy on Wil Trace. He died of a viral infection, and throughout his body were exit wounds, where animals had eaten their way out of him without a trace of how they got into him. They tried to take blood samples of the Ontongard, but the samples all disappeared, and there were strange invasions of mice and bugs. Janet Haze was a halfway point between the two. Her body showed signs of infection, and all her blood samples vanished. Pack knows Pack. The Ontongard and Pack hate each other on sight."

Ukiah looked at her, stunned. "Yes. That's the beginning of it."

"And Pack knew you in the park at night. The Ontongard knew you in a room full of cops. All your blood samples at the hospital vanished, contaminated mysteriously with bugs."

He startled. "They were?"

She nodded. "I checked last night, after you left. Whatever Pack and Ontongard are, you are too. And that's not completely human, is it? That's what you suddenly realized yesterday. I saw you being taken away to be killed, and you weren't as rattled as you were last night. It hit me after I tried to figure out why. Once you approach it with the right mindset, all the clues are there, waiting to be seen."

He nodded. "I thought I was different because I was raised by wolves. Then last night, I realized how blind I had been. The Pack had set it all up, spelled it all out, even underscored a few points, but I didn't get it."

"I've had all night and all this morning to think about it, Ukiah. I don't care what you are. I love you. I want to be with you. It was agony to think I might never see you again."

"Are you sure? Our children would be Pack too, and their children too."

"If we have any." She looked pained. "If you're not human, there's a chance that we won't have any."

She had considered more of this than he thought possible. He stroked her cheek. "I was created to have children with a human. The problem will probably be *not* having kids with you."

"That is an age-old human problem I can cope with." Indigo murmured and pulled him onto the bed.

While still sprawled on his bed, they ordered Chinese to be delivered. It was a small feast with pints of General Tso's Chicken, Mopo Tofu, Orange Beef, Stir-Fried Shrimp Rice, Won Ton Egg Drop Soup, and Crab Ragoon. While Indigo was in the shower, the bags of food were delivered. Ukiah carried it to the attic game room and unpacked them onto the coffee table.

Indigo followed his calls up to the attic and laughed in surprise. "This is pig heaven. I should have guessed." She walked out to stand under the basketball hoop. "Is this regulation height?"

"Yeah." Ukiah served himself out of every container. "Max put it in this spring after one too many jokes about the ceiling at the Super Bowl party."

She came to check out the wall of electronics. "Max sure loves techno toys." She fingered the edge of the seventy-two inch flat screen TV. "This must be amazing to watch."

"Since Max put the system in, he has gotten kind of 'volunteered' to host football parties." Ukiah sat back into the leather couch, balancing his plate as he watched her explore the room. Indigo had only put on one of his black tracking T-shirts and her panties. She looked so sexy he considered forgetting about the food.

She stopped by the bookcase and eyed Max's collection of photo albums. "Are any of these of you?"

"I'm in the last two albums, there on the bottom."

Indigo pulled the last two and came to slide into his lap. She flipped the first open and Max's wife looked out at them. Ukiah reached out and flipped quickly through the book. "I'm toward the end somewhere. I really don't look at this one much."

They hit the photos of the wrecked car and Indigo stilled his hand. "This is the accident, isn't it?"

"Yeah." He slid his fingers from the cold vinyl. "Max took pictures after they pulled it out of the lake."

Black muck and slimy trails of algae covered the crumpled Porsche. Max had taken almost a whole roll; twenty-three compulsive shots, walking a slow circle about the car. It made the car somehow lurk on the page. Five pages of death on wheels. The twenty-fourth photo took a page by itself, even though there had been two empty slots after the car. According to the nearly invisible counter at the bottom, it was actually taken prior to the pictures of the car. It was of the fresh grave with the massive headstone. "Aileen Bennett, Beloved Wife, 1965–1998" and "Max Bennett, Beloved Husband, 1965–"

Indigo shivered in his arms and flipped the otherwise blank page. The next page was also blank. "No more?"

"He skipped a few pages." Ukiah flipped over the next five empty pages. "I think he has a roll of film he never developed that he left space for. Here, this is where the pictures with me start." He tapped the first photo, him looking unsure at the camera, looking only twelve. "I remember Mom Jo giving him this photo the first time he came to the farm, so I think this was what he used as a reference when he worked my case."

"Who is this kid with you here?" She pointed to the second photo, taken at a party.

"Johnny Libzer, the first case that I worked on with Max. The family asked us back a week later for this party. It was kind of embarrassing how much fuss they put up."

The initial few pages, he noticed for the first time, focused on the people they had found. Sometimes Ukiah was in the frame, sometimes not. They were stilted, forced, posed things that Ukiah vaguely recognized as a typical snapshot. Max, though, liked to take "unguarded moment" pictures, and took them in quality par to a professional. Slowly Max's normal photos drifted in and took over—and for a while they focused only on Ukiah. Ukiah on a lookout point, eyes closed in focus, nose to the wind that blasted back his hair. Ukiah lost among the giant hemlocks of Cook Forest, looking at the camera with wolf intensity through a screen of ferns. Ukiah supporting one of the Boy Scouts he rescued from the Yellowstone wildfire, both covered with black soot.

Ukiah on one of the large stone outcroppings at McConnell's Mill, muddy from two days of searching the creek bottoms, asleep, half-curled about recently found, blonde moppet Sarah Healy.

"These are beautiful," Indigo whispered as she reached the last page. "Do you think I could get copies?"

"I guess so." Ukiah handed her the next album. "I'm afraid I took a lot of the photos in this one, and it shows."

In the second book, Max expanded first to Ukiah's family and then to their range of friends. Mom Lara asleep on the front porch with Cally in her arms, the sunlight brilliant in her hair. Mom Jo perched in the tree house. Chino blending with the woodwork. Janey, regal and proud. Kraynak breathing smoke like a dragon. Their Friday night poker gang, lit only by the hanging light, caught in midlaugh.

Ukiah's photos were clumsy imitations. He had tried for Max's style but missed somehow. Looking at them now, Ukiah realized that one of his mistakes had been that he tried too often for a subject in motion. Parts were blurred, details were lost. He needed to catch the subject in a moment of stillness, wait until they stopped.

The last photos had actually been taken by a professional. They were used in a magazine, accompanying a story on the agency. He and Max had taken the photographer on a search-and-rescue into a freshwater marsh. On black-and-white film, he had caught the marsh's stark eeriness and the grueling nature of the track. Ukiah had had to all but crawl through every inch of the trail, and only Max's backup from a punt-boat had kept him going until they found the missing girl. They were, Ukiah realized, the only pictures of Max and him working together.

Indigo shook her head. "It's strange to flip through the two albums and see Max come back from the dead." She opened the first book and then laid beside it the second one. The gravestone on a sterile page. Max leaning against the Cherokee, laughing as Ukiah sprawled muddy and exhausted on the hood. "You love him, don't you?"

Ukiah nodded. "When I was young, going to church, doing stuff with the scouts, playing baseball, I saw the other kids with their dads and I wanted"— he scrambled for the right word—"needed so bad to have a father too. I'd make up stories for myself about what my father was like." He shrugged. "Maybe it was like a chick imprinting. Max was the first guy to show up and feed the need. Somewhere along the way, he's become all the father that I wanted, needed." He grinned and whispered. "But don't tell Max. It's not a *manly* thing to talk about."

"Sometimes," she whispered back as she kissed his neck, "it really shows that you were raised by two women."

It was nearing two o'clock when they disentangled themselves from the couch.

"Are you going to be in trouble for taking such a long lunch?"

Indigo shook her head. "I've been pulling fourteen-hour days this week so far. When I said I was taking a long lunch, the only thing that they said was not to go out alone. They've tightened up security on the offices and are double-teaming everyone. Things are tense right now."

Ukiah considered his new memories. "This is really weird for the Ontongard. Normally they would do anything not to attract attention to themselves.

They have time and patience usually to do things right. It's how they've stayed invisible for so long."

Indigo shrugged. "Statistically, they couldn't stay invisible forever. Wil Trace almost disappeared mysteriously with his death blamed on the Pack. They didn't count on the speed trap. They didn't expect you to be at the police station. Those two points are the only things that brought them to the forefront."

"And Doctor Haze."

Indigo's eyes narrowed as she considered the dead robotics engineer. "Doctor Haze is a tricky mystery. If you assume that the Ontongard were going to use her, the question becomes how. She was working on several top-secret projects with broad military applications, but the more we looked at those, the less likely they were the target. Her family is comfortably wealthy, but not the Rockefellers. She has an uncle who is a judge on the state court, but his caseload has nothing of importance right now."

"The Ontongard work in the far future. They might have been setting up with something five years from now being the target. What are the projects she was working on?"

Indigo winced slightly. "I can't discuss them with you. I can tell you that they're years from being in a working prototype stage, and Doctor Haze was barely involved in them until recently. She was only bumped up the promotion ladder a few weeks ago when her immediate supervisor was killed."

A Pack memory clicked and whirled in Ukiah's mind, and he almost spilled Indigo onto the floor when he bolted up.

"What is it?" She studied his face. "Are you all right?"

He took her hands. "What I say to you next is part of not being human. Rennie didn't *tell* me anything—

well, not much. What he did was give me his memories. Doctor Haze's supervisor was Doctor Sam Robb. Rennie killed him because he was an Ontongard. Rennie screwed with the gas main on the Robb's house, and it blew up."

She nodded slowly, no doubt on her face. "It did. We suspected arson, but the explosion destroyed most of the evidence."

"Rennie was in Schenley Park when Janet Haze was killed because he suspected that the Ontongard might approach her. He had come to check her out, and the place was crawling with police. He followed the chaos into the park and found us before the police."

"Then the company is the focus."

Ukiah nodded, wishing Indigo could tell him about the projects. Pack memory might be triggered again. "They must be interested in one of her projects."

Indigo looked at the ceiling for several minutes, thinking hard. "This looking into the future is difficult. A band of alien terrorists like the Ontongard could be interested in any one of the projects, depending on their having the patience to wait through development. I can't see the connection, though, of taking the FBI agents."

"Haze's company hasn't finished any projects?"

She looked at him. "You think it might be something already developed, in place, and shelved?"

He shrugged. "They hurried with Haze. It was just a week or two between her supervisor being killed and her first being approached." He remembered the books on immortality, and the photograph. "And they approached her, courted her, instead of just taking her. What they're doing with the FBI agents is their normal procedure."

"Taking her would have triggered almost as many alarms as they're triggering now."

He shook a finger to indicate time was an important point. "If the target date was five years out, then a kidnapping and release wouldn't damage things horribly. It would have been smoothed over and forgotten. But if the target date is now, they couldn't grab her and hold her. They can do it with the FBI agents, because there's no real connection between the agents and Haze's company. It's relatively safe for their plans to take the agents."

"And there is a sense of desperation to this. Like everything is coming to a head. Things have gone wrong for them, and they're scrambling."

"So, has the company finished any projects lately, something they're about to ship or release?"

"Just one, but I doubt that would invoke any interest in a gang of covert terrorists. It's not even top-secret."

"What is it?"

She picked up the remote, flicked on the television, and punched in a number. The NASA channel came up, showing the desolate red Mars landscape, moving by ever so slowly. "They built the Mars Rover."

Tribot, the company Doctor Janet Haze had worked for, was housed in an unassuming yellow brick three-story building between Centre Avenue and Baum Boulevard in Oakland. Indigo pressed the buzzer on the street entrance and talked to a receptionist over the attached intercom before the door unlocked with a *thunk*.

The receptionist was young, pretty, and flustered. "Special Agent Zheng, we weren't expecting the FBI today. Who should I tell that you're waiting? Mr. Lang again?"

Indigo shook her head. "We would like to see someone familiar with the Mars Rover."

Startled, the receptionist picked up her phone, dialing a quick three-digit extension. She swung in her chair so her back was to them and spoke quietly into her headset. Still Ukiah heard. "Mr. Lang, Special Agent Zheng is out here wanting to see someone about the Mars Rover. The Rover crew is all in the War Room. Should I send them down there? I don't know. Yes, sir." She turned back and smiled. "Mr. Lang says you're to go down and see the Rover crew."

The receptionist gave them directions down to the War Room. Indigo apparently recognized the landmarks given because she nodded at certain points. As they hurried through the offices, Ukiah suddenly caught a familiar smell. He paused, sniffing, and comparing the faint scent to his great store of known odors.

The musky scent, he realized, belonged to an Ontongard. He patted his hip, reassuring himself he was armed, then followed his nose through the maze of cubicles and offices. He found himself at the doorway of an inner core office. The reek of Ontongard made the hair on the back of his neck rise.

"What is it?" Indigo asked.

Ukiah leaned back to eye the nameplate beside the door. *Sam Robb.* "This was the office of Doctor Haze's boss, the Ontongard insider before Rennie killed him."

The room was a dark cubbyhole. Not a room people would fight to fill. It had not been cleared after Sam Robb's death, stocked full of papers, books, charts, graphs. Ukiah noted, however, that there were no personal items. No framed pictures. No posters or artwork hung on the wall. Nothing pleasing or odd sat on the desk, attracting the eye. When tracking missing persons, Ukiah found knickknacks and useless clutter to be the greatest clues into people's minds and habits. All the clues he normally looked for revealing the inner personality were missing.

"Did Robb's family come and clear out his office?" he asked Indigo.

"Robb didn't have family. No next of kin or emergency contact information was ever provided. It was one of the quirks of his death that kept the case open. We kept finding holes and outright lies in his employment records."

"How did he get work at a company that does top-secret projects?"

"That's what the FBI would like to know. Someone let him slip through, maybe for money."

Pack memory served up a disturbing alternative. "Or they were Ontongard too."

Indigo didn't answer, but her eyes went cold.

The War Room was a high-tech conference room. White boards hung on the walls with almost every inch covered in techno-babble. Each person had their PDA linked to screens embedded into the top of the table, and computer gibberish scrolled up and down. An air of frantic activity clung to the twenty employees gathered in the room. Only one or two glanced up as Ukiah and Indigo entered.

One of them recognized Indigo. "Special Agent Zheng? This is not a good time."

"Doctor Elsie Janda," Indigo said to Ukiah. "She's now project leader on the Mars Rover project. Doctor Janda, this is Ukiah Oregon. He's working as a con-

sultant on the case." Indigo glanced about the room.
"Is there something wrong with the Rover?"

The woman managed a weak smile. "We're trying
to decide that right now. NASA called us about an
hour ago. There was an unexplained course devia-
tion. Nothing major, except that the Rover doesn't
seem to be responding any more to their course
corrections."

"So they've lost control of the Rover?"

The woman shook her head. "Lost control is too
strong for the present situation. The onboard computers will go a long way to keep it from damaging
itself. I'm sure we'll be able to correct the problem
shortly."

Ukiah tilted his head to see a screen as the user
scrolled through the lines and lines of code. The code
reminded him of the scrap of paper that had vanished from Doctor Haze's bedroom. He pulled out
his own PDA and scribbled down a piece of his
memory. "Excuse me, would this suggest anything to
you?" He handed his PDA over to the project leader.

The woman frowned at it. "Well, the first are all
modules of the Rover programming. I don't recognize the second set."

Ukiah took back his PDA. "This list was at Doctor
Haze's place when she died. It's quite possible that
she somehow sabotaged the Rover using this list."

"Janet?" The woman's surprise seemed real. "Sabotage the Rover? She lived for the Rover. She said it
was going to put her in the history books, her ticket
to immortality."

"Was immortality important to her?" Indigo asked.

"She hated obscurity," Doctor Janda said. "We
were the ones that called the police on the day she
died. It was too unlike her to miss a chance in front
of the cameras. All the local stations had interviews

lined up with her, and some of the nationals too. When she didn't show, and no one picked up the phone at the house, we knew something went really wrong."

"So there's no chance that the Rover has been sabotaged?" Indigo pressed.

Doctor Janda exchanged guilty looks with some of her programmers. "Someone used Janet's passkey and passwords the night after she was killed. We didn't think to report it because all that was accessed were old Rover files. Some of her stuff, and some of Doctor Robb's diddles."

"Diddles?" Indigo and Ukiah asked in duet.

"He was weird—brilliant but weird. He'd waste time coming up with alternate codes to get equipment to do the weirdest stuff. Like this." Doctor Janda pulled out a diagram and pointed to a mass of circuitry. "This is the short-range radar unit. Sam came up with a diddle that made it act like a radio transmitter, sending out a repeated message signal."

"What was the signal?" Ukiah asked.

The project leader shrugged. "Who knows? A soda jingle maybe. Sam always said it was 'Wake up and come here.'"

Don't wake the sleepers.

Ukiah blinked. The Pack had said it a dozen times, kind of like "God be with you," and he hadn't thought to ask. Don't wake which sleepers? Pack memory supplied the answer; the crew of one hundred thousand on the main invasion ship. Pack memory also maintained that they were dead. Prime had killed them when he sabotaged the ship by first wiping out all crew wakeup programs and then blowing the torpedoes while still in their launch tubes.

How could you wake sleepers who were dead? Ukiah searched back through the memories to find the source of the quote. It was a fragment of Prime's last thoughts and words as he filled the hypodermic dart that transformed Coyote from wolf to alien being. The true phrase had been "must not/don't allow/forbid those sleeping to be awakened." Prime had repeated it like a chant. What blazed bright in Prime's heart at that moment was the realization that he had to become what he hated in order to fight on past death. He had previously vowed to struggle to his own death, and that would be where it stopped. What had changed his mind was lost in the flashes of pain's blackness. What was passed on to the Pack was the knowledge he had to become a lesser evil to fight a greater evil.

Coyote made his Get and abandoned them, stringing them out behind him. Their wolf-bred instinct, however, drew them together and they worked to make a culture for themselves. The Pack clung to the moment of Coyote's creation, because in it was validation for their own acts of violence and Getting.

So they took their maker's chant and made it their motto, forcing it into a rough English translation: "Don't wake the sleepers." Wolflike, though, they had never questioned what it meant truly. What sleepers? How could they be awakened if they were dead?

"You okay?" Indigo asked, touching his elbow, drawing him back to the room full of puzzled programmers.

He nodded vaguely. "This course change. Do you know where the Rover is going now?"

"Well . . ." Doctor Janda shuffled through paper on a side desk to pull out a map. She talked as she hunched over the map, skimming fingers over valleys and mountains. "We think it has somehow deviated back to an old course path. There were several camps as to what should be explored. Lots of big-money special interest groups had different ideas on what the mission should be, what was to be explored. In the end, it was the luck of the draw, you know, window of opportunity, and if the Lander sets down where it was supposed to."

"And?" Ukiah pressed.

"Navigating Mars isn't like a jaunt on the moon, or even Earth. Clouds obscure landmarks, and dust storms habitably change them beyond recognition." The project leader paused to finally locate what she was searching for. "Here's the landing site." She traced a meandering line and then tapped on the map. "This is where the course change came in. See this line? This was one of the original mission paths; it leads up to this crater. It looks like the Rover has merely defaulted back to some prototype code."

"This looks like an impact site." Indigo ran a finger along the curved wall of the indicated valley. Ukiah stared at the sight with his stomach turning to lead and sinking down through his guts.

"Sure is!" Doctor Janda smiled, oblivious to Ukiah's distress. "Something large hit it about three hundred years ago." The right time frame for the crater to have been made by the main invasion ship. "Astronomers of the time made note of a flash of light on Mars. There was a lot of interest in studying this crater, but just before the Rover was launched, information from the Hubble telescope indicated that this area would be difficult to transverse. The Rover probably can make it, but no one wanted to take the risk of sending it all that distance to get stuck the second day out. Not with the primary mission being to return mineral samples to Earth."

"How long will it take for the Rover to get into the crater?" Ukiah asked, trying to fight down his growing panic.

Doctor Janda chewed on her bottom lip, eyes squinted as she thought. "Three days—probably. But we're hoping to upload a course correction and get it back on its original mission."

Three days.

"Can you turn off Sam Robb's diddle?"

Doctor Janda looked at him in surprise. "Um, no. We need control of the Rover to do that."

Indigo glanced at him, and her eyes widened slightly. "Thank you, Doctor Janda." She caught Ukiah by the arm and guided him toward the door. "We'll let you get back to work. I'll be contacting you later."

Outside in the hall, Indigo gazed up at Ukiah as he leaned heavily against the wall. "What's wrong?"

"My father's people came to invade Earth. A hundred thousand warriors. We thought Prime reduced the main ship to space dust, but he didn't. The ship is on Mars. It made that impact crater. And if the Ontongard has gone through all this to get the Rover to the ship, then they believe that they can bring those warriors to Earth. I need to go find the Pack and talk to them."

He pushed off the wall and started for the door.

"Why the Pack?" Indigo kept pace with him. "What can they do?"

"I don't know, but Indigo, do you think that anyone else is going to believe that there's an alien invasion ship sitting on Mars and that its sleeping crew is about to be awakened by the hijacked Mars Rover? Hell, it sounds like they don't even know that the Rover has been hijacked."

She considered it. "No. They've searched that crater with everything man can turn on Mars. The Hubble telescope. SALT. There's no sign of a space ship."

"The ship has shields against electronic and visual detection," Ukiah said.

"Surely the Rover isn't sophisticated enough to pilot an alien space ship to Earth. Hell, if the shields are anything like those in the movies, the Rover won't even be able to get through to the ship."

They passed the receptionist and went out into the afternoon heat.

"Pack memories are so weird." Ukiah struggled to explain. "It's like that old story about five blind men and an elephant, each describing the animal by the piece he's standing next to and failing to see the rest. I can wonder 'why can't the humans see the ship?' and the answer 'because of the shields' comes back. I can tell you where the shield control panel is, how to fix the shields, how to sabotage them, the standard protocol in emergency situations dealing with shields. But what can the Ontongard do with the Rover with the shields up—I don't have the faintest."

She rubbed her face. "I have to get some sleep. This has gotten too weird for even me. We have three days to stop the Rover. You talk to the Pack tonight, and tomorrow we'll figure something out."

He pulled her close and kissed her. "Want me to drive you home?"

She nuzzled into him. "No. It would just strand me in the South Hills. Drop me downtown and I'll pick up a company car."

"Why not your motorcycle?"

She laughed. "They asked me to ride in something a little more sturdy until this blows over. This time, when you get done with the Pack, give me a call."

"I could be real late," he warned.

"Then I'll be slightly incoherent. Wake me and talk to me, okay?"

*   *   *

Finding the Pack was easy this time. They scattered and reformed like a flock of birds, but not without coordination. Long ago Rennie had marked out sites to gather, and they cycled through them with the phases of the moon. It was full moon, the sixth month of the year, and thus they were at Rochester Inn.

Ukiah parked his motorcycle in the vast gravel parking lot and pushed his way into the crowded bar. A big-screen TV was playing a baseball game, and as he entered, there was a roar as a fly ball was caught and the score remained deadlocked at the top of the ninth. The air stank of beer, sweat, cigars, whiskey, and an underlying scent of Pack. He brushed through people, learning odd bits of information from them as he worked his way to the Pack.

He found the Pack taking up the back corner of the bar, several tables pushed together and scattered with dirty dishes and beer bottles. The Pack had sensed him coming and had a chair ready for him beside Rennie.

"The memory work?" Rennie asked as Ukiah straddled the chair.

Ukiah nodded. "Worked great. Worked well enough for me to figure out what the Ontongard are up to. We're screwed."

Rennie frowned and the table stilled. "What do you mean?"

"Prime didn't blow the ship. It's on Mars. The damn Rover that Janet Haze helped build is on Mars. They're going to wake the sleepers."

"That can't be," Hellena whispered.

"They've already taken control of the Rover. They might have already awakened them."

The Pack stood as one and pushed their way through to the big-screen TV. A fly ball had just been hit deep into center field and the outfielder was scrambling. Bear got to the TV first, reached out, and changed the channel as the outfielder missed the ball. There was a howl from the fans, drowned quickly by a snarl from the Pack.

Bear hit the local early news first, doing the headline news. They played updates on the FBI killings—Warner's body had apparently turned up while Indigo was with him. The dead FBI agent's picture vanished to be replaced with the Mars Mission logo. "Late this afternoon, NASA reported that they lost control of the Mars Rover. Attempts are being made to reestablish control." They went to a press conference where a thin, nervous man explained to the local affiliate the exact time and place that they lost control.

"Hex must have known since the beginning that the ship wasn't destroyed," Rennie raged. "That bastard! No wonder he's always been so smug. All his little plots and deals—they never made sense without knowing this. This is what he's been working toward."

"I don't get it," Bear murmured. "If the ship's been up there all this time, and the Ontongard have always had the remote key, why do they need the Rover?"

"Listen to the background," Hellena suddenly hissed.

There was a strange warbling noise, repeated over and over again. It was, Ukiah realized, Sam Robb's "wake up and come here" signal. Ukiah frowned, the Pack memory recognizing it as familiar but slow in revealing the information to him.

Rennie growled beside him, recognizing it first. "The shutdown code for the ECM shield. The shield must have gone up when the ship crashed, and the remote key had been rendered useless. Normal security protocol. Origination of the shutdown code has to be within the short-range weapon perimeter. That's what they need the Rover for. Once the shield is down, they can wake the sleepers with the remote."

His words triggered memories and Ukiah groaned aloud.

"What is it, cub?"

"Janet Haze had the remote key. That's why the Ontongard are kidnapping the FBI agents. When the key didn't turn up in police evidence, they assumed it was turned over to the FBI. But FBI doesn't have it."

"They don't?"

"I found it and didn't know what it was until now. They can't wake the sleepers. They can't control the ship."

"You have the remote key?" Rennie repeated with amazement. "And you didn't realize it?"

"I didn't have Pack memory earlier," Ukiah reminded him. "I put it in a safe place until I had time to figure out what it was."

"Then there's lots of hope here." Rennie laughed. "This is the first time the Pack's got their hands on that damn remote, and we'll make the most of it. Go smash the bloody thing, cub, and scatter the pieces in the river. The rest of you, if Hex's here in Pittsburgh making Gets, then they're controlling the Rover from somewhere in Pittsburgh, maybe from that ugly yellow building in Oakland. If we stop the Rover, then the shields stay up. Screw the bastards every way we can."

"At least until the colonization of Mars starts."

"We'll fight that war when it comes. Tonight we fight this war."

Ukiah glanced up at the TV screen, and his knees almost buckled under him.

"What?" Rennie looked too at the screen where the story had changed from the lost Rover to the newest of the kidnapped FBI agents.

"Indigo," Ukiah could only manage a whisper, staring up at her photo. "They've taken Indigo. They're going to try to make her a Get." He turned to Rennie. "You've got to help me find her."

"Cub, the FBI and the police are going to turn the city upside-down to find her. No one else but the Pack will be looking for the Rover control system. If she dies, she dies. If we don't stop that Rover, all of mankind will die."

He wanted to beg, to plead, to point out that they had three days to stop the Rover, but he couldn't. Pack memories supplied too many details on Prime's home world, an entire race supplanted by the Ontongard. Much as he loved her, Indigo's life couldn't weigh against all the lives on the planet. He slowly nodded. "You're right."

Rennie gripped his shoulder and gave him a slight shake. "Look for her. If you find her in time, we'll come and help you free her."

Max answered the phone with "Bennett," which meant he was driving.

"Max. Where are you?" Ukiah hiked quickly across the bar's parking lot. Dusk was setting in quickly, bleeding the light from the sky.

"Wheeling."

Ukiah swore, stopping beside his bike. "Still? I need you."

"What's wrong?"

"The Ontongard, they took Indigo. I need to find her now, before they kill her."

There was a long silence from Max. "Kid, I won't be back for another two hours, even at eighty miles per hour."

"I know. I know. I'm heading downtown to get a trail on them. It might take me that long just to get a trace. I'll call you when I know more."

"Do that."

Ukiah hung up and glanced at the darkening night sky. Never before did it seem to press so close or hold so much menace.

He found Kraynak and asked to see the dead FBI agents. Kraynak refused him at first, and Ukiah hounded him out into the night, a small covered porch where the smokers practiced their habit in a smoke-free world.

"Damn it, Kraynak, just let me see their clothes. What can it hurt?"

"Lately, the mind boggles." Kraynak lit a cigarette, the match flaring in the shadows. The swirl of smoke and the glowing end marked the detective as he stood silently considering. "Okay, kid, on one condition. You said that Bennett was down in Wheeling but hauling ass to get in here. If I let you in, you wait for him, because he'll be all over my ass if you go off alone."

Ukiah shook his head. "I can't do that. They're playing with a type of germ-warfare virus, Kraynak. The minute they inject her, she's dead. There's no cure. There's no hope. If they did it like they did the others, they injected her with an immune-suppression drug when they grabbed her. They'll give it time to work and then they hit her with the virus. When they do that, she's as good as dead. I can't wait."

Kraynak considered him, then slipped his PDA out

of his pocket, consulted, and muttered darkly. "There was a syringe found at the kidnapping site. Come on, kid, let's see what you can do."

The clothing was a barrage of information. Death, illness, fear, dirt. They tumbled over Ukiah's senses in a rush. He picked out the shirt and handled it, closing his eyes against the room, to Kraynak's rasping, smoky breathing, to the musty air, the harsh overhead lights. He was his fingertips, and the cloth was rumpled pages of an encyclopedia. There was the blood from the head wound, fibers from a car's trunk, the crushed leaf juice from Schenley Park, the dry gray dust from the abandoned office building, sweat tainted with fear and then illness, deodorant and after shave now days old, vomit, and dirt.

Dirt.

Black oily dirt. He restlessly rubbed his fingers over the spot, then lifted it to his nose and smelled deeply, focusing only on the dirt. It was familiar. He willed the memory of it forward.

During their second year, when he was doing part-time work with Max, a child had gone missing, and he had tracked it cross-country to an abandoned lot. There, concealed by an overturned refrigerator stacked high with tires, he had found the boy's body.

On the steps up to the house, during the track across the dry, autumn landscape, and in the lot, there had been black oily dirt. It rained out of the sky from a local incinerator, so very fine that no one seemed to notice it.

He pulled himself up out of the focus and checked the other pile of clothes. Black oily dirt. He bolted for the door, shouting, "They're in Kittanning."

"How do you know?"

"There's a tire incinerator there. The dirt gets on everything."

"Ukiah, there's more than one of those things in the area."

"Then I might be wrong, or I might be right. I have to go."

"Ukiah, wait!" Kraynak shouted, but Ukiah left him behind, running down the halls of the police station.

He was out into the night and to his bike. He paused to flip out his phone and punch Max's speed dial number. It rang once.

"Bennett."

"They're in Kittanning."

"Damn, we're still over an hour out, and that's on the other side of Pittsburgh, like fifty miles out. You've got your gun and a jacket?"

"I've got my gun and extra clips. There's no time to fetch a jacket, Max. I have to go now."

"Call me back when you find out where in Kittanning."

"Okay. See you later."

As he hung up, he heard a sound. He turned and made out Bear standing in the shadows.

"Kittanning," Bear nodded. "Hex is the only one that makes Gets. He'll be there. It's been a long time since we've put our teeth in his face."

Ukiah straddled his bike. "Then the Pack will be there?"

"They will have to be gathered together first."

"I can't wait for them any more than I can wait for my partner." Ukiah pulled on his helmet.

"Go. We'll be there when you need us."

Ukiah peeled away into the night. Kittanning was up the Allegheny River, a straight shot on Route 28 with only a handful of red lights the whole way. On his bike, late at night on the fairly smooth road, he could whip through the dark at 200 miles per hour if he pushed it hard. Only it left his backup far behind.

One blurred sign had read 43 miles. His speedometer read 180 most of the way. Fifteen minutes later he arrived in Kittanning. He rode the empty streets, nose to the wind, senses focused for the trace of Ontongard. When he found the building, he killed the engine and coasted into the shadows.

Max answered the phone on the first ring.

"I'm in Kittanning. They're in a building on the corner of Washington and Fifth, along the river."

"I'm still at two-hour ETA to get there, kid."

"I know. Call Kittanning and the state police and the FBI. See if you can get them out here. If nothing else, there's probably going to be some shooting."

There was silence from Max, then, "Damn it, Ukiah, be careful."

"I will," he promised and hung up. *I promise to carefully get my ass shot off.*

They weren't expecting trouble, and so he got into the door and through the first three Ontongard with ease. He cringed as he pulled the trigger, knowing in his soul that he was committing murder. As Indigo would no longer be her true, calm, loving self, these creatures were no longer human. They had been twisted and molded against their will. But he couldn't ignore the fact that they were like Pack. They were like Rennie and Hellena. They were like himself. He chanted to himself, "Don't wake the sleepers."

Beyond the three there was a long hall and then a door opening onto a steel catwalk. He loaded a fresh clip, shoving the warm, mostly spent clip into his back pocket. He moved out onto the catwalk, his pistol braced with both hands.

Ukiah's skin crawled as the short hairs along his arms and back lifted with awareness of Hex. He was here, the Ontongard's master.

Indigo was there too. They had her tied to a support beam, one arm free to facilitate the injection. She wore only his black T-shirt and faded jeans; they had taken her from her home, sleeping and waiting for his call. The one long lock of hair spilled forward, screening her face from them. She was still and seemingly fearless.

Ukiah spotted Hex as he reached the stairs leading down into the vast factory floor. He wore a white silk shirt, its left sleeve rolled up, and one of his Get was tying a tourniquet about the bared arm. The Get watched Ukiah come. Without looking himself, Hex drawled, "Get that dog. Do it as quietly as possible."

Instantly the Get rushed toward him, a wave of bodies. There were too many of them. He emptied his gun as they flooded toward him and went down hard under their assault. A moment later they had him pinned on the ground, one pushing a shotgun over the others' shoulders to wedge the barrel tight to his head.

"Wait." It was a quiet, calm command, but his attackers froze instantly, as if every muscle had locked in their bodies. Footsteps rang in the sudden silence and Hex came into view.

Hex was tall, thin to the point of gaunt, weirdly shaped about the head and face. His eyes were a solid black, no iris, no whites, just blackness. His hair hung black and straight, but it was stiff, as if it were of bristles instead of normal hair.

He studied Ukiah, then looked up to scan the catwalk, the building, maybe even the streets outside.

"You're alone. The Pack doesn't hunt alone. What are you doing here?"

Ukiah panted, trying to think and not to think at the same time. Pack memory told him that Hex might be able to read Ukiah's thoughts. A plan came to him and he shunted it away quickly, before it could be discovered.

The shotgun was cocked by one of his Gets, but Hex spoke as if he had the gun in his hands. "I'm told that this hurts immensely."

"We know what you're up to," Ukiah growled. "And we know you're screwed royally. We've decided to add to your misery."

Hex sniffed, finishing tightening the tourniquet as if he were straightening a necktie. "You're bluffing."

Ukiah forced himself to laugh. "She can't get it for you. The FBI doesn't have it. They never had it."

Hex stopped, his head lifting to stare at Ukiah. "What are you talking about?"

"You screwed yourself good this time. You were so sure that the FBI had your toy that you've done everything but paint a bull's-eye on yourself. God, we've gone so long as your whipping boy, but now you've done it good. The FBI knows about you now. They hate you and they'll hunt you down like the monster you are."

The Ontongard leader turned and walked away.

Ukiah thrashed against those holding him, straining to get closer to Indigo, to place himself between her and Hex. "You can make her into your Get, but she won't be able to fetch it for you."

He risked a glance at Indigo. Her face was steeled to neutral. Her eyes flared with emotion when his met hers, pain that went deeper than any emotion he had ever seen register on her face, and then was gone, controlled and banished.

Hex returned, carrying a length of two-by-four in his hand. The Get holding Ukiah heaved him suddenly up and forward. "Doesn't have it?" He struck Ukiah with a casual backhanded blow across the face with the two-by-four. "Can't get it?" Again the two-by-four struck. "My toy?" A whimper of pain leaked out of Ukiah with the third blow. "Stop dancing around the pronoun and give the name."

"The remote key. Janet Haze had it in the woods and lost it. Only she couldn't remember that, could she? You killed her because she screwed you to hell and back."

The Ontongard leader stood looking at him, still holding the bloody two-by-four. It was quite possible, Ukiah realized suddenly, that he was about to be beaten to death with it. His eyes wanted to steal over and look at Indigo again, but he controlled them. He mustn't let Hex know how important she was to him.

"Shaw was in the park. He found it, didn't he?"

Certain that Hex could spot a lie, Ukiah kept to the truth. "For the first time the Pack controls the key."

Hex looked down at him with what might be a glare. The all-black eyes made it hard to read. Into that silence Ukiah's phone chirped. It had chirped a second time when one of the Get pulled it from Ukiah's pocket and pressed the answer button.

"Talk," Hex commanded.

He almost said his name, but swallowed it. "Yes?" It was the Pack leader. "Where are you?"

Hex, hearing Rennie's voice, reached out and took it from the Get. "Shaw, you have something of mine. I have something of yours. I'm sure that you remember what I did to the last little one you were so stupid to Get." An image flashed into Ukiah's mind and he almost vomited. A child served like a roast pig, skin golden crisp and pulled back from joints, mint sauce on the side. "I suggest a trade. I'll even throw in an FBI agent. It seems I don't need her."

Rennie's answer was clear. "Go to hell."

The Ontongard leader held out the phone. Without warning the shotgun was placed above Ukiah's foot and the trigger pulled. The pain struck Ukiah with the noise, a deafening thunder and ring of the shotgun's report and the pain of dozens of pellets ripping his foot apart. Ukiah screamed, trying not to look, but his battered flesh reported the damage. His boot had been peeled away, along with much of his flesh. Bone was exposed to air, ripped free of flesh, and broken.

After Ukiah's scream fell to a whimper, Hex put the phone back to his ear. "He's a cute little puppy dog, Shaw. If I have to, I'll blow him full of holes."

"I'm not far behind him, and I'll pay you in kind for anything done to him."

"Growl, dog, growl. That's all you've done for hundreds of years."

The Get, though, were moving. They produced a length of chain and secured Ukiah's arms and legs tightly, as he struggled weakly to get free. The chain was looped back to a support beam and padlocked there. One Get vanished and reappeared with cans of gel fuel.

"I'm done growling." Rennie's voice was calm. "I'm going to tear your throat out."

"Agree to the trade, Shaw, or there won't be anything to salvage of him."

"You've gone mad if you think I'll trade the world for the life of one Get. Kill him. Scatter his ashes to the wind. You'll never see that remote key again."

Hex flung the phone away. He turned and struck Ukiah with the two-by-four, again and again. Ukiah writhed under the blows, trying to pull his chained hands over his head.

Suddenly Hex caught him by the hair, jerked him up to look him in the face. "Where is it?"

A pressure struck Ukiah full in the forehead. His mouth opened and the words rushed out. "It's in the tree—" He snapped his Judas jaw shut, biting his tongue deep in the effort.

Hex pulled him closer. "You know, don't you. Where is the key?"

The desire increased, like a scream of pain presses to be released. He fought the desire.

"You said 'in the tree.' You will tell me where it is." The alien caught Ukiah's chin and wretched his head up—locking their gaze. "Again. Where is it?"

At my home, he wanted to scream, *with my moms and sister*, but he bit relentlessly down on his tongue. No. Don't tell. Never tell. Die first.

"Where is it?"

He howled, in pain for a moment, then it deepened as he found some secret refuge inside him. It was a wolf's howl of misery, of defiance?—no—a call to the Pack. He howled till the air was gone from his lungs. Then he breathed deep and started to howl again. Call the Pack. Call the Pack and they'll kill this torturer of cubs.

Hex growled and snatched the shotgun from his Get. He chambered a shell and shot Ukiah in the chest. Again. And again. And again until Ukiah lost count, pain and noise blurring together. When it stopped, the ringing of the report went on with the pain. Ukiah fought for breath, refusing to give in until he was sure Indigo was safe.

Hex turned away. "Burn them both."

Ukiah flailed on the floor. He had to save Indigo.

"No." His voice wasn't much more than a croak. "You can't hurt her."

"I can't?" He lifted up the shotgun to point at Indigo.

The words were impossible to form. "She's carrying," he gasped for a breath and forced the rest, "my seed. She's my mate. I'm Prime's son."

Pack memory translated the disbelief, then dismayed revelation flashing across the alien's features. He wiped blood from Ukiah's face and tasted it. "You're Prime's brat, a God damn breeder and I just blasted you full of holes!"

Out in the night, a wolf howl lifted, deep and angry.

Hex screamed with anger, turned, and shot one of his own Get. He emptied the shotgun into the hapless man, then used the gun like a club. Finally he flung the gun aside.

He stooped down beside Ukiah. "You're going to help me take this world." He reached down and plucked up a squirming ball of fur. It was, Ukiah realized distantly, one of his mice memories already forming from the blood pooling about him. "One way or another." Hex shoved the mouse into a pocket and reached down, snatching up two more. "Bring them both. Hurry."

There was an explosion at the door that Ukiah had come through earlier. Hex glanced toward the noise and fled in the other direction, running before the Pack.

The remaining Get scurried to free them. Ukiah could only lie and watch them fumble with the blood-slick links. He felt like he was under water, trying to suck air through a layer of water. The pain was gone and there remained just a growing coldness. Things seemed to be traveling away from him,

as though he was slowly falling down a well. Dimly
he was aware that they had undone Indigo's chains,
and that she fought them silently, savagely. Then the
Pack was there and Hex's Get became instantly dead
bodies strewn haphazardly on the floor.

"Go after Hex," Rennie snarled. "Run him down
and kill him."

The Pack went, nose to the wind to catch the trail.
Indigo came and gathered him into her arms, a furnace of heat against his cold skin. There were tears
in her eyes, turning them to pools of mercury. Rennie
crouched beside Ukiah. "Cub?"

Ukiah fought for the surface of the well. "I told
Him—I told Him—who I am—Indigo my mate—
with my seed. Keep her safe."

Rennie touched his bloody cheek. *I'll keep her safe.
You can stop fighting and rest.*

Ukiah looked over to Indigo and lost himself in
her eyes and died.

CHAPTER NINE

Monday, June 22, 2004
Pittsburgh, Pennsylvania

Ukiah came awake with the thunder of guns echoing through his head, as if the report had been stuck in his ears until he was aware enough to register it. It faded to oppressive silence. He listened for some time to his ragged breathing and stumbling heartbeat. Eventually they strengthened and steadied, becoming monotonous.

Then he noticed he was cold, weak, and naked. He opened his eyes. Smooth white porcelain pressed against his cheek and filled his vision. He could see a sliver of the room beyond the wall of porcelain. An unfamiliar bathroom spread out around him, smelling of disinfectant and enclosed air.

What am I doing here?

It was his first conscious thought but there were no answers forthcoming. He remembered sitting in his moms' kitchen, Max about to serve him eggs— then nothing—not even choppy flashes of unattached memories. His mind had been wiped clean. No clue remained why he was sleeping naked in a strange bathtub.

What happened to me?

There was movement and three black mice scurried along the lip of the bathtub to his face. One,
braver than the other two, came up to rest tiny paws
on his nose and eyed him closely.

Are you mine? he wondered. *Are you memories I lost?
What happened?*

Suddenly he felt a wave of mice pour across his
body, heard their tiny feet magnified by sheer numbers into a weak rumble. They crowded onto the
edge to press close to his face, weaving and bobbing.
Bursts of images careened through his mind.

Flashes of pain, of an alien's face, of the smell of
Indigo, like flashbulbs, exploded across his senses
and were gone. He latched firmly on one thought
and moaned in agony. Indigo! The Ontongard had
Indigo!

He waved weakly at the mice, trying to get them
out of his way. They fled to the other side of the tub.
He clawed at the slick surface, finding all his muscles
weirdly weak. It was as if the Pack had gassed him
again. Had they?

He got up on the edge of the bathtub. Hundreds
of small objects he hadn't noticed before rained off
him, pinging off the ceramic floor. He caught one
after it dribbled to a stop. It was a tiny gray metal
ball, smaller than a pea in size. He frowned at it until
enlightenment dawned on him. They were shotgun
pellets. The Ontongard had obviously used a shotgun
on him, many times.

He toppled onto the floor. The bath mat had a big
H with Hilton written through it. He could see into
the next room now, obviously a hotel room with the
standard two beds, chairs, and a TV set.

He was at the Hilton?

Someone moved in the next room. He recognized
the person as Pack before they came into view. Hel-

lena stopped in the bathroom door, looking slightly bemused at him.

"You're awake." She lifted him with surprising ease, carried him like a child into the next room. One of the beds was already turned down. She laid him in it and tucked the sheets about his chest.

Although he couldn't see them, he was aware of the wave of mice following after them. Their numbers finally impressed on him the fact that he had been hurt badly.

"I need to find Indigo," he whispered to Hellena.

"You've already found her," Hellena soothed. "You were a knight without armor, riding to the rescue. You saved her, and now you need to heal. You're feather light from all the blood you lost."

The mice joined him on the bed, their thoughts on food. He could feel their hunger along with his own. "I'm starving."

She laughed and picked up the phone. "Hello? Yes, this is Suite 320. Can I still get breakfast? Good, I want four of the works. Pancakes, sausage, orange juice, anything that looks like breakfast, please bring it up. Also, can I have a plate of cheese? Cubed. Thank you." She hung up and smiled at him in her maternal way. "There. It will be up in a few minutes."

He looked around the room. "Why are we here?"

"We're hiding." She tweaked the blankets closer to his chest. "Hex now knows that you exist and that you alone know the location of the remote key. He would kill to get ahold of you."

Remote key? What was a remote key? Pack memory called it up, and he realized it was the strange object he had found in Schenley Park. The implications cascaded down on him. The key was only good if the ship had survived. If the ship had survived, then the sleepers could be woken. If the sleepers woke, Earth was doomed. He shuddered at the casualness with which he had slipped the key into his stash hole.

"You'll be cold until you eat." Hellena misunderstood his shudder. "Your body used most of its energy up healing itself. You're not completely healed yet, but your body needed to let you wake up to take fuel in."

Ukiah indicated the mice with his eyes. "What about them?"

"When you're completely healed and they are fully fed, you can take them back in. If you tried now, the system's wide energy drain would kill you again."

"Again? I was dead?"

She shrugged slightly. "It happens. You were dead in Schenley Park when Rennie and I first found you."

Obviously I have to rethink some of my past. How many times he had woken up cold and starving with no clue as to what had just happened? The first had been with Joe Gary, with the rifle hole that had seemed like it should have gone straight through him, but hadn't. There had been the motorcycle accident last winter, the one he had never told anyone about, waking alongside the road with his neck hurting as if he'd broken it. There had been the blankness of his early childhood. Had he been killed, left for dead, only to revive with no memory at all?

He moaned as it suddenly hit him; if he had rescued Indigo and then died, Indigo would think he was dead forever. She would tell Max. Max would tell his moms.

"I need to call my moms, and Max, and Indigo. I need to let them know I'm okay."

Hellena caught his hand as he reached for the phone. "You're not okay, not yet. A kitten could kill you by just playing with your mice. When you're dead, you're helpless. Wait."

"They think I'm dead."

"And they've thought that way for a full day now. A few more hours won't add or subtract from that first blow of grief."

He considered, then shook his head. "My moms and Indigo, yeah, I think they can take it. I'm afraid for Max. I'm afraid that he'll blame himself and do something stupid. Please."

Her dark eyebrows drew together in worry, but finally she nodded. She dialed the number and held the phone to his ear. Max's wireless phone rang three times and then dropped Ukiah into the voice mail. He entered Max's security code and worked through the stored messages. Most of them were from Kraynak, abrupt requests for a return call. The last hinted that Max wasn't even carrying his phone. Ukiah deleted all traces of his call from Max's system and exited.

"I thought those things were supposed to be more secure," Hellena murmured as she hung up.

"If you have the security code, then you can do anything with them."

"Do you know the code from overhearing it, or did your partner tell it to you?"

He looked at her, surprised. "If he trusts me with his life, why wouldn't he trust me with his privacy?"

They heard a knock on the door of the adjoining room. Hellena leaned down and produced a shotgun from under the bed. She undid the locks on the bedroom door, stalked out to the adjoining sitting room. She stood for a moment silent beside the door. Ukiah found himself trying to sense what stood beyond the far door. Pack? Ontongard? Human?

Hellena judged it to be human, because she called softly, "Who is it?"

"Room service. You ordered some food."

"Wait a minute." Hellena tucked the shotgun behind a chair beside the door and came to shut the door to the bedroom. Ukiah could hear her undo all the security locks and chains and opened the door. "Just leave the cart, if you can."

"Okay. When you're done, just push it outside. Please sign here."

A moment later the outside door closed and Ukiah relaxed. Hellena redid the locks, pushed the cart into the bedroom, and locked that door too. The smell of food was maddening. The mice abandoned him in a wave to rush the cart. She laughed and set the dish of cubed cheese on the floor for them.

"You know," Ukiah tried to sit up and failed, "as a private detective hired to find someone, I usually check hotels first."

"Humans use hotels." Hellena helped him to sit and stuffed pillows behind him. "The Pack normally hole up in abandoned buildings or head out to a national park."

"Why aren't we, then?"

"Necessity. The rest of the Pack are looking for the Ontongard. I couldn't take care of you alone elsewhere. Here I have running hot water, food delivery," she set a plate of pancakes down in front of him with a flourish, "and, if necessary, a security team who will view me as right, because I'm the paying customer. The suite gives me two sets of locked doors they have to get through, and being off the ground floor means they won't come in through the window."

Ukiah attacked the pancakes as he considered the slight Pack woman. Unsaid, but implied, was the fact that she was the last line of defense before the Ontongard reached him. She seemed in her late twenties, but she appeared early in Rennie's memories, making her at least a hundred. There was no clue as to how she had been made into Pack, she had just appeared at a Gathering, awkward and shy. To give Rennie credit, he had loved her on first sight, and had stayed true to her through the course of a century. Memory led to memory, and Ukiah was suddenly recalling what it was like to make love to her.

Blushing, he devoted himself to the sausages, and recalled only his own memories.

He didn't finish the breakfast, although he made impressive inroads on the four meals. At some point he was chewing—and then he was asleep.

Ukiah woke with a stranger standing over his bed.

He yelped in surprise and tried to fling himself aside. Steel-strong hands caught hold of him, clamping over his mouth, smothering an instinctual growl.

"Hush, cub, we don't want to bother the neighbors. It's just me." It was Rennie's soft brogue, his scent, his pack awareness pressed against Ukiah, but it wasn't his face.

Rennie?

Aye, cub, it's me. I'm wearing a guise, nothing more.

The words *guise* and *Rennie* connected to spill out borrowed memories. A shearing pain as chin and cheek bones rearranged themselves under flesh to copy another person's appearance. The taste of blood that provided the pattern to be copied. Of looking into a mirror and being startled by one's own appearance.

Ukiah studied the broad Asian face, complete with almond-shaped eyes, and nodded. Rennie released him and settled on the edge of the bed, dropping keys in a loud jangle onto the nightstand.

"Why do you look like that?"

"Just being careful not to lead anyone back to you," Rennie said. "If we'd left with your loved ones, you'd be six foot under right now, but we don't truly have time to keep an eye on you ourselves right now."

Ukiah frowned, momentarily confused. Oh yes, Hellena said he'd been killed, not that he remembered it happening yet. "So why are you here?"

"Where's the remote key?"

"I put it where it should be safe," he hedged, not wanting the Pack at the farm.

"Hex took three of your memories. Any place *you* know of is no longer safe."

Ukiah sat up in a bolt of terror—and fainted. A few moments later he woke again, aware that there had been a dilation of darkness. He started to sit up again. "My moms and sister, I have to warn them."

Rennie pinned him to the bed with frightening ease. Ukiah hadn't realized how weak he still was. "We warned your one true love, and she was making arrangements to protect your family even before we took your body. We take care of our own, Cub, and that includes their families."

"It's in my tree house. There's a knothole that I've used over the years as a treasure chest. I put it there."

Rennie flashed white, straight teeth. "Ahhhh, the tree house. Your love told us that they had only gotten 'in the tree' out of you. With all of Schenley Park to choose from, I'm sure that Hex is howling in frustration. Your love seemed confused by the reference. Would your family be too?"

"They would know. Max would too. There's The Tree for me, and then all the rest in the world. Indigo has been in the tree house, but I didn't explain how important it is in my life. I should. She should know these kinds of things."

Rennie laughed and tousled Ukiah's hair. "If you had to have a woman, at least you picked one with steel in her gut. She wept for you, and then turned her cold vengeance on those that hurt you. She ordered for Tribot to be seized. She's found two of Hex's dens already—broke them open and all the Get have been killed in gunfights. Word is that she's tracing all Tribot's financial backers and having the IRS go over them with a fine-tooth comb. Hex will be sorry he ever woke her anger."

"She's going to get herself killed."

"Oh no, not a possible carrier of Prime's grandson. His Get would rather shoot themselves than hurt her. What a wonderful truth you wove to protect her. Then you finished it off by pledging us to her."

"I did?" Ukiah shook his head. "I don't remember."

"You did. We've kept an eye on her for you, but to be truthful, it's been a great satisfaction to watch her wreak her carnage on Hex."

It occurred to Ukiah that the activities listed would take up days. "How long have I been out?"

"It's been two days. You woke up yesterday once, and now."

"So, if the Ontongard got the memories to work for them, they have the remote key."

"We don't think they'll be able to get the memories to work in that way. We've handled your memories here, and they've proved most stubborn at cooperating."

"Yours wasn't a ball of laughs either."

"But mine was built of fractured DNA. You could force it to break and submit. Your memories are seamless, unbreakable little buggers. While they like Hellena, even she can't take them in. We thought it was because you were near at hand, but those we took out still refused."

"So they don't work."

"Not as memories."

"What else would you use them for?"

"There are three other ways of using them that I can think of—and unfortunately they can try all three."

"Oh God, I'm even afraid to ask."

"The first is they could make Get out of them. One mouse could make one Get, and because you're a breeder the success rate would be close to guaranteed. Your Get receives your memory, but it would also have your will and determination. Hex would have to torture the information out of it."

"Oh Jesus, no." Ukiah started to get up and got pushed down again. "I can't let him do it."

"It's been two days. If he's managed to grab a human, it's done. There's a chance that your love has harassed him too hard to give him time, but there's nothing you can do."

"What's the second way?"

Rennie indicated his borrowed face. "A single mouse would provide enough information for a host of Ontongard to wear your guise."

"Why the hell would they want to look like me? What good would that do them?"

Rennie tightened his hold on Ukiah's shoulder. "While your family might think you're dead, Hex knows you've survived what he did to you. He might seek hostages to lure you back to him."

Ukiah nearly howled then, and fought Rennie's hold. "Let me up, damn it! Let me up!"

"I told you, your Lady of Steel made arrangements to move your family." Rennie growled softly. "Now hold still. You're only hurting yourself."

"What about Indigo? What about Max?"

"We're watching your love, don't worry about her."

"And Max?"

Rennie took a deep breath and let it out, much the same way Max often did when he conceited a point that he didn't want to give in on. "We'll find your partner and protect him, cub. We're gathering the entire Pack to search out Hex. The Hell Hounds have already arrived. We can spare the manpower."

"Promise me."

"We'll find him. We'll protect him."

Ukiah collapsed back into the bed. Darkness pulsed at the edge of his vision in time with his heartbeat. Much as he wanted to get up, he realized he couldn't. "What's the third way?"

"The third is to grow the mouse in a full human. It would take time, but Hex is used to having centuries to work with. It would give him a breeder to work with. It would be probably his best bet because it won't have your memories—thus your hard-won strength of character—and will be pliable in Hex's hands."

"No memory?"

"To grow that much, the mouse would have to dump its memory storage. The more it grows, the less memory it has. To go from mouse to adult human, it would wipe out everything."

"Is this just theory, or have you done this before?"

"We grew Bear back from a mouse. It took about twenty years. When he was full grown, we gave him Pack memory from one of his Gets, which was the best we could do."

His life, Ukiah decided, had gotten very twisted lately.

There was a knock at the door. Rennie lifted his

head, nose flaring, eyes narrowing. Then the Pack leader relaxed. "That's Hellena with supplies."

She had bought clothes for him to replace the blood-soaked tatters of his own clothes. She also brought bags of produce and cheese bought at the Strip district, and greasy bags of hot food from the Strip's food vendors.

"When you wake up, you should be back on your feet completely." Rennie indicated the key ring with his eyes. "I've brought your bike back from Kittanning and parked it at the Kaufmann's garage, top level. Very nice bike."

"Thanks." Ukiah yawned deeply. "If you find one of my Gets, you're not going to hurt it, are you?"

"Of course not." Hellena took away his plates and pushed him back into the bed. "They would be Pack. Pack takes care of Pack." She tucked the blankets about his chin and kissed his forehead. "It keeps us human."

He woke alone. Hellena and Rennie were gone, and all his mice too. For a moment he thought the two Pack members had taken the mice with them, then realized that, during his last sleep, they had all merged back with him. With a slightly fuzzy focus, he could remember all of the showdown between himself and the Ontongard.

He was stiff and sore, and covered with scars, but he was intact. He took a long hot shower. It was only as he dressed that he noticed the note written on the Hilton's stationery, in elegant cursive handwriting. Pack memory told him was Hellena's. It read: We fear the remote has fallen into the Ontongard's hands. We must find Hex or all will be lost. Take care.

The Ontongard had been to the farm.

He snatched up his key ring, wallet, and wireless phone and headed out to find his motorcycle. Minutes later he was streaking out of Pittsburgh toward home.

Dead dogs littered the front yard. Pools of blood marked where something larger had been killed and taken away. The house was abandoned, starkly empty, a shell of what it had been. There was no clue as to where his family had gone.

He climbed up into the tree house and checked the stash hole. Rennie had been there, an Ontongard, and Max. Who had been first? Rennie was obviously the last. Had Max come out to the tree house, following something Indigo told him, and found the key? Or had the Ontongard found the key, and Max come later?

Max's phone still didn't pick up. He flew back down I-79 to Pittsburgh, frantic now for Max.

The office had been trashed. He picked his way through the wreckage, trying not to cry. The grandfather clock had been smashed, the Frank Lloyd Wright desk overturned, the drawers broken. Paneling had been torn from the wall. He wandered up to his room and found all his clothes on the floor, the inside of the closet torn apart. He picked up one of his tracking T-shirts. It had been torn out of spite. He went through his whole collection of tracking T-shirts until he found two intact. He took off his stiff new shirt and put one of the black T-shirts on.

The four garage doors stood open and all of the vehicles were gone. The gun safe was empty except for Max's phone, its low battery message flashing. The floor safe had been pried up and carried away.

He collapsed onto the front porch and called Indigo. Her voice message system picked up, stated that Agent Zheng was not taking calls, and hung up. He called directory assistance, got the FBI front desk number, and put a call in.

"FBI."

"Can I speak with Special Agent Zheng?"

"I'm sorry, Special Agent Zheng is not taking calls. Is there anyone else that can help you?"

"This is her boyfriend. Is there any way I can please talk to her?"

"Sir, I have had people call claiming to be every possible member of her family and ask for her. If you want an interview with her, I suggest you try the public relations office. Do you want me to connect you?"

"No."

He hung up and noticed that the last three days of newspapers were on the porch. He picked up the one following the night he was killed. It unrolled to a quarter-page picture of Indigo holding his body. "FBI Agent Saved, Rescuer Killed."

God, what a nightmare. The world about to be invaded, his family missing, Max missing, Indigo unreachable.

He regarded his phone. He had fifty-seven numbers in memory. The first three were home, the office, and Max. Number four was Chino.

Chino answered on the third ring. "Hey hey hey— who the hell is this? You're using Ukiah's phone."

"Chino, it's Ukiah. I need to find Max."

"This is a trick, isn't it? I saw what happened out at Ukiah's moms'."

"What happened, Chino?"

"Hey, Ukiah is dead. I saw him. I kissed his soul farewell. The man is dead."

"Chino, look, okay, let's forget who I am. Do you know that the office has been trashed?"

"Huh?" There was a pause as Chino missed the change in subject and needed to backtrack mentally. "Max warned me to stay away from it."

"Well, the place is a wreck. The bad guys came and went. If you can't believe I'm Ukiah, can you at least call a locksmith and get the front door fixed? It's busted and standing open. See if you can get a carpenter to fix the paneling. The damn bastards tore it off the wall. Hire a maid to clean the kitchen. They dumped all the food out three days ago, and it reeks. Might as well stock it again too. Get a pen and I'll give you the petty fund's PIN number and leave the ATM card for you to pick up." He gave him the PIN number and reached back and stuck the ATM card in the mail slot. "It's in the inside mailbox. And can you send someone out to my moms'—Ukiah's moms'—and get the dogs buried. There's a rock about a hundred feet north of the kennels. That's where we buried the other dogs that died. Can you get someone to bury the dogs back there?"

There was long silence, and then a frightened "Ukiah, that's you, isn't it?"

"Yes, Chino, it's me. It's hard to explain, but has anything about me ever been normal?"

"No, man."

"Have you seen Max? His phone is here at the office. I've been trying for three days to get ahold of him. All the cars are gone too."

"I don't know shit about the cars. I was with him in Wheeling when you called. We flew back from West Virginia and still got there far too late. You were cold, oh so stone cold. Shit man, you were a good kid, no one should have took you down like that. Agent Zheng said that you were taken down because you had something that you'd hidden and wouldn't cough it up. Said you had hidden it in a tree, and just like that Max had to leave for the farm."

Max had the key. Ukiah closed his eyes and wondered if this was a good thing or a bad thing. "What happened at my moms'?"

"You don't know?"

"Not a clue, except there are dead dogs everywhere."

"FBI scrambled a team out to your place to move out your folks. They were giving the wolves one last run when a car pulled up. Six men got out. One was wearing your face. Your moms almost went out to him when the wolves took him down, tore him to shreds. You know what they say, can't fool animals. That started a gunfight."

"What happened to my moms?"

"The FBI came out on top. Six-zip. Thanks to the wolves. They got around to looking close to the one wearing your face. The build was wrong, you know, wrong size shoes, wrong size pants, slightly too tall. Creepy shit."

"Did Max go out to the farm soon after that?"

"Yeah. We hit it right after the mop-up of the bodies. No one had told your moms anything yet. It was all 'do this, do that,' with no why. Max told them about you. They took it hard and then the FBI took them away."

"But they're safe, they're not hurt, right?"

"They're fine, man. You know that Max wouldn't take another step until he was sure they were okay."

"Yeah. Did he go out to the tree house?"

"Is it in that great big tree out back?"

"Yeah."

"Sure did. Was that where you hid the thing? In a tree house?"

"Yeah. I couldn't tell them where it was, not with it on top of my folks."

"I hear you. Look, don't worry about the office or the dogs. I'll take care of it. I'll put out the word that you're back and looking for Max."

"Thanks, Chino."

"Take care of yourself, kid. A lot of people love you."

Number five was Janey's home phone and she didn't answer. Her answering machine picked up and Ukiah left a stilted awkward message.

Number six was their lawyer, who didn't believe him until Ukiah recalled the various degrees on his wall and started to give, in order, the names of his classmates listed under his graduating class photo. He promised to contact the *Pittsburgh Post-Gazette* and have a retraction story printed. He also stated that since Ukiah's body was taken before anyone official reached the scene, he hadn't been declared dead. There was no paperwork there.

Feeling somewhat better, Ukiah decided to take on the FBI directly.

Outside the FBI offices was a news truck, which Ukiah skirted. Inside the receptionist looked somewhat harassed. She told him firmly that Agent Zheng wasn't taking visitors.

"I'm Ukiah Oregon. I was killed three days ago rescuing Agent Zheng. Can't you at least let her know that I'm back from the dead to visit her?"

She looked a little more rattled. "Pardon me?"

Ukiah took off his shirt, exposing his scabbed-over wounds. "I was killed, shot seven times, and I'm back from the dead."

"I'm sorry, she isn't taking visitors. The message was explicit."

Ukiah decided to continue undressing. It wouldn't be worth getting shot storming the FBI offices. Naked, maybe no one would assume he was carrying a concealed weapon.

"Excuse me, what are you doing?"

"I'm going to see Agent Zheng. I do hope she's really here and that's not some idiot line you've been chanting."

"She's here, but she's not seeing anyone."

Ukiah placed Max's door jammer up to the electronic lock and pushed the button. The door buzzed, and he jerked it open and he was inside, moving quickly. He dropped the jammer and headed for Indigo's office.

A high, piercing alarm went off. Within seconds he was surrounded by tense men and women in black pantsuits pointing Smith & Wesson revolvers at him. He walked forward slowly, hands upraised. "Look, I just want to see Special Agent Zheng."

At least they didn't shoot him. Instead, a tight knot of unarmed men tackled him in unison, forty feet from her office.

"Indigo!" he shouted as they took him down. "Indigo!"

They wrenched back his arms and handcuffed him. "Clear!"

She came out of her office, gun ready.

"Indigo," he whispered, looking into her steel gray eyes. "Please, Indigo, please talk to me. My moms are gone. Max is missing. The dogs are dead. The key is gone. All I want is to talk to you."

She looked down at his chest. One of the scabs had broken and was seeping a trickle of blood. She looked back to his face. "Ukiah?"

"Indigo, it's me. I've tried to call, but I couldn't get through. Please, I didn't know what else to do."

She uncocked her gun and handed it to the agent beside her and dropped down in front of him. Her eyes were filled with tears as she lightly touched his battered chest. "Oh, Ukiah, you were dead. I saw him kill you. After the Pack came, I held you and wept. You were dead."

"I was," he whispered.

"How can you be alive again?" She looked up into his eyes.

"I'm Pack, remember?" he whispered for her ears alone. "Remember I told you about Pack living a long time? This is why. We heal all damage done to us, even after our hearts stop beating. You have to burn us to keep us down. That's what the gel fuel was for."

She stroked his cheek, her eyes soft liquid gray. "I learned the meaning of heartsick, to watch him beat you and not be able to do a thing, say a word."

"I couldn't let them hurt you. I love you, Indigo. I would do it again to keep you safe."

She kissed him, and part of his world was right again.

They took off the handcuffs and let him up. Someone retrieved his clothes and produced a first-aid kit. They called his moms first, Indigo doing all the talking at first, confessing falsely that she had made a horrible mistake in telling people that Ukiah was dead when in fact he was alive. She gave him the phone then, but all he could do was listen to his mothers cry until he distracted them with talk of burying the dogs. They were at a safe house on a lake, they told him, with its own private beach. Cally was happy digging in the sand. She had slept through most of the chaos of the gunfight. They had decided, until his body was found and a funeral could be set, that they wouldn't break the news to her. Now she wouldn't have to know. He promised to drive up shortly and be with them.

After this call, Indigo cycled quickly down Ukiah's phone list with her steel command voice. Instead of trying to convince each person that she was actually a person back from the dead, she was able to say, "This is Special Agent Indigo Zheng of the FBI. I'm trying to reach Max Bennett or discover the whereabouts of his company vehicles. Can you help me?"

Usually this was followed with, "Yes, I was the one Ukiah was protecting. Yes, he was a good kid. The paper unfortunately jumped the gun; the paramedics were able to revive him. He isn't dead. Yes, that's right. He's still in critical care. I'm sorry, I can't give out that information. Do you have any idea how I can reach his partner, Max Bennett?"

"You know, you are an amazing liar," Ukiah said after she hung up with Max's accountant. "What information can't you give out?"

"People want to know where they can visit you and send flowers."

They hit pay dirt on the eight call—Kraynak. He wasn't home, but his niece informed Indigo that the Hummer was in the Kraynaks' garage.

"I'll go out and get it." He kissed her and reluctantly let her go. "You keep on calling. And make sure I can get in the front door this time."

Kraynak lived in Beechview, technically still within the Pittsburgh city limits, but only by a few feet. Ukiah pulled up and parked his motorcycle on the left side of the narrow one-way street, behind Kraynak's battered Volkswagen van. The street was lined with nearly identical three-story brick houses with wide porches. Kraynak's porch was scattered with toys, and his sheepdog barked furiously as Ukiah rang the doorbell.

"Kitchen!" Kraynak shouted in the house and opened the door, still looking behind him at his dog. "Kitchen! Alicia, come get this dog!"

He turned and went slack-jawed.

Ukiah supplied the dialogue: "Ukiah, you're dead! No, I'm not. Yes you are, I saw you, you're dead. Okay, I was dead but I got better. Blah, blah, blah, etc, etc, etc. Hey, come on in."

Kraynak blinked, then laughed somewhat nervously. "I guess you've heard that a lot today, eh?"

He hadn't moved, however, to let Ukiah in. His gray shaggy sheepdog showed a better sense of hospitality by rambling over to stick his nose into Ukiah's hand.

"Hey, Radar." Ukiah rubbed him behind his shaggy ears. "Good dog. Sorry, no treats today."

Tension went out of Kraynak's pose and he swung open the door. "Come on in, kid. Radar, kitchen!"

The front door opened into the living room. Comfortable overstuffed furniture crowded around the walls, leaving paths to the rest of the house. A baseball game played on the television in the corner. Snacks, bottles of microbrewed beer, and gun magazines lay scattered on the coffee table in front of the couch. Obviously Kraynak was making the most of his day off.

Kraynak flicked off the TV and twitched a gun magazine off the couch. "Sorry, kid, but I heard about what happened at your moms'. My kids and wife are home. I can't afford inviting trouble in."

"Agent Zheng called and got Alicia. She said you weren't home, but the Hummer was in your garage.

I came over to pick it up. I need to find Max. I think he's in trouble."

Kraynak shook his head. "You think you know someone. I would have bet even money that Max would have moved heaven and earth to track down your missing body. But he said he knew how you died, when you died, and even why you died. He didn't need your body to mourn, just knowledge. If it had just been you getting killed, I think he would have been okay. What hurt him was what they did to what he had left. What they did to your moms' and his house. They threaten everything he's built since his wife died. I tried to talk him out of trying to find them, but he wouldn't listen to me, he even stopped carrying his phone. I don't know where he went, kid, but he's probably heading for deep shit."

"He took the Cherokee?"

Kraynak nodded. "He said it would stand out less. The Hummer is out in my garage and Janey has the sedan. He said that the Pack took your bike, and that kind of bugged him too, but I can see why they did."

"Can I swap my motorcycle for the Hummer, store it in your garage?"

"Sure, kid, anything to help."

Ukiah unlocked the Hummer and climbed into the driver's seat. He flipped on the deck and keyed up the tracking program. The agency owned a dozen tracers, split up among the three cars. He cycled quickly through the list. Four showed up on the map firmly in Beechview with him. Five were parked at Janey's place in Squirrel Hill. The remaining three weren't on the local map, and he had to flip up to the southwestern Pennsylvania map for them to show up.

Narrows Run Road, out toward the airport.

He checked several times as he started up the Hummer and slowly eased it out of the narrow garage and into the equally narrow alley. The Cherokee didn't seem to be moving. There was no way to tell if Max was even in it anymore, but it was his only lead.

Max had left the radio on, as usual. Top story of the hour? "Legal representatives of local hero, Ukiah Oregon, announce that the private investigator hadn't been killed in the rescue of Special Agent Indigo Zheng as earlier reported." Minutes later his phone rang with the first of many seeking interviews with him. After the first dozen, he turned it off.

The Cherokee sat parked squarely among hundreds of other cars in the airport parking lot. It wasn't the expensive lots near the newer airport terminal, but one of the failing cheap lots near the old abandoned terminal. Ukiah pulled the Hummer up behind the Cherokee and killed the engine. There was no sign of violence, no air of destruction and ruin. He climbed down out of the Hummer to circle the Cherokee warily. Its security system was active, double-locked by the remote and door code. Ukiah disarmed the security system with the remote on his key ring. No one but Max, himself, and Chino had used the door handles in the last few days. No sign of blood on the font driver seat. He leaned across and turned on the deck.

"Hey, get away from the car!"

Ukiah leaned back out of the car. The parking lot attendant was coming toward him quickly, a huge bruiser of a black man with a shaved-top hair cut, goatee, and more body parts pierced than Ukiah wanted to count.

Ukiah indicated the Cherokee. "This is my car."

"The hell it is." The attendant was almost on him.

"I can prove it. I have an owner's card."

The man scowled at him but slowed his charge to a reasonable walk. "You ain't the man that left it here. He paid me up front."

"Late thirties, white, brown hair graying at the temples, about a head taller than me?"

The attendant nodded slowly. "Yeah, that's the man."

"That's my partner, Max Bennett. Nobody has seen him for three days. When did he park the car here?"

"Early yesterday morning."

Ukiah produced his copy of the Cherokee's owner card. "It's a company car, but I own half the company. This is my card." He gave the man his business card. "If you see my partner, I want you to call me. I'm very concerned about him."

The attendant eyed him. "He didn't skip with all the company money, did he?"

Ukiah laughed dryly, shaking his head. "I wish. We're private investigators and we got involved in a very dangerous case. Did my partner tell you where he was going, give any indications of when he was coming back?"

A 747 thundered overhead, so low it looked like it would land in the parking lot. With back thrusters whining, it slipped over the slight hill to presumably land safely.

The man studied the business card, waiting for the rolling jet thunder to abate before speaking. "He said he wanted to get breakfast down the street at the Bob Evans and that he'd be back for the shuttle out to the terminal. He walked off and didn't come back."

Ukiah glanced up the road to the large red restaurant. It was a short walk. There were a number of hotels scattered about it. Maybe Max had checked into one of them and used the airport parking lot as a cover. Over a day, though? No. Not the Max he knew. Something had gone wrong.

"Did you notice anyone following him? Were there any police cars or ambulances that showed up yesterday that you noticed?"

The man considered him. "You really are worried about the dude? No, I didn't see anything."

Ukiah pulled a couple of tens out of his wallet. "I'm not going to be able to take the car right now, so this should cover it for a little longer." He waited until the man acknowledged the first payment. "If you remember anything new or see my partner," he handed him the rest of the money, "there'll be more of this. He's in a lot of danger and I need to find him fast."

"No, no, I don't need the money." The man waved off the bills. "I'll let you know. No sweat. Your partner tipped me big to keep an eye on the car for him. More than enough to keep an eye out for him too."

Ukiah pocketed the money. "I'm going to check out the car and then go down to Bob Evans. I'll rearm the security when I'm done."

"Cool." The attendant noted an arriving customer and started off. "Take care."

Both the right and left shoulder holsters were gone. Max's favorite two pistols and the shotgun were missing from the gun safe. All the preloaded 9mm and .357 Magnum magazines, plus a box of shotgun shells, were gone from the ammo box. Max's trench coat, which could cover all three guns nicely, was missing too.

Another jet passed overhead, looking impossibly large to be in midair. He could feel the rumble of the engines in his bones. He glanced at the hotels. How could anyone sleep through such noise?

He shook his head and considered the missing

guns. Max wouldn't take a shotgun to go eat breakfast, not while carrying two pistols already. Max had
lied to the attendant. Ukiah scanned the area. Where
could Max go in a short distance so heavily armed?
Why hadn't he parked closer to the site?

There was only one logical answer. The old abandoned terminal. It was surrounded by acres of
cracked and weedy parking lot. A lone car would
have stood out, begged to be noticed. A quick jaunt
over the four-lane highway and he'd be in.

Ukiah shook his head. "Oh, Max. You went in and
didn't come out." He flipped out his phone and
called Indigo. Her voicemail answered on the first
ring and informed him that Special Agent Zheng was
not taking calls. He swore, noticing that the attendant
was heading back toward him. Indigo must have
been hit by the new wave of reporters chasing after
the story of his resurrection. The communication barrier was back up.

The attendant came up to him and indicated a
large panel truck with his eyes. "A dude on a Har-
ley's been sitting behind that truck watching you for
the last five minutes. I didn't realize it at first, but
he's definitely watching you."

Ukiah threw out his senses and caught the tingling
of Pack presence. "I see him. He's a friend. Don't
worry."

It was Bear, looking bored.

"I don't know how you do that," Ukiah said. "I've
been keeping watch on someone following me."

"You watch with your eyes." Bear tapped his tem-
ple and then his chest. "You have to feel with your
soul. I can let you roam far ahead of me and with
my soul follow."

Ukiah nodded, realizing that the Ontongard could
track him as easily. He jerked his head toward the

old terminal. "Max went in yesterday. His truck's still here. I can't get through to my lady of steel. Where's the Pack?"

"Scattered far and wide. You think this is the On-tongard's lair?"

He glanced back over the terminal. "Could be. Someone has Max in there."

"You waiting for the Pack this time?" Bear asked, starting up his big bike. It rumbled to life, competing in noise and vibration with a DC-9 coming in for a landing.

Ukiah considered this. After last time, would he rush forward again? He had been barely in time to save Indigo. Rushing ahead had hurt like hell, but waiting would have cost him her life. Still, if he hadn't died, then Max wouldn't have gone off alone to be captured and maybe killed.

He sighed. "No, I've got to go in now. I need to find him."

Ukiah saw a host of entrance options as he walked across the parking lot. Rental cars this way. Arriving passengers that way. Departing passengers over here. Each sign pointed to a different level or wing of the old terminal.

The first door he came to was just beyond an empty circular fountain. It was an odd outcrop of a building, separated from the terminal by a five-lane crescent of departing passenger traffic. A half-circle in design, it fit neatly, although weirdly, into the crescent. The door had been glass, but a sheet of plywood was fixed over it.

He ran his fingers over the door handle. Max had touched it, but had he entered through this door? Ukiah tried the door and found it unlocked. A stair-well took up the breadth of the tower, leading down into some space under the roadway. It was cave-black beyond the slant of sunlight from the open door.

Would Max have gone down these steps? The door was unlocked, providing easy access. Max would have been looking for things hidden, which the darkness suggested in plenty. Ukiah closed his eyes and focused on the scents coming up from below: damp mold, dust shifting down from a failing roof, Ontongard's musk, and faintly, finally, the smell of human urine.

Ukiah considered for the first time that the Ontongard had his three memories. Obviously they had used one to make guises of himself. That left two mice that could be used to make Gets. Ukiah sniffed the scent of urine uneasily. Had the Ontongard kidnapped victims to be made into Gets?

He checked the inside door handle. It worked easily. He would be able to get back out. He stepped into the dark stairwell and let the door swing shut behind him. After a moment his eyes adjusted to the darkness and he could see that there was a faint light coming from below. He crept down the steps.

Water dripped somewhere in the darkness, and the echoes told him that the room was vast. Far to the right of the staircase, a single lightbulb gleamed. Across from the door, HERTZ was spelled out in giant letters and beside it was a ticket counter still littered with information packs.

Ukiah stalked toward the light. Signs pointed out GROUND TRANSPORTATION, BAGGAGE CLAIMS, and REST ROOMS. The single lightbulb, he noticed, was off a strand of recently run Romex cable, stapled haphazardly to the ceiling tile. The white cable ran off into the darkness, but pointed in a straight line at the next distant light.

At the third light, he found where they had jumped Max. They had hurt him, pouring his blood out onto the moldy carpet. Judging from the number of kicked-over chairs, torn, rotting carpeting, and smears of blood, it had been a long wrestling fight. Max's trench coat lay in a rumpled heap on the floor, surrounded by a halo of Max's belongings. His wallet, the cash gone but the credit cards intact. Ukiah slipped it into his own pocket. Car keys. Those too he picked up. Random electronic gadgets that Max forever had stuffed into his pockets—those Ukiah left behind. One, however, was a small mag flash light, which Ukiah used to spot the other belongings. Max's black suede PDA case blended into the background so well that Ukiah almost missed it. So did the case of Max's stash gun. Ukiah snatched them up, hoping that, while he worried over Max's belongings, Max himself wasn't being killed elsewhere. The blood, though, was from yesterday, old and dried.

He did a quick last sweep, bending down to run the light under the still-standing row of chairs. There he found the remote key. He picked it up, shaking his head. Max had to have thrown it under the chairs while they had wrestled him to the ground. The near cave darkness had cloaked the key from the Ontongard. Ukiah slipped it into his pocket, feeling like he had wasted too much time already.

He found Max's blood trail and took off at a trot.

They had put Max in a ten-by-ten foot office converted into a cell. The Romex line had been diverted to put a light into the room The lock had been installed recently, the sawdust on the floor still smelling of cut wood. Max had bled on the floor, urinated in the corner, slept on one bare table. The room was now empty. The door leaned at a drunken angle, its hinges popped off but its dead bolt still locked. The dust layering the information desk beside the door had been disturbed; guns and the cured leather of holsters had been placed on the top and removed.

Where was Max?

Ukiah clung to the knowledge that the door had been forced from the inside. Max had probably escaped and, hopefully, had even recovered his weapons that had been stacked by the door. Ukiah searched the floor for a blood trail out, but Max had stopped bleeding. Taking out the flashlight, Ukiah swept the area. Across the wide hall, he noticed a sparkle of glass. He crossed the hall, keeping the light trained on the item until he saw it clearly.

He moaned in pain.

A hypodermic syringe gleamed on the dark carpeting. He didn't want to touch it, learn its truths. He forced himself to pick it up. Max's blood tipped the needle. He pulled out the plunger and ran the tip of his pinkie on the inside edge. The ghost impression of Ukiah's blood coated the inside of the syringe. The Ontongard had found a human to make into Ukiah's Get.

Ukiah clutched the syringe tightly until it shattered in his hand, driving tiny slivers of glass into his palm.

It was useless to deny it. The Ontongard had injected Max a full day ago. His Max was dead, gone, wiped clean and replaced with a copy of himself. Even if Max's body was walking, his soul was gone.

CHAPTER TEN

Wednesday, June 24, 2004
Moon Township, Pennsylvania

Ukiah sat, grief-stricken, bordering on forever. Max was dead. Ukiah couldn't function, couldn't think, could barely even breathe. He thought he knew grief, but this was too huge and awful for him to even see the edges of it. Eventually he realized that he had held a palmful of blood that had slowly changed into a mouse. Whiskers fine as spider legs tickled his fingers, searching for food. He numbly plucked out the shards of glass and reabsorbed the mouse.

What should he do? He had lost the race this time, lost it so badly he couldn't find the finish line. What should he do?

He got to his feet. He would have to find his missing Get. *Follow with your soul,* Bear had told him. Ukiah closed his eyes and felt for the distant echo of himself. Forward and up, the shadow of his soul was impossible to miss.

Max made one mean Get.

Ukiah found the site of the first gunfight in Baggage Claim Area C. Max hadn't been hit; none of his blood stained the floor. He had unloaded his SIG-

Sauer P210 into three Gets from the cover of a half wall that separated Area C from Area B. The spent 9mm rounds glittered on the dark floor. The short wall was peppered with shotgun pellets from the Gets' weapons. The Gets lay drained of blood and covered with anxious mice. The nine rounds from the Sauer were split evenly between the Gets. Max had reloaded, dropping the empty, expensive magazine on the ground in a clear indication of his mindset—he wasn't worrying about coming back out of the terminal.

The single 9mm shells resting on the chests of the dead Gets indicated that Max used the new clip to fire a coup de grace square between their eyes while standing over them.

Ukiah judged that Max had killed the Gets within the hour. Only temporarily dead, it still would be a day or so before the Gets recovered from the damage Max had inflicted.

The gunfire must have summoned the second wave of Ontongard Gets. Max laid waste to them in Baggage Claim Area A. The Sauer one-third empty, Max had changed over to the Desert Eagle. Almost two dozen rounds of the spent .357 Magnum casings littered the floor, with two spent magazines dropped wastefully to the side. These Gets had also been finished off with a bullet between the eyes.

The last of the Gets had been solo, armed only with a knife. Why had it come alone after the others had been slaughtered? Max had emptied his shotgun into it, square into the chest. Ukiah winced at the pulverized flesh, his chest aching in sympathy. Why had Max killed this one so cruelly? It was unlike Max. It was even unlike Ukiah.

Ukiah played the flashlight over the dead body. Its memories skittered before the sweeping beam of light. It wore Nike shoes, blue jeans with torn-out knees, and a blue T-shirt, now torn to ribbons. Ribs gleamed white where flesh had been torn away. Ukiah shifted the light higher to see if Max had felt compelled to add the forehead shot. The light fell on the face, and all became clear.

It was one of Hex's Gets wearing a Ukiah guise.

The likeness was perfect. It was the face he had seen in the mirror thousands of times, except this one was pallid and lax in death. He could see no flaws; nothing to say this wasn't him.

Looking very closely, Ukiah could see that the hair was a shade too light in color. It wasn't his glossy black, but a dark brown. It wasn't something a normal person would notice in the dim light, pressed by enemies. Wearing his guise, Hex's Get had come alone to gain Max's trust and then knife him in the back.

What stupidity. Max would have known instantly that this was a fake. At least Ukiah thought he would. Ukiah hunched beside the disguised body and wondered. Max, even with new Pack senses, might have been fooled for several minutes. Time enough to be killed.

How close had the battle been? It depended on if Max had the Pack memories. Ukiah remembered how lost he had been just days ago, ignorant of the players and even of the game. Without the Pack memories, Max might not have realized there were any disguised Gets in the wings or how to tell them from the real thing.

Ukiah thought back to when he had woken up in the hotel. What had been his last genetically encoded memory? Max feeding him in his mother's kitchen. Grief sudden and hard bent him over, and he smoth-

ered a howl of despair that ripped out of his Pack-
tainted soul.

*No, don't think about it. Push it away. Think of what's
at hand.* It was the only way he could function. He
strove to focus on how the memory of that breakfast
related to him receiving the Pack memory. It came
after. That had been the morning after he had been
so sick. So Max had Pack memory.

Ukiah hunched in the dark, covering his tear-
burning eyes. Maybe he should just pull out and
leave this to the Pack. They would blow it all to bits
with joyful abandon.

No, Max was his Get. He had a responsibility, like
a father to a son.

The lights had been set so that the frozen escalator
was entirely in darkness. He crept up the uneven
steps, making sure the next step was actually there
before moving up. He had images of the Ontongard
removing a middle section and him falling to a temporary death. Halfway up he tripped over another
Get disguised as Ukiah. This one had a canister of
the gas Rennie had used on him when the Pack kidnapped him. The Get had all nine rounds of the Desert Eagle emptied into it. It also was still slightly
warm. He was getting closer.

Ukiah took the gas and hurried up the rest of the
steps. The escalator took him up to ground level,
opening onto the wide main hallway of the terminal.
Signs indicated that straight ahead were the gates
with their waiting areas, behind him was check-in,
the ticket counters, and the main terminal entrance.
Toward the gates, he could feel a single Pack life,
scared and hurt. He started to trot. Sunlight filtered
through the filthy windows lining the waiting areas.
The light reached across the chair-strewn waiting

areas to just touch the edge of the forty-foot-wide hallway. He kept to the edge, jogging in and out of the slants of light, each patch of darkness blacker still because of the sudden flashes of light.

There was the deep boom of a shotgun up ahead and Ukiah started to run. After a hundred feet he hit the reek of gunsmoke and fresh blood. It was the only warning he got before colliding suddenly with Max, standing in the darkness.

Ukiah rebounded off his partner into the sunlight, stunned that he almost missed Max in the dark. He reached out his senses, searching for Pack presence in Max. There was none. Max seemed to be totally and only Max. Ukiah almost wept in relief and happiness. "Max! You're okay!"

Max backpedaled into the next slant of light, dismay open on his face, jerking up the shotgun to level at Ukiah's chest. Dismay fled before anger. "Damn you murdering bastards!"

Ukiah's hands went up in a show that they were innocent of weapons. *If Max isn't Pack, he can't tell I'm the real Ukiah. This isn't good.*

Sprawled behind Max was a dead fake Ukiah. A shotgun fired at point-blank range had punched a hole in its chest. Ukiah winced, trying not to look at it. *Definitely, not good.*

"It doesn't work!" Max growled through teeth clenched tight in rage. "I know you're not him. Try anything, and God forgive me, I'll shoot you like the others."

Max was splattered with blood, and it was clear he had been dragged through hell. Three days of stubble darkened his face. His nose had been broken, and both his eyes were bruised deep purple out to the edge of their sockets, masking him into a large rabid raccoon. His short hair stood up and out in various patches. He had not changed his clothes since Ukiah saw him four days ago. The military starch was long gone. What was left of his clothing was torn, bloody, mold-stained, and drenched with fear-tainted sweat.

The shotgun had drifted upward and pointed at Ukiah's face. He cringed at the double-barrel stare. "Say something," Max shouted. "Don't just stand there looking at me!"

Ukiah shrugged, not sure why Max wanted him to talk. It would be safer for Max just to shoot him, though it probably would be a hard thing for Max to do—even after the third time. "I don't know what to say, Max. Coming back from the dead is hard enough to explain in a hundred words or less. Add a couple of bloodthirsty copies of myself into the mess and—" He motioned faint helplessness with his hands. "What can I say?"

"Say anything. I might believe you."

And unbelievably, it sounded like he might. Was Max just sick of killing Ukiahs, and desperate for any reason not to do it again? Or had Ukiah triggered a gut feeling that the disguised Gets never reached? He stood dumbfounded, separated from Max by darkness. Finally, he found his voice.

"Max, if I could talk all day, you'd have no doubt. There are a billion words and phrases between us, but I don't know which single one you'd believe right now. You're just going to have to trust me, or shoot me—and all the others like me."

Max stared at him, then motioned downward with the shotgun. "Get on your knees, hands behind your head, cross your legs." As Ukiah complied, Max stepped behind him, bringing up the shotgun. Ukiah squeezed close his eyes, bracing for the shot. It would hurt, he told himself, only for an instant—and then he would heal.

Max took a long, shuddering breath, and ran a hand across Ukiah's back. It puzzled Ukiah until he realized that Max had just swept his hand over the lettering of his tracking T-shirt *Private Investigator, Bennett Detective Agency.* "Why are you wearing this?"

It was a numb, unreadable question.

Ukiah floundered for an answer. Putting on the T-shirt had been some gut action he hadn't thought out. "I don't know. I missed you. I was so lost and alone. Maybe, wearing my tracking shirt was as close as I could get to having you with me."

"Oh hell, get up."

Ukiah got up slowly, unsure of what was coming next.

Max startled him by pulling him into a rough hug that went on and on. "You saw me and *joy* went across your face. There's no other word for it. And I thought, 'That was Ukiah's true smile, his true eyes filled with happiness. This is Ukiah.' But I knew it couldn't be you. Oh kid, you were hard and cold when I got to Kittanning. You had to be one of the fakes, only better than the others."

Ukiah laughed into Max's shoulder with pure relief. "It's me. It's me."

"The more you talked, the more I knew it had to be really you. You could never talk your way out of a paper bag. Oh kid, I missed you. Don't you ever pull this dying shit on me again."

Ukiah shook his head. "No, I don't want to do that again."

Max let him go, sobering. "I'm serious, Ukiah. I never want to see you lying dead again. It was like my wife all over again, only worse. I had months to brace myself to see her and it was awful." He looked away, shaking his head.

It certainly was his Max. Ukiah caught his arm, flipped it palm up, and pushed the torn sleeve up to his elbow. An angry puncture mark scarred Max's forearm. "Why aren't you dead—or worse?"

Max laid a rough palm on Ukiah's cheek. "Because the answer to the question 'would you ever hurt me?' is an emphatic no, not even on the viral level. They shot me full of your blood and left me to change. I thought I was dead, one way or another. Then, out of the wound crawled this black worm, thin as a hair and slimy. It had to be the weirdest, grossest thing that ever happened to me. I really just wanted to rip it out of me, but it was already coming out, and I was afraid I'd break it off inside me. It took forever for all of it to crawl out, and then it turned into this." Max reached into his breast pocket and pulled out a sickly runt of a mouse by the scruff of its neck. "Even the littlest part of you recognized me and refused to hurt me."

Ukiah accepted back the memory with great relief. "Oh thank God. I didn't think I could live with myself if they made you my Get." He closed his hands about the mouse and reabsorbed it. "Come on, let's get the hell out of here."

On the edge of his hearing, he suddenly caught a thin wail of misery. It was underscored by a weird, stabbing ghost pain. It was as if part of him was standing far away, lost, frightened, and hurt. The feeling pulled at him, a desperate needing. "What is that? Did you hear that?"

Max paused, listening intently. The wail came again and he nodded. "It sounds like someone in pain."

They looked at each other, and knew that they

couldn't leave without finding the person. They moved down the corridor, counting up the gate numbers. The cry came infrequently but grew louder, clearer. It was the wail of a baby. Toward the end, Ukiah found himself all but running toward it, unable to resist the pull.

"Whoa, whoa, whoa!" Max warned quietly behind him.

The corridor ended in a huge round room, an arc of departure gates. Just before the corridor opened into the sun-filled room there was a set of rest rooms. Ukiah followed the sound into the men's room.

When he pushed open the door, a stench hit him, making him gag. Balanced on a row of sinks sat a battered Quaker Oil box. A newborn infant had been left naked inside, untended for a long period of time. The infant had fouled itself many times and the smell was overpowering. The baby boy shook its tiny fists and wailed with hunger. There were no baby supplies in sight: no bottles, clothes, blankets, cans of formula, or diapers. There was just the battered Quaker Oil box and the baby.

"Oh, poor thing," Ukiah crooned, gathering the infant up, trying to ignore the mess. The baby quieted immediately, looking at him with huge black eyes. Coming from it was the pure oneness, the sense of "This is right" that Ukiah had felt dozens of times over the last few days, only from tiny little mice.

"Oh, God, no!"

Max spun from the door he had been guarding. "What is it?"

"This is me, Max. This baby is me."

"What?"

"They took one of my memories, Max, and made a copy of me. This is me."

"Oh, Jesus Christ on a donkey," Max swore. "Well,

regardless if it's you or someone else, we can't leave it here with these monsters. Clean him up a little and let's get out of here."

Amazing, the sinks had running water. The Ontongard apparently had reconnected this rest room. Ukiah ran the water, hoping it would get warm, but it didn't. "This is going to be cold, little one, but you need to be quiet, okay?"

The baby regarded him seriously and accepted the chilly bath with grace. There were no diaper sores that Ukiah had expected from such filth, until he remembered that this was a Pack baby. He took off his shirt and wrapped the now shivering child in it. Hunger came from the infant with alarming intensity.

"Max, do you have a candy bar or anything?"

"Ukiah, it's a baby. They drink milk and maybe some cereal. You should know that after Cally."

"It's a Pack baby, Max. I think it will digest about anything you put into it."

Max slipped out a Snicker's bar and threw it across the room to Ukiah. "Well, he's welcome to it. Watch he doesn't choke on the nuts."

Ukiah cut the candy bar up with his Swiss army knife, paring off the chocolate layer, and fed the slivers to the infant. Slowly the intense hunger abated.

Why, though, was he worrying about the baby? It had been just a splash of his blood three days ago. It was a mouse, just changed slightly, and larger. It was him, operated remotely. It was—a baby. He lifted it to his shoulder and it nuzzled into him. With a sigh of contentment, it fell into trusting sleep.

"Come on, kid, let's get out of here. I hate to remind you, but if the Ontongard get hold of you, they can make hundreds of those babies."

*   *   *

So they ran. Ahead came the sounds of gunfire. Sporadic at first, then building. Max caught Ukiah's arm and they stopped.

Panting, Max glanced back the way they had come and toward the growing gunfight. "We don't want to get in the middle of that."

Ukiah pointed down the corridor past the escalator. "We could stay on the main level and go out past check-in."

Max shook his head. "If their main stronghold wasn't downstairs or down this wing, then it's back toward check-in. At this old terminal, they had foot traffic bottleneck through security just beyond the escalator. People flying out would check their bags and then go through security. People flying in would go down the escalator and pick up baggage, rent cars, and such, without having to pass through the security check area."

In other words, there was only one way out past check-in, and that was most likely where the Ontongard were.

"Let's try these doors," Ukiah suggested.

Each waiting area had four sets of doors. Through the filthy windows, it was clear that the doors opened into midair, some thirty feet or so from the ground. Once upon a time, umbilical corridors connected the doors to jumbo jets. Now the heavy steel doors were locked tight.

"Damn," Max swore at the last door as it too proved to be locked. "We don't have time to sit and try to pick the lock." Only in the movies could a lock be picked in mere seconds. The gunfire grew louder. With a growl of anger, Max picked up a chair and flung it at a window. The chair bounced harmlessly off with a loud hollow *thunk*. Max swore, pulled out the Sauer and emptied it into the window. Nine tiny thumb-sized stars appeared in the glass.

"Oh, give me a break," Max moaned.

"Someone's coming." Ukiah shifted the baby on his shoulder to draw his Colt.

Someone was running, light and quick, through the slats of light. It was Rennie, carrying a shotgun and bleeding from a thigh wound.

"Cub!" Rennie called as he spotted Ukiah "You've got luck a mile long and whisker thin. I see you found your partner. I don't suppose you found the damn remote key too?"

"Of course I found it. It's what I do."

"It's what he's good at," Max added.

"Yes! We'll win this one yet." Rennie glanced at Ukiah again, eyes narrowing as he took in the sleeping baby on Ukiah's shoulder. "What is this?"

Ukiah flinched back as the Pack leader reached out for the child. "It's mine."

"I won't hurt the babe," Rennie promised quietly. "Let me see him."

Reluctantly, Ukiah handed the infant over.

Rennie took his Memory gently. "It's been such a long time since I held a baby. Not since Bear blew himself up. It's an awe-inspiring thing, to see the smallness that will one day be a tall strong man. Look how tiny his hands are! Surely in a baby, you can see the face of God."

"Ukiah thinks the baby is his," Max ventured.

Rennie gave a short laugh. "Oh, it's the Cub's. Even if you can't smell the Cub's scent or sense his blood in the child, surely you can see the Cub in the baby's eyes and hair. The Ontongard must have tortured the Cub's Memory and then stuffed it well to grow it so quickly."

"Tortured?" Ukiah claimed back the infant. "What do you mean by that?"

"We age fairly slowly, Cub, except when we're hurt. Our cells are forced to divide quickly and recklessly in order to heal the body. With the deterioration in the quality of the cell copies, we age. For the Ontongard to get a mouse to grow to this size in three days, they would have had to hurt it over and over again, providing it with all the food it could eat."

Ukiah laid a protective hand on the baby's head. "They weren't taking very good care of it when we found him."

Rennie shrugged. "It's a Pack baby. It will survive just about anything. The Ontongard could afford to neglect it when other projects took precedence. Well, finders keepers, losers weepers." He chuckled happily. "Nip that little breeding project in the bud. Provided, of course, we get you three out of here."

"We can go back the way you—" Ukiah started but his sentence was clipped short by an explosion deep in the belly of the terminal.

"Nope," Rennie stated cheerfully as dust swirled around him. "No can do."

"You blew up the way out?" Max gasped.

"We plan on blowing up the whole place. That was just the start. We were sure that the Ontongard had the key, so our only hope was to stop the Rover. The Ontongard are controlling the Rover from here, so we're going to blow up everything."

With logic like that, Ukiah thought, *no wonder the FBI had all the Pack members on their most wanted list.*

Rennie glanced at him. *The Ontongard outnumber us ten to one. It's unlikely we'll win today, but there's a chance we'll do enough damage as we go down that we'll stop them for now.*

Ukiah blushed and looked away. The other Pack members came straggling in. They were splattered with Ontongard blood, and sported dozens of bullet holes and shoulder-riding mice themselves. Mixed in with Dog Warriors were men and women he recognized only from Rennie's memories. Hell Hounds. Wild Wolves. Devil Dogs. Not all five gangs, not all members of four present. *Where are the others?*

We couldn't reach the Demon Curs, Rennie answered him. *Some were too scattered around Pittsburgh to show up in time. Two have fallen already.*

"Well," Bear drawled, "they know we're here."

"Most of Pittsburgh knows you're here," Max commented.

The Pack laughed at him, reloading guns and patching wounds.

"Stay here," Rennie ordered Ukiah and Max. "We'll go ahead and see if we can slip you out before we level the place. And, Cub, break the damn key."

Bear took off, running off into the darkness, and the others followed with practiced grace.

Ukiah handed the baby off to Max and dug the key out of his pocket. He spent several minutes trying to snap it in two, or even bend it. He laid it on the floor and beat at it with a chair. It didn't bend, break, or scratch. Nothing in Pack memory said it was indestructible, but also there was nothing saying it was easily breakable either. It seemed, in fact, designed to be somewhat idiot-proof and thus very durable.

He eyed it. It would have been so much easier if Prime had just broken the remote key so long ago. Why hadn't he?

Of course, there was no answer—or more correctly, the answer was lost along with massive amounts of Prime's blood.

Ukiah tried for information in another manner. Had Prime access to the key after they came to Earth?

Yes, there was one clear memory of Prime casually picking it up, as he reminded Hex that the directives were clear: in case of emergencies, a breeding program was the first thing to establish.

Prime was guarding his thoughts from Hex, and thus his plan was unknown to his children. The breeding program had been a distraction, because he went off to sabotage the Ovipositor. So the real plan must have been to send Hex away, so Prime could play with the remote key. If he was bothering with the key, then he had known the main ship was on Mars. If he had followed his normal mode of operations, then he would have made the destruction of the main ship his top priority.

There were no clues, though, to support this theory at all—thus the Pack ignorance of the main ship's survival. Prime's only warning that remained was the enigmatic "Don't wake the sleepers," and that had been misunderstood completely.

So what had Prime done with the key?

Ukiah had learned over the years of investigating that it was pointless to guess at what people had done. Usually, though, it wasn't difficult to discover what they *could* have done, and then do a process of elimination on their possible choices. He rummaged through Pack memory, discovering that Prime's options were slim: the remote key could not reach through the shielding.

It couldn't reach through the shielding.

If Prime had any plan involving the remote key, then when he started, the shields must have been down. The landing on Mars hadn't triggered the automatic defense program, or the shields would have been up. Hex wouldn't have raised the shields; such an act would have stranded him on Earth until the humans developed space flight. Prime must have used the remote key to raise the shields, rendering the key useless.

Starting the automatic defense program, however, was a single command. Prime could have triggered it seconds after he picked up the remote key. There had been numerous distractions for Hex on the scout ship. Why not use one of them? Why had he sent Hex off to start the dangerous breeding program?

Prime always made backup plans. Plans upon plans. The breeding program had been a distraction, but layers of sabotage had still been created to deal with it. If Prime hadn't finished before Hex returned, Prime's mutated genes would have been used. If a child were created, he had planned to kill the mother as soon as possible. If he couldn't do that, the problem would still have been solved when he blew up the scout ship.

Layers on layers.

The shields must have been a default plan. What would take a long time and probably meant the destruction of the main ship?

Asked correctly, Pack memories supplied the answer: the correct codes, programmed into the remote key, then uploaded to the ship, would trigger total destruction. It would take hundreds of commands to override all normal safety procedures so that the destruct sequence could be sent and fully obeyed. One missed safety procedure would render the whole process null. Worse, the system might automatically clear itself of earlier acts of sabotage, and the sleepers would be awakened.

Ukiah studied the key. It had essentially two levels. The first was a top buffer, the active code, what would be loaded onto the ship's computer when the uplink was established. The second area was a densely packed set of possible commands. The lower sets of these were common commands; "Give status report," "Raise shields," and "Wake all sleeping crew." "Wake all sleeping crew" was the command loaded in the active code area.

If Prime had spent a long time coding in a new set of commands, it would be a higher set. Ukiah considered the key. Like humans' computers, the alien's computers had developed on the simple electric principle of on and off. They too had counted in binary at first and the storage of the device was an exponential of two—a high exponential. One of all these memory slots had Prime's destruction code locked into it. Which slot?

Ukiah hunted through Pack memory and found nothing. He wished he could explain the alien device to Max. The language, the equipment, the concepts were all so foreign. Even with Prime's memories, Ukiah could barely understand how the item worked.

Forget the item, he told himself, focus on the man. What did he know about Prime? Alien memories slipped by, sights seen by alien eyes, the Earth experienced by an alien taste. Prime hadn't seen the lush Oregon wilderness as a place fit for saving. He would have loved better the mountains of New Mexico. The countless animals hadn't stirred him. Truly, Ukiah's mother had been the first thing on the planet he had seen fit for saving. He had seen beauty in her.

Ukiah shook his head. No. That didn't lead to anything. Which number would Prime have selected. He moaned inwardly. Prime number.

He checked his memories. Yes, Prime's name had come from his father, not from the Pack.

Which Prime number?

Ukiah decided on the highest one inside the set of possible slots.

There, like a birthday present waiting to be opened, was the first instruction set. *"Prepare to upload new safety overrides . . ."*

Had Prime finished it? Ukiah prayed that Prime had, because Ukiah knew he couldn't finish it. The destruction sequence seemed to be complete. If it was, why hadn't Prime uploaded it? What was missing?

Prime probably would have set the active code to "Raise shields" until he could finish the destruction sequence. That way, if something were to go wrong, Prime could quickly trigger the shields, and Hex couldn't wake the sleepers. After he had programmed in the code, but before he had changed the active code, the shields had been raised.

Ukiah rubbed his forehead. Why? Why? Then it hit him. Prime had been overly cautious—he had laid too many plans. He had taken too long setting the sabotage on the main ship and had run out of time. The scout ship had been launched before the destruction of the main ship had been triggered, and the damage hadn't been complete because he hadn't finished.

Prime wouldn't have loaded the code into the active buffer until he was sure, 100 percent. He had finished the code, but had taken too long. The shields were raised instead. Hex had killed Prime, and a long wait to wake the sleepers had started.

Ukiah dropped Prime's program into the active code, overriding the "wake the sleeper" code. If he had a chance, he was going to finish what his father had started. As an afterthought, he also overwrote the "wake the sleeper" code with Prime's program. Hex, if he checked, would easily catch the substitution and be able to write a new program. It would take time, and time was what they needed.

Ukiah slipped the remote key back into his pocket. The baby woke in Max's arms and started to cry. Fear radiated out of it, striking Ukiah seconds before the sense of Ontongard. He turned and out of the shadows came a host of Hex's Gets.

"Come with us," one Get intoned, without his words registering on his face, as if he were merely a radio, the voice of Hex piped through him. "Come now, or die."

A door, cloaked by the dark and clutter, seemed as if it should lead to a closet. Instead it gave access to a maze of halls and blank doors—secret passages for airport security and maintenance. They were hustled to a vast upstairs room. Cables snaked from computer to computer. Racks of equipment, empty pop bottles, and greasy pizza boxes littered the floor. The Ontongard had lined up a row of seventy-two-inch flat screen televisions and fed onto them a processed version of the NASA channel, with its live Rover coverage. The result was a huge and grainy picture of Mars, as if you had been suddenly transformed into a small alien being squatting on the surface of the red planet.

Hex paced before the televisions. He turned as the Gets brought in Ukiah, Max, and the baby. "Breeder, Get, Memory. A nice collection of breeding stock, one would hope. Soon to be unnecessary, one would also hope." He stopped pacing to focus on Max. Ukiah tried to edge sideways, to shield Max from the alien gaze. "There's something wrong with our happy family picture. Your blood failed to create a Get."

"Thank God," Max muttered.

"I refuse to bend to you," Ukiah growled. "I refuse down to every cell in my body."

Hex looked down at Ukiah. "I can kill you even more painfully this time, and the next time, and the next time, until I reduce you down to only memories."

Ukiah winced. Obviously refusing wasn't the wisest answer.

And all his memories will hate you, his Memory unexpectedly retorted from Max's shoulder. *We'll hunt you down and sear you from this planet like a weed.*

Hex laughed. "Don't make threats at me, Memory. By the time you can do any hunting, you will believe I'm your father."

Never! We'll tell ourselves the truth every waking moment of the day, every sleeping moment of the night. We were the Cub and Hex unmade us. We will never forget, even after we've forgotten everything else.

Hex shook his head. "Where did this insanity in Prime's blood come from? I thought it was just a temporary illness in him, something that would have been worked out of his system if I had felt like giving him the time to live. Then his Gets turned up as rabid dogs, nipping constantly at my heels as I tried to finish my mission. And now his son and all his parts—rebellious, traitorous little shits. One wonders if your bloodline is worth trying to use at all. Surely all you will breed will be tainted with your father's insanity."

Forewarned this time, Ukiah managed to silence his son's next outburst with *Hush, go to sleep,* and Max held a peacefully sleeping baby.

"Prime destroyed the scout ship," Ukiah replied. "And even after the Rover reaches the main ship, you can't wake the sleepers. I'm all you have."

Hex waved away the problem. "Getting up to

Mars to lower the shields was the hard part. If I can't get the key back, I'll jury-rig something. I had rough copies made before I realized that I could just modify the Rover's existing equipment. I hate the idea of trusting everything to an untried copy of the key, but in theory it will work. I've got time to fiddle until it does work. One way or another, I will get the damn ship to Earth. Still, it would not do to dispose of you too quickly. I could try for a hybrid with your Memory, half you and half me. That might solve the insanity problem."

Max took a quick step backward, shielding the baby with his hands.

There was a deep roar below them. The floor heaved up and fell. The lights flickered, browned out, and then steadied. Dust rained down from overhead.

"Go kill those damn dogs!" Hex shouted, and Gets rushed down a staircase on the far side of the room, almost directly opposite from where they had been brought up.

Ukiah thought he heard a distant voice, a cry of dismay, then Rennie's mind touched his.

Cub? He has you?

He does. He stands close to me.

Damn! Your life is safe, but not your soul. Did you do as I asked?

I couldn't.

Rennie broke off the contact instantly and down in the guts of the terminal came a wolf howl. A chorus of wolves went up. It sang to Ukiah of fear, of determination, of hate for an ancient foe.

The Gets had stopped their activities at the computers, heads lifted to listen to the wolf song.

Hex, however, stared at Ukiah. "What did Rennie Shaw ask you to do?"

I had a rough copy made, Hex had said. *In theory it should work.*

"What did Rennie Shaw ask you to do?" Hex asked, moving closer.

Ukiah cringed, remembering being struck full on by the two-by-four.

A weirdly human smile played at Hex's mouth. "I'm sure we can find one of those lying around here. Now, for the last—"

Hex turned suddenly to look back at the wall of TV screens. The Martian landscape had flickered and vanished. Now, displayed across the TV, was the main ship, ugly in the way only a race with no regard for beauty could create ugly. Huge, mottle-colored, it bristled with weapons that Ukiah knew from Pack memory; weapons that even now humans couldn't withstand. He felt a howl of despair beat against his lips, and he swallowed hard to keep it from escaping. He reached out to Max, touched him on the elbow to get his attention, and nodded toward the far staircase where the sounds of fighting had resumed.

"Get one of the duplicate keys," Hex ordered.

"I'll offer a trade," Ukiah all but shouted, bringing everyone's attention on him. "Rennie ordered me to break the remote key, but I didn't have a chance." He backed up slowly. "If you let us go—me, my partner, my memory—I'll give it to you."

"Why would you die to protect it before and not now?"

"I died to protect my mate. I used the key to stall you, so you wouldn't hurt her. If you have a duplicate key, there's no reason for us to die now. Just let us go, and I'll give you the original key. You don't need us anymore."

"You're bluffing," Hex snarled. "You don't have it."

Ukiah pulled the key out of his pocket and held it up. Behind him, the Pack flung themselves against the locked entrance, the wood groaning was it was tortured out of shape. He changed his grip on the key, thumbs pressed hard at its center point. "Now, let us go, and I'll throw it to you. Try anything, and I'll snap it in half."

"You've been dealing with humans much too long," Hex drawled. Like a multiheaded snake striking, there was a sudden blinding motion from all the Gets. One fired a shotgun that caught Ukiah in the side, flinging him sideways into the wall, while others leaped forward.

There was a rush of bodies from the stairwell, and the Pack spilled into the room. The Gets reached Ukiah first, ripped the key from his hand, and flung it across the room to Hex. As the Gets checked the snarling fury of the Pack, Hex slammed the key into the console slot and turned it. Tones started to play in the room, heading out to distant Mars. Bear broke free of the Gets and leaped on Hex, and they went down in a snarling mass.

The fight rolled over Ukiah, then left him behind. Rennie appeared to suddenly haul Ukiah to his feet and slam him against the wall. His large hands closed hard on Ukiah's throat. "What the hell have you done? Have you betrayed everything to try and save one life?"

"I had to give it to him," Ukiah choked, trying to keep his mind blank. Hex mustn't be warned. "I had to."

"I should have killed you the first time I saw you," Rennie roared.

"You've lost, you stupid cur!" Hex was shouting

at Bear. "You had no hope of winning, you rabid dogs! I'll have you all flayed alive and laminate your skins. Stop her!"

Hellena had broken free of the Gets and raced to the instrument panel, hand outstretched for the key. She was going to be able to yank it free before the command was done.

"No!" It was a duet of voice and mind, Hex and Ukiah shouting the same word. Hellena spun like a hard-twisted puppet, her eyes meeting Ukiah's with surprise, and then a bullet exploded her head, spraying gore onto the control console.

"No," Ukiah repeated, softer, this time in denial.

She'll get better, he chanted to himself, *she'll get better.*

There was a sudden strange stillness in the room as everyone looked at Ukiah, puzzled by his outburst. Hex twisted in Bear's stranglehold to look from Ukiah to Hellena and then to the console, where the key continued to upload its long complicated program in musical tones. Understanding dawned on his alien face.

"He's changed the code! Stop the signal! Stop the signal!"

The fight took a sudden hard change of direction, as the Ontongard struggled to reach the key and the Pack fought to stop them.

"You've changed the code?" Rennie released his grip, his eyes wide with amazement.

"He had another key. A copy. It could have worked. I had to give him the booby-trapped one and hope he'd use it without checking."

The key finished and dropped silent. On the screen, harsh brilliant light began to fill the ship's view ports, spilling out into the Martian dusk. The image began to tremble as the great redirected engines shook the ship.

"What did you do?" Rennie breathed, his eyes riveted to the screen. "How could you know how?"

Ukiah gave him the answer in the form of a question. *If the first attempt didn't destroy the ship, Prime, what can you do from Earth? What would take time to set up? Time during which you couldn't dare be caught, so you allowed a monster to be conceived.*

Correctly asked, Rennie only needed a moment to think. *Close all the engine exhaust ports, disable the emergency damper system, and then fire the engines at full.*

Don't wake the sleepers, Ukiah replied.

Rennie smiled full with evil delight, then frowned, glancing at the screen filling with light. The pack leader caught Ukiah's shoulder and gave Max a hard push toward the door. *"Run!"*

Ukiah could sense Rennie barking silent orders to the Pack. Even as the threesome started to run, the Pack opened an exit, heaving and flinging themselves and Ontongard out of the way.

"What?" Ukiah shouted as they cleared the door. "What did I miss?"

"The sleepers were Plan A for taking over the human race. If they're gone, *you* become Plan A."

The Rover control center was, it turned out, in the observatory level of the old terminal. Escalators led down to the great concourse and beyond were a row of doors to the outside. They stumbled down the uneven stairs, the fight following close on their heels. As they sprinted toward the doors, Rennie flung away his shotgun.

"What are you doing?" Ukiah cried.

"I'm trying not to get killed by the cavalry," Rennie snapped. He yanked open the center plywood-covered door and pushed Ukiah out into the open.

Thirty-odd police cars were jammed into the five-lane half-circle departing zone, their lights almost blinding after the darkness of the terminal. A hundred police, it seemed, crouched behind the squad cars, shotguns and service revolvers aimed at Ukiah.

Ukiah jerked up his hands, cringing. *Oh, this is going to hurt.*

"Hold your fire!" Indigo's voice boomed across a megaphone. "He's one of ours!"

Max, carrying the baby, was pushed through the door next. He too paused, stunned by the array of weaponry aimed at him.

"Hold your fire!" Indigo chanted.

Rennie stepped out behind them, caught hold of their arms and hustled them to the curb. Even as they reached the cars, the fight burst out of the doors. Tight knots of three and four combatants roiled through each of the five doors, spilling out quickly until the entire war spread across the sidewalk.

"This is the FBI!" Indigo boomed across the megaphone as Ukiah and the others dropped down beside her, panting from running. "You're under arrest! Put down the weapons and don't move!"

"Who are the good guys?" the officer beside Indigo asked her.

Indigo turned her gray eyes to Ukiah.

"Shoot them all," Rennie whispered to him.

Ukiah quailed at the thought, then nodded as a policeman beyond Indigo suddenly cried out in pain, shot by the Ontongard. "Shoot them all, sort them out later."

"Return fire," Indigo commanded.

The thunder of gunfire was long and deafening. Ukiah crouched behind a cruiser's tire as the thunder went on and on. Mars glistened in the evening sky and, for a moment, seemed brighter and larger than ever before.

They bagged the dead as quickly as possible, wearing leather gloves to snatch up mice and ferrets gathering around the bodies. Ukiah and Rennie picked out the Pack dead and gathered up the Pack's collection of mice. Indigo had the dead Pack members moved to a temporary holding area; officially their bodies were to be moved to the coroner's office after the Ontongard were dealt with, but when that time arrived later the next day, they were gone.

Once the Pack was cleared away, Indigo started on the Ontongard. "These people are carriers of a highly deadly virus transmitted through the blood," she told the coroner who just arrived, having only been called after the Pack dead had been culled. "Have them fingerprinted, a dental print made, and then cremate all the bodies."

She made a point to single out Hex's body. "Make sure this one is first to be cremated."

Ukiah watched them carry Hex away. "That's cold. You know they're still alive."

Indigo looked away. "What they did to you was cold. What they tried to do to me was cold. What they did to Wil Trace and Agent Warner was cold." She shook her head. "This is the only justice that makes sense. I'm not going to risk the lives of these officers over and over again. What would a jail term be to the Ontongard? Would they even serve it? What about the other prisoners? How would you protect them from the Ontongard? If we gave them a trial and found them guilty and sentenced them to death, how would we carry it out? Our Constitution, made for men, bans burning people alive, and nothing else would kill them. They're not human, Ukiah, and we can't treat them as such."

"I'm not human either, Indigo."

She looked at him with tears in her eyes. "Yes, you are, because you allow yourself to be one. You've taken a name and place in our society. You've got a birth certificate, Social Security number, you've registered for the draft, you pay your taxes, and you obey the law. You've said, 'These are my mothers. These are my friends. This is my lover.' You take photographs, have favorite clothes and favorite foods. Everything you've ever done has made you part of mankind. Even the Pack, with all their lawlessness, have kept their names and wear their gang colors as a signal of 'this is who we are within your society. We are the lawless ones that run on the fringes, expect trouble from us.' They have friends. They take lovers. As long as there has been the FBI, there has been a Pack file. They're human because they make themselves human.

"But the Ontongard—" She shook her head. "They held me for four hours, Ukiah, and not once did any of them give a glimmer of having a soul. You saw how they were, human-shaped appendages for Hex, a group mind working as one spread-out body. They don't have names anymore. The one or two we've managed to capture understood the concept, but refused to apply it to themselves. They don't collect personal effects. You'll find more stuff in a doghouse than where Ontongard have lived for weeks. They don't have friends and lovers. They eat what is at hand. Sometimes it's pizza, but often it's bulk dry dog food. They're not human, Ukiah, and I'm not going to treat them as such."

What justice would make sense? Pack memory told him how impossible it was to keep Pack in normal jails. Intricate escape-proof cells would have to be built, and scattered wide to keep the Ontongard separated and isolated from other prisoners. A thousand in all would need to be built and then maintained for hundreds of years.

"You're right," he sighed. "We can only ignore them, or deal with them thoroughly. Doing things halfway would only lead to dead law officers and Ontongard still roaming free."

She took his hand. "Do you hate me for this?"

He laughed and put his arms about her. "How could I hate you when I love you so much? Besides, I don't think the Pack would let me get another girlfriend. They like you. They call you the Lady of Steel."

She hugged him tightly. "The last three days, there was always a Pack member on the fringe of my vision. It was like you were hovering over me, protecting me." Reluctantly, she released him. "I have work to do. It will take me the rest of today and all of tomorrow to fill out the paperwork. After that, if you don't mind the wait, I could take vacation time and we could go together up to the safe house and get your moms."

"I'd love that."

A smile came to her gray eyes, and she went off to wreak her cold vengeance on the remaining Ontongard. As Ukiah watched her compact figure move among the tall burly policemen, Max drifted over to stand beside him.

"You and Agent Zheng." Max smiled at him. Besides the baby, he now also held diapers, baby clothes, a can of formula, and a baby bottle. "I see it, but I still have trouble believing it."

"She's the most amazing and beautiful woman there is."

"They all are when you're in love with them. Here, take the baby. Arn Johnson had some extra baby things in his squad car and he let me have this stuff. Did you know he and his wife had triplets?" Max shook his head. "And he always seemed like such a sane man." He held up a small disposable diaper. "I can't believe that as small as this is, it's going to be too big."

"He'll grow into that size." Ukiah laid his Memory on the trunk of a squad car and found that he hadn't forgotten how to diaper an infant.

"Not today, I hope."

Ukiah shrugged, reaching for the T-shirt. "I don't think so. Anything is possible." The T-shirt read "Daddy's Pride and Joy." He picked up the clothed baby and held him at arm's length. Serious black eyes studied him in return. Beside him, Max read the instructions on the formula can out loud.

"Max, it just suddenly hit me."

"What?"

"I've got a baby."

Max gave a tired, weak laugh. "You certainly do."

"This is—like—forever."

Max caught Ukiah's slightly panicked look and patted him soothingly on the shoulder. "Don't worry, we'll work it out."

CHAPTER ELEVEN

Wednesday, June 24, 2004
Moon Township, Pennsylvania

While things were still in full chaos, Max slipped them away from the police and FBI. It would be better to go, he pointed out, before anyone thought to ask exactly where the baby came from. Retrieving both the Hummer and Cherokee, they drove to the offices. By then, Ukiah could do little more than slump over the steering wheel of the Cherokee.

Max opened the Cherokee's door. "You okay?"

"I'm wiped, and I know there's nothing here to eat."

Max laughed and tousled his hair. "Just hold on, it will only be a little while longer."

Chino appeared minutes later with a plate of sushi from the corner Japanese restaurant. "Oh man, you look like the walking dead. Max too. Where did you find him? Shit, have you been shot again? What the hell happened? Hey, did you hear about the spaceship?"

"Spaceship?" He barely tasted the twelve pieces of California and tuna maki as he wolfed them down, one bite per piece.

"It's on all the channels. The Rover malfunctioned

and stumbled onto this alien spaceship on Mars! Then the dude blew up! They're playing it again and again. Hey, where did the baby come from? Max told me to go get a carseat, but I thought he was shitting me."

"It's a long story. Where's Max?"

"Taking a shower. He says you're moving out as soon as he's got some clothes packed. The house is full of workmen and cleaners. He doesn't want you to come in, so stay put. I'm running over to Babyland on Penn Avenue. It shouldn't take me more than a couple minutes to get a carseat."

Ukiah shifted over the central console to the passenger side and napped while waiting. He was vaguely aware when Max returned, opening the hatch to load suitcases. It was Chino's return, with bags of fast food, that woke him up.

"I thought you might still be hungry." Chino grinned as he installed the carseat. "Cute kid. Whose is it?"

"Mine."

"Ukiah's."

"You dog!" Chino's smile melted to puzzlement. "So, who's the mother?"

Ukiah glanced helplessly at Max.

"We'll explain later." Max slammed shut the hatch. "I'll call you tomorrow about the rest of the work that needs to be done here. Watch your step, things still might be a little hairy for a while."

"Where are you going to be?"

"It'd be better if you don't know."

Max went out by the zoo, then up through Etna. At one point he stopped and switched the license plates. They went through a McDonald's drive-through in Allison Park, cut through the small town of Mars, and finally they stopped at the Residence Inn in Cranberry Township.

"Here?"

"This is a family place." Max slid on sunglasses to hide his two black eyes. "We'll blend in here. Kind of."

Max went in alone and checked them in as three adults (thus creating a paper mother) and a child under the name of John Schmid. They parked in the back and took the elevator, unseen, up to the fourth floor. The suite had two bedrooms, a kitchenette, a living room, and two complete baths. The "do not disturb" sign was a magnet that stuck to the steel door and stated "no service." Ukiah numbly stripped, showered, pulled on a pair of shorts Max had packed for him, and crawled into the bed of the smaller bedroom. Max stayed awake to set up the crib that housecleaning delivered to the door, fed the baby, changed its diaper, and tucked it into the crib. Then he too collapsed in the larger bedroom.

There was a mega-watt streetlamp right outside the window. With the curtains drawn, it was impossible to tell night from day. Ukiah woke from a shared dream of being small and helpless. For a moment he laid curled in the unfamiliar bed, fearful of the Ontongard's return. Then, as he woke up fully and realized what his memory had endured, he went to the crib, full of anger and guilt.

"Hey, little one, it's okay. You're safe." He lifted the baby out and cradled it to him. Where they touched flesh to flesh, they were so identical that he could barely determine where his body stopped and his memory's started. The baby's fists were covered with saliva and sour milk. The tiny head had minute traces of baby powder. Still, Ukiah could feel the pain of the baby's gas bloated stomach as if it was his own.

Max came out of his bedroom still looking jumpy. He wore drawstring sweatpants and a white sleeveless undershirt that left little doubt to the hardships he'd suffered the last few days. He held his SIG-Sauer carefully pointed at the ceiling. He relaxed after scanning the room and finding only Ukiah and baby. "I forgot how often those things ate."

"I'm hungry too."

Max laughed and returned the Sauer to its holster under his pillow. "I'll see what we can get delivered."

A short conversation with the front desk produced the number of a Chinese restaurant that delivered. Max called in an order, and then fiddled with baby bottles and formula.

It hurts. The baby whimpered into Ukiah's mind. *It hurts.*

"I know, pumpkin," Ukiah murmured, nosing into his memory's soft black hair. "If you just burp, it will stop hurting."

Max took the baby, expertly tucking him onto his shoulder, and produced a wet burp with a couple of well-placed pats. "We need a name for him."

"How about Max?" Ukiah carefully accepted the baby back from Max, mindful to support the wobbly neck and head.

"Thanks, but no," Max said with great sincerity. "My older brother is a junior, and it drove me nuts with big Bob and little Bob, Bob and Bobbie, Senior and Junior. If our partnership is to be a long one, let's not complicate it with that." Max considered a moment, and then suggested, "John Oregon would be nice and simple. Face it, kid, not much about his life is going to be simple."

Gas gone, hunger became the baby's complaint. "Is that bottle ready?"

"It should be." Max lifted the bottle out of the water, tested on his wrist. Satisfied with the temperature, he handed it to Ukiah. "John? Jim? Tom?"

Ukiah looked down at the baby as it ate greedily. "What do you think, little one?"

Eyes as black as his own regarded him. *Kittanning.*

"Kittanning?"

It was where I was born.

"He says he wants to be called Kittanning."

Max scowled at Ukiah. "Why does your life have to be so weird?"

"Sorry."

"Kittanning. Kittanning Oregon. Kit. Kit Oregon. Okay. It works."

The phone rang. Max eyed it a moment before picking it up. "Yes?"

A woman's voice asked, "You ordered Chinese food to be delivered?"

"Yes."

"It's here. I'm sending the delivery man up."

"Thank you."

They waited, tense, to the silence, the soft chime as the elevator opened down the hall, and then footsteps approaching the door. A soft knock. "Chinese?"

Max looked at Ukiah.

"It's a human," Ukiah whispered. "He has food. There's no one else out there."

So Max opened the door, took the offered bag, and paid in cash. They listened to the retreating footsteps, the chime of the elevator, and then the silence.

"How long are we going to hide out?" Ukiah asked.

"A day or two. Maybe a week." Max unloaded the bag. "We need to get hold of Leo and make sure no one can take the baby. Kittanning. There's the whole mess of you coming back from the dead." He paused to turn on the television. The Martian landscape appeared on the screen. As they watched, the alien ship, repulsive to the human eye, flickered into existence.

Max turned the channel. The alien ship loomed in the Mars Rover's cameras, huge and menacing, its true dimensions lost as it towered over the Earth vehicle. Next channel. The blinding explosion, seconds of brilliance before the Mars Rover vaporized in the destruction of the alien ship, followed by the gray static. Next channel. A frame by frame analysis of the sequence. Channel after channel. All normal programming preempted. Photos enlarged until they were blurred. Computer modeling done in an attempt to grasp the true dimensions of the now vanished ship. Shots of Mars through the Hubble telescope, showing a massive dust storm, blurring all features. Experts from every field across the world were being interviewed, offering no real explanations.

"Okay, we might be hiding out longer than a week," Max finally said.

"I'm sorry, Max."

"Hell, kid, considering all the ways this could have turned out, I think we got a pretty good deal."

They slept. They ate. They watched the endless coverage on the spaceship, because there was nothing else to watch. Finally, Max went out and bought a DVD player and a couple dozen comedies. Life, he said, had been too exciting lately for thrillers. They packed up Kittanning and their guns and cautiously ventured out each day to let the cleaning staff in.

They made their phone calls while out driving. Indigo paid them compliments on neatly vanishing and arranged to meet them at the Grove City Outlet Mall, just off of I-79, halfway to the safe house on Saturday afternoon. Chino reported that the work was proceeding on the office and that no one seemed interested in him, the offices, or their location. Leo, their lawyer, was much less optimistic; while fathers were optional, the legal system mandated that newborns came with birth mothers. He promised to work on a solution.

By Saturday, Max still looked like a raccoon, but not a single bruise remained on Ukiah.

The safe house was a lovely craftsman cabin with faded blue siding, set on the shore of a lake. Maple and oak trees stood close to shelter it from the sun and wind, but beyond it was the wide openness of water and sky. When they arrived, Ukiah's moms and Cally came out in their summer dresses to fuss over him. When they were done, Max and Indigo distracted Cally off to the beach, and Ukiah lifted the sleeping Kittanning out of the car.

"Who's this?" Mom Jo whispered.

"This is my son. His name is Kittanning."

The song of wolves woke him. The wind was up, tossing the treetops, rushing thin veils of clouds across the star studded sky. Ukiah found Mom Jo on the back porch in her flannel bathrobe, staring out over the lake.

"There aren't any wolves in Pennsylvania," she breathed.

"Yes, there are," he said, feeling the faint prickle of Pack presence. "They just walk on two legs instead of four." He started down the steps, out into the wild night.

She reached out and caught him by the shoulders.

"I know they're calling you. Just remember to come back."

In the dark, with his other family nearby, he finally found the courage to ask the question he wanted to ask all day. "Does it bother you, Mom, that I'm not human?"

She laughed into his hair. "Oh, Mowgli, my little wolf boy, I knew you weren't human when I saw you sitting in the snow, eating that rabbit. Go on, run with your gray brothers. Just remember to come back to me."